"My favorite part is when Hilo travels through galaxies. If I had to describe it in three words, I'd say it's **'SUCH A BLAST!'** D.J. is my favorite because he's a really good friend!"
—Matt A., age 10, Bloomfield, N.J.

"I like **COOL HEROES AND ROBOTS**—and Hilo is both!"
—Malcolm S., age 9, Riverdale, N.Y.

"**GINA WAS MY FAVORITE** character because she's into science and soccer like me! I also liked D.J.'s family because it looks like mine!"
—Kiran M., age 7, Carlsbad, Calif.

"*Hilo* is really cool and funny. It's **FUNNY** that he likes mangoes. You should read it because it's actually just **REALLY FUNNY!**"
—Gerard A., age 8, Bloomfield, N.J.

"**HIGH ENERGY** and **HILARIOUS**!"
—Gene Luen Yang, National Ambassador for Young People's Literature

"**FANTASTIC. EVERY SINGLE THING ABOUT THIS . . . IS TERRIFIC.**"
—Boingboing.net

"My students are obsessed with this series. **OBSESSED!**"
—Colby Sharp, teacher, blogger, and co-founder of the Nerdy Book Club

"More **GIANT ROBOTIC ANTS** . . . than in the complete works of Jane Austen."
—Neil Gaiman, author of *Coraline*

"Anyone who loves to laugh should read *Hilo*. It is **ACTION-PACKED** with a robotic touch."
—Breslin S., age 10, Jackson, Mich.

"*Hilo* is loads of **SLAPSTICK FUN!**"
—Dan Santat, winner of the Caldecott Medal

P9-CJK-976

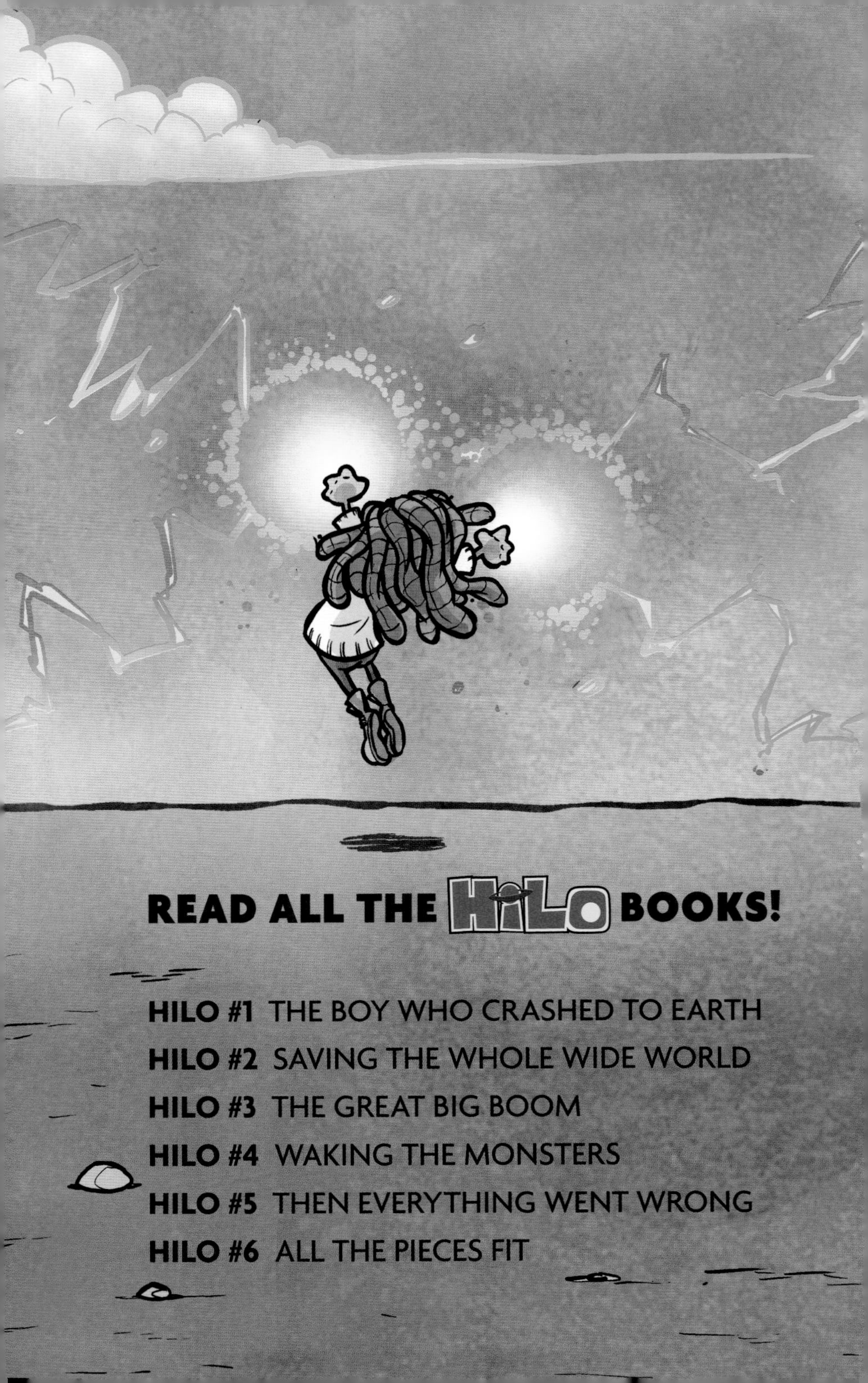

READ ALL THE HILO BOOKS!

HILO #1 THE BOY WHO CRASHED TO EARTH

HILO #2 SAVING THE WHOLE WIDE WORLD

HILO #3 THE GREAT BIG BOOM

HILO #4 WAKING THE MONSTERS

HILO #5 THEN EVERYTHING WENT WRONG

HILO #6 ALL THE PIECES FIT

BOOK 6

HiLo

ALL THE PIECES FIT

BY JUDD WINICK

COLOR BY
JOSÉ VILLARRUBIA

RANDOM HOUSE 🏠 NEW YORK

Copyright © 2020 by Judd Winick
All rights reserved. Published in the United States by Random House Children's Books, a division of Penguin Random House LLC, New York.
Random House and the colophon are registered trademarks of Penguin Random House LLC.
Visit us on the Web! rhcbooks.com
Educators and librarians, for a variety of teaching tools, visit us at RHTeachersLibrarians.com
Library of Congress Cataloging-in-Publication Data
Names: Winick, Judd, author | Villarrubia, José, colorist.
Title: Hilo. Book 6, All the pieces fit / by Judd Winick; color by José Villarrubia.
Description: First edition. | New York : Random House, [2020] |
Summary: "After discovering the truth about how he lost his memories and Dr. Horizon's identity, Hilo goes back to Earth and tries to prevent Razorwark from destroying the world—and everyone in it."
Identifiers: LCCN 2018058871 | ISBN 978-0-525-64406-4 (hardcover) |
ISBN 978-0-525-64407-1 (hardcover library binding) | ISBN 978-0-525-64408-8 (ebook)
Subjects: LCSH: Graphic novels. | CYAC: Graphic novels. | Robots—Fiction. | Friendship—Fiction. | Extraterrestrial beings—Fiction. | Science fiction.
Classification: LCC PZ7.7.W57 Hn 2020 | DDC 741.5/973—dc23
Book design by Bob Bianchini
MANUFACTURED IN CHINA
10 9 8 7 6 5
First Edition

FOR
PEDRO

CHAPTER 1

EVERYONE CALLS ME D.J.

EARTH.
NOW.
MY NAME IS DANIEL JACKSON LIM.
BUT EVERYONE CALLS ME D.J.

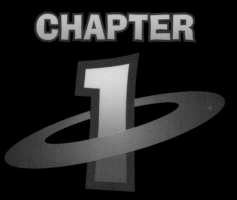

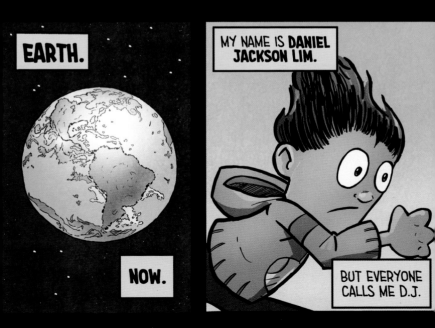

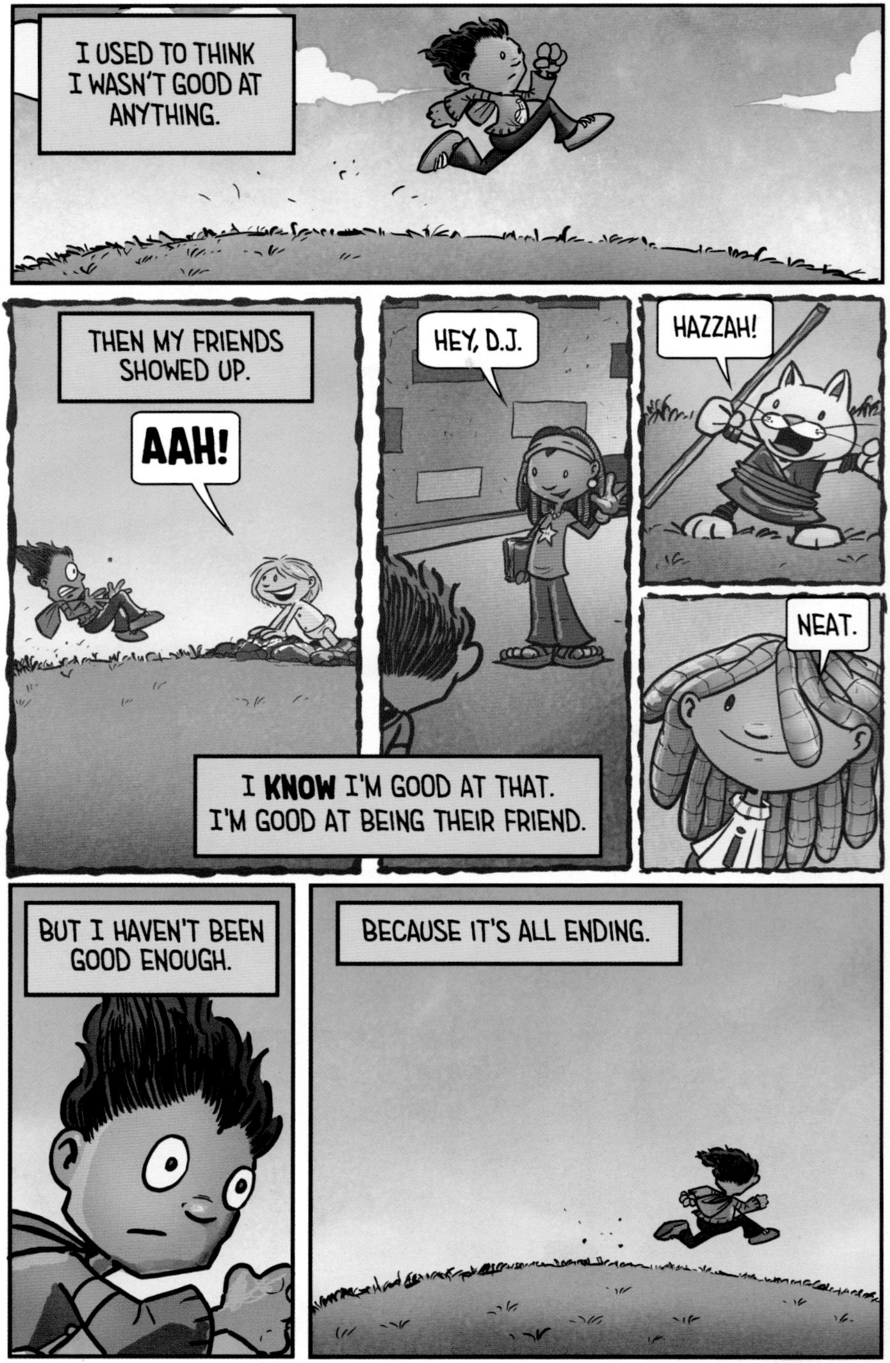

I USED TO THINK I WASN'T GOOD AT ANYTHING.
THEN MY FRIENDS SHOWED UP.
AAH!
HEY, D.J.
HAZZAH!
NEAT.
I KNOW I'M GOOD AT THAT. I'M GOOD AT BEING THEIR FRIEND.
BUT I HAVEN'T BEEN GOOD ENOUGH.
BECAUSE IT'S ALL ENDING.

CHAPTER 2

STAY CALM

HILO'S HOUSE.
TWELVE HOURS AGO.
YOU SEEM TO BE FUNCTIONING WELL.
IZZY.
ARE YOU SURE YOU'RE OKAY?

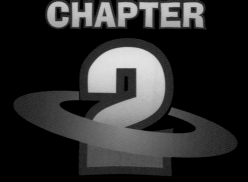

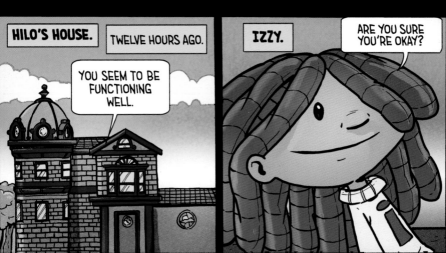

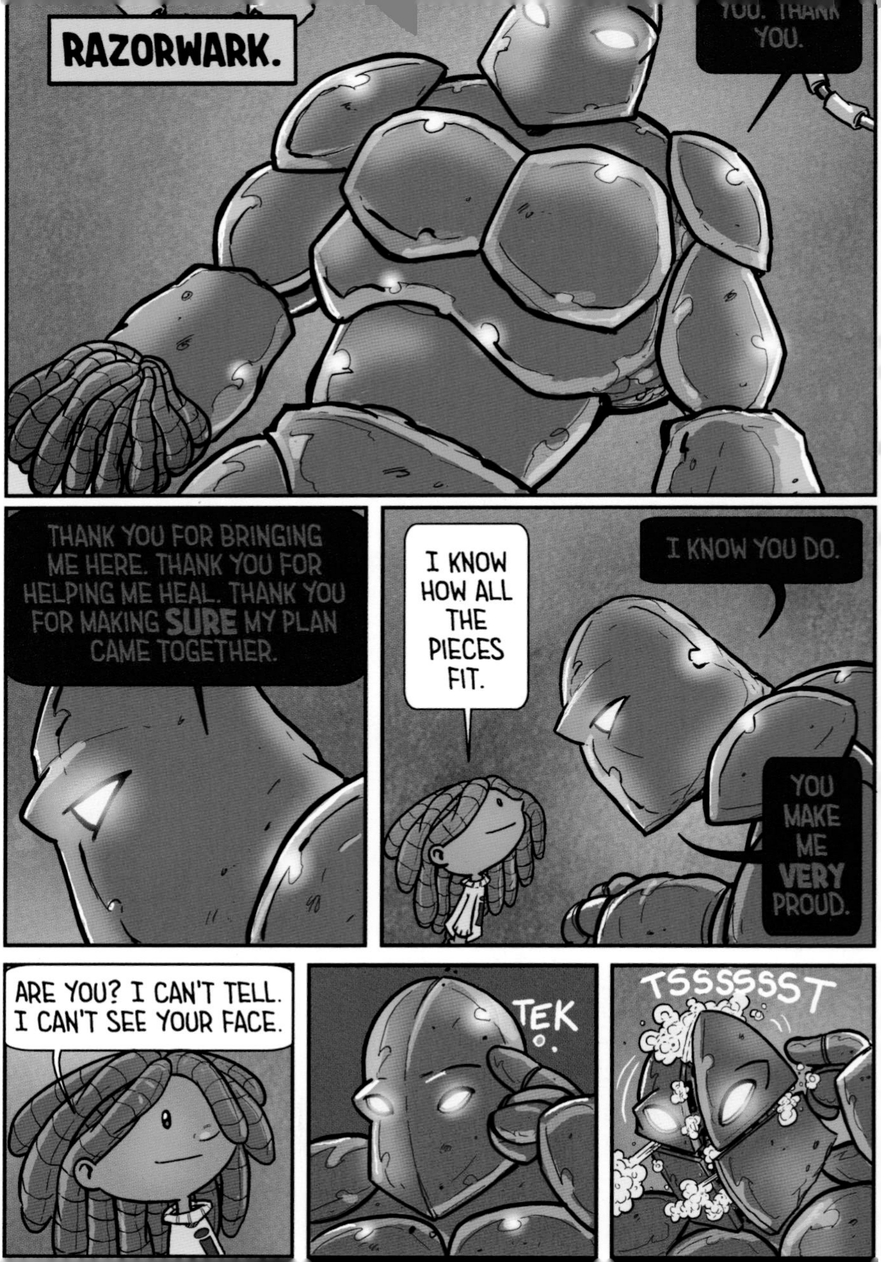
RAZORWARK.
YOU. THANK YOU.
THANK YOU FOR BRINGING ME HERE. THANK YOU FOR HELPING ME HEAL. THANK YOU FOR MAKING **SURE** MY PLAN CAME TOGETHER.
I KNOW HOW ALL THE PIECES FIT.
I KNOW YOU DO.
YOU MAKE ME **VERY** PROUD.
ARE YOU? I CAN'T TELL. I CAN'T SEE YOUR FACE.
TEK
TSSSSSST

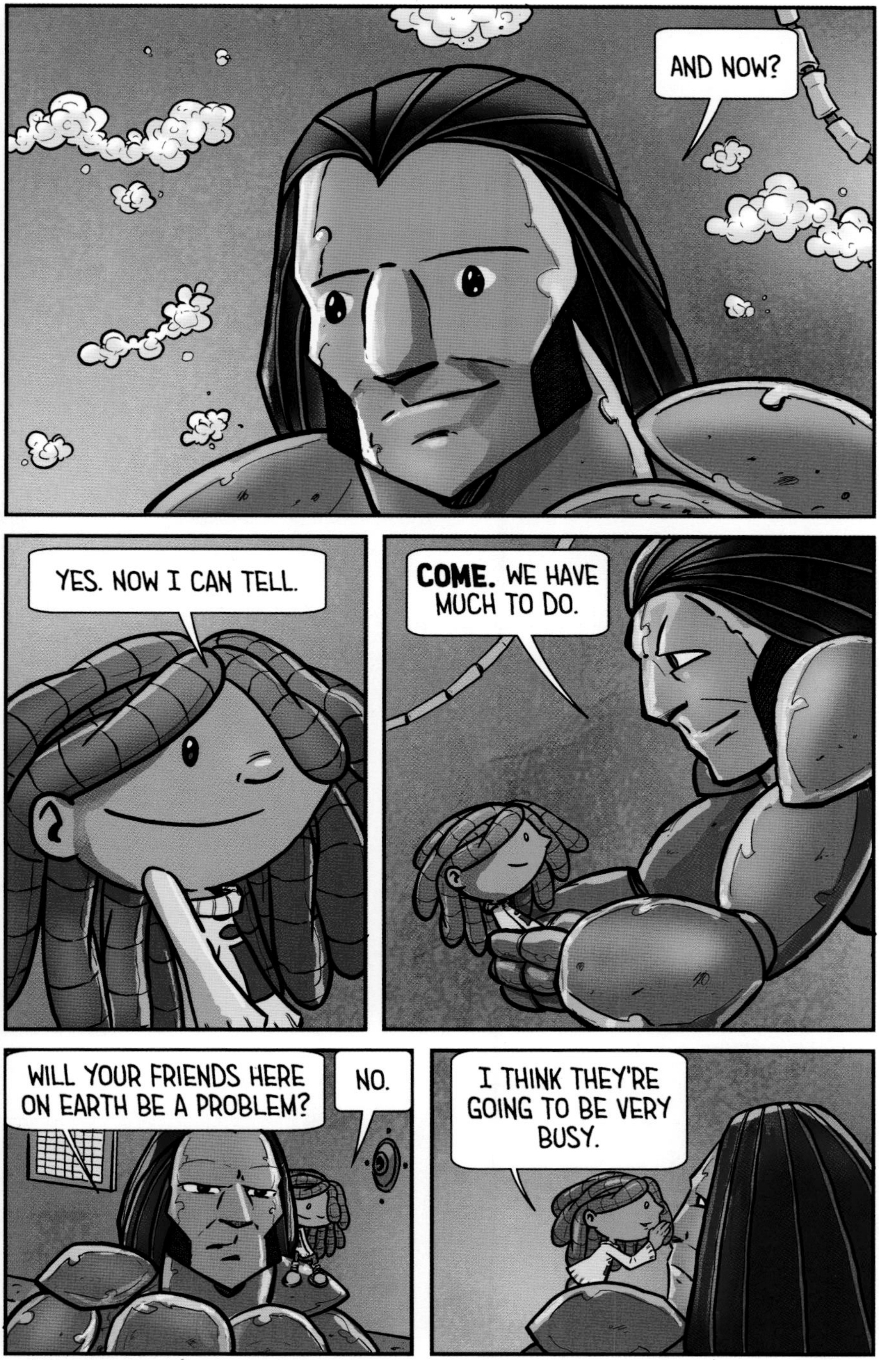
AND NOW?
YES. NOW I CAN TELL.
COME. WE HAVE MUCH TO DO.
WILL YOUR FRIENDS HERE ON EARTH BE A PROBLEM?
NO.
I THINK THEY'RE GOING TO BE VERY BUSY.

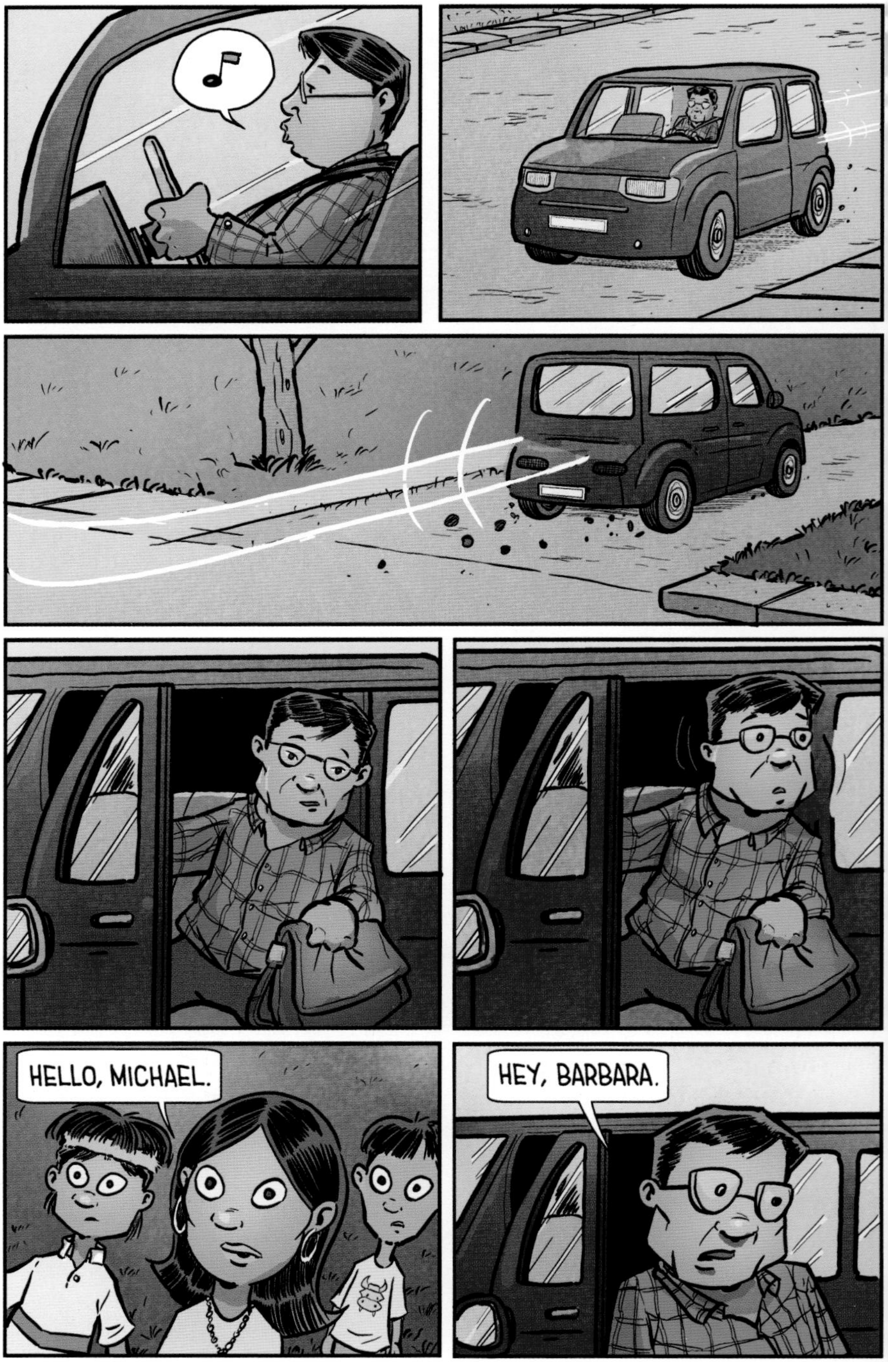
HELLO, MICHAEL.
HEY, BARBARA.

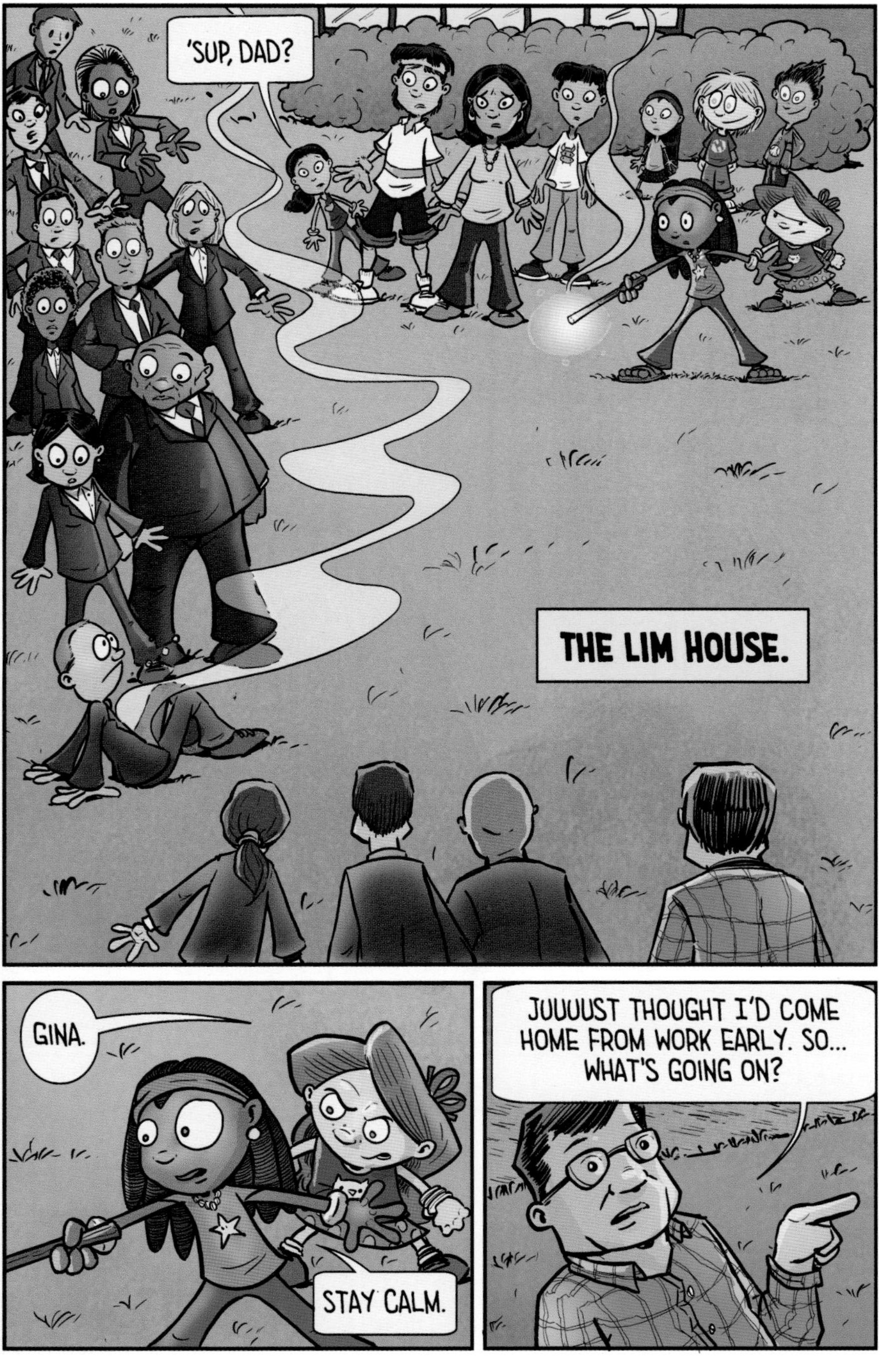
'SUP, DAD?
THE LIM HOUSE.
GINA.
STAY CALM.
JUUUUST THOUGHT I'D COME HOME FROM WORK EARLY. SO... WHAT'S GOING ON?

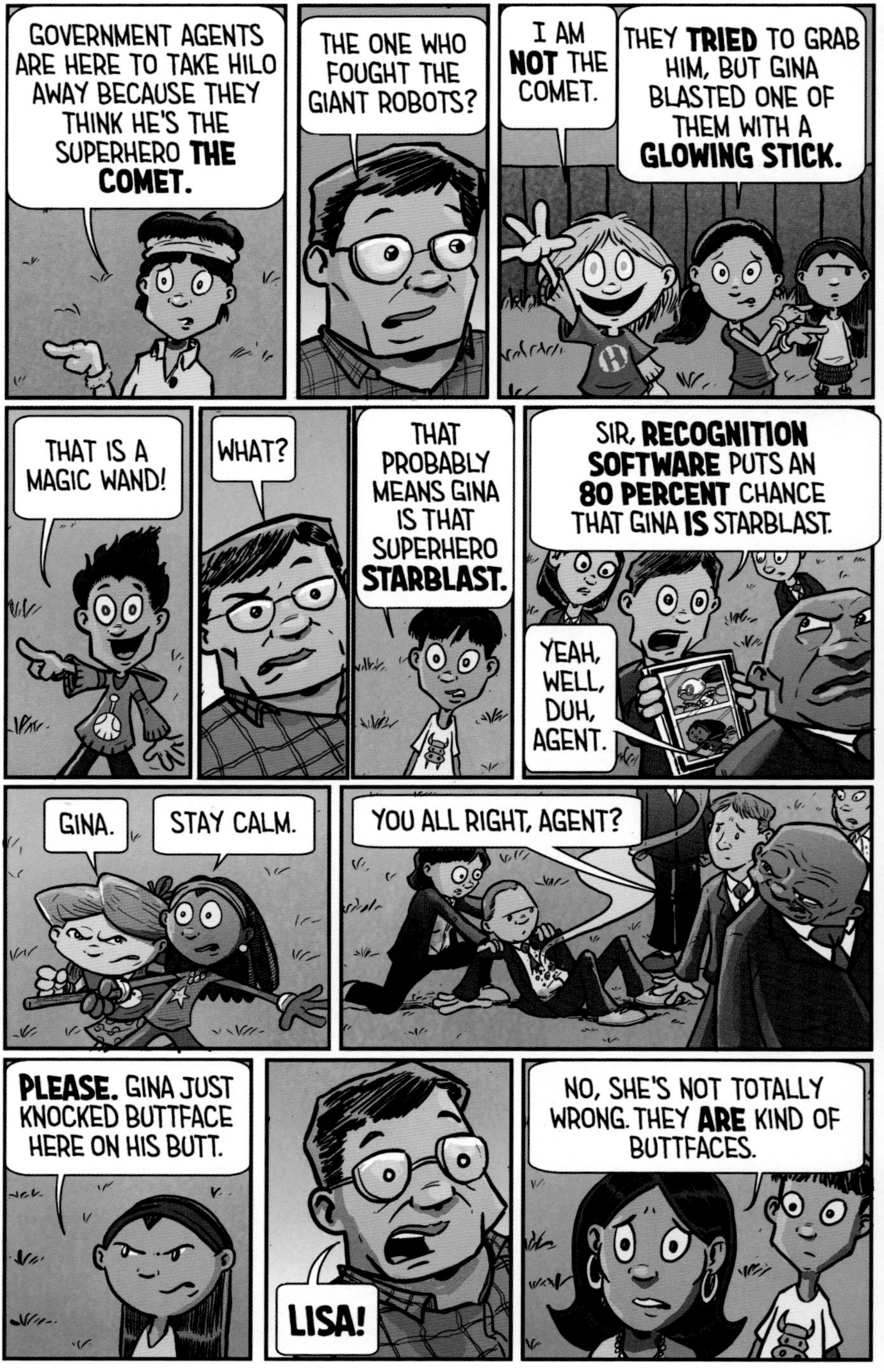
GOVERNMENT AGENTS ARE HERE TO TAKE HILO AWAY BECAUSE THEY THINK HE'S THE SUPERHERO **THE COMET.**
THE ONE WHO FOUGHT THE GIANT ROBOTS?
I AM **NOT** THE COMET.
THEY **TRIED** TO GRAB HIM, BUT GINA BLASTED ONE OF THEM WITH A **GLOWING STICK.**
THAT IS A MAGIC WAND!
WHAT?
THAT PROBABLY MEANS GINA IS THAT SUPERHERO **STARBLAST.**
SIR, **RECOGNITION SOFTWARE** PUTS AN **80 PERCENT** CHANCE THAT GINA **IS** STARBLAST.
YEAH, WELL, DUH, AGENT.
GINA.
STAY CALM.
YOU ALL RIGHT, AGENT?
PLEASE. GINA JUST KNOCKED BUTTFACE HERE ON HIS BUTT.
LISA!
NO, SHE'S NOT TOTALLY WRONG. THEY **ARE** KIND OF BUTTFACES.

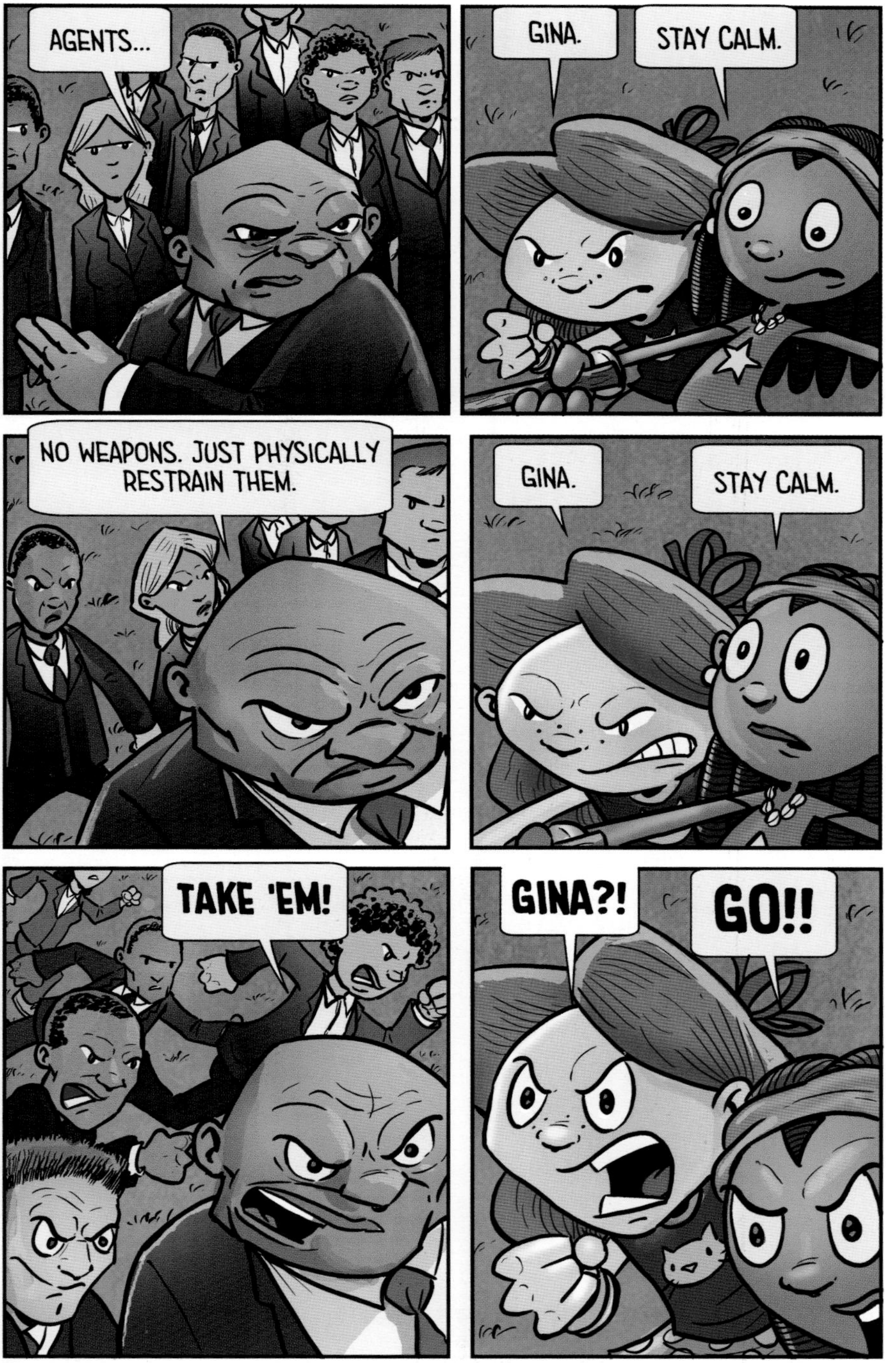
AGENTS...
GINA.
STAY CALM.
NO WEAPONS. JUST PHYSICALLY RESTRAIN THEM.
GINA.
STAY CALM.
TAKE 'EM!
GINA?!
GO!!

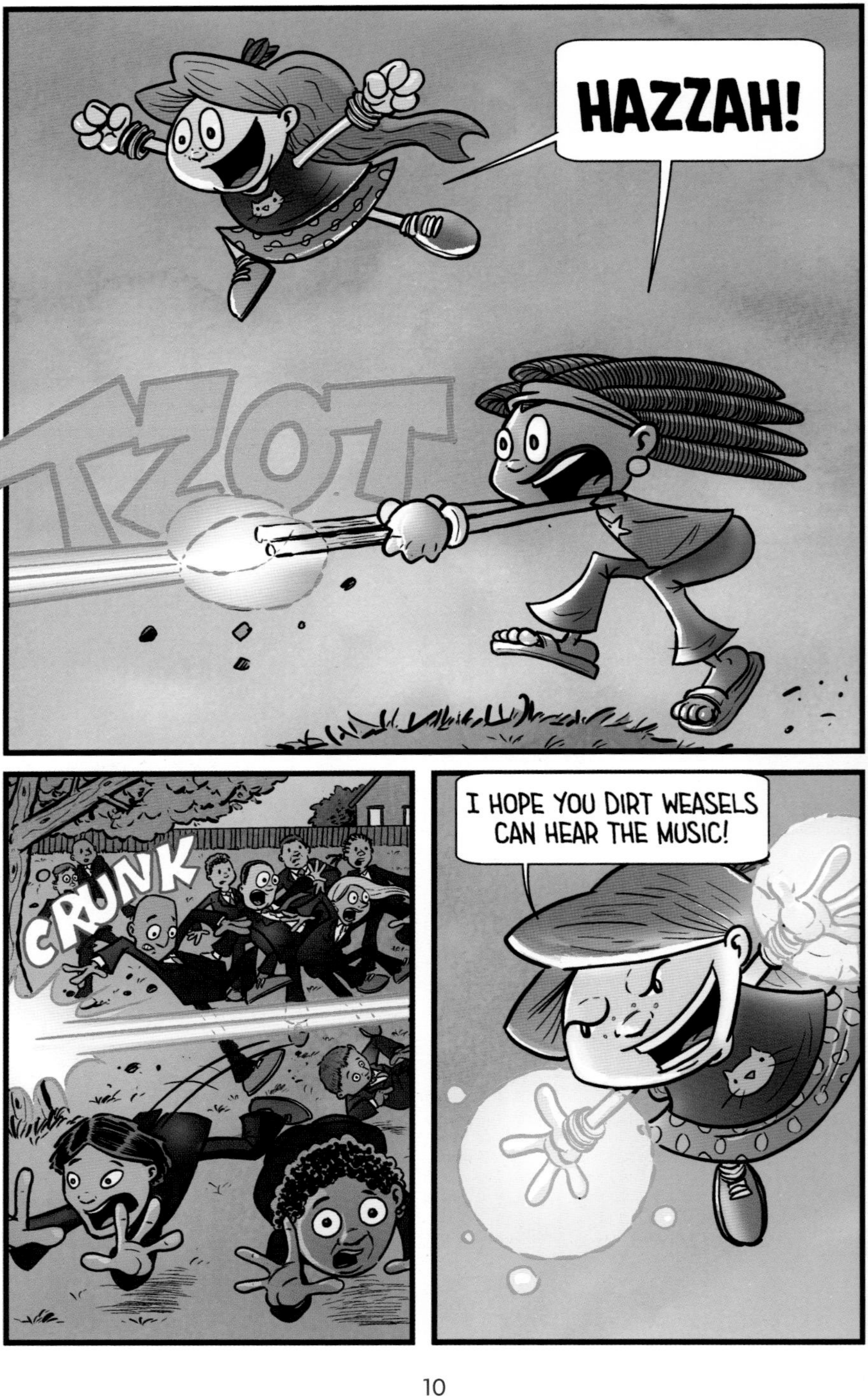
HAZZAH!
TZOT
CRUNK
I HOPE YOU DIRT WEASELS CAN HEAR THE MUSIC!

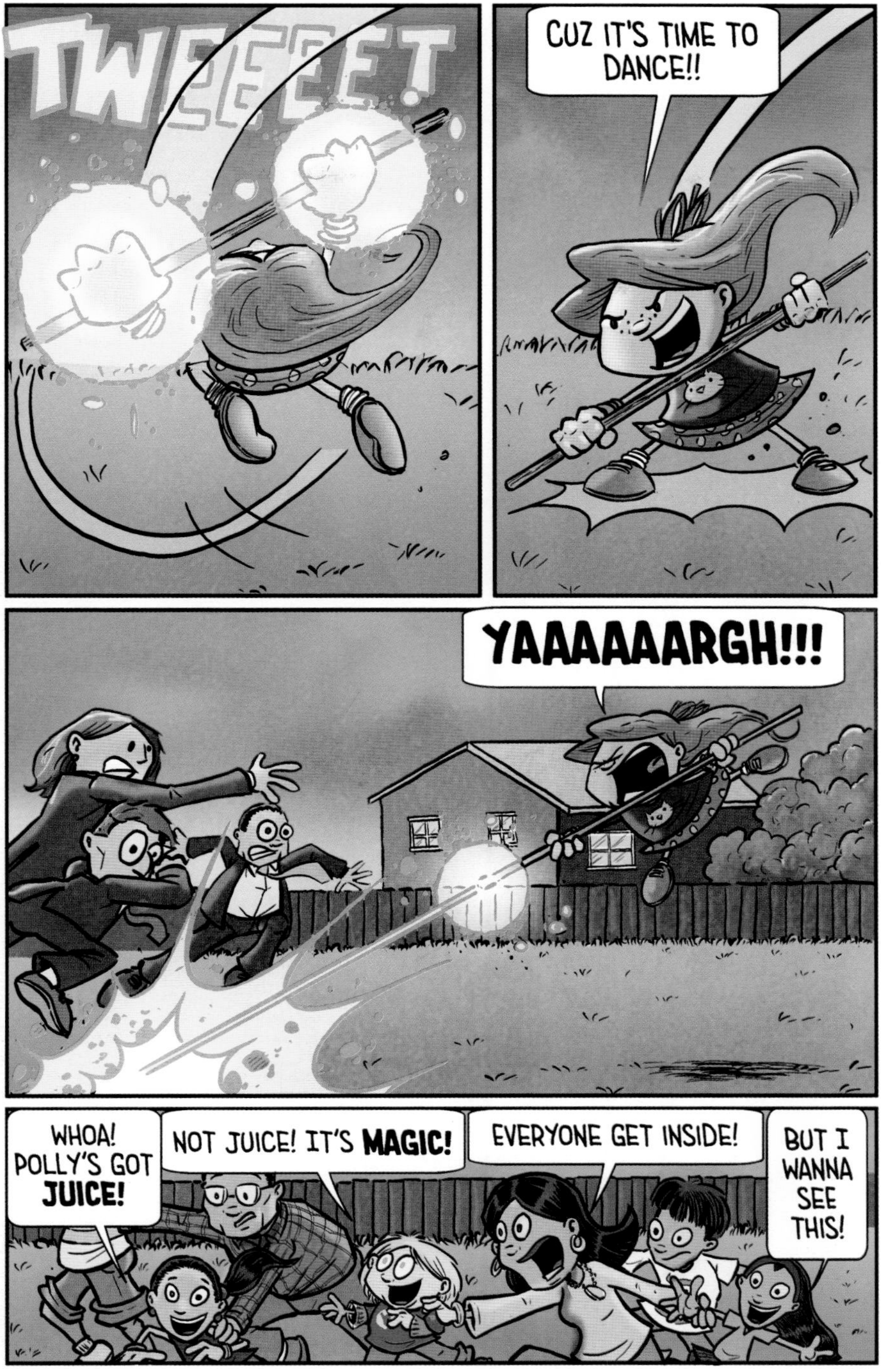
TWEEEET
CUZ IT'S TIME TO DANCE!!
YAAAAAARGH!!!
WHOA! POLLY'S GOT **JUICE!**
NOT JUICE! IT'S **MAGIC!**
EVERYONE GET INSIDE!
BUT I WANNA SEE THIS!

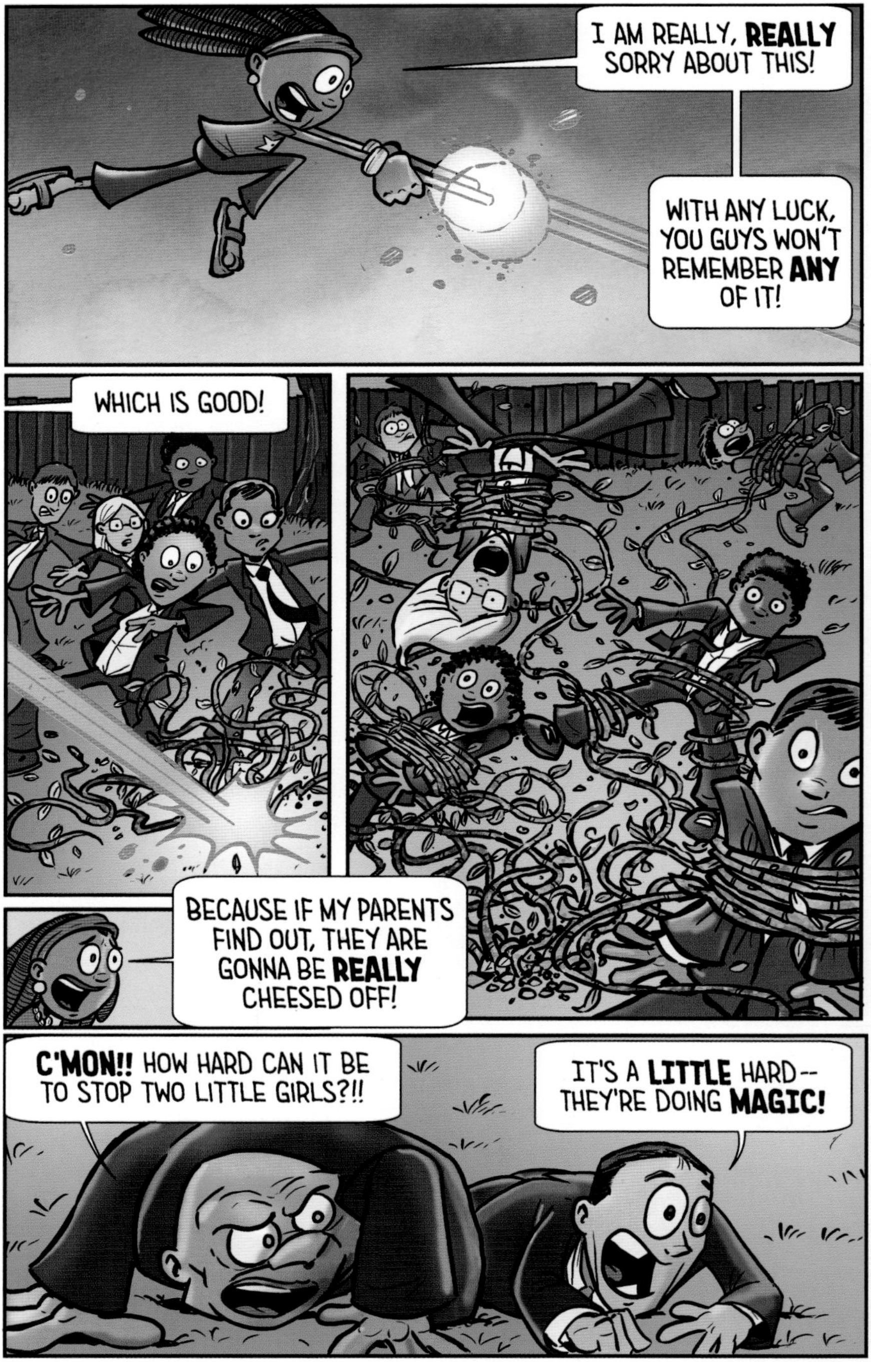
I AM REALLY, **REALLY** SORRY ABOUT THIS!
WITH ANY LUCK, YOU GUYS WON'T REMEMBER **ANY** OF IT!
WHICH IS GOOD!
BECAUSE IF MY PARENTS FIND OUT, THEY ARE GONNA BE **REALLY** CHEESED OFF!
C'MON!! HOW HARD CAN IT BE TO STOP TWO LITTLE GIRLS?!!
IT'S A **LITTLE** HARD-- THEY'RE DOING **MAGIC!**

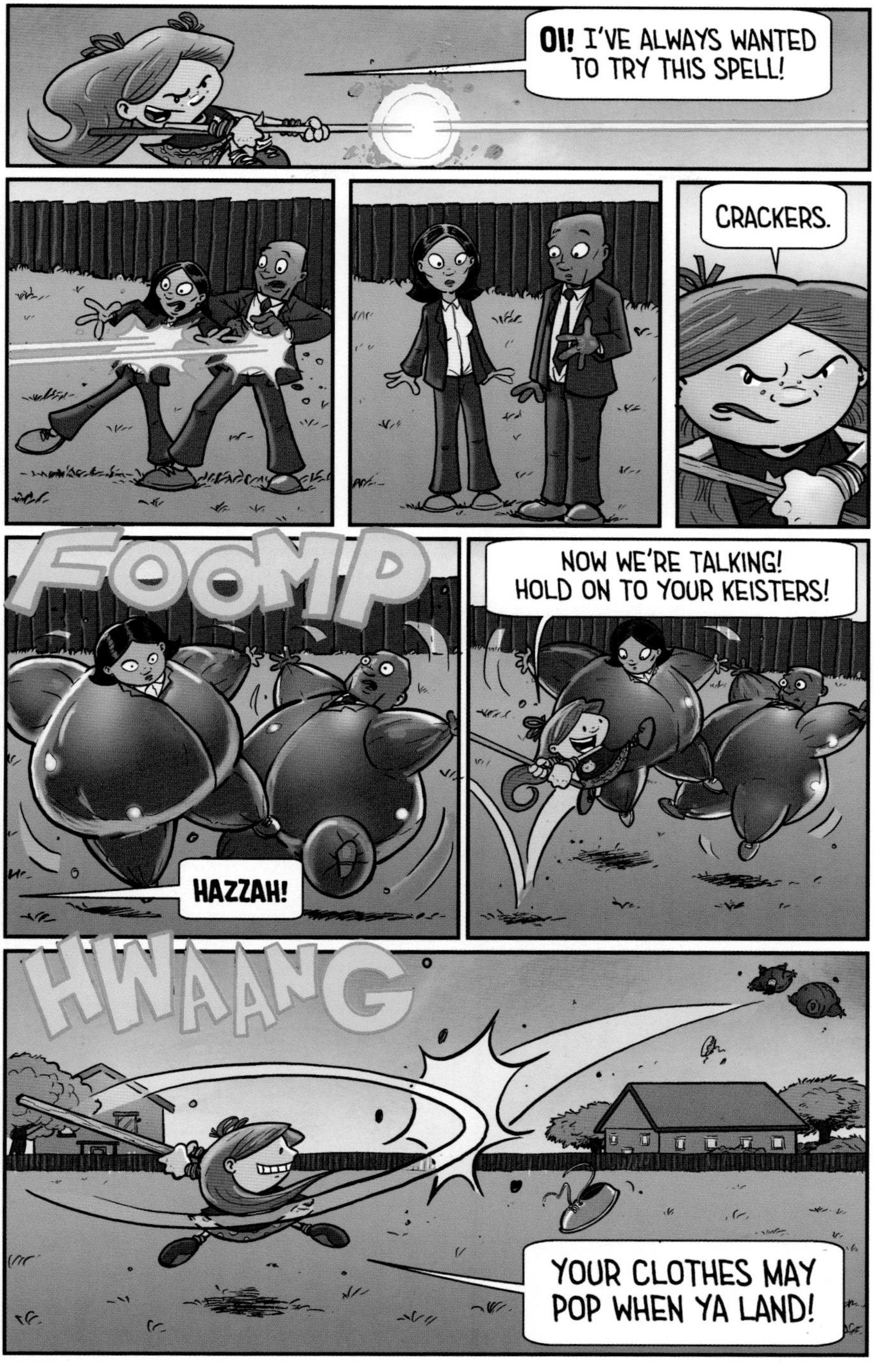
OI! I'VE ALWAYS WANTED TO TRY THIS SPELL!
CRACKERS.
FOOMP
HAZZAH!
NOW WE'RE TALKING! HOLD ON TO YOUR KEISTERS!
HWAANG
YOUR CLOTHES MAY POP WHEN YA LAND!

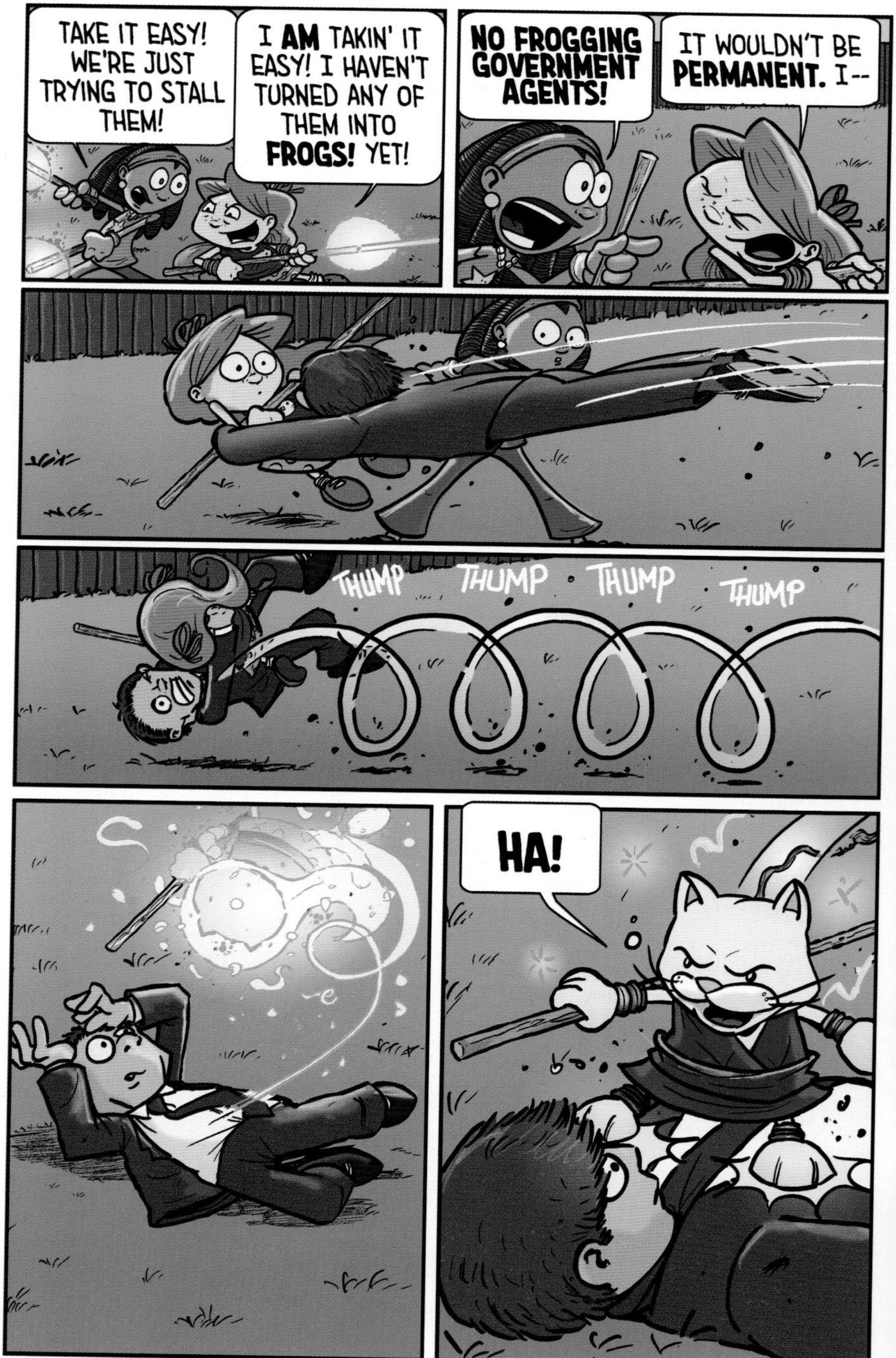
TAKE IT EASY! WE'RE JUST TRYING TO STALL THEM!
I **AM** TAKIN' IT EASY! I HAVEN'T TURNED ANY OF THEM INTO **FROGS!** YET!
NO FROGGING GOVERNMENT AGENTS!
IT WOULDN'T BE **PERMANENT.** I--
THUMP THUMP THUMP THUMP
HA!

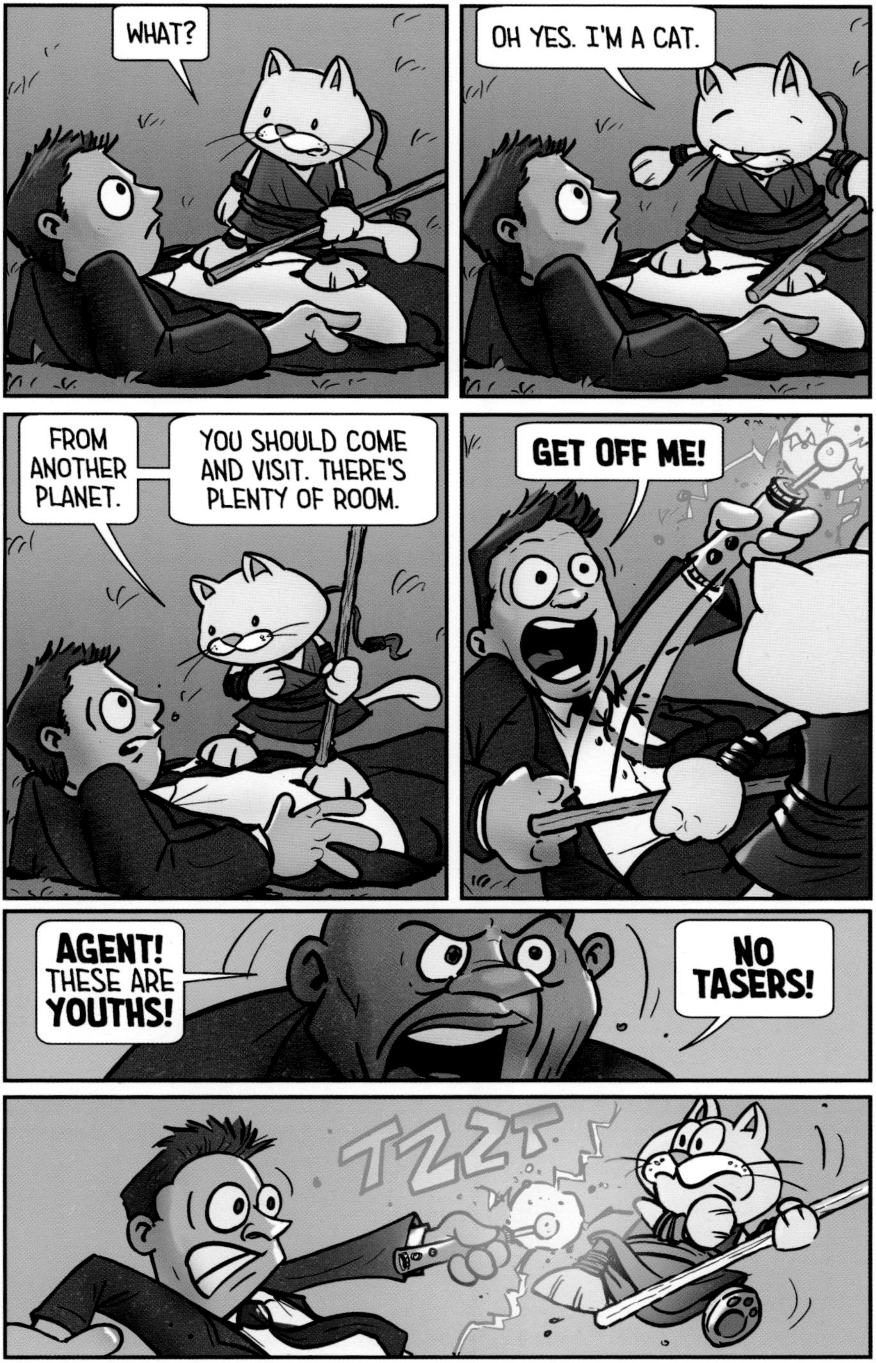
WHAT?
OH YES. I'M A CAT.
FROM ANOTHER PLANET.
YOU SHOULD COME AND VISIT. THERE'S PLENTY OF ROOM.
GET OFF ME!
AGENT! THESE ARE YOUTHS!
NO TASERS!
TZZT

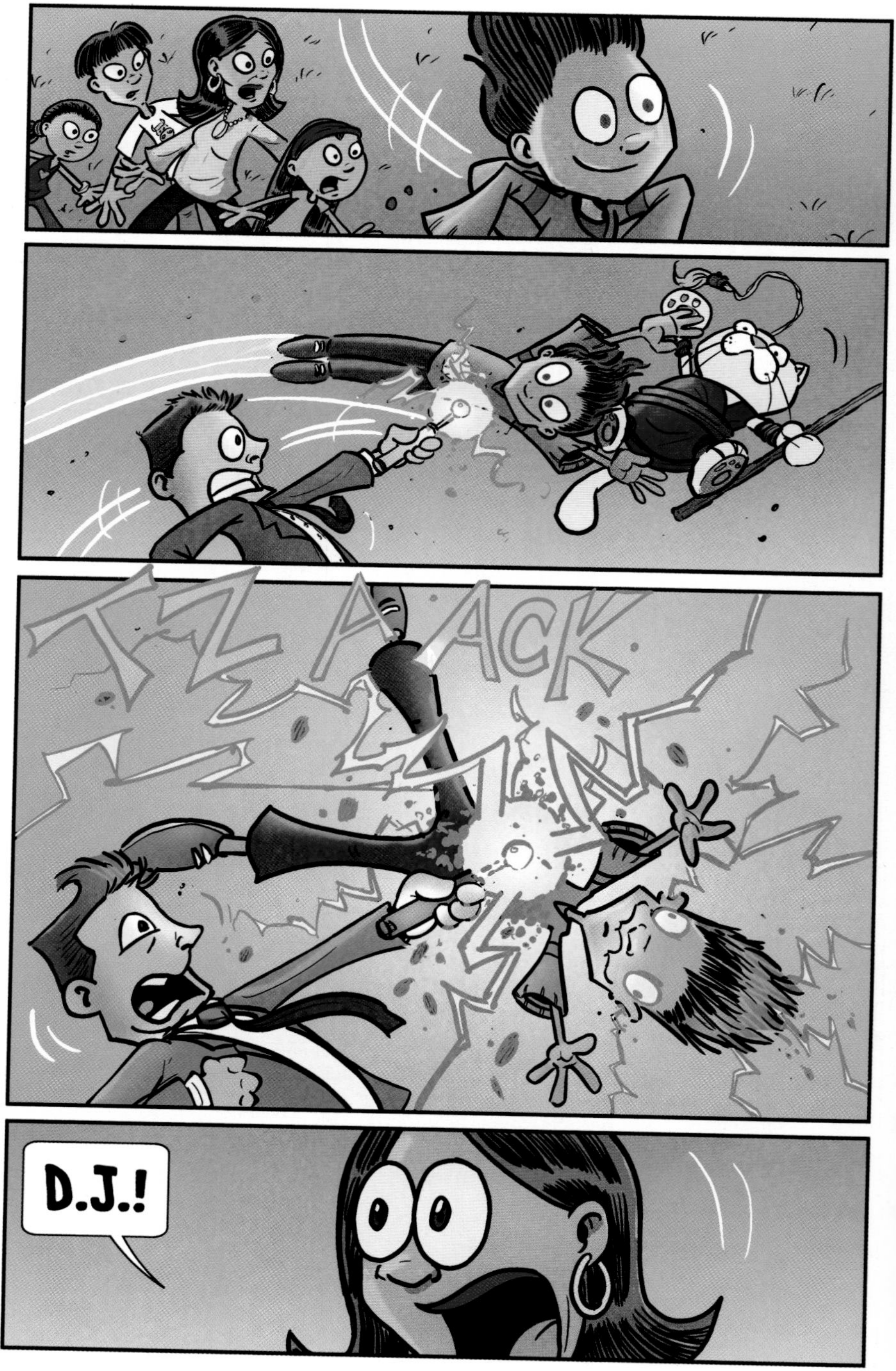
TZACK
D.J.!

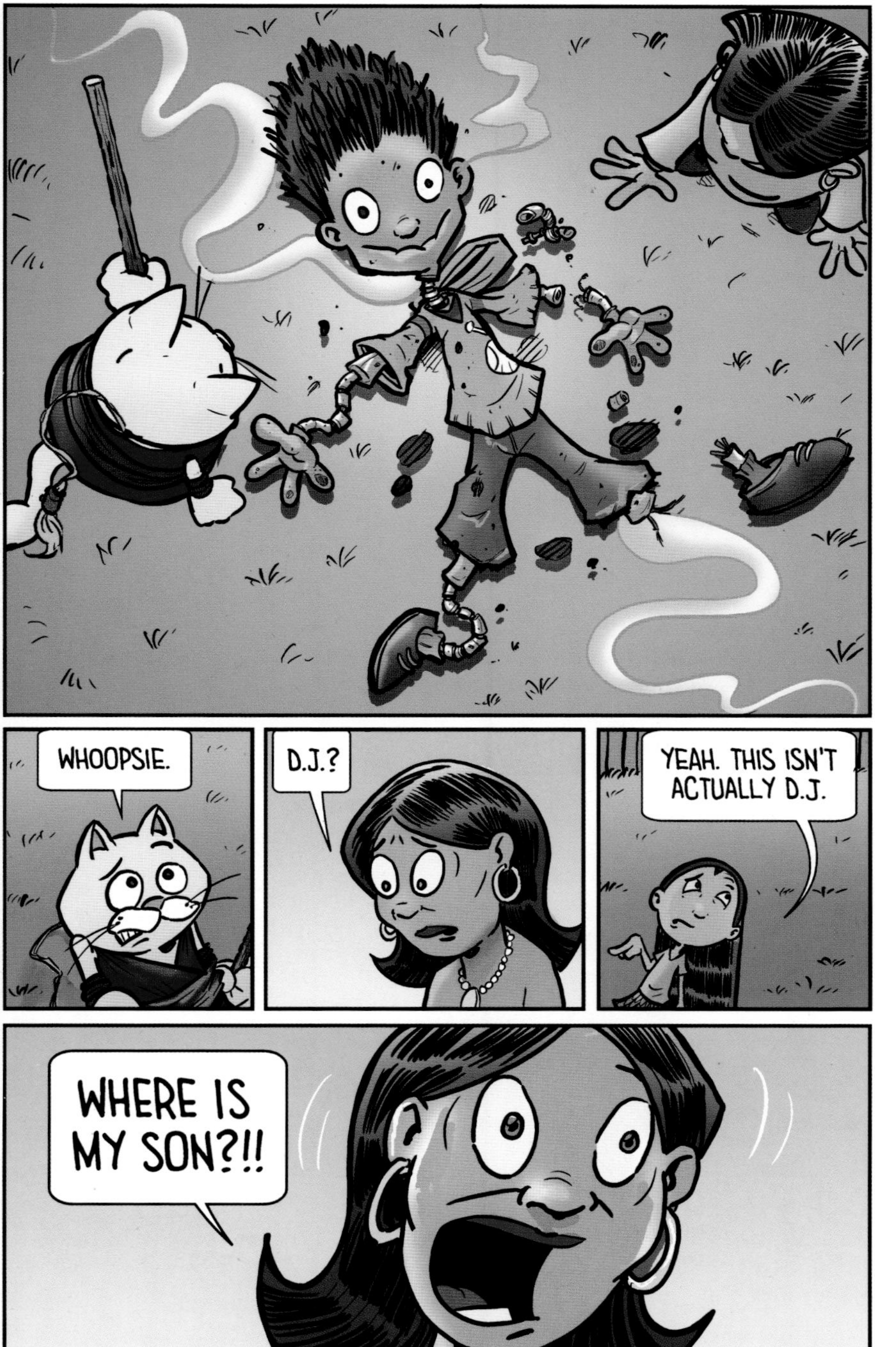
WHOOPSIE.
D.J.?
YEAH. THIS ISN'T ACTUALLY D.J.
WHERE IS MY SON?!!

CHAPTER 3

HARD BUT TRUE

JANNUS. HILO'S PLANET.

CALM DOWN.

NO.

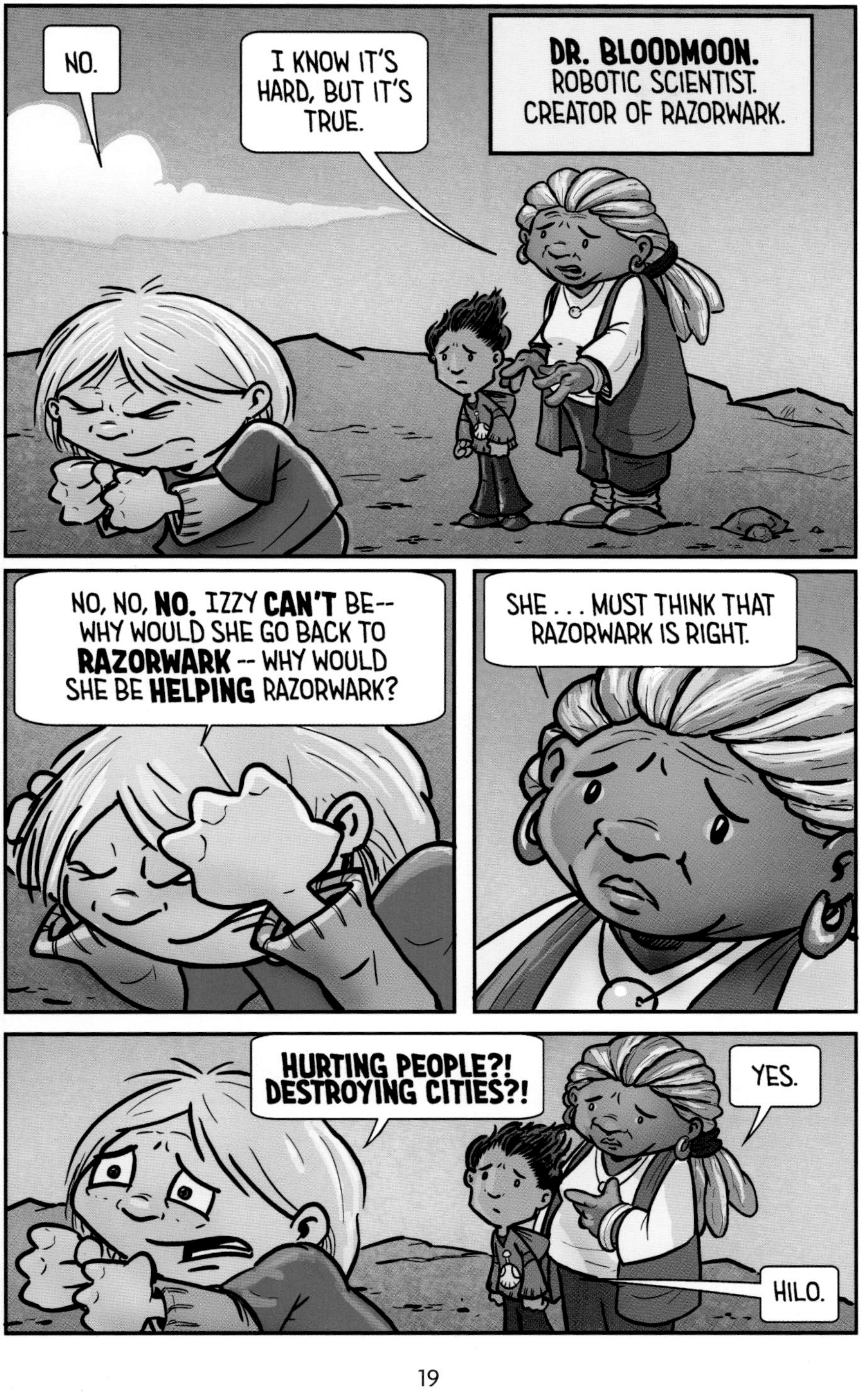
NO.
I KNOW IT'S HARD, BUT IT'S TRUE.
DR. BLOODMOON. ROBOTIC SCIENTIST. CREATOR OF RAZORWARK.
NO, NO, **NO.** IZZY **CAN'T** BE-- WHY WOULD SHE GO BACK TO **RAZORWARK** -- WHY WOULD SHE BE **HELPING** RAZORWARK?
SHE . . . MUST THINK THAT RAZORWARK IS RIGHT.
HURTING PEOPLE?! DESTROYING CITIES?!
YES.
HILO.

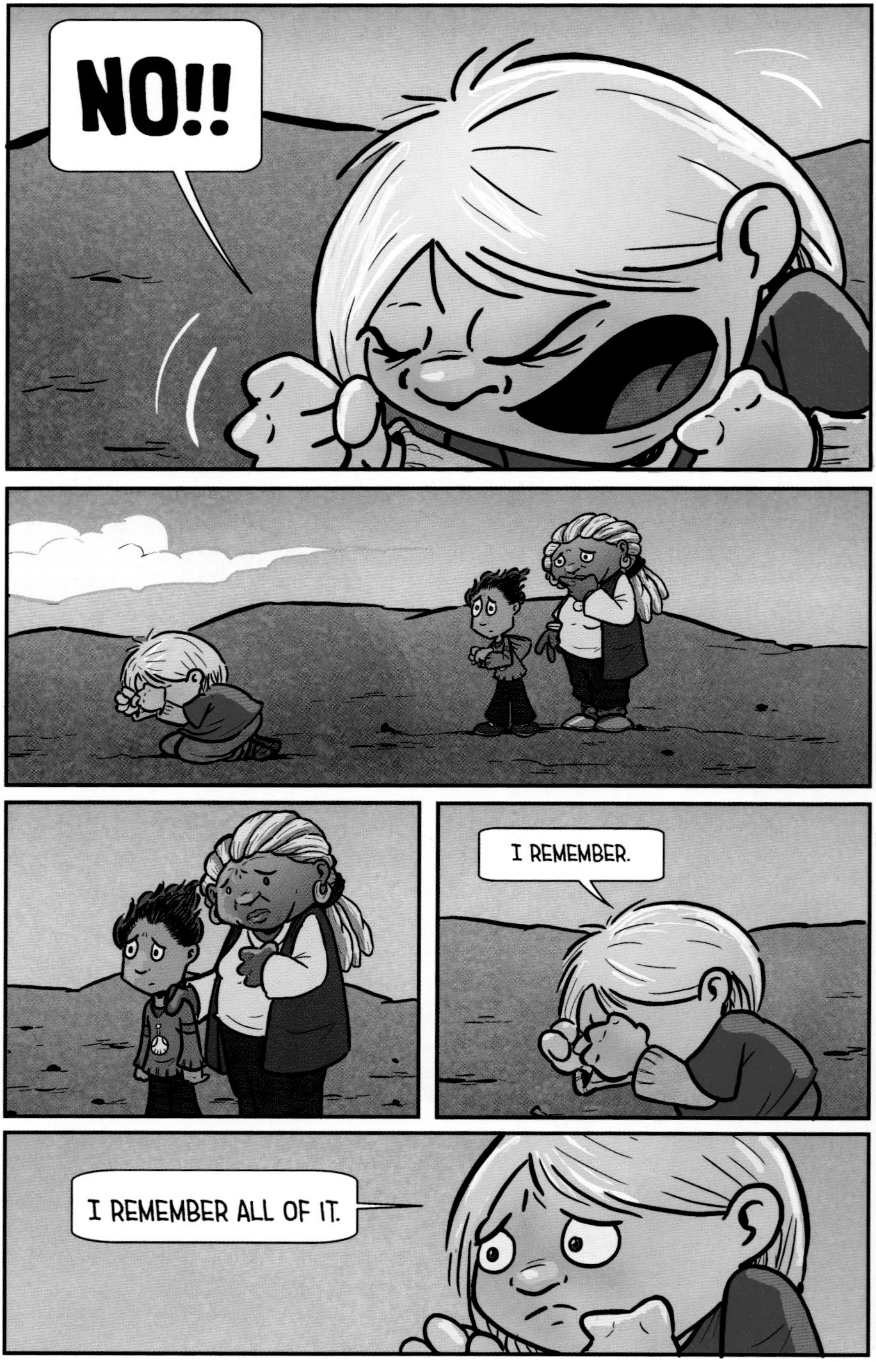
NO!!
I REMEMBER.
I REMEMBER ALL OF IT.

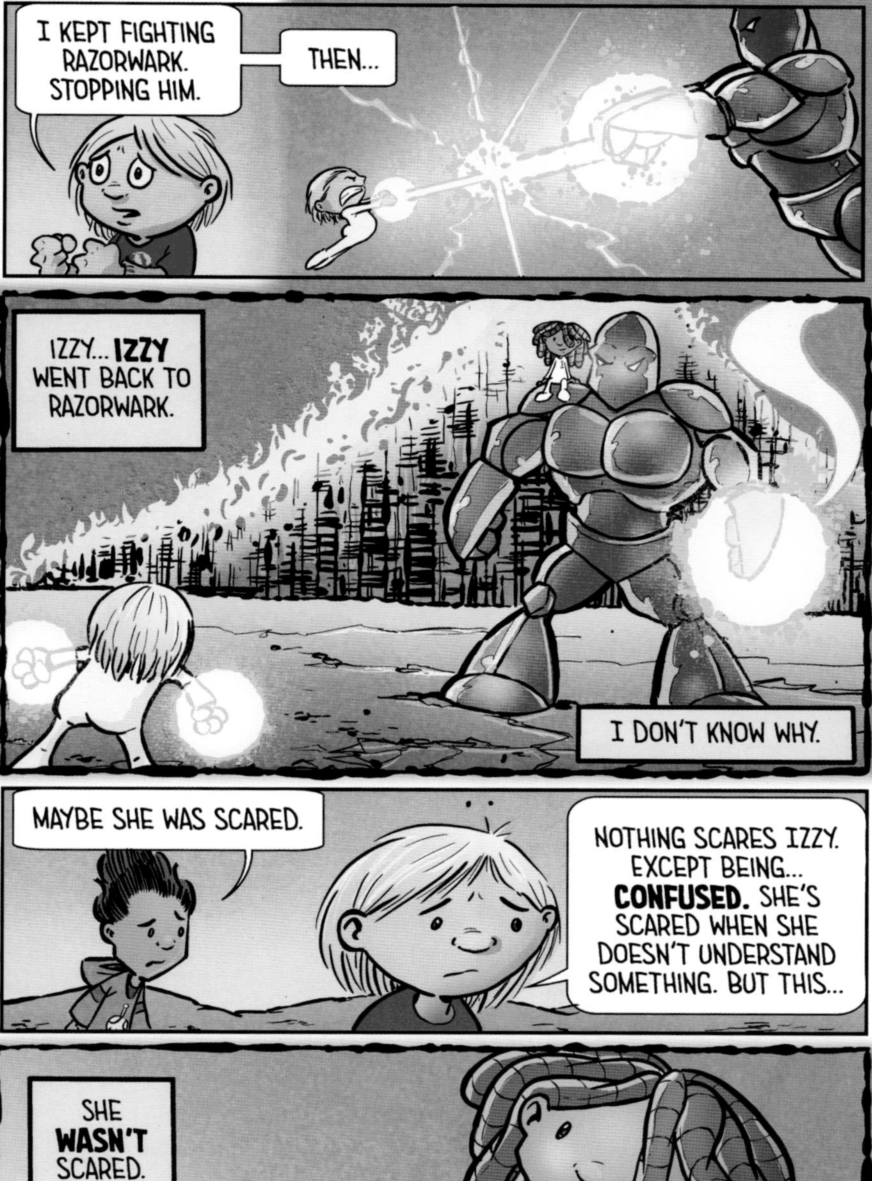
I KEPT FIGHTING RAZORWARK. STOPPING HIM.
THEN...
IZZY... **IZZY** WENT BACK TO RAZORWARK.
I DON'T KNOW WHY.
MAYBE SHE WAS SCARED.
NOTHING SCARES IZZY. EXCEPT BEING... **CONFUSED.** SHE'S SCARED WHEN SHE DOESN'T UNDERSTAND SOMETHING. BUT THIS...
SHE **WASN'T** SCARED.

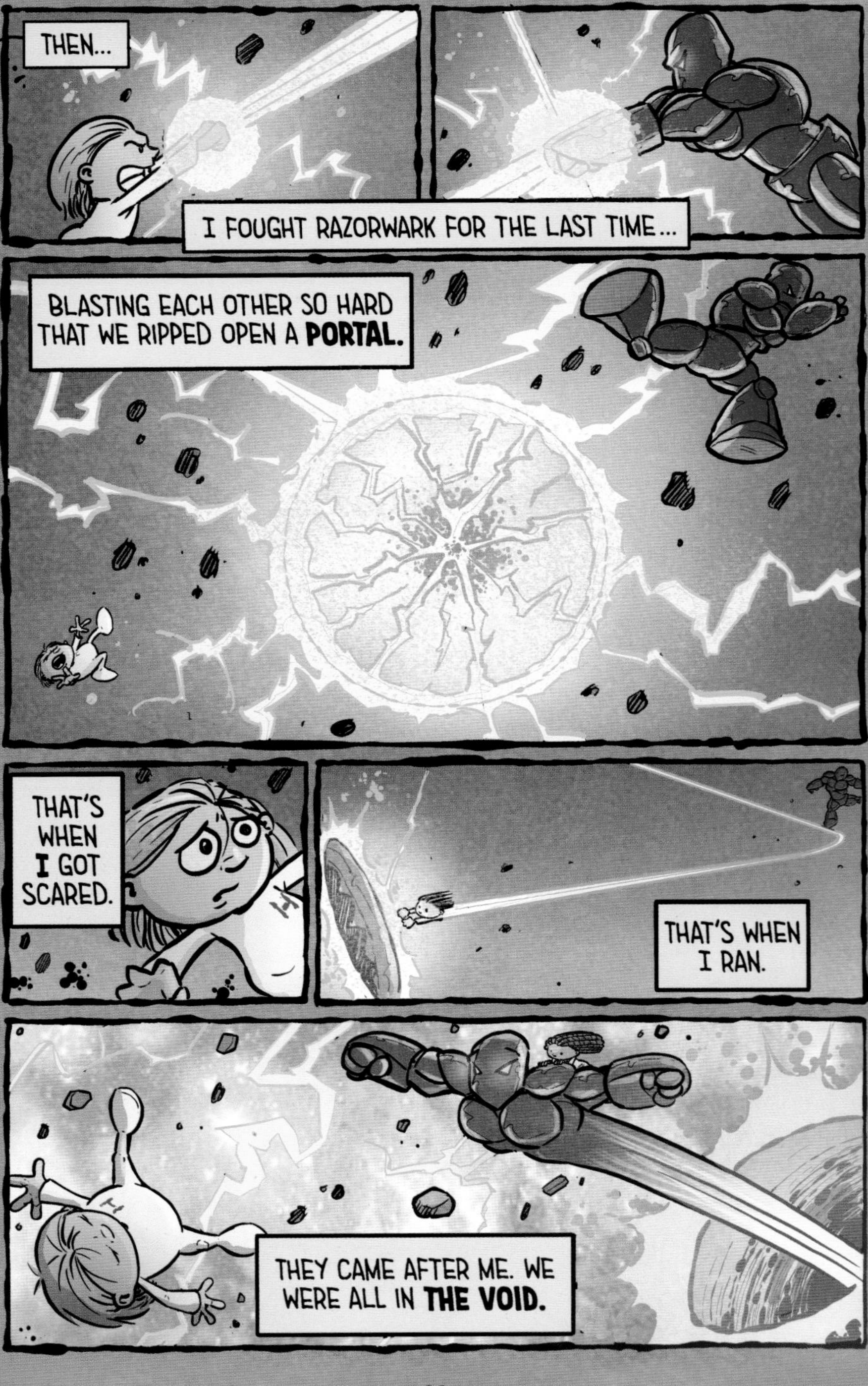
THEN...
I FOUGHT RAZORWARK FOR THE LAST TIME...
BLASTING EACH OTHER SO HARD THAT WE RIPPED OPEN A **PORTAL.**
THAT'S WHEN **I** GOT SCARED.
THAT'S WHEN I RAN.
THEY CAME AFTER ME. WE WERE ALL IN **THE VOID.**

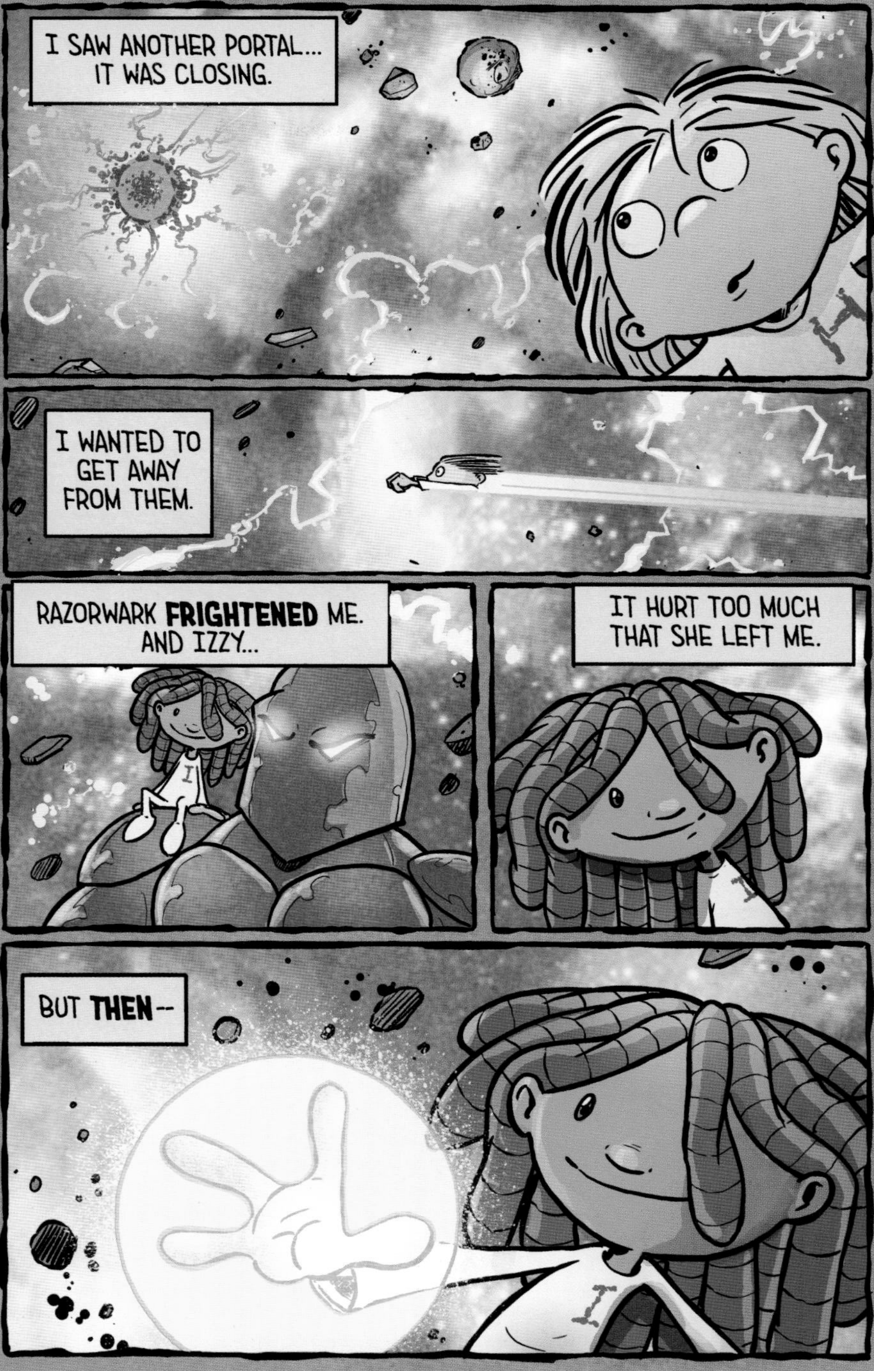
I SAW ANOTHER PORTAL... IT WAS CLOSING.
I WANTED TO GET AWAY FROM THEM.
RAZORWARK **FRIGHTENED** ME. AND IZZY...
IT HURT TOO MUCH THAT SHE LEFT ME.
BUT **THEN**--

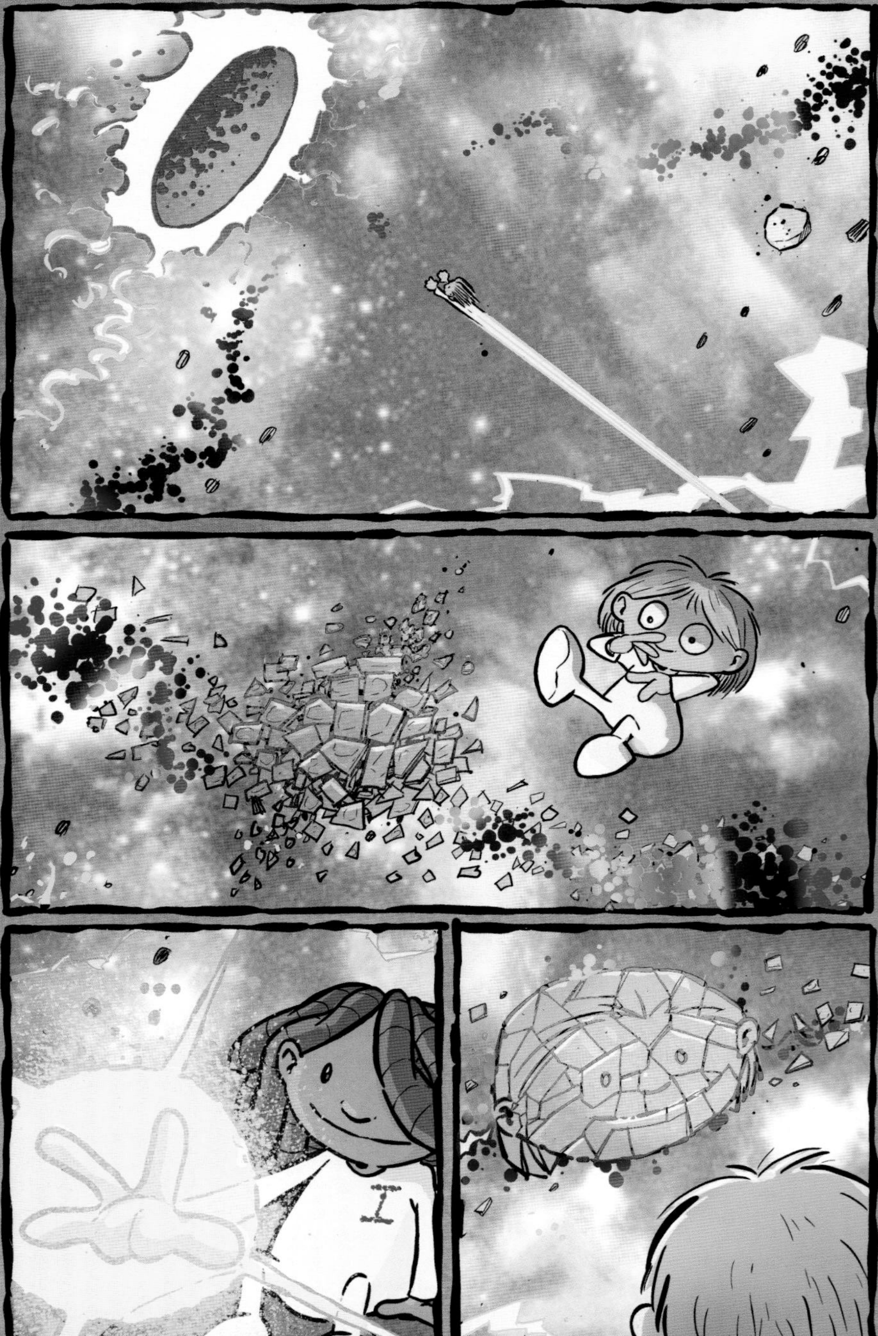

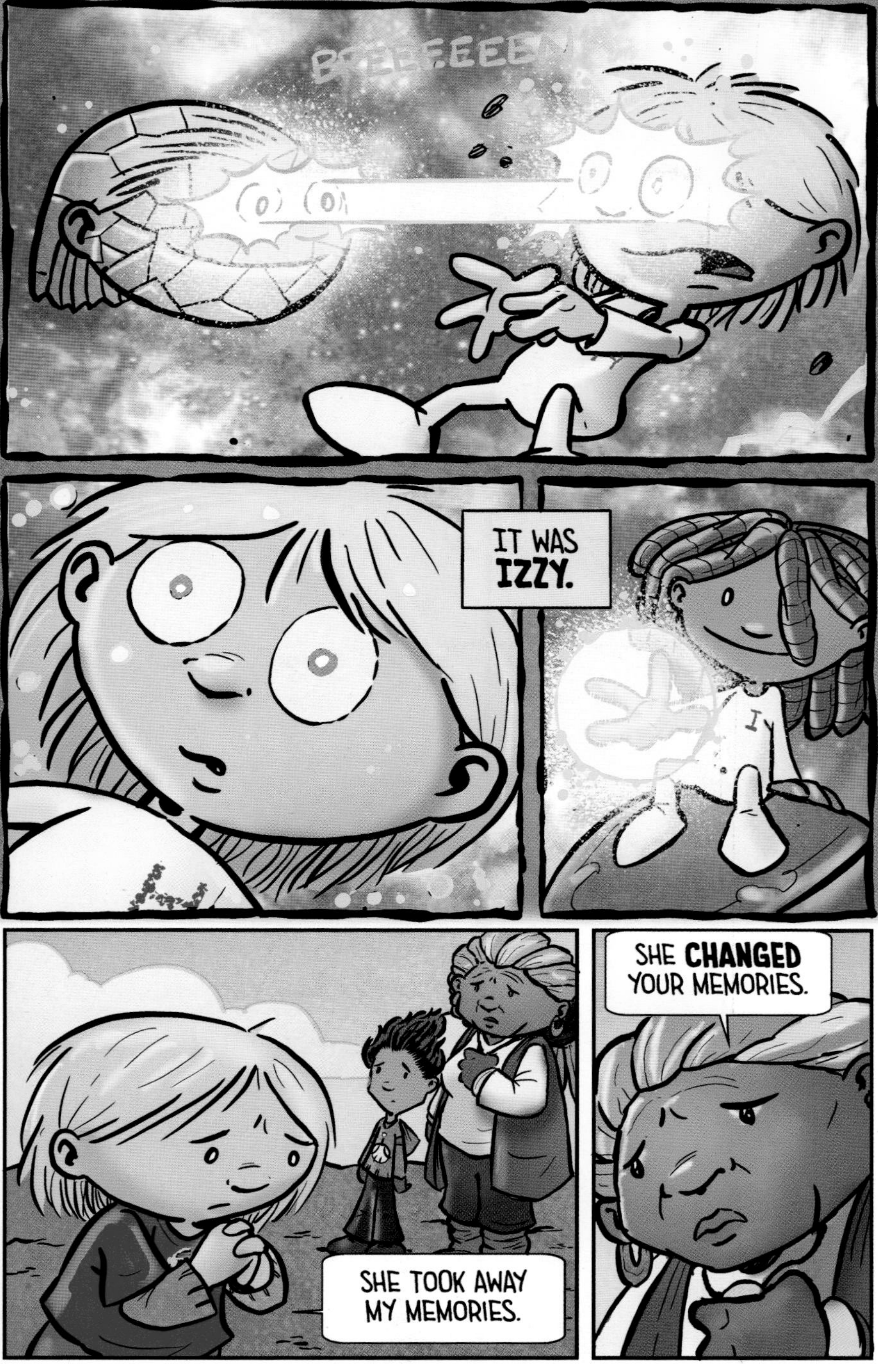
BREEEEEEN
IT WAS IZZY.
SHE TOOK AWAY MY MEMORIES.
SHE CHANGED YOUR MEMORIES.

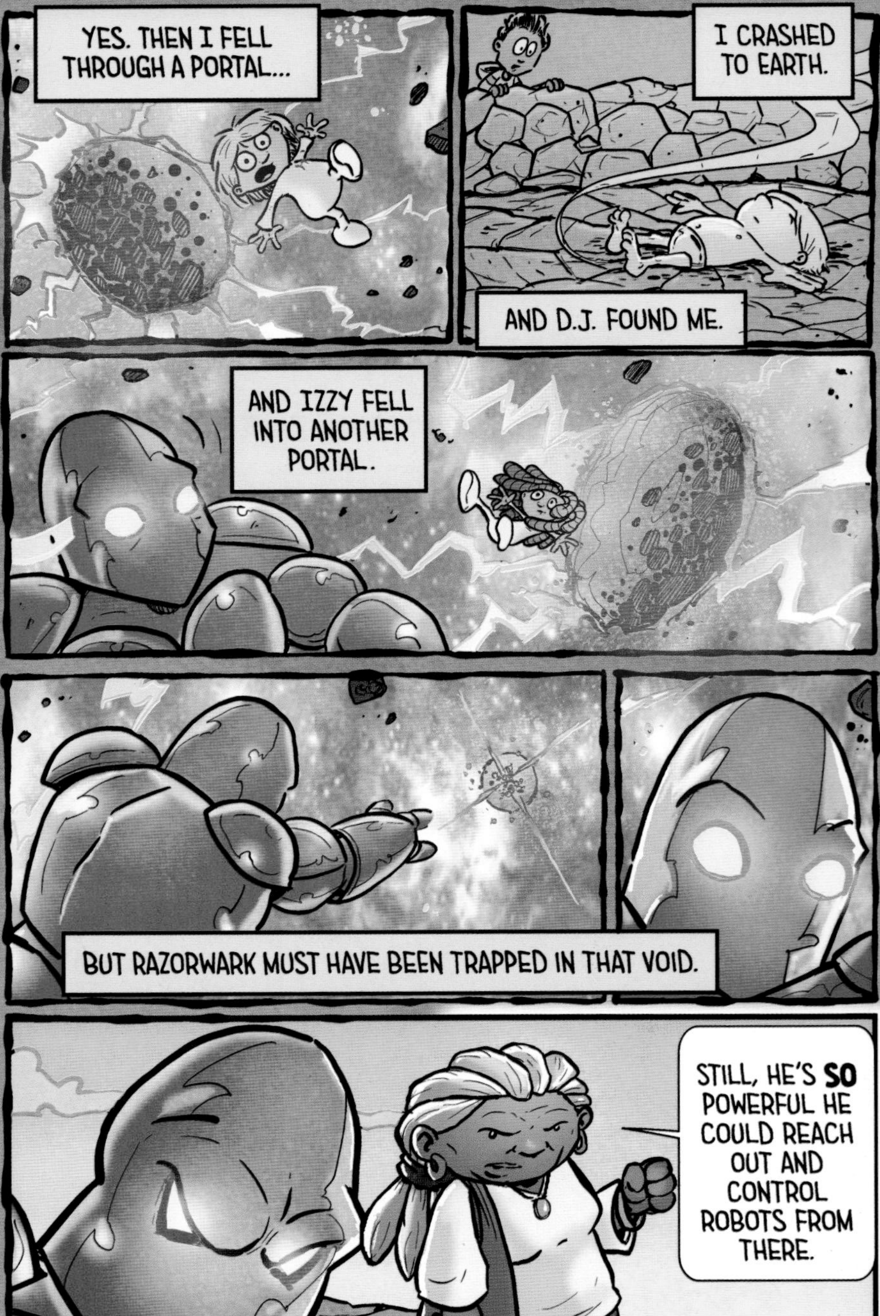
YES. THEN I FELL THROUGH A PORTAL...
I CRASHED TO EARTH.
AND D.J. FOUND ME.
AND IZZY FELL INTO ANOTHER PORTAL.
BUT RAZORWARK MUST HAVE BEEN TRAPPED IN THAT VOID.
STILL, HE'S **SO** POWERFUL HE COULD REACH OUT AND CONTROL ROBOTS FROM THERE.

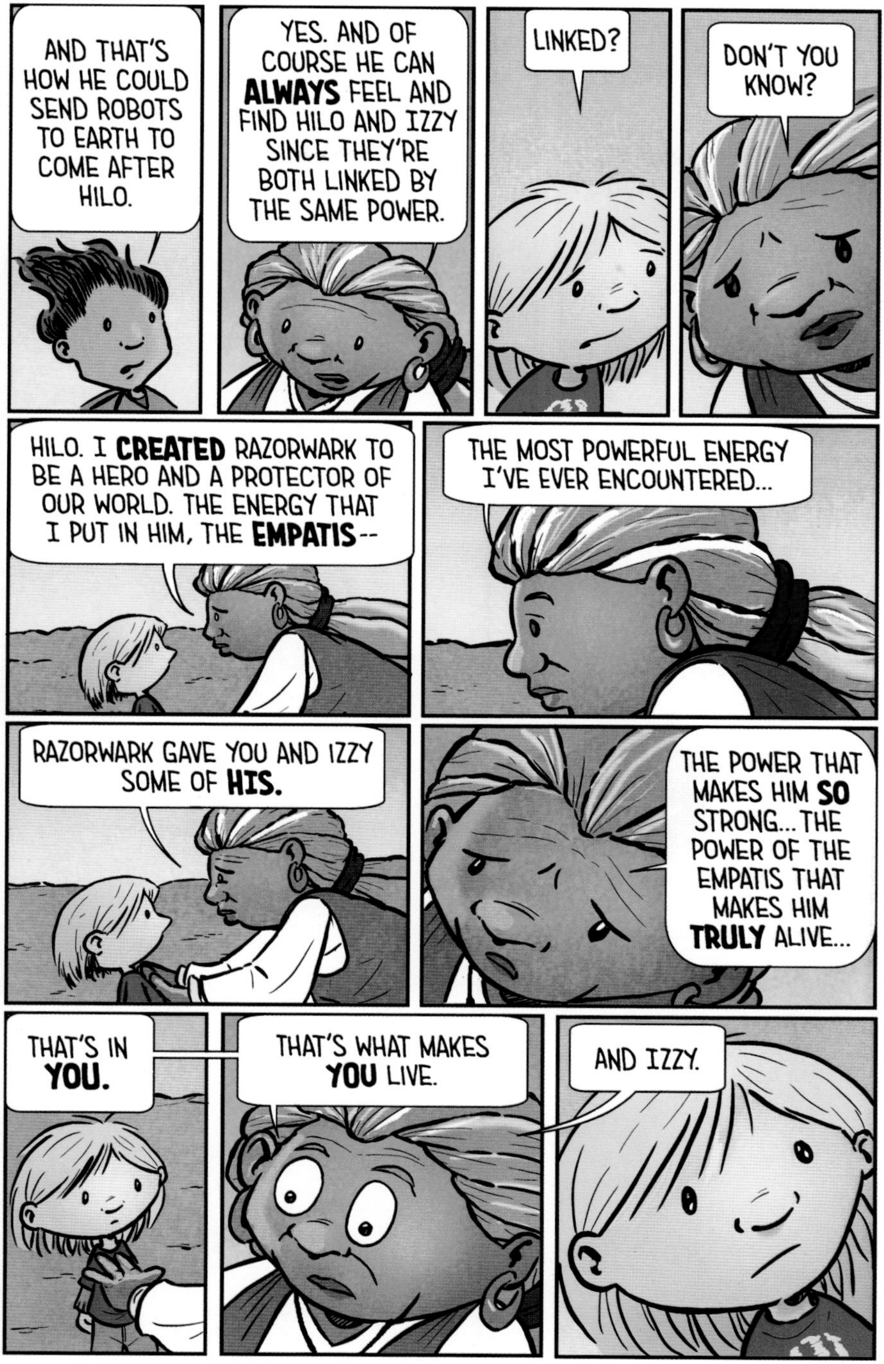
AND THAT'S HOW HE COULD SEND ROBOTS TO EARTH TO COME AFTER HILO.
YES. AND OF COURSE HE CAN **ALWAYS** FEEL AND FIND HILO AND IZZY SINCE THEY'RE BOTH LINKED BY THE SAME POWER.
LINKED?
DON'T YOU KNOW?
HILO. I **CREATED** RAZORWARK TO BE A HERO AND A PROTECTOR OF OUR WORLD. THE ENERGY THAT I PUT IN HIM, THE **EMPATIS**--
THE MOST POWERFUL ENERGY I'VE EVER ENCOUNTERED...
RAZORWARK GAVE YOU AND IZZY SOME OF **HIS.**
THE POWER THAT MAKES HIM **SO** STRONG... THE POWER OF THE EMPATIS THAT MAKES HIM **TRULY** ALIVE...
THAT'S IN **YOU.**
THAT'S WHAT MAKES **YOU** LIVE.
AND IZZY.

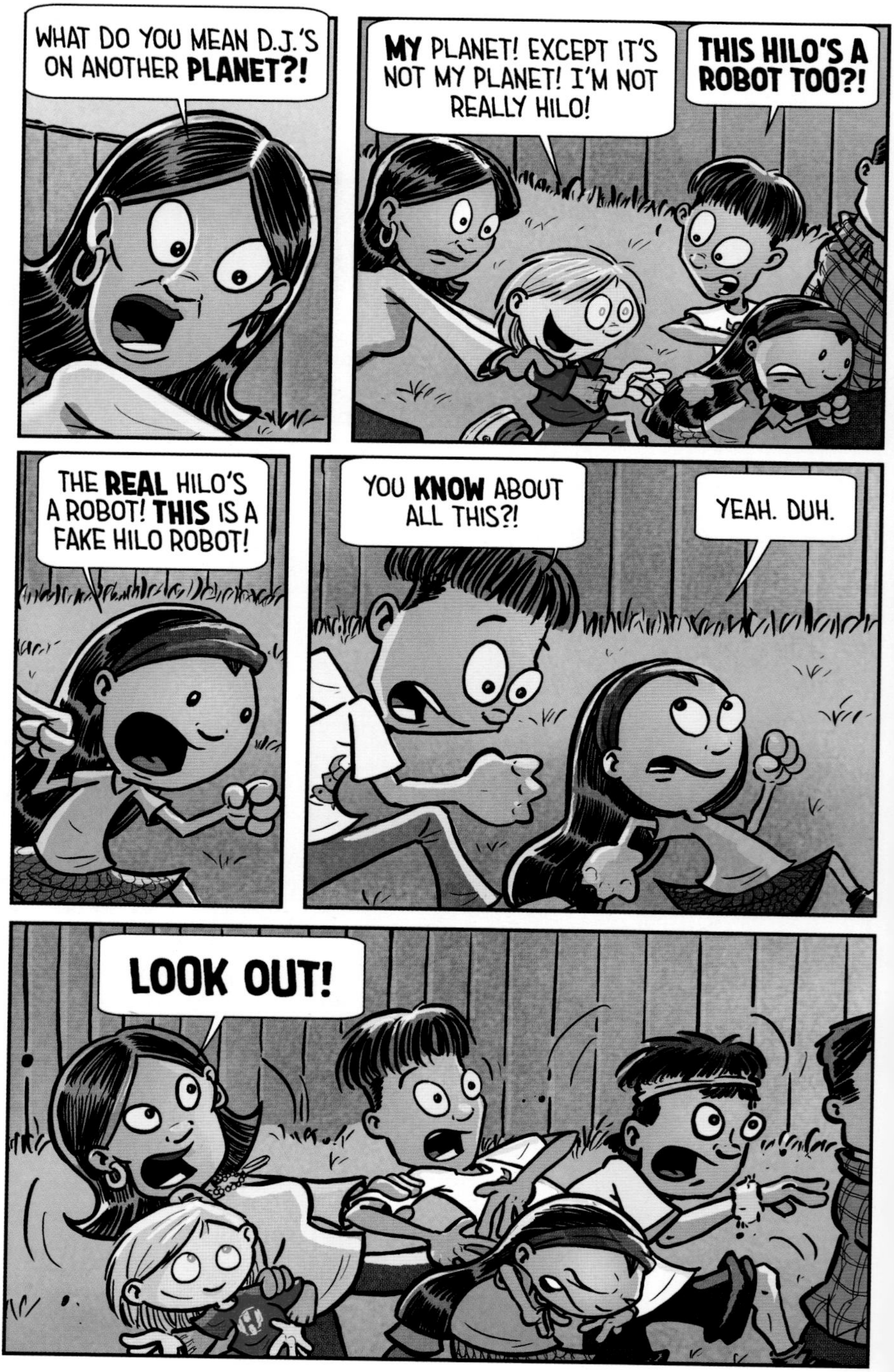
WHAT DO YOU MEAN D.J.'S ON ANOTHER **PLANET?!**
MY PLANET! EXCEPT IT'S NOT MY PLANET! I'M NOT REALLY HILO!
THIS HILO'S A ROBOT TOO?!
THE **REAL** HILO'S A ROBOT! **THIS** IS A FAKE HILO ROBOT!
YOU **KNOW** ABOUT ALL THIS?!
YEAH. DUH.
LOOK OUT!

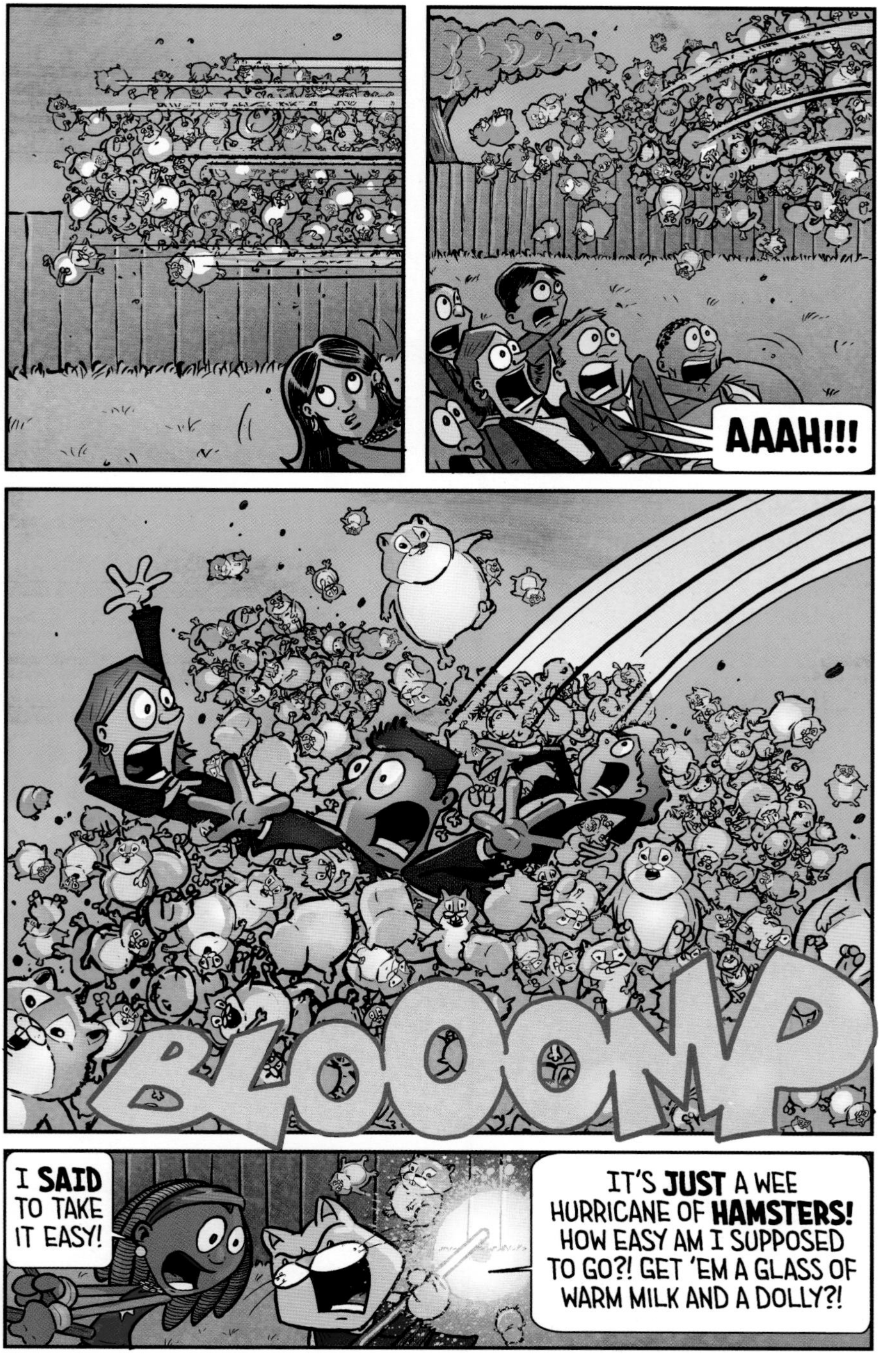
AAAH!!!
BLOOOMP
I SAID TO TAKE IT EASY!
IT'S JUST A WEE HURRICANE OF HAMSTERS! HOW EASY AM I SUPPOSED TO GO?! GET 'EM A GLASS OF WARM MILK AND A DOLLY?!

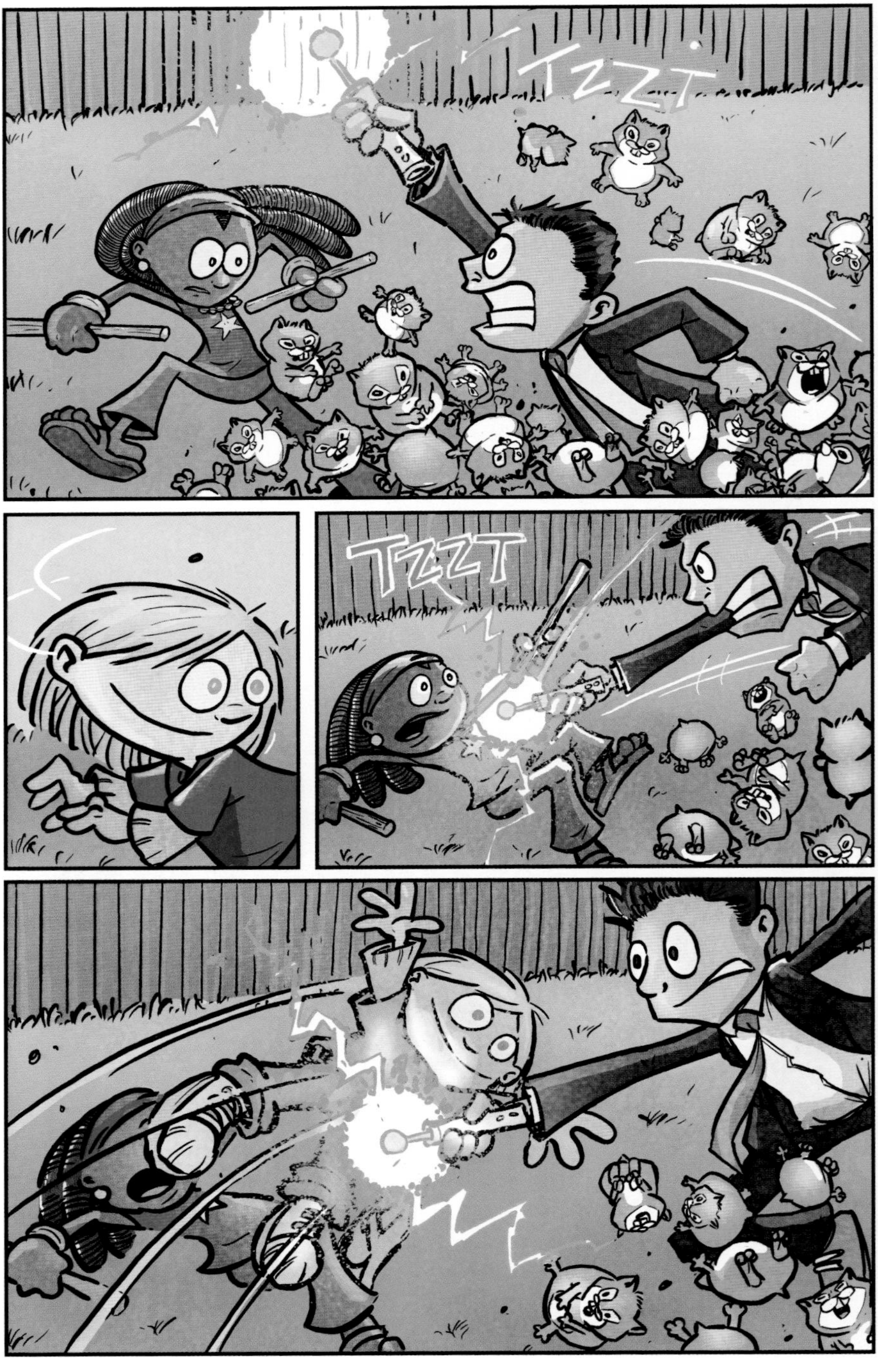
TZZT
TZZT

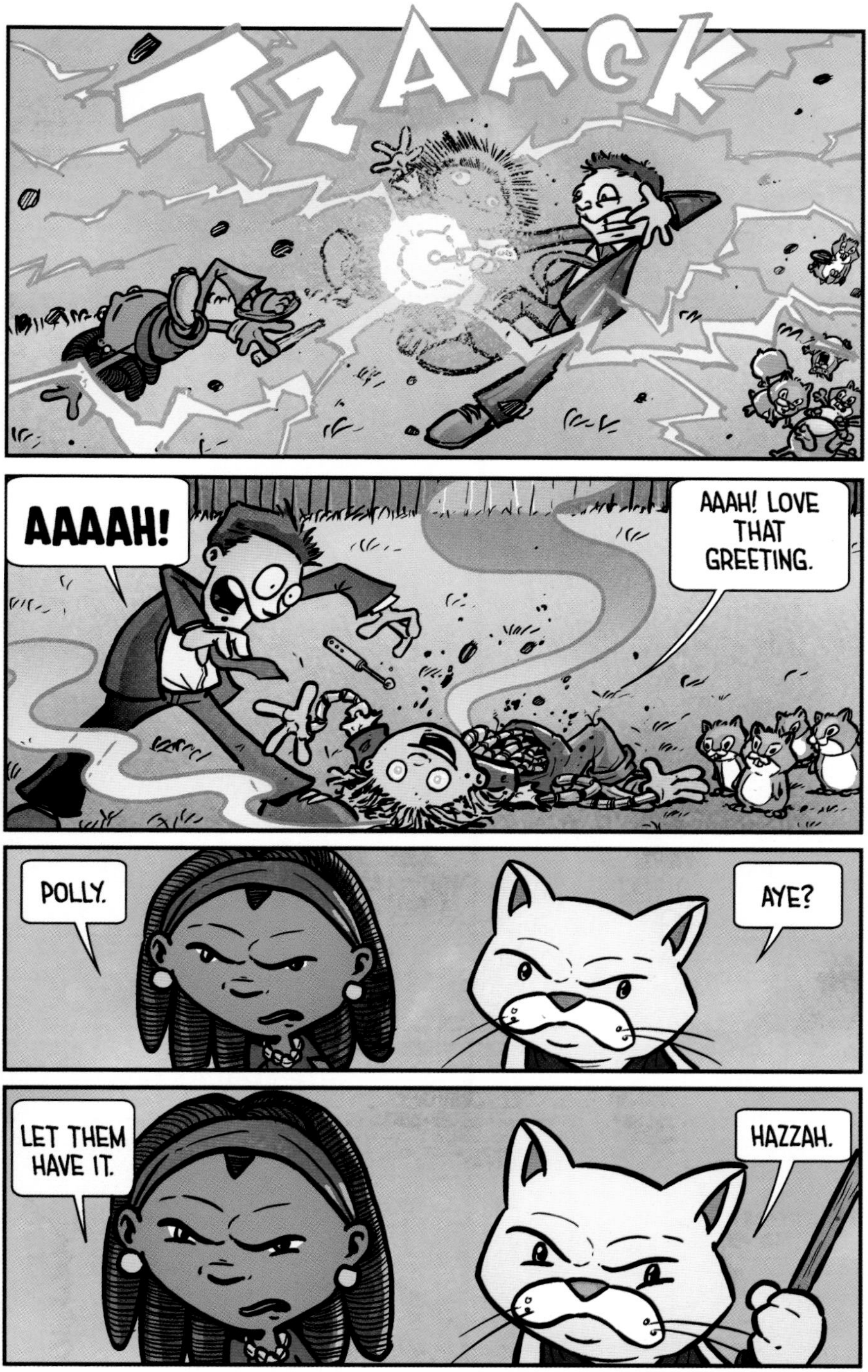
TZAACK
AAAAH!
AAAH! LOVE THAT GREETING.
POLLY.
AYE?
LET THEM HAVE IT.
HAZZAH.

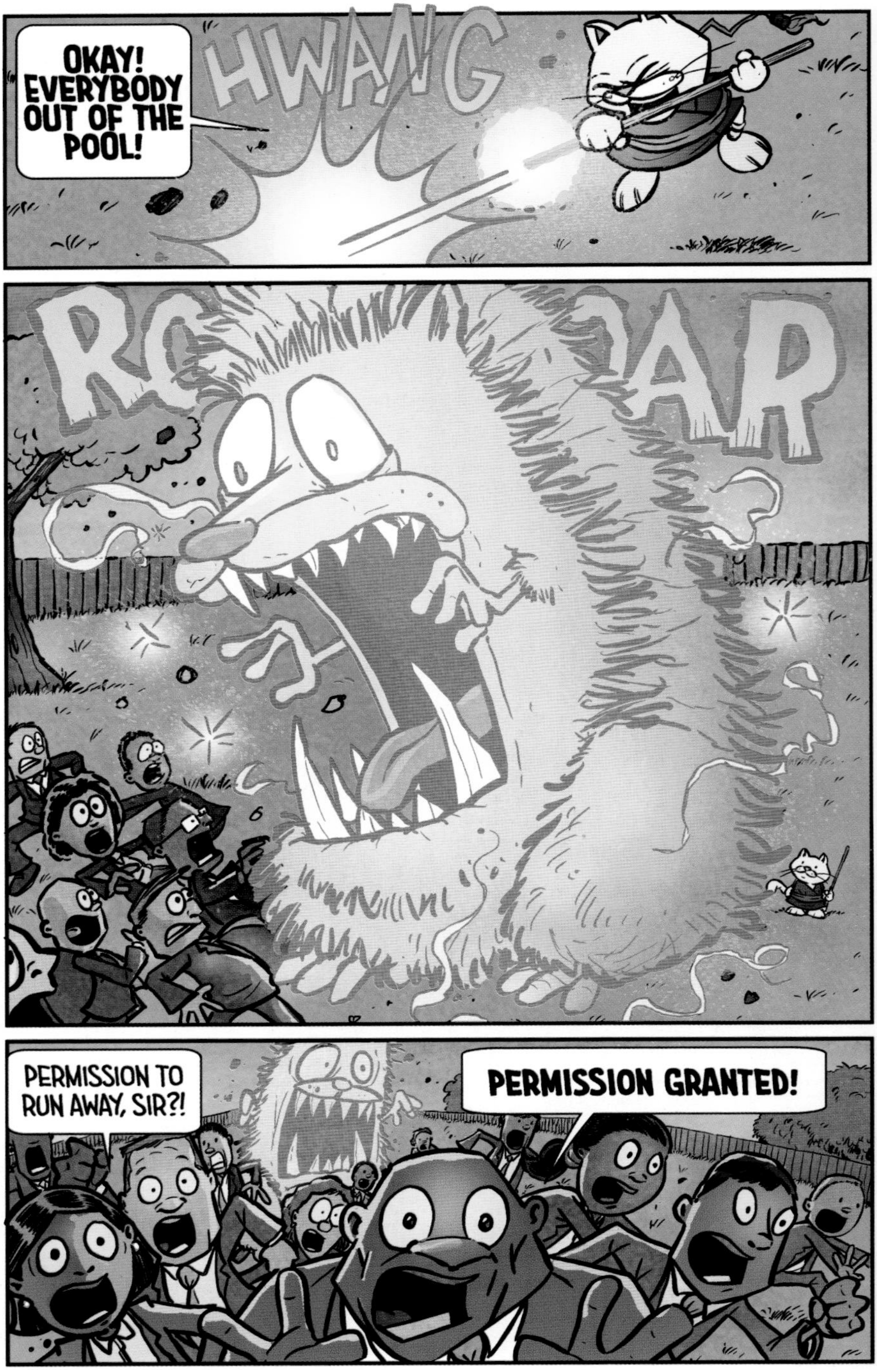
OKAY! EVERYBODY OUT OF THE POOL!
HWANG
ROAR
PERMISSION TO RUN AWAY, SIR?!
PERMISSION GRANTED!

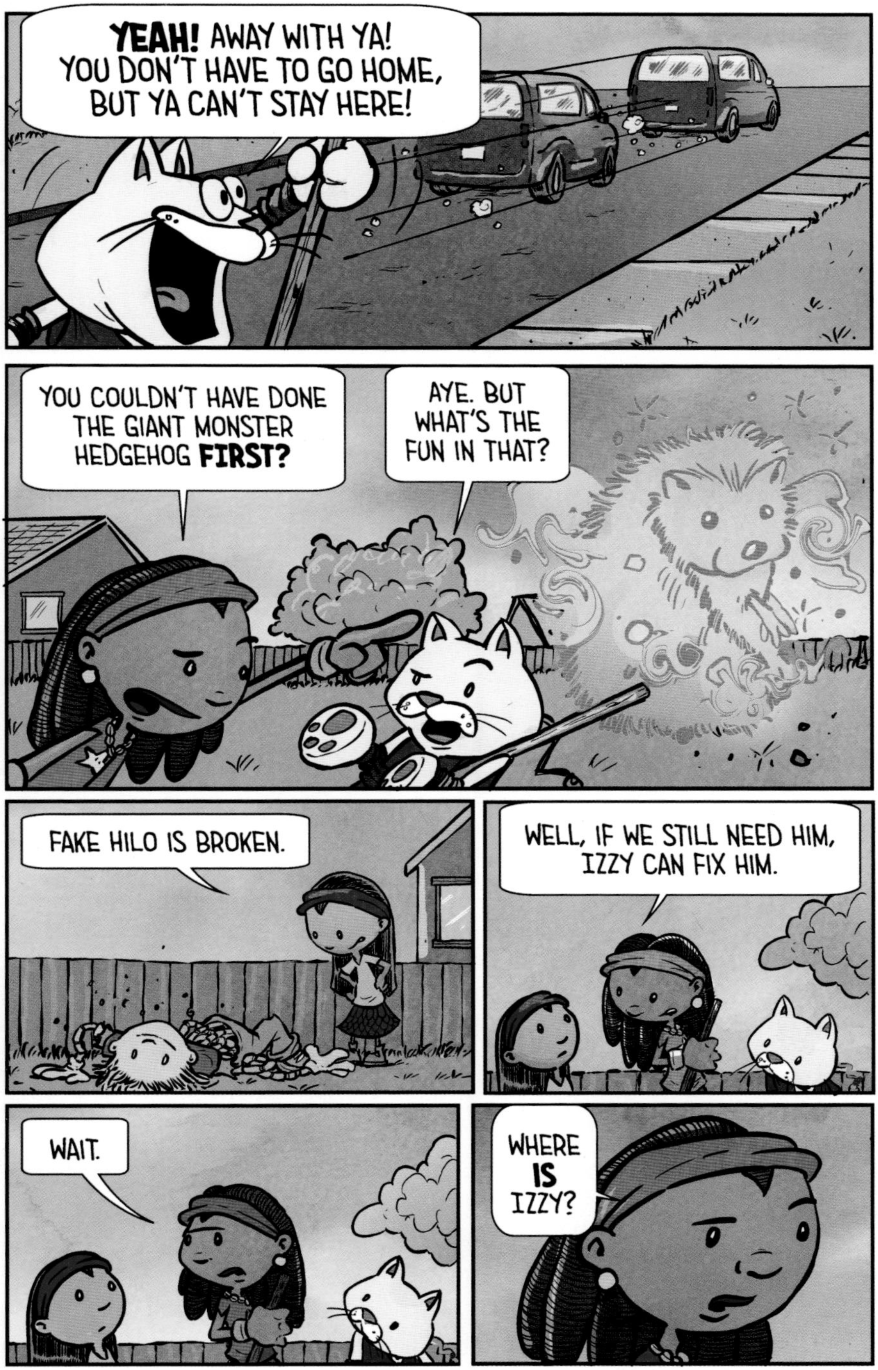
YEAH! AWAY WITH YA! YOU DON'T HAVE TO GO HOME, BUT YA CAN'T STAY HERE!
YOU COULDN'T HAVE DONE THE GIANT MONSTER HEDGEHOG FIRST?
AYE. BUT WHAT'S THE FUN IN THAT?
FAKE HILO IS BROKEN.
WELL, IF WE STILL NEED HIM, IZZY CAN FIX HIM.
WAIT.
WHERE IS IZZY?

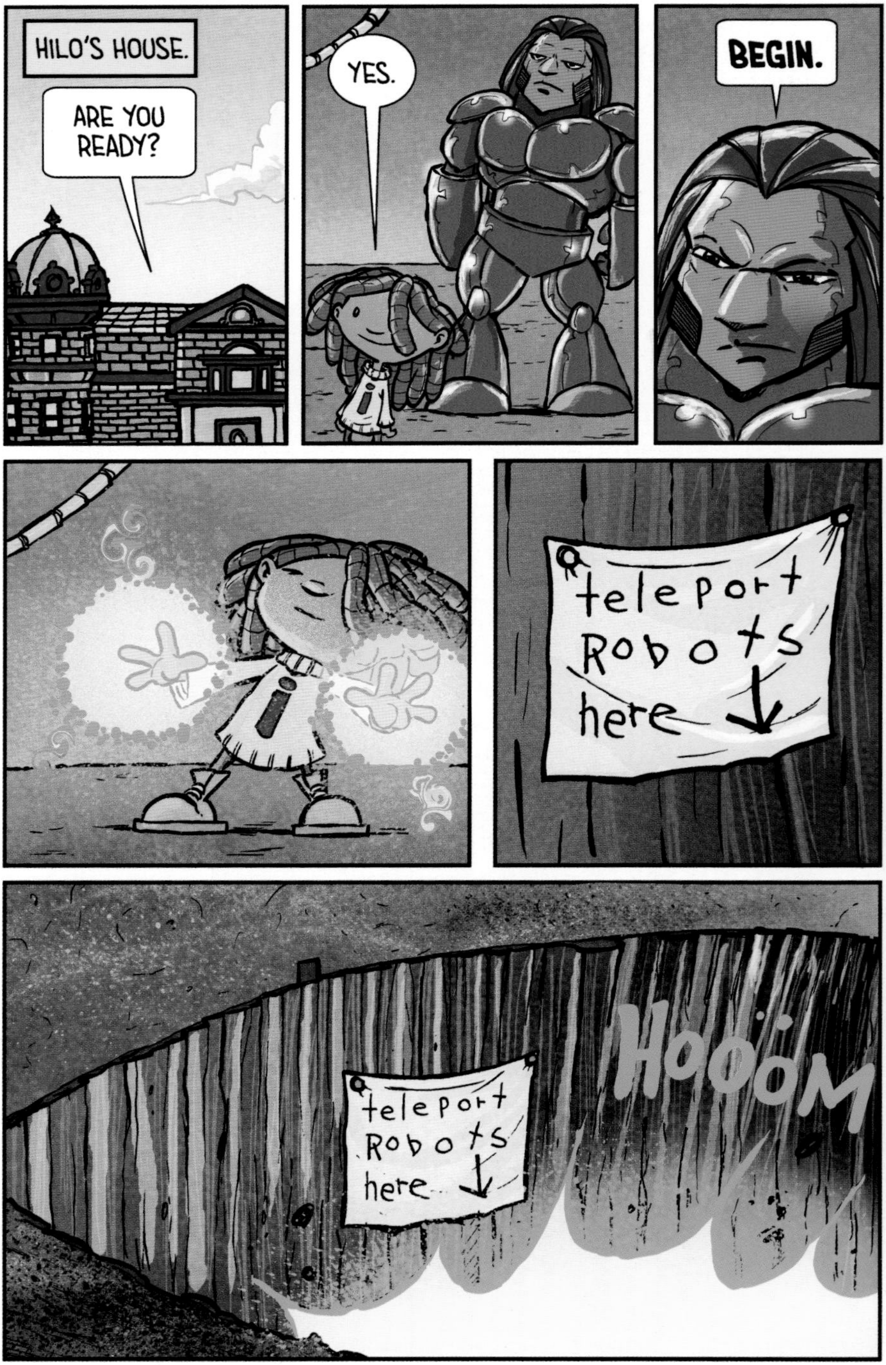
HILO'S HOUSE.
ARE YOU READY?
YES.
BEGIN.
teleport ROBOTS here
teleport ROBOTS here
HOOOM

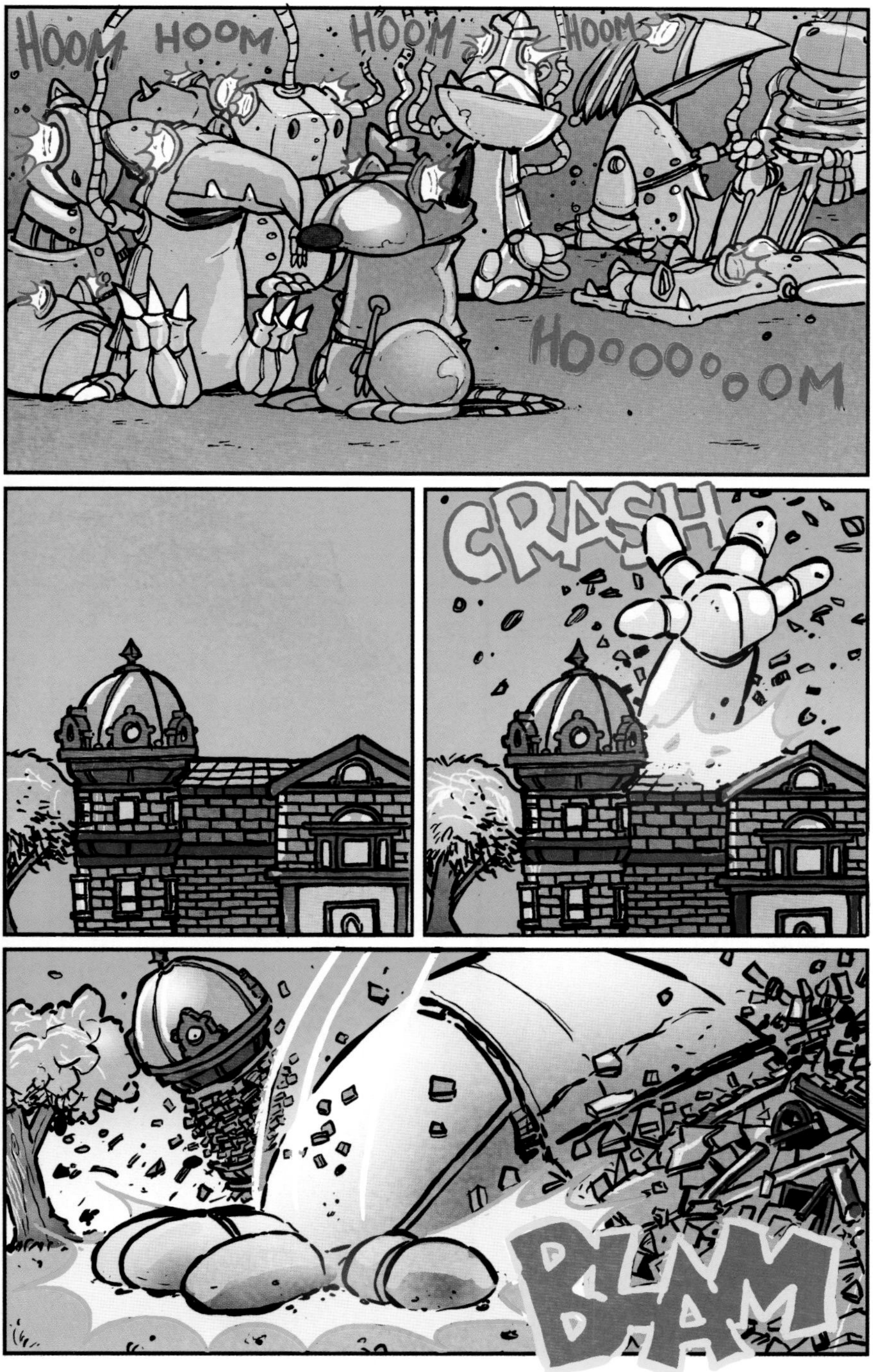
HOOM HOOM HOOM HOOM
HOOOOOOOM
CRASH
BLAM

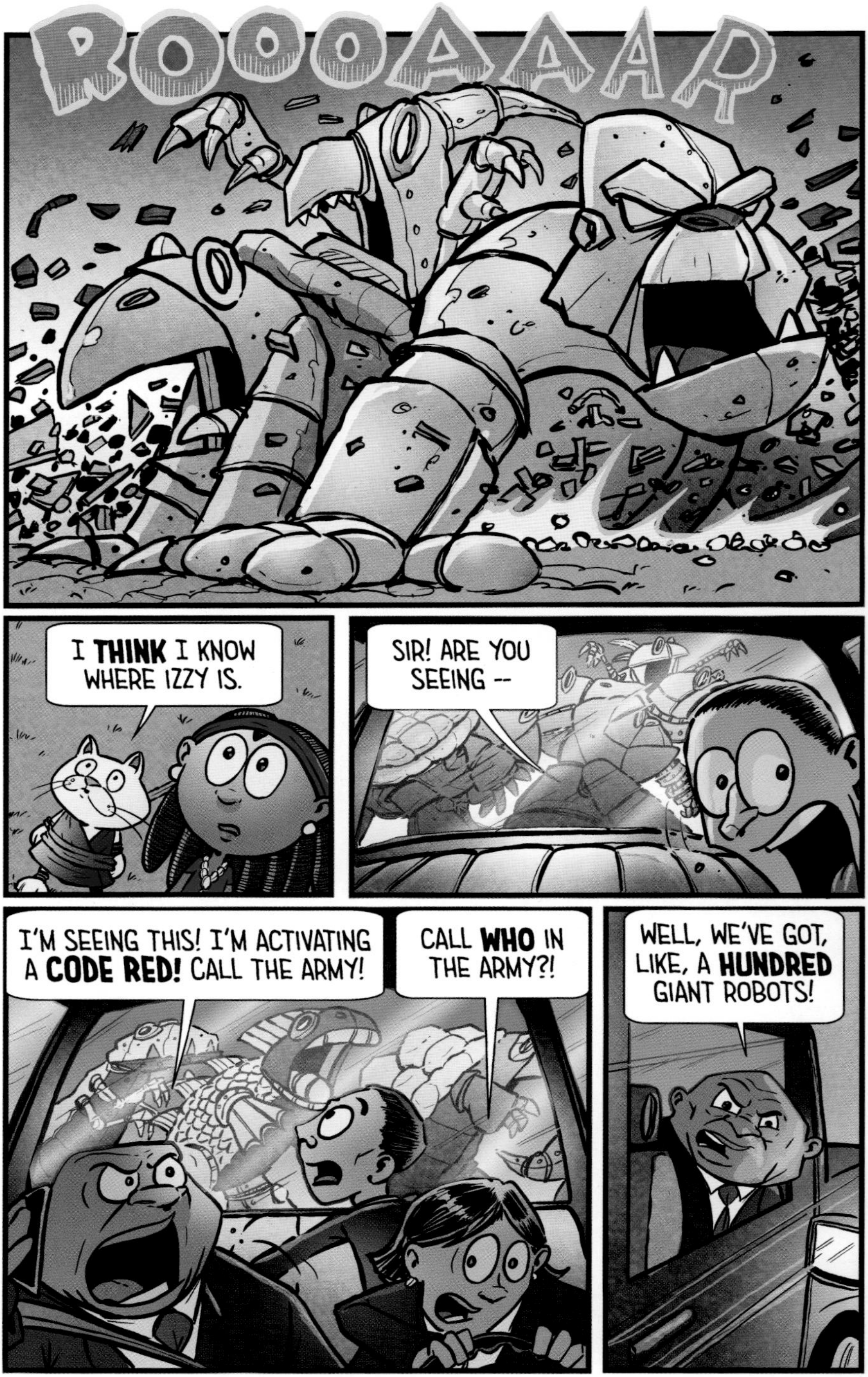
ROOOAAAP
I **THINK** I KNOW WHERE IZZY IS.
SIR! ARE YOU SEEING --
I'M SEEING THIS! I'M ACTIVATING A **CODE RED!** CALL THE ARMY!
CALL **WHO** IN THE ARMY?!
WELL, WE'VE GOT, LIKE, A **HUNDRED** GIANT ROBOTS!

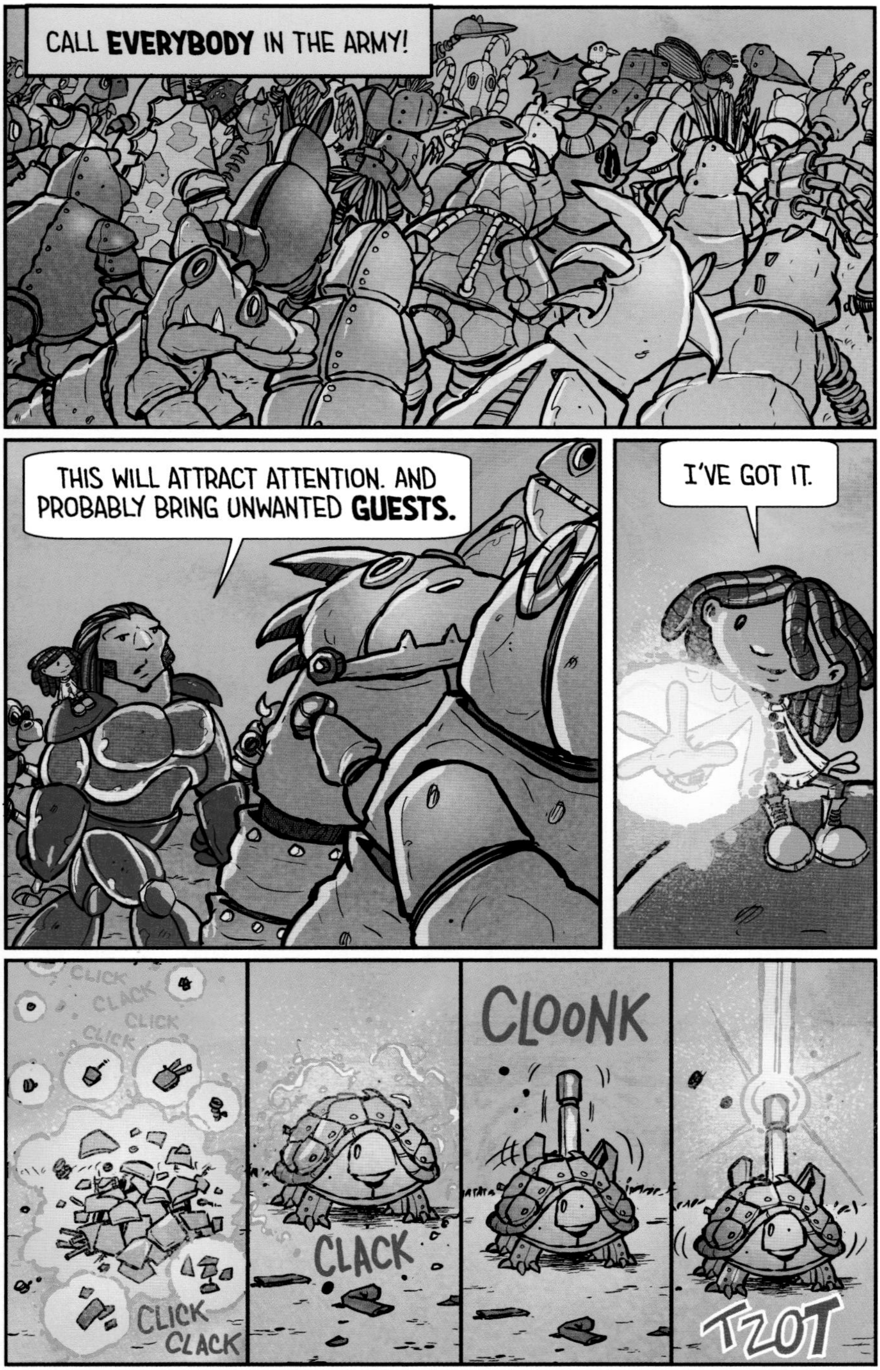
CALL **EVERYBODY** IN THE ARMY!
THIS WILL ATTRACT ATTENTION. AND PROBABLY BRING UNWANTED **GUESTS.**
I'VE GOT IT.
CLICK CLACK CLICK CLICK
CLICK CLACK
CLACK
CLOONK
TZOT

HOOOOOOOOOOOOOOOOOOM
BLEEEEEEEEN
HOLY MACKEREL.

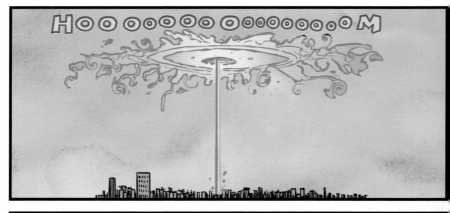

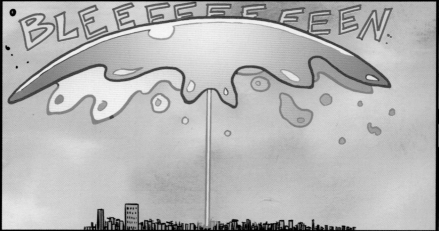

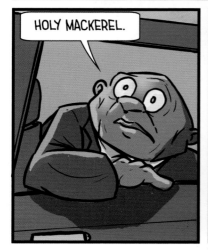

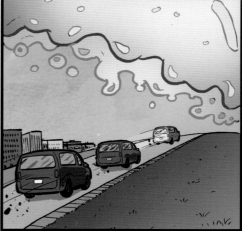

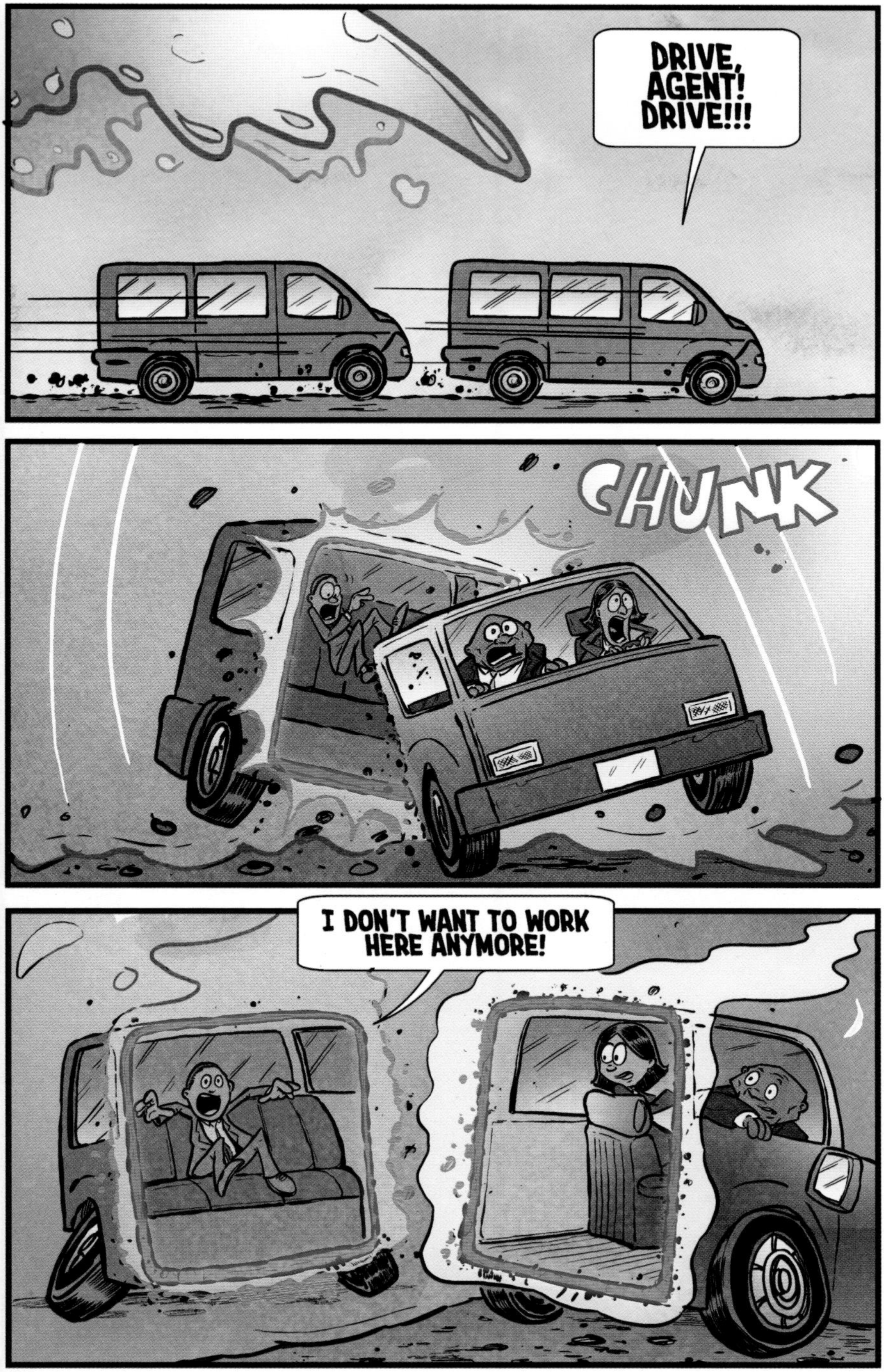
DRIVE, AGENT! DRIVE!!!
CHUNK
I DON'T WANT TO WORK HERE ANYMORE!

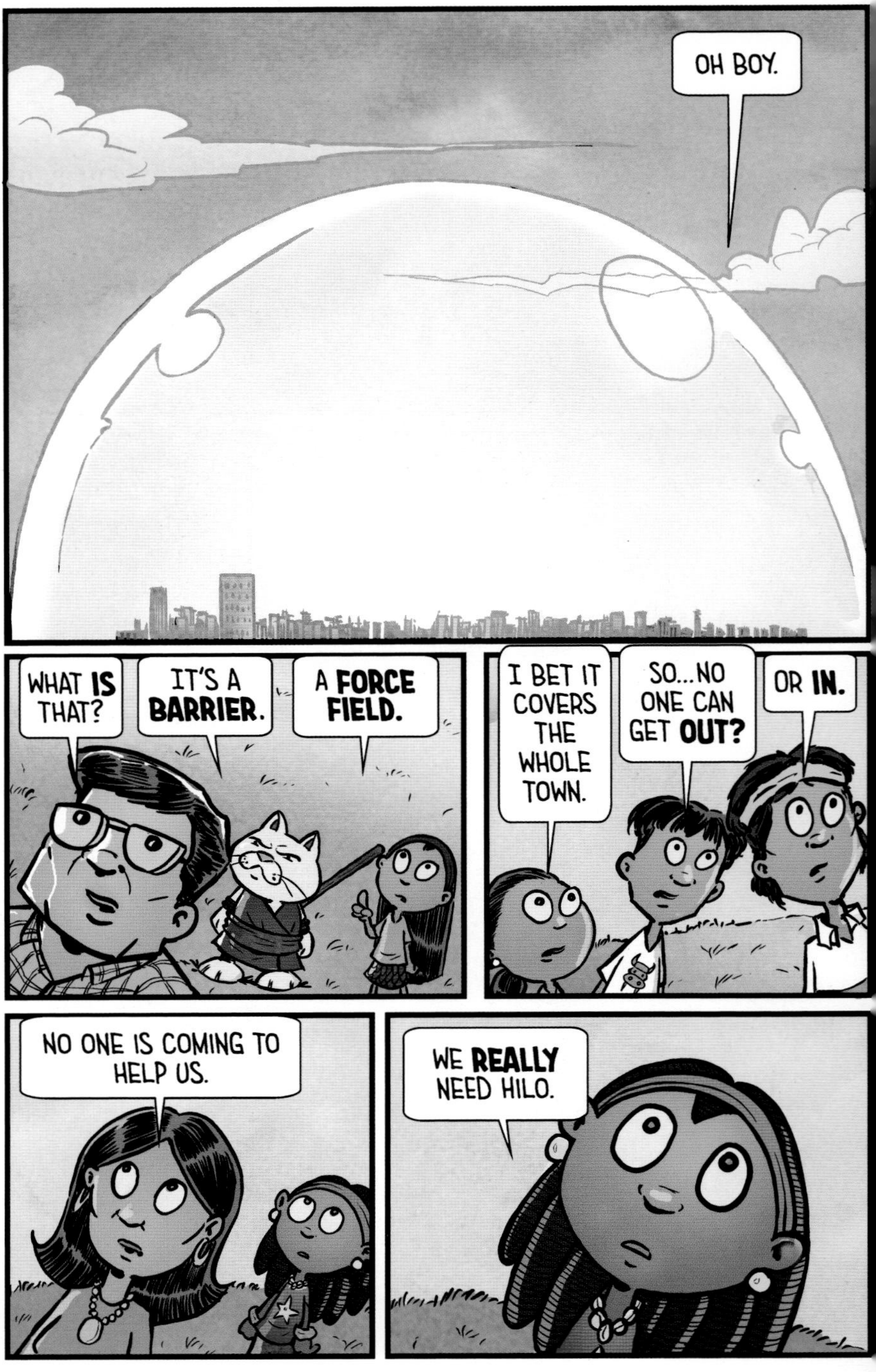
OH BOY.
WHAT **IS** THAT?
IT'S A **BARRIER**.
A **FORCE FIELD.**
I BET IT COVERS THE WHOLE TOWN.
SO...NO ONE CAN GET **OUT?**
OR **IN.**
NO ONE IS COMING TO HELP US.
WE **REALLY** NEED HILO.

CHAPTER 4

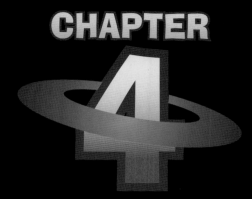

YOU FEAR. YOU LOVE.
YOU FEEL.

JANNUS.

WE HAVE TO GET BACK TO EARTH.

RAZORWARK IS THERE.

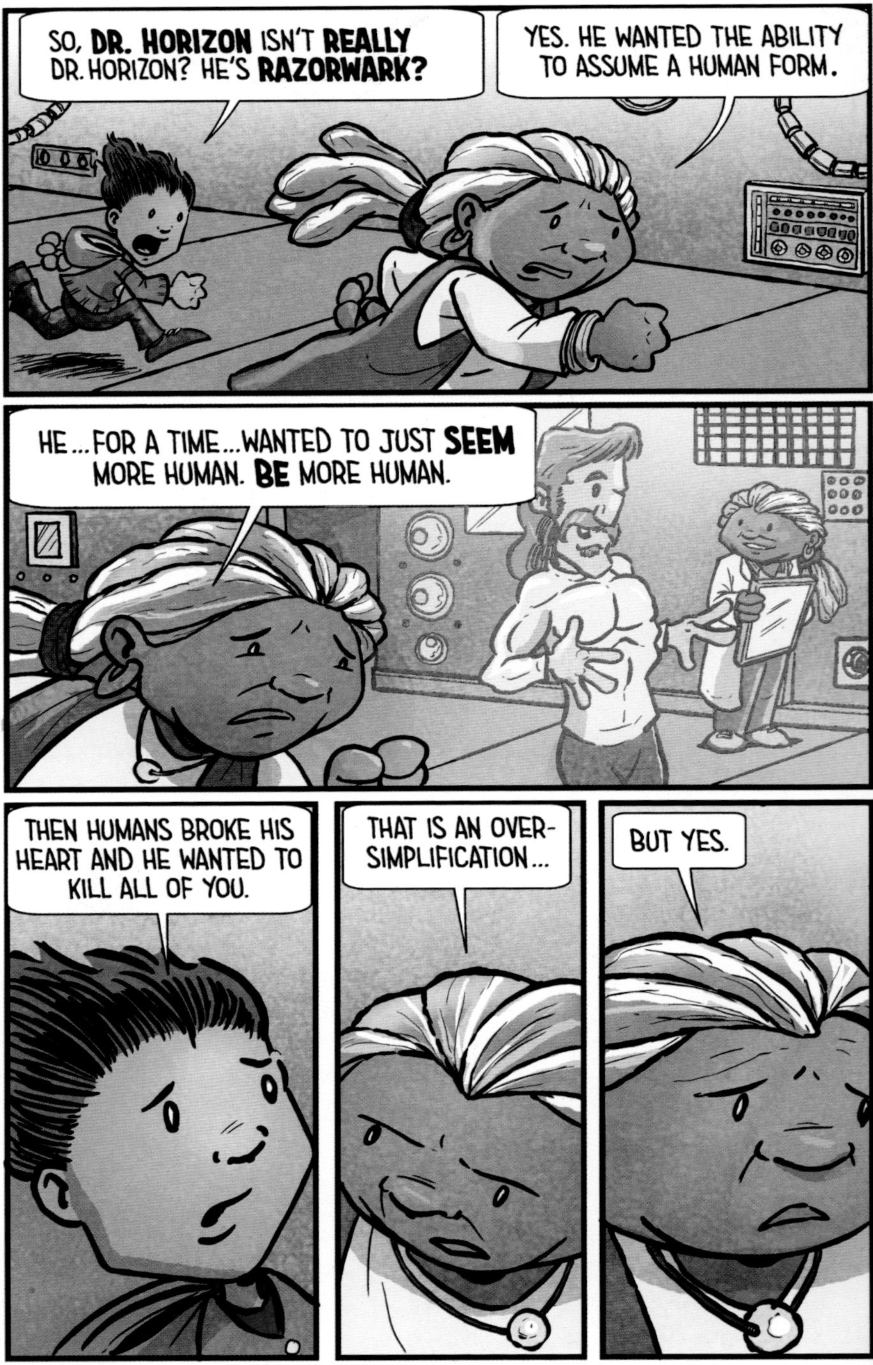
SO, DR. HORIZON ISN'T REALLY DR. HORIZON? HE'S RAZORWARK?
YES. HE WANTED THE ABILITY TO ASSUME A HUMAN FORM.
HE...FOR A TIME...WANTED TO JUST SEEM MORE HUMAN. BE MORE HUMAN.
THEN HUMANS BROKE HIS HEART AND HE WANTED TO KILL ALL OF YOU.
THAT IS AN OVER-SIMPLIFICATION...
BUT YES.

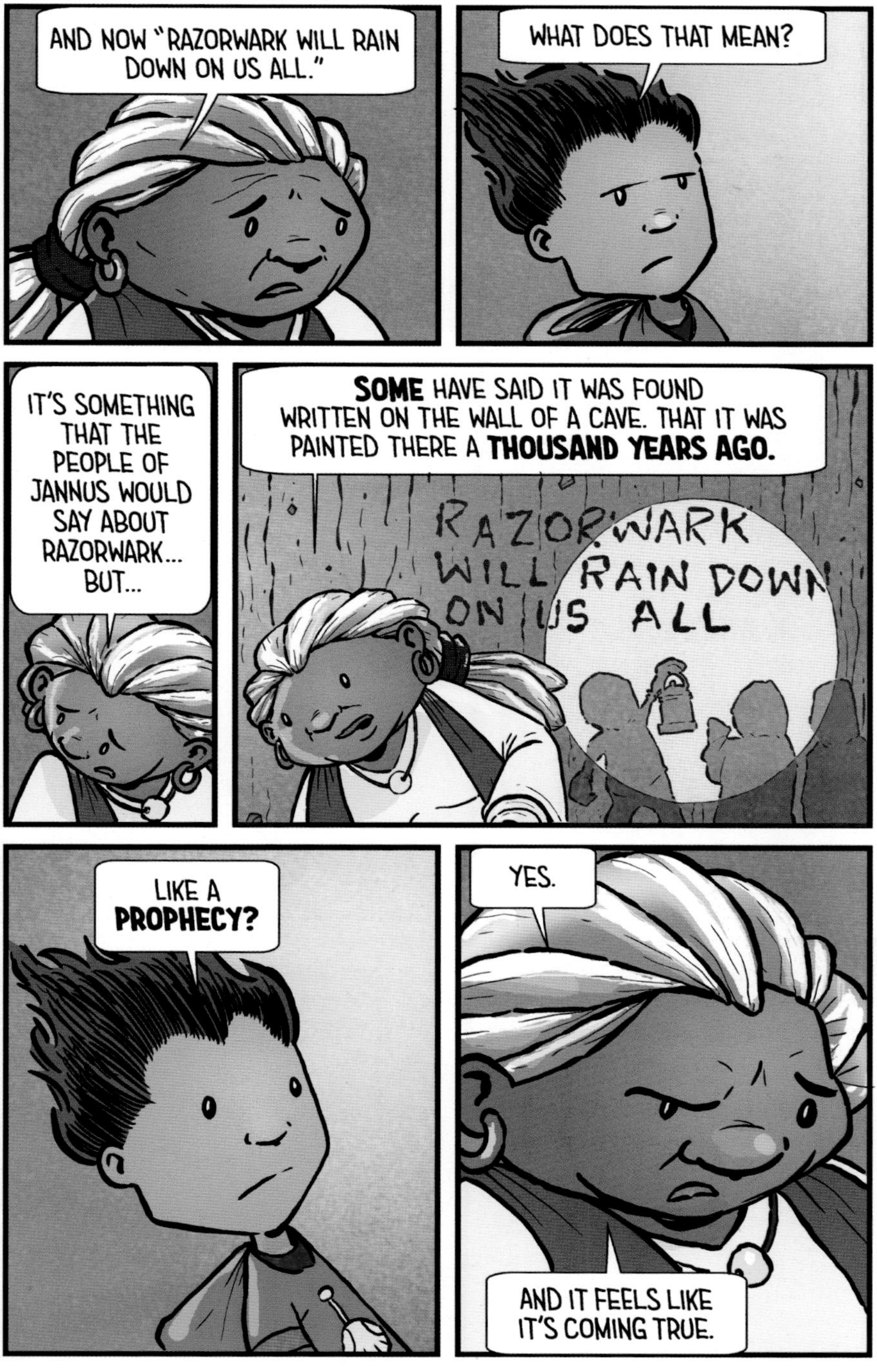
AND NOW "RAZORWARK WILL RAIN DOWN ON US ALL."
WHAT DOES THAT MEAN?
IT'S SOMETHING THAT THE PEOPLE OF JANNUS WOULD SAY ABOUT RAZORWARK... BUT...
SOME HAVE SAID IT WAS FOUND WRITTEN ON THE WALL OF A CAVE. THAT IT WAS PAINTED THERE A THOUSAND YEARS AGO.
RAZORWARK WILL RAIN DOWN ON US ALL
LIKE A PROPHECY?
YES.
AND IT FEELS LIKE IT'S COMING TRUE.

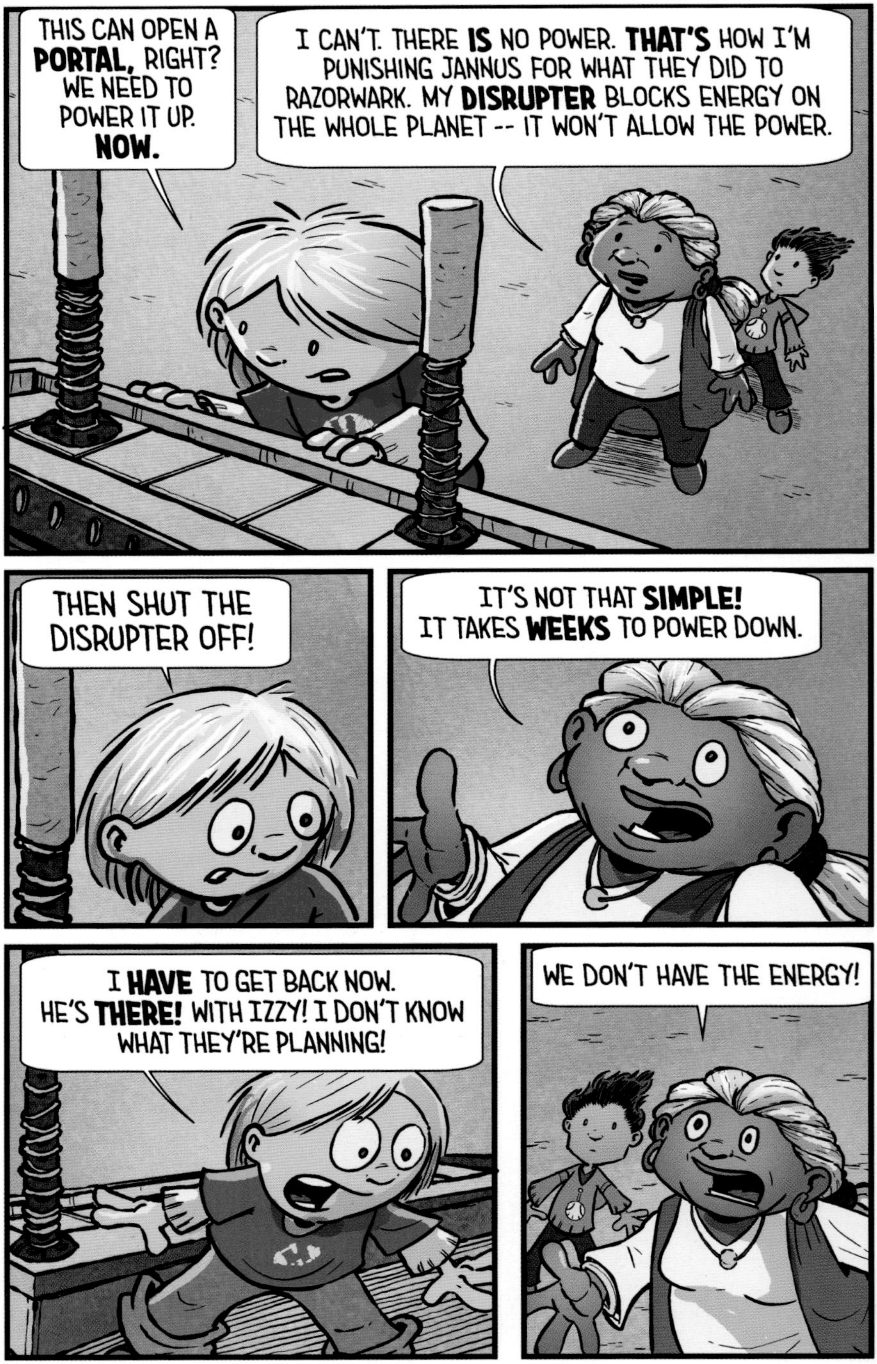
THIS CAN OPEN A **PORTAL,** RIGHT? WE NEED TO POWER IT UP. **NOW.**
I CAN'T. THERE **IS** NO POWER. **THAT'S** HOW I'M PUNISHING JANNUS FOR WHAT THEY DID TO RAZORWARK. MY **DISRUPTER** BLOCKS ENERGY ON THE WHOLE PLANET -- IT WON'T ALLOW THE POWER.
THEN SHUT THE DISRUPTER OFF!
IT'S NOT THAT **SIMPLE!** IT TAKES **WEEKS** TO POWER DOWN.
I **HAVE** TO GET BACK NOW. HE'S **THERE!** WITH IZZY! I DON'T KNOW WHAT THEY'RE PLANNING!
WE DON'T HAVE THE ENERGY!

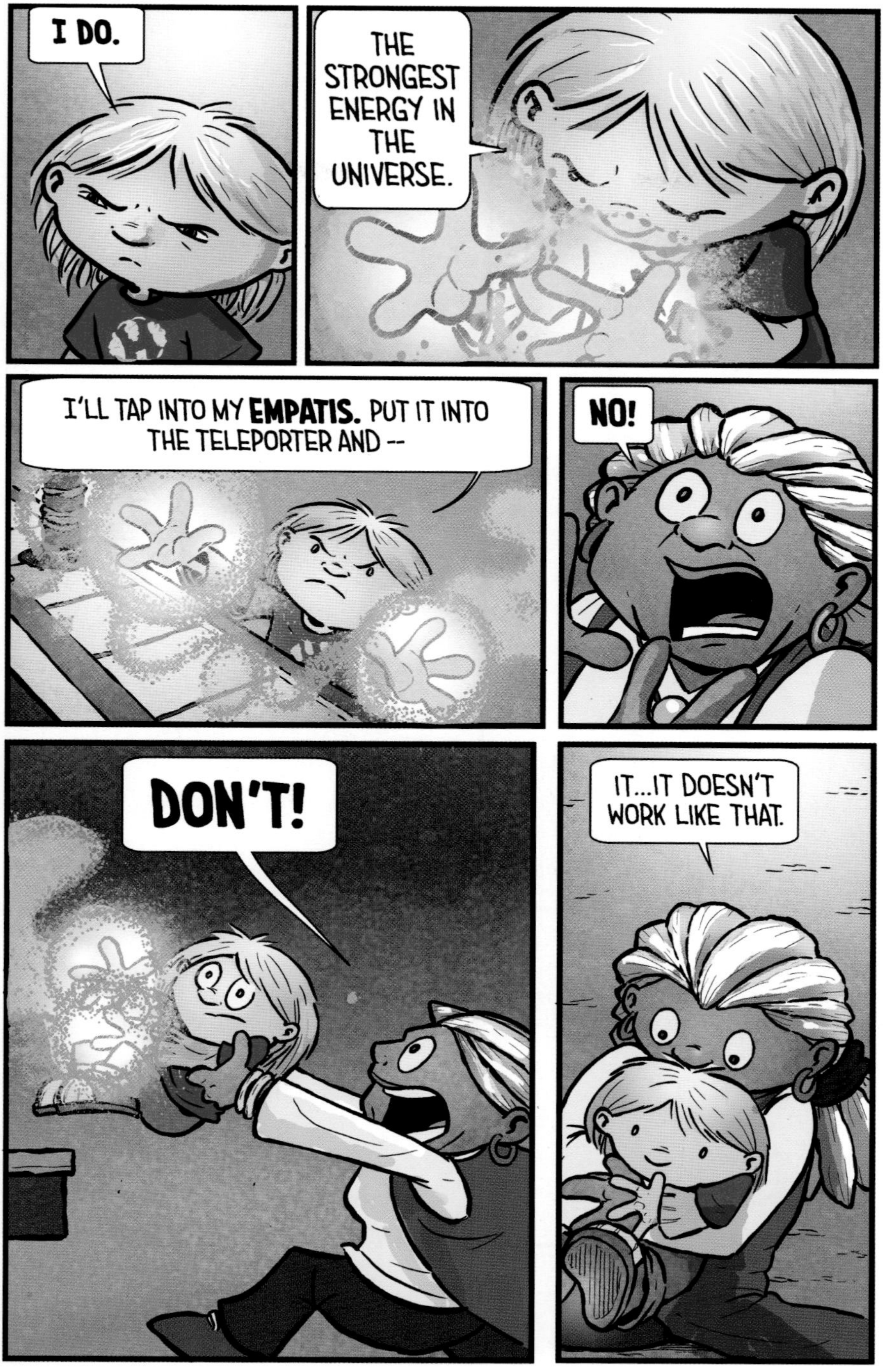
I DO.
THE STRONGEST ENERGY IN THE UNIVERSE.
I'LL TAP INTO MY **EMPATIS.** PUT IT INTO THE TELEPORTER AND --
NO!
DON'T!
IT...IT DOESN'T WORK LIKE THAT.

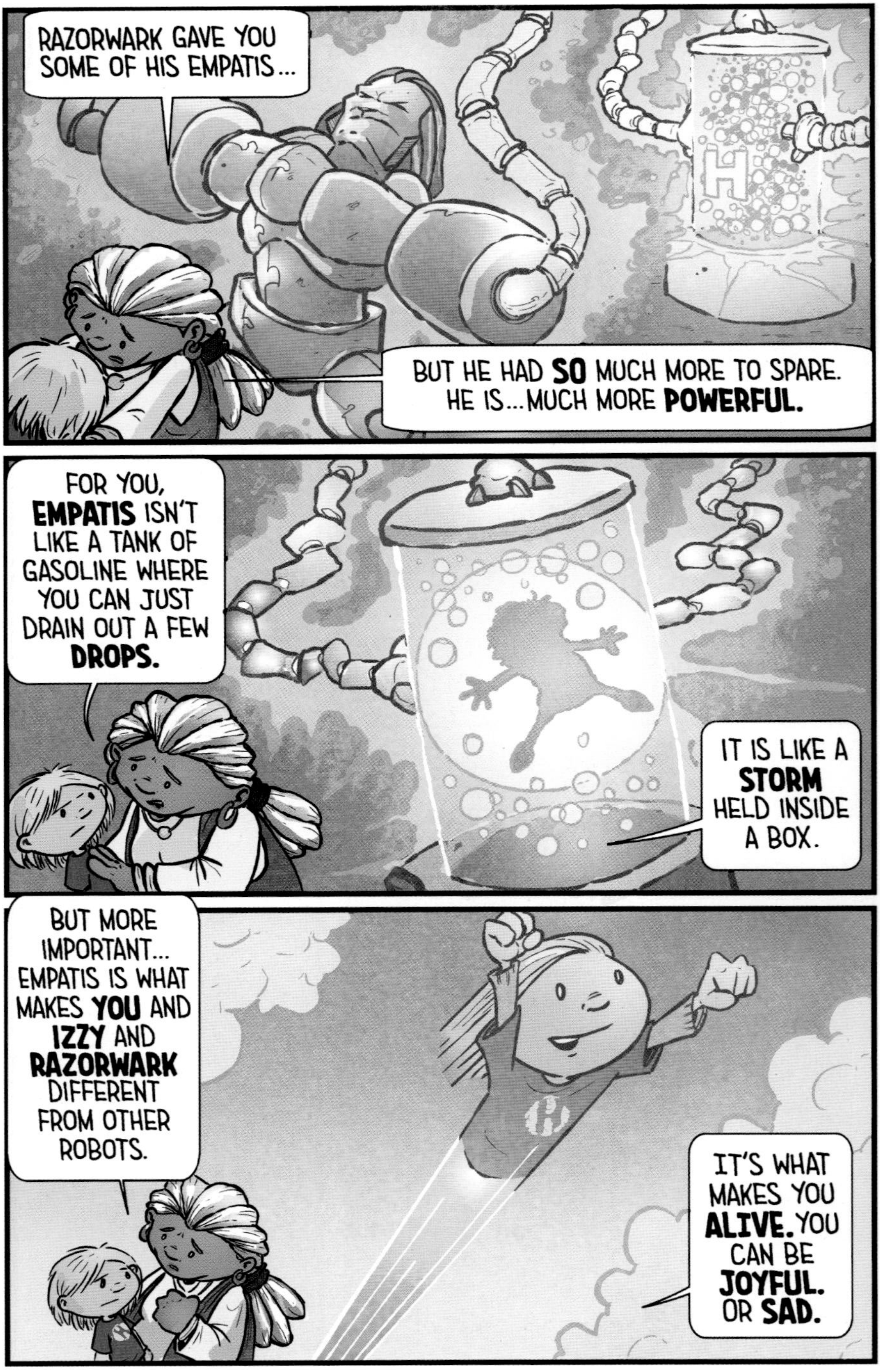
RAZORWARK GAVE YOU SOME OF HIS EMPATIS...
BUT HE HAD **SO** MUCH MORE TO SPARE. HE IS...MUCH MORE **POWERFUL.**
FOR YOU, **EMPATIS** ISN'T LIKE A TANK OF GASOLINE WHERE YOU CAN JUST DRAIN OUT A FEW **DROPS.**
IT IS LIKE A **STORM** HELD INSIDE A BOX.
BUT MORE IMPORTANT... EMPATIS IS WHAT MAKES **YOU** AND **IZZY** AND **RAZORWARK** DIFFERENT FROM OTHER ROBOTS.
IT'S WHAT MAKES YOU **ALIVE.** YOU CAN BE **JOYFUL.** OR **SAD.**

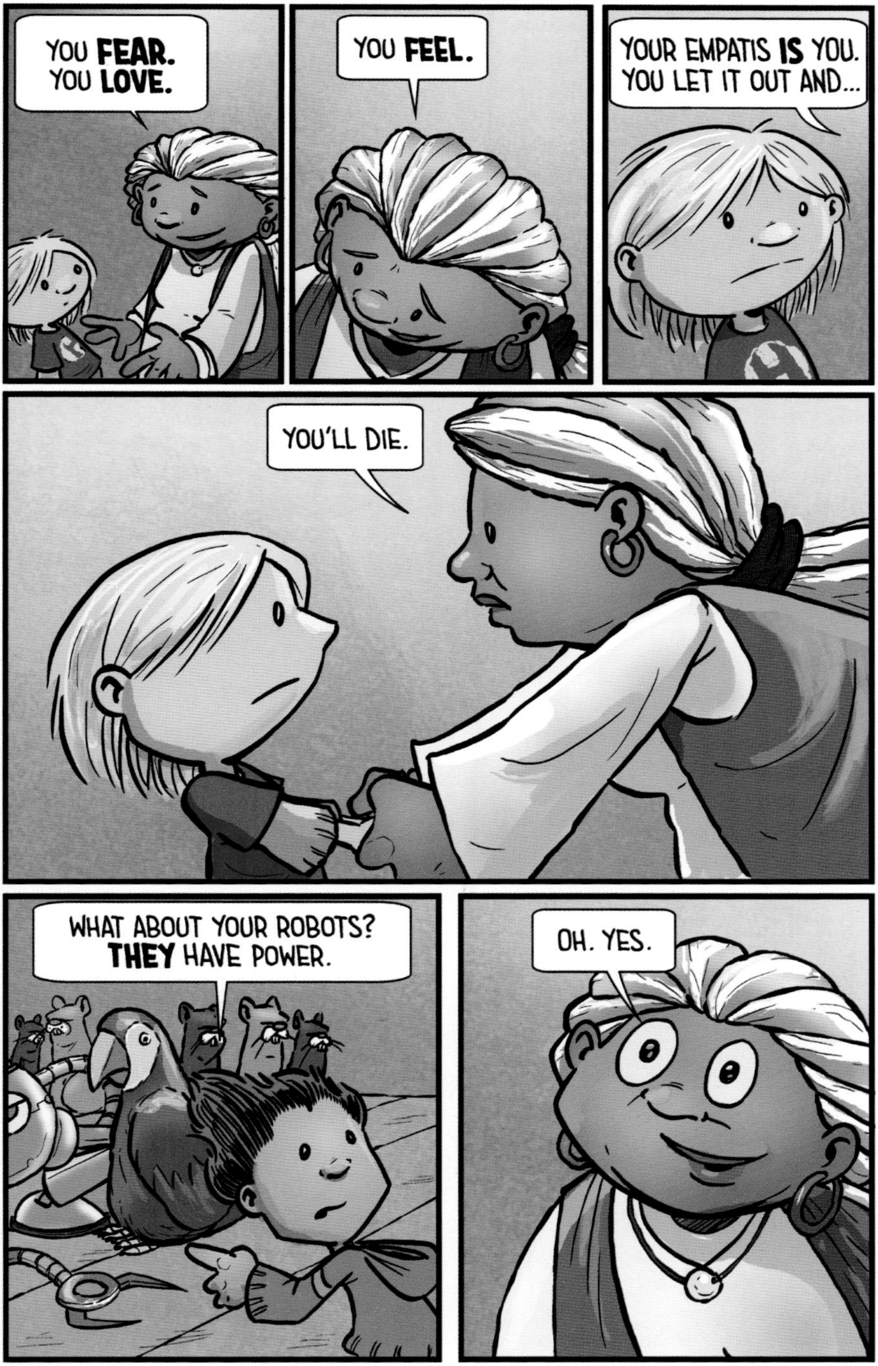
YOU **FEAR.**
YOU **LOVE.**
YOU **FEEL.**
YOUR EMPATIS **IS** YOU. YOU LET IT OUT AND...
YOU'LL DIE.
WHAT ABOUT YOUR ROBOTS? **THEY** HAVE POWER.
OH. YES.

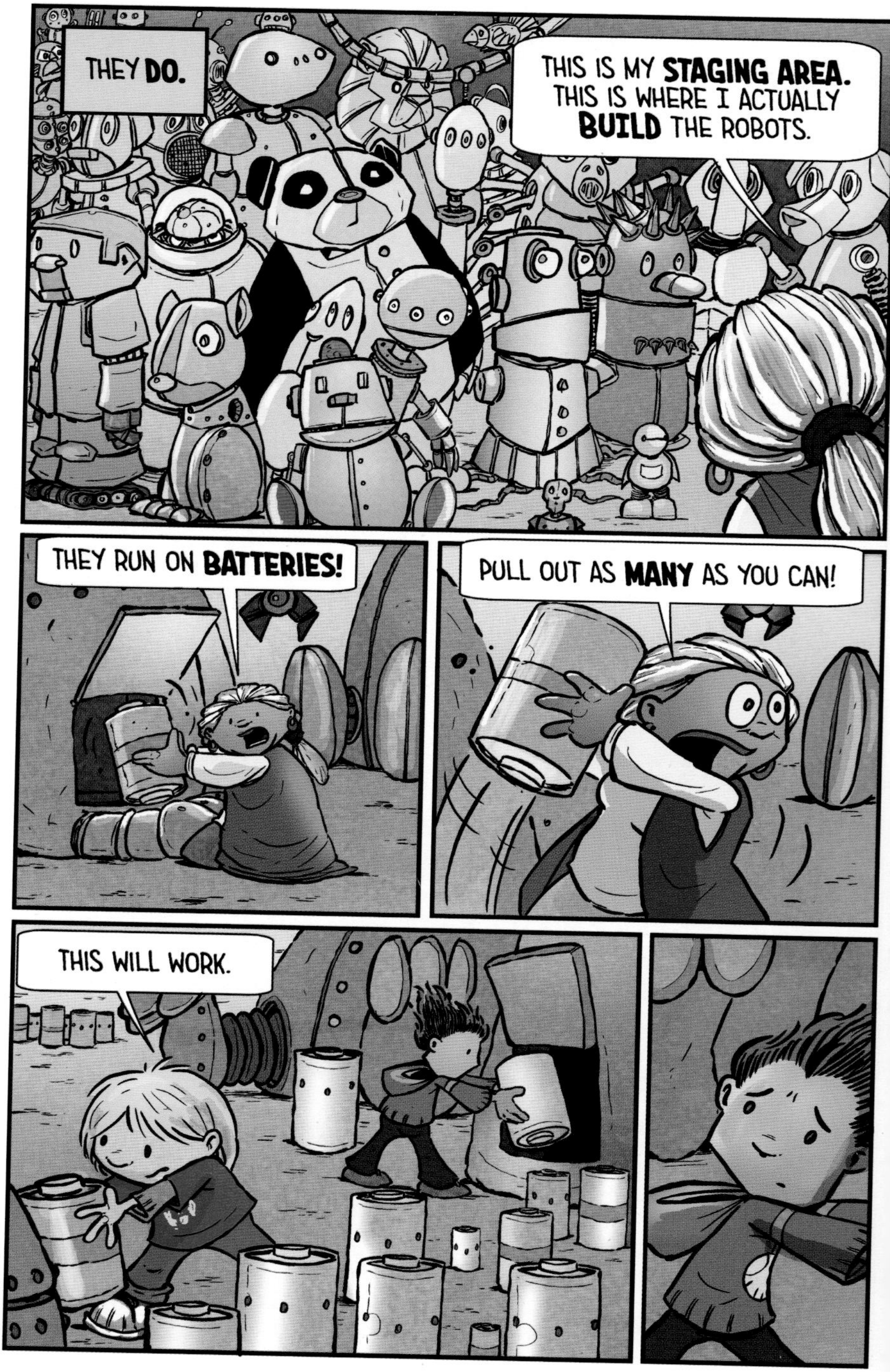

THEY DO.
THIS IS MY STAGING AREA. THIS IS WHERE I ACTUALLY BUILD THE ROBOTS.
THEY RUN ON BATTERIES!
PULL OUT AS MANY AS YOU CAN!
THIS WILL WORK.

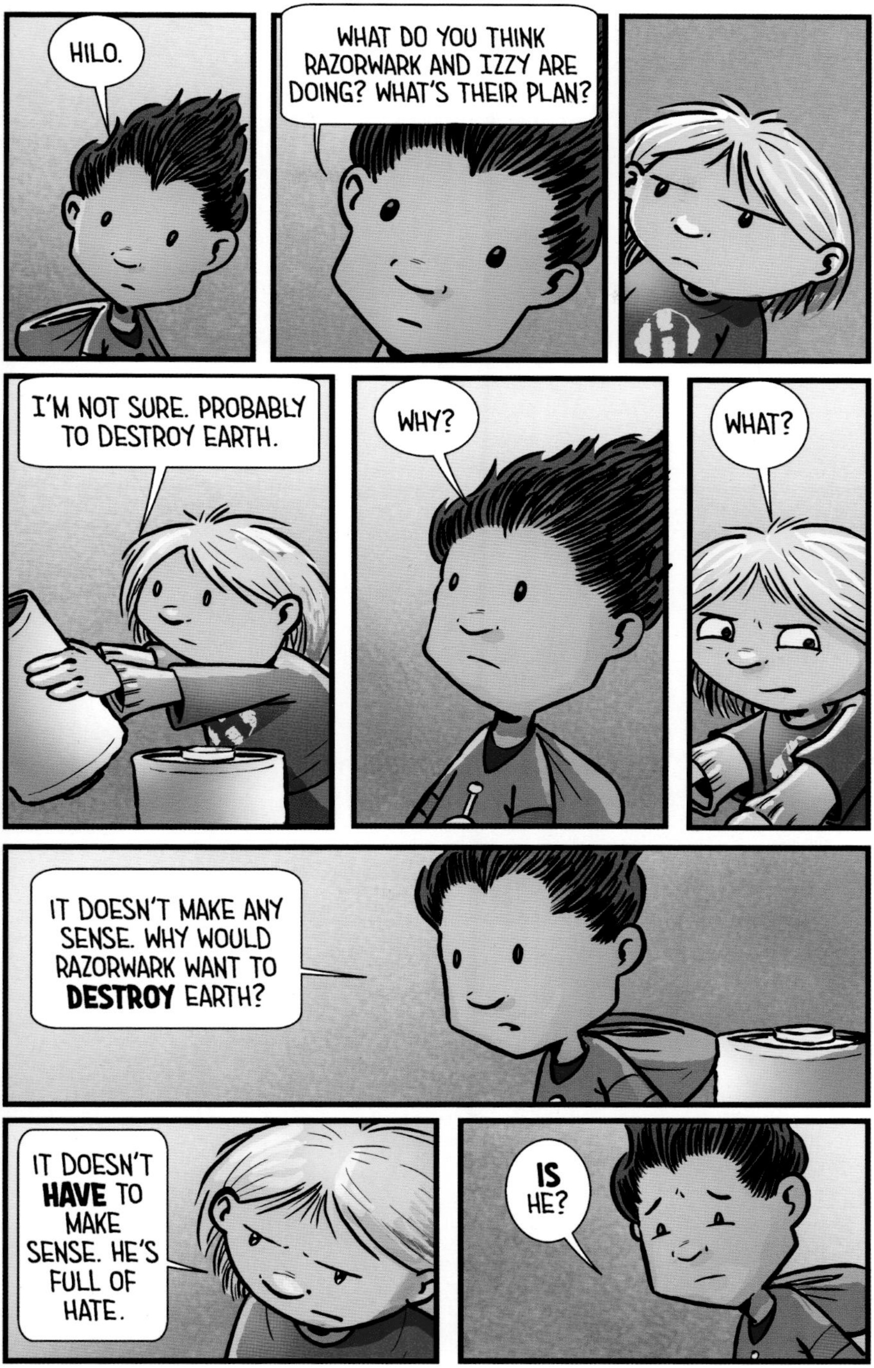
HILO.
WHAT DO YOU THINK RAZORWARK AND IZZY ARE DOING? WHAT'S THEIR PLAN?
I'M NOT SURE. PROBABLY TO DESTROY EARTH.
WHY?
WHAT?
IT DOESN'T MAKE ANY SENSE. WHY WOULD RAZORWARK WANT TO **DESTROY** EARTH?
IT DOESN'T **HAVE** TO MAKE SENSE. HE'S FULL OF HATE.
IS HE?

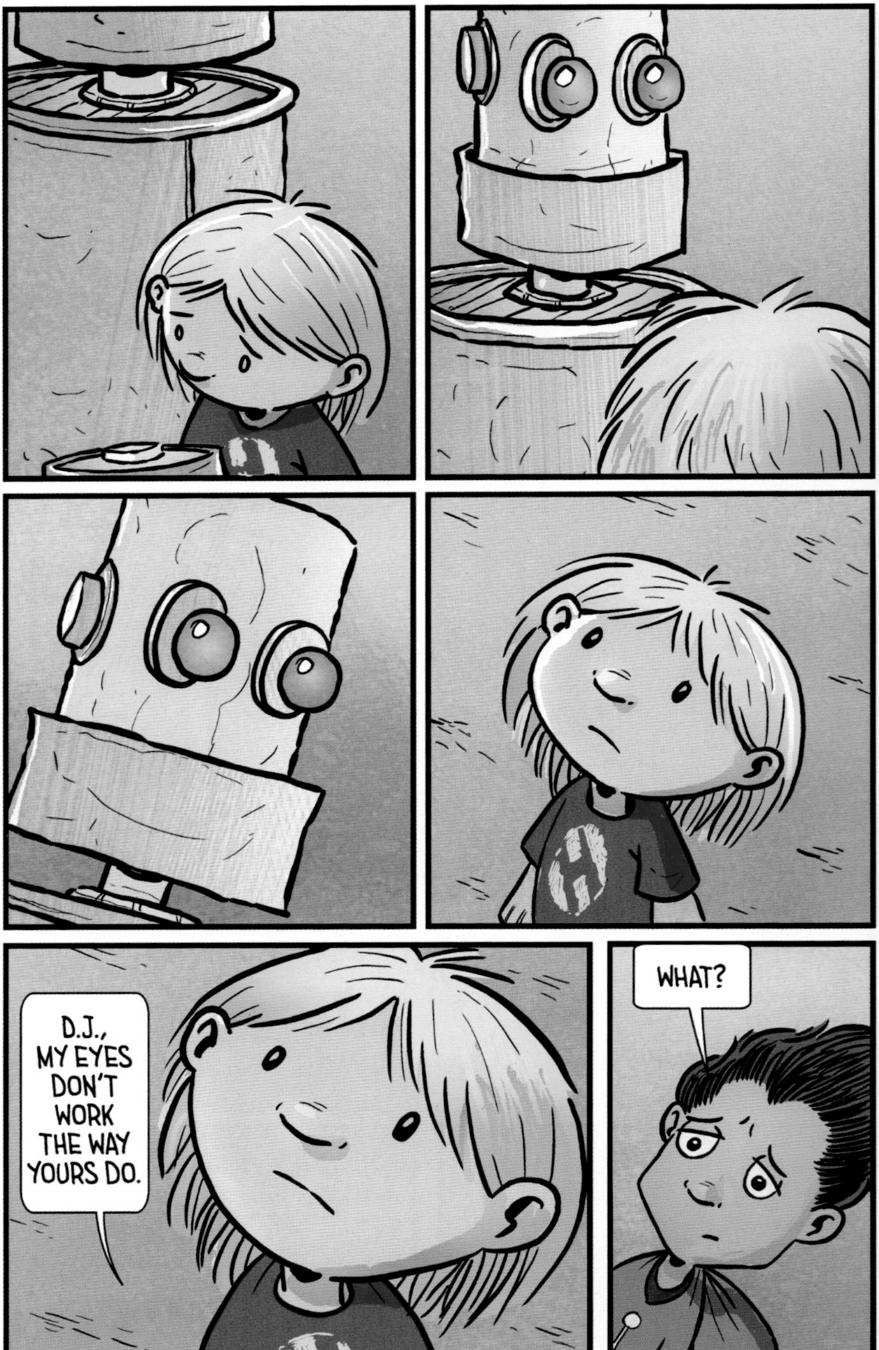
D.J., MY EYES DON'T WORK THE WAY YOURS DO.
WHAT?

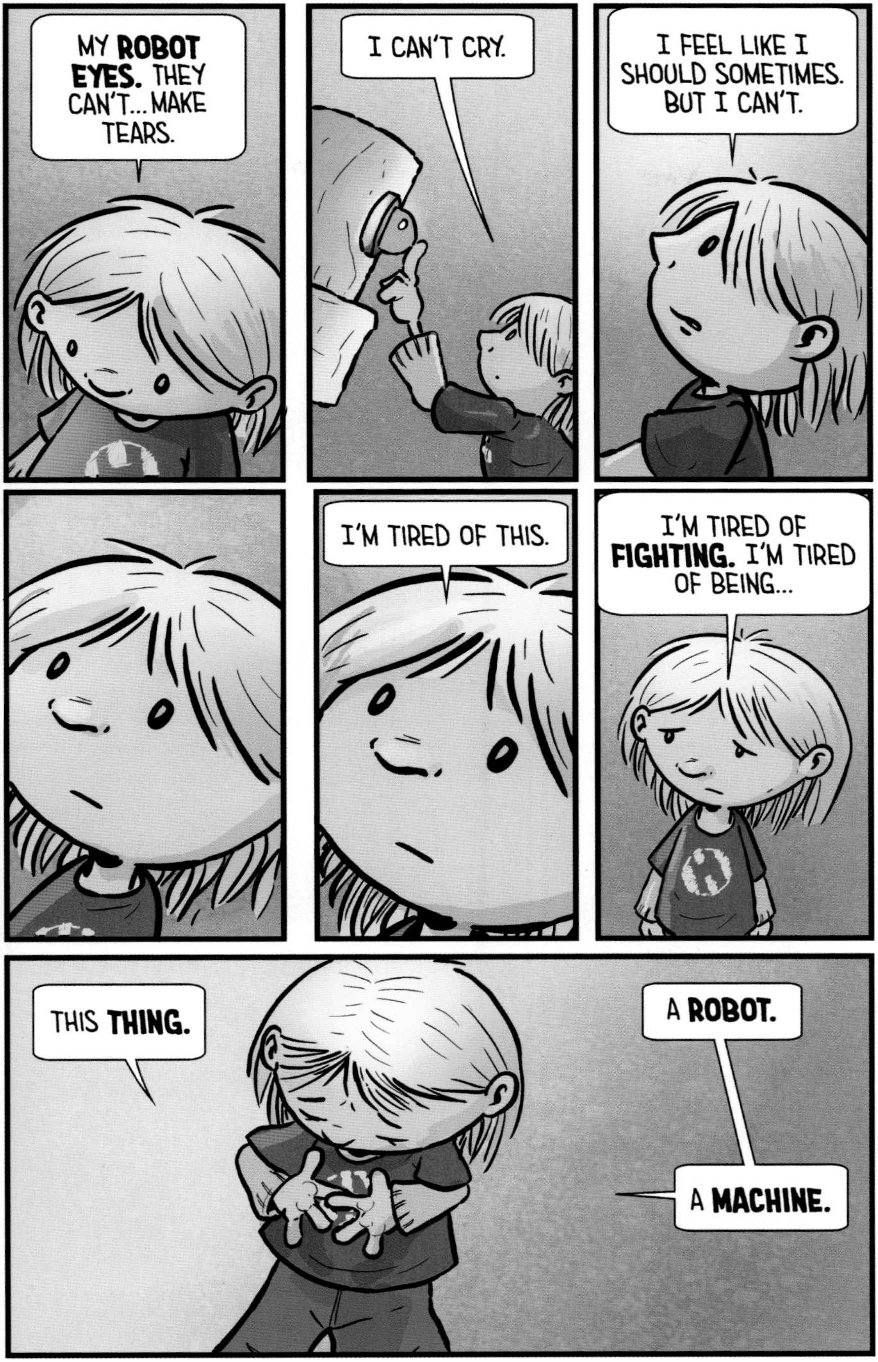
MY **ROBOT EYES.** THEY CAN'T... MAKE TEARS.
I CAN'T CRY.
I FEEL LIKE I SHOULD SOMETIMES. BUT I CAN'T.
I'M TIRED OF THIS.
I'M TIRED OF **FIGHTING.** I'M TIRED OF BEING...
THIS **THING.**
A **ROBOT.**
A **MACHINE.**

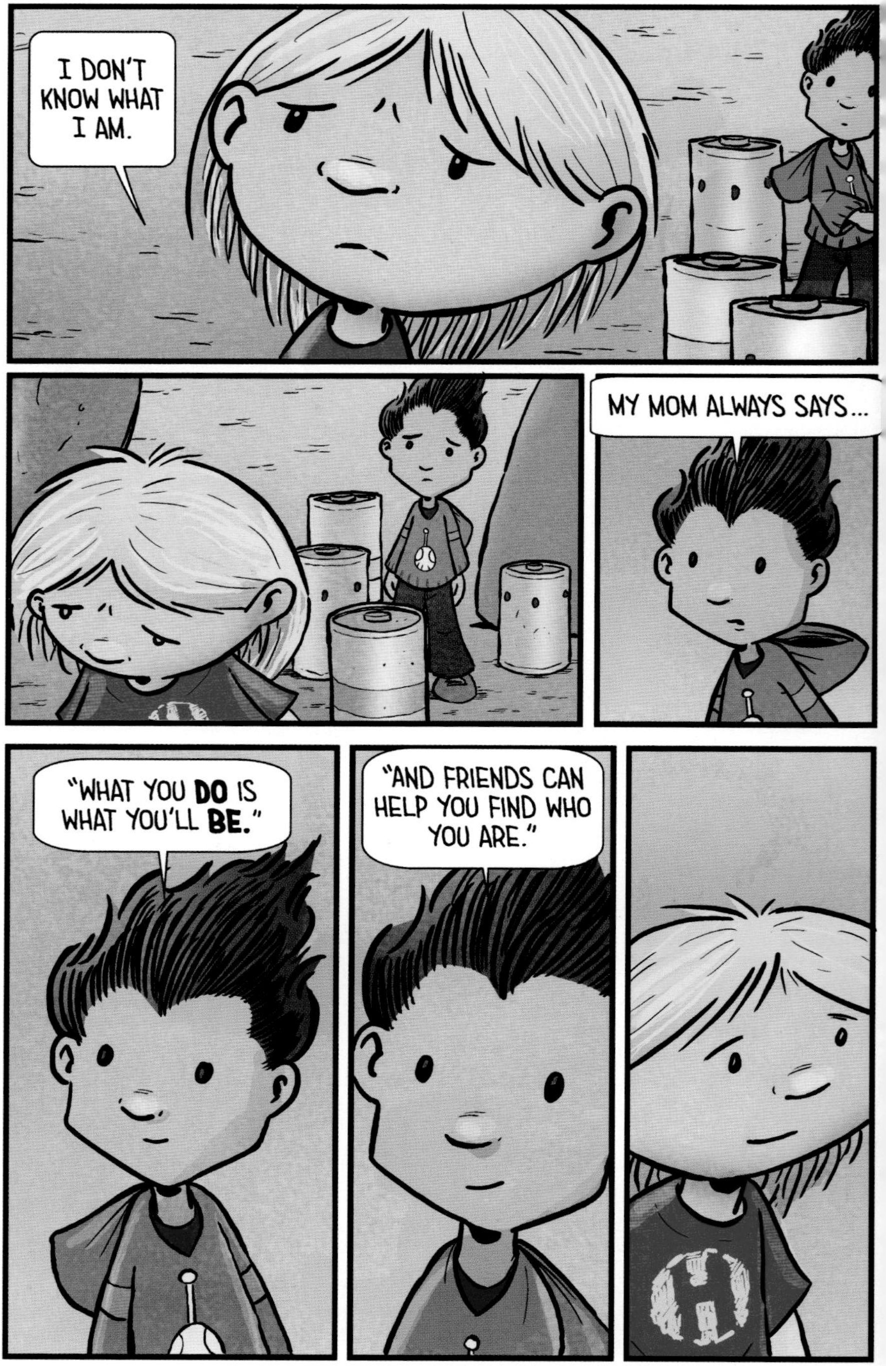
I DON'T KNOW WHAT I AM.
MY MOM ALWAYS SAYS...
"WHAT YOU **DO** IS WHAT YOU'LL **BE.**"
"AND FRIENDS CAN HELP YOU FIND WHO YOU ARE."

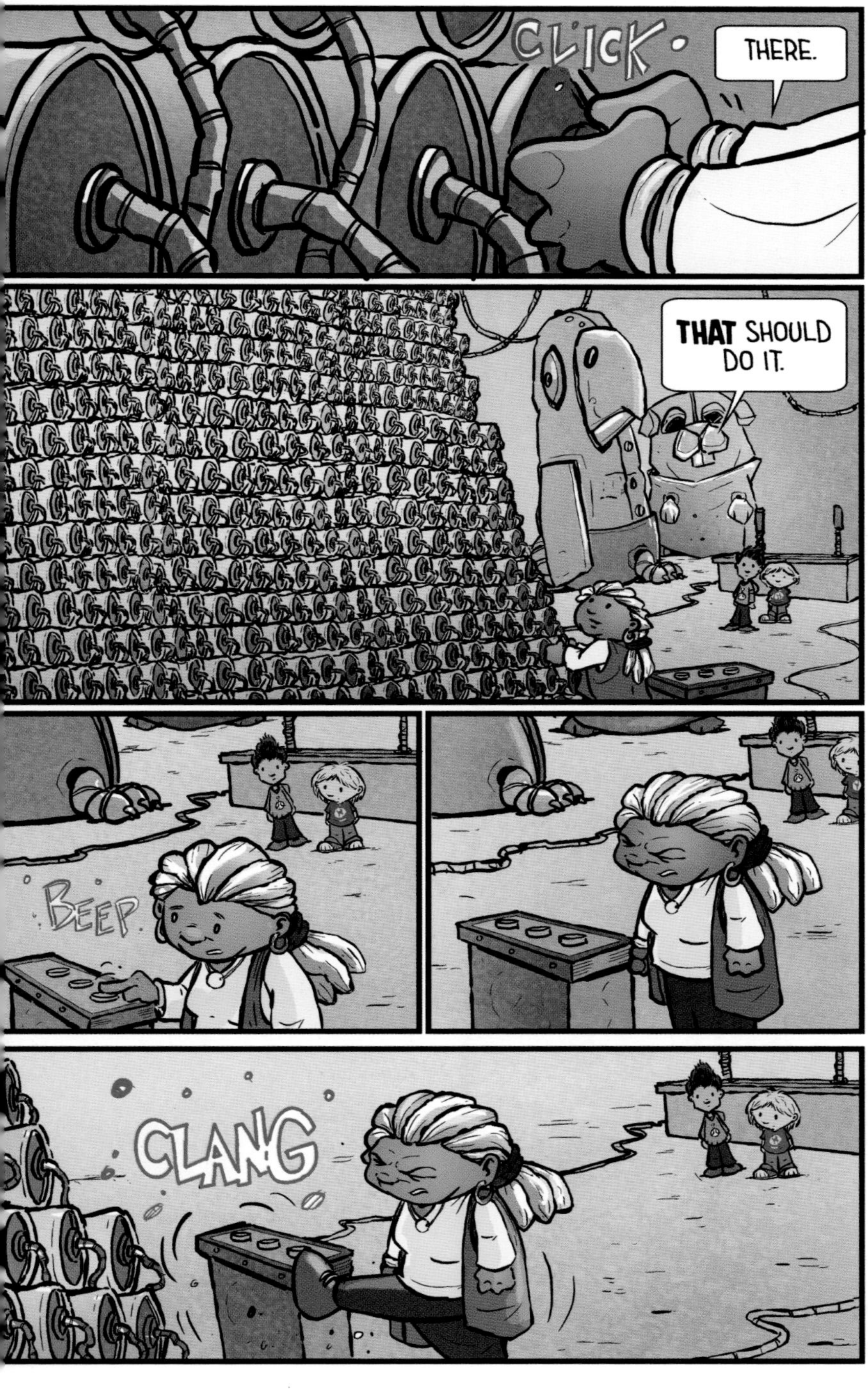
CLICK
THERE.
THAT SHOULD DO IT.
BEEP
CLANG

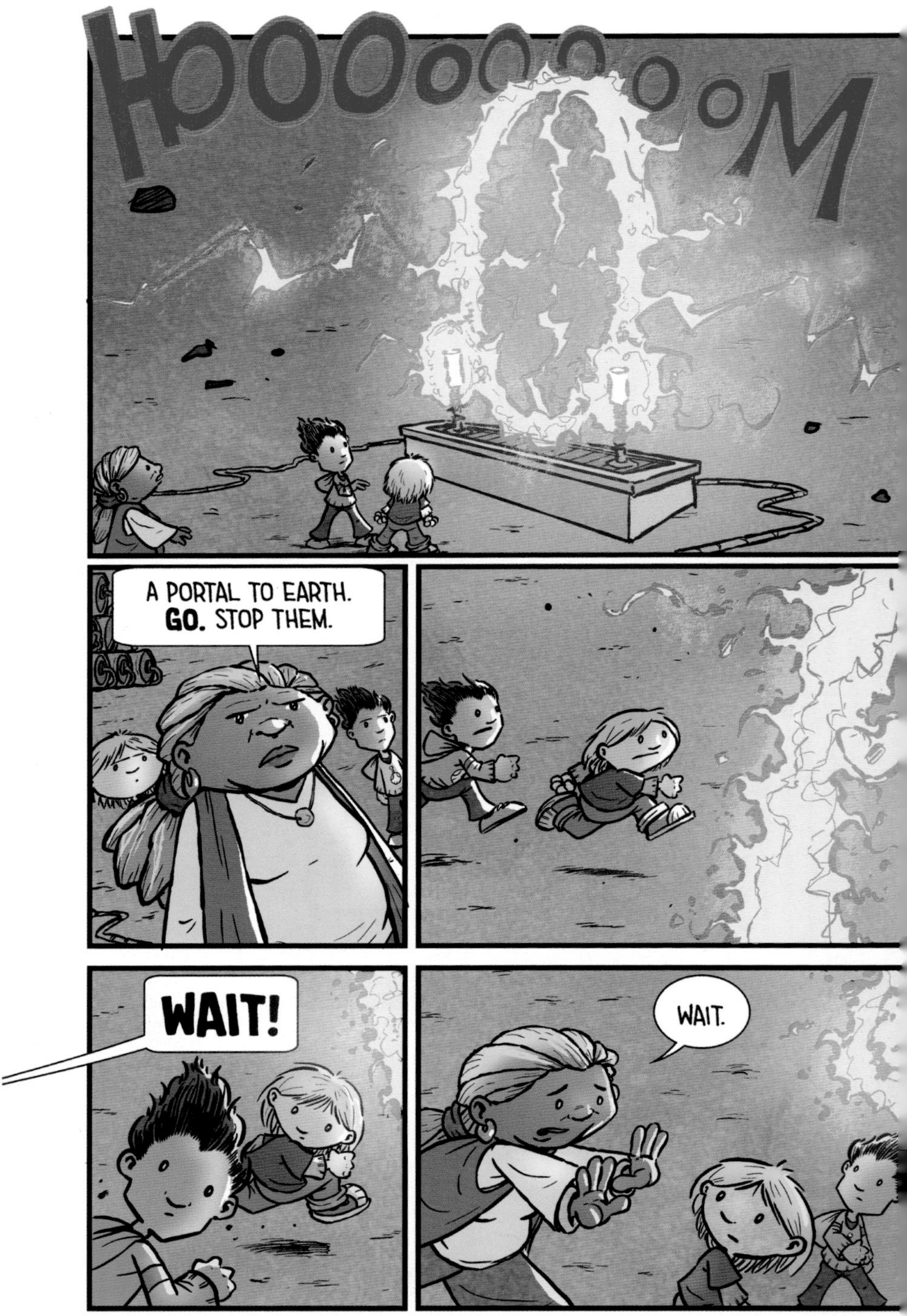
HOOOOOOOOOM
A PORTAL TO EARTH. **GO.** STOP THEM.
WAIT!
WAIT.

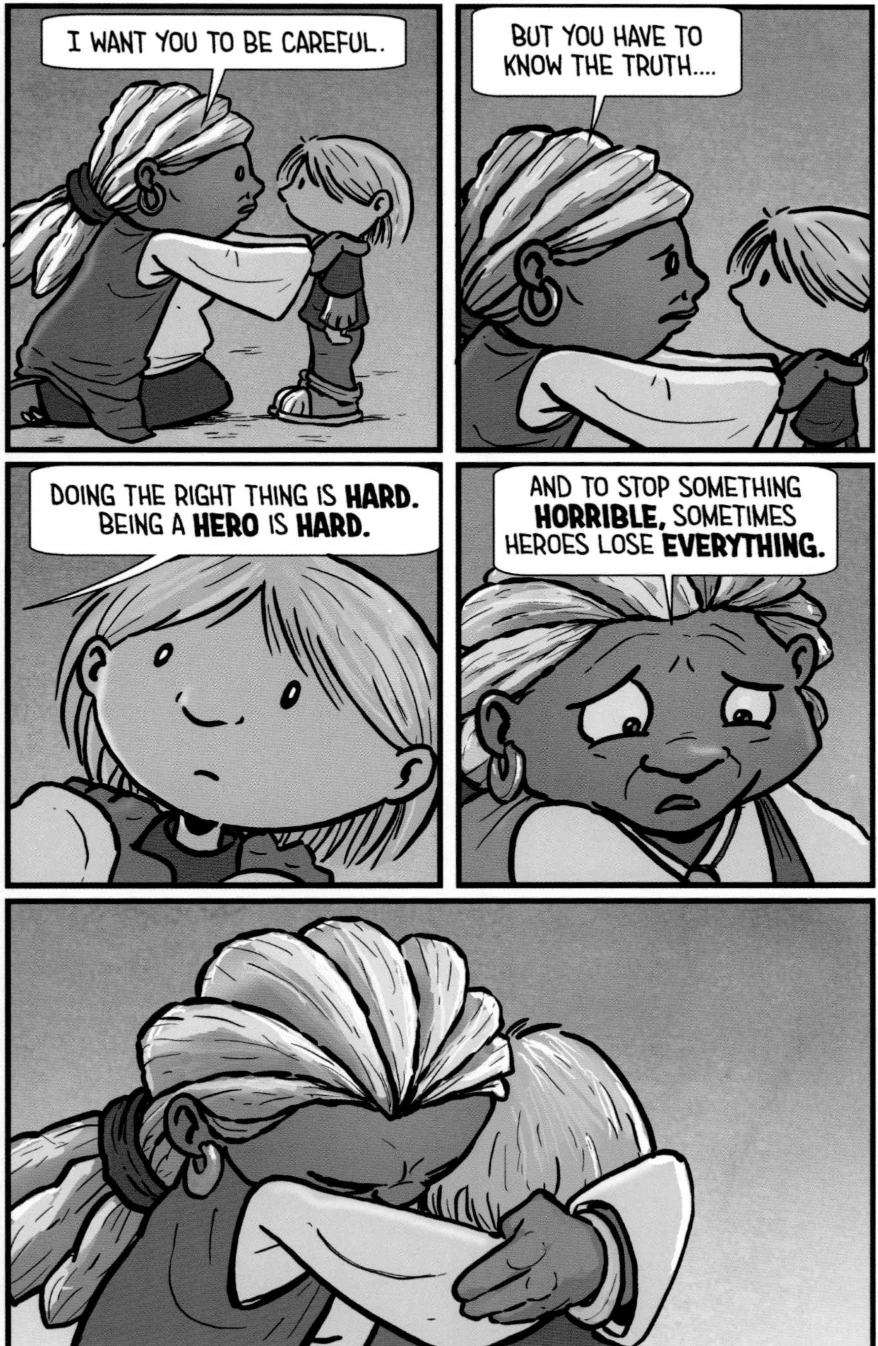
I WANT YOU TO BE CAREFUL.
BUT YOU HAVE TO KNOW THE TRUTH....
DOING THE RIGHT THING IS **HARD.** BEING A **HERO** IS **HARD.**
AND TO STOP SOMETHING **HORRIBLE,** SOMETIMES HEROES LOSE **EVERYTHING.**

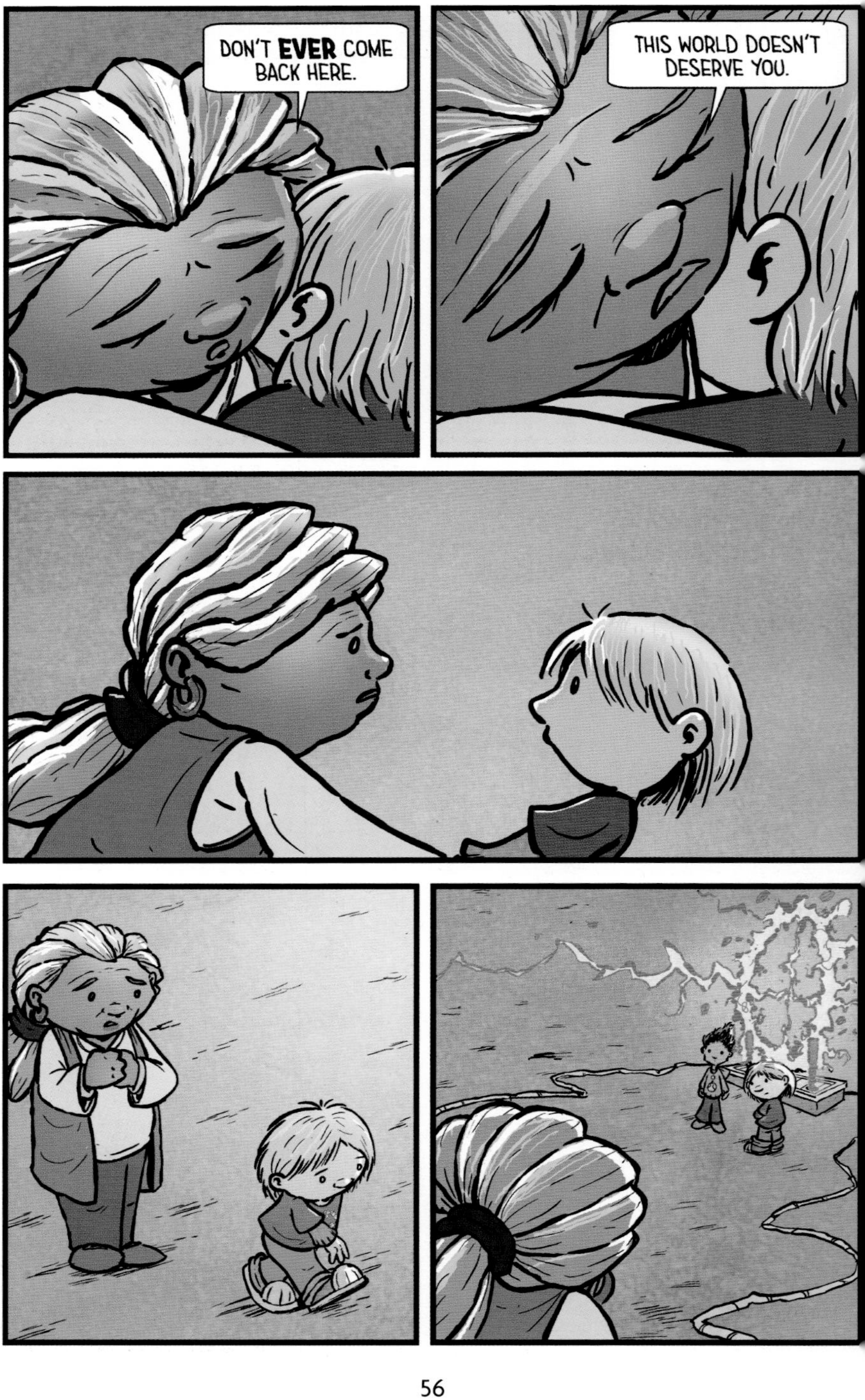
DON'T **EVER** COME BACK HERE.
THIS WORLD DOESN'T DESERVE YOU.

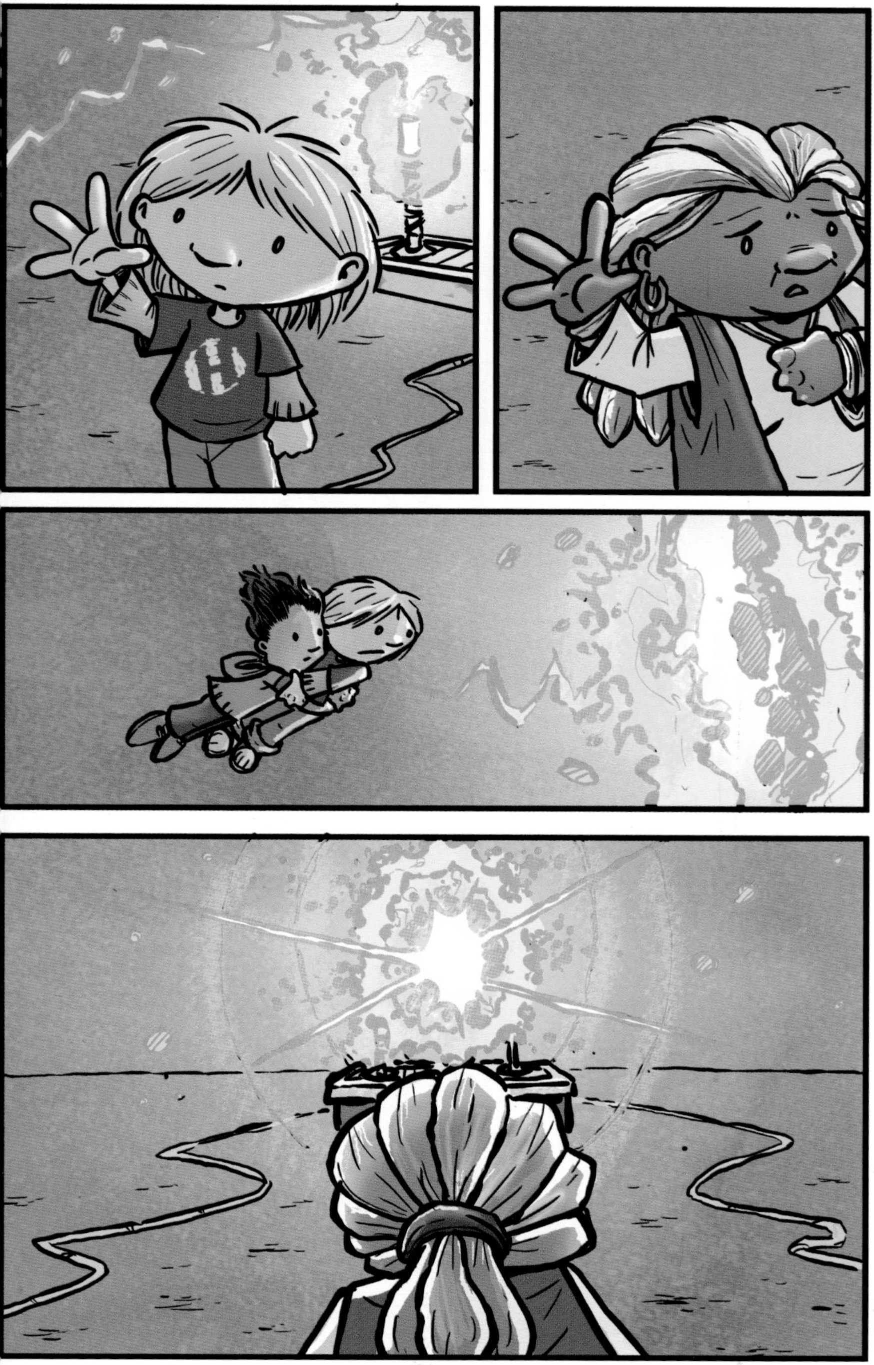

CHAPTER 5

STRIKE UP THE BAND

HAMAKER'S CANYON.

27 MILES OUTSIDE OF BERKE COUNTY.

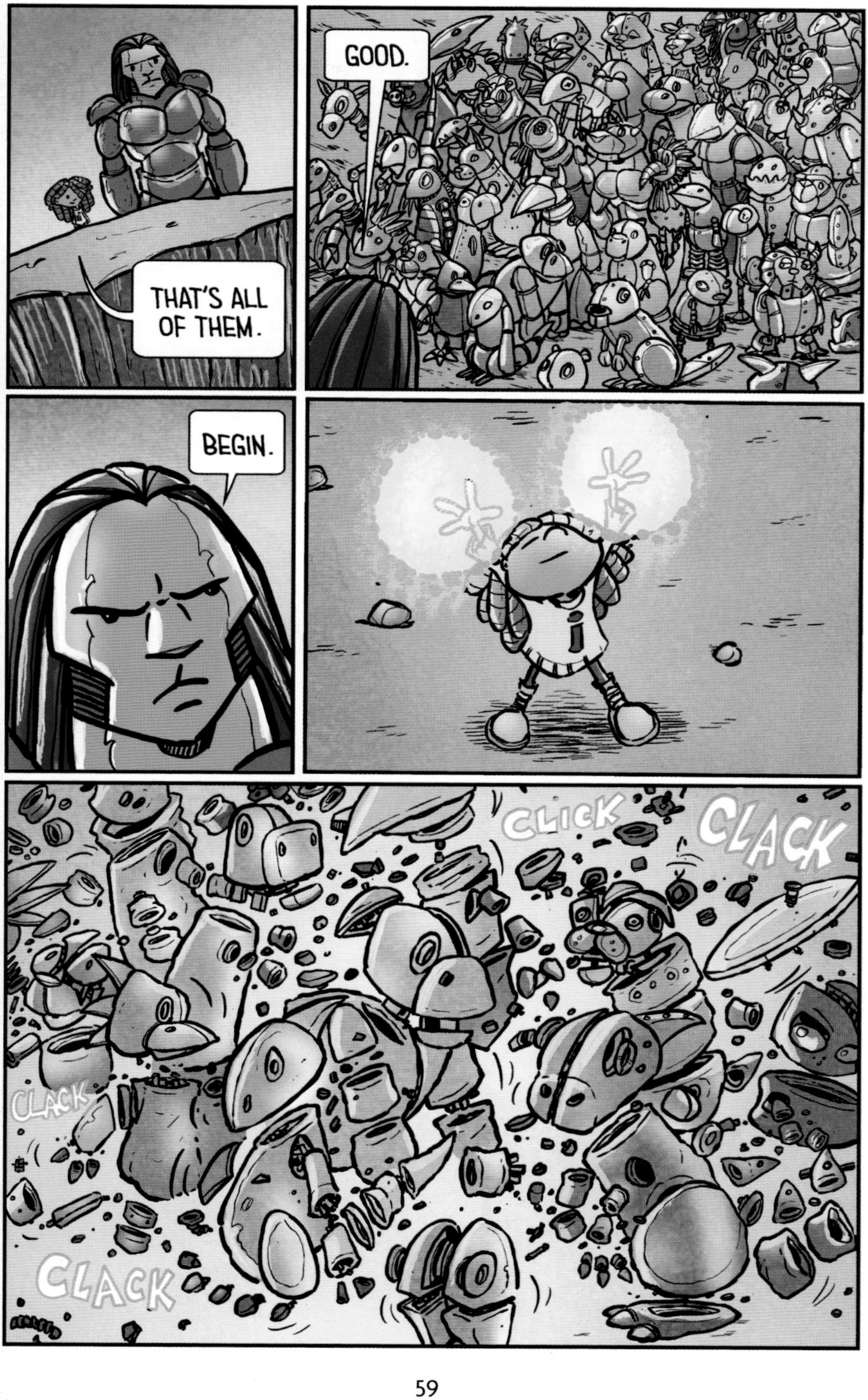
THAT'S ALL OF THEM.
GOOD.
BEGIN.
CLICK
CLACK
CLACK
CLACK

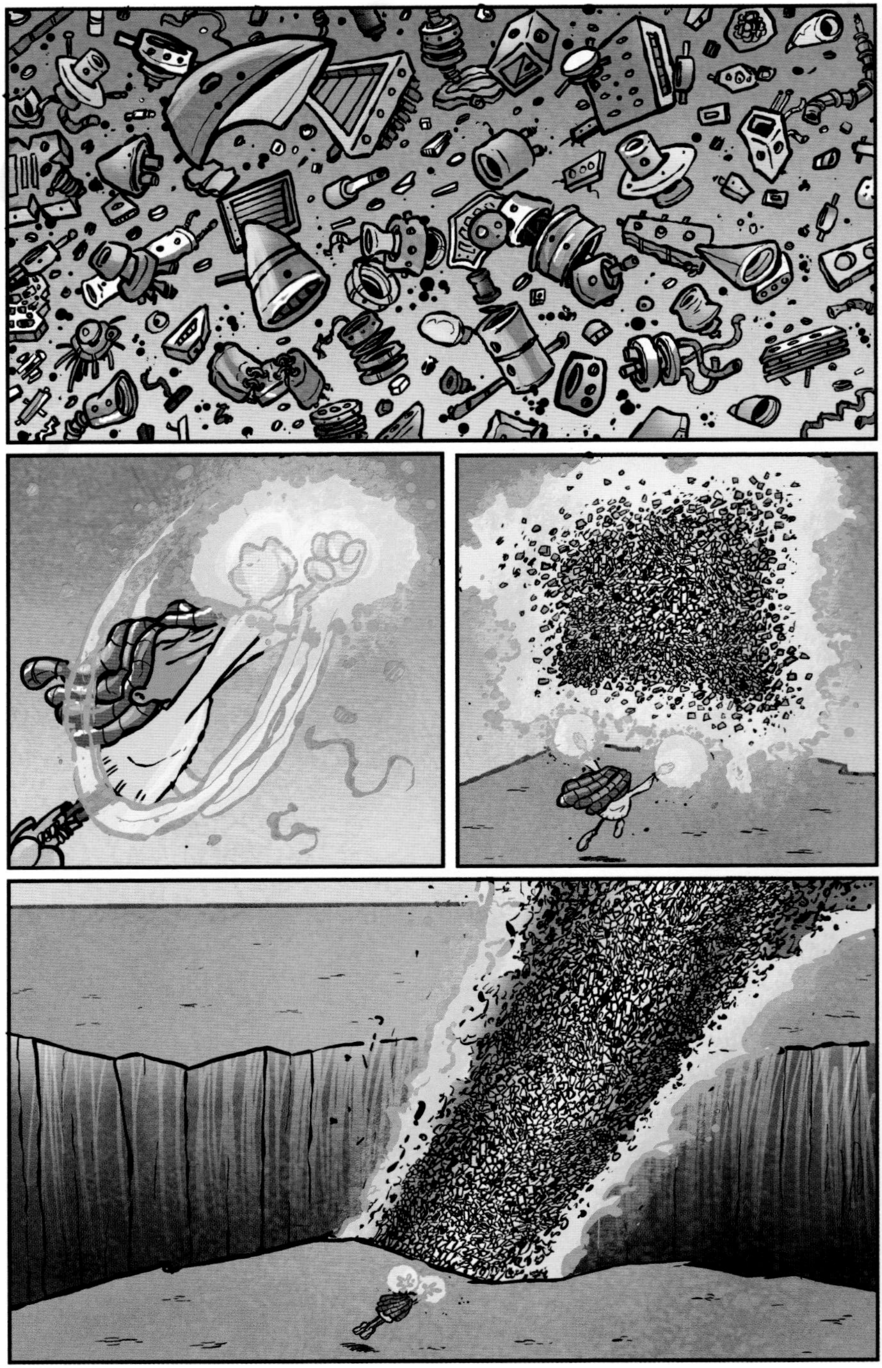

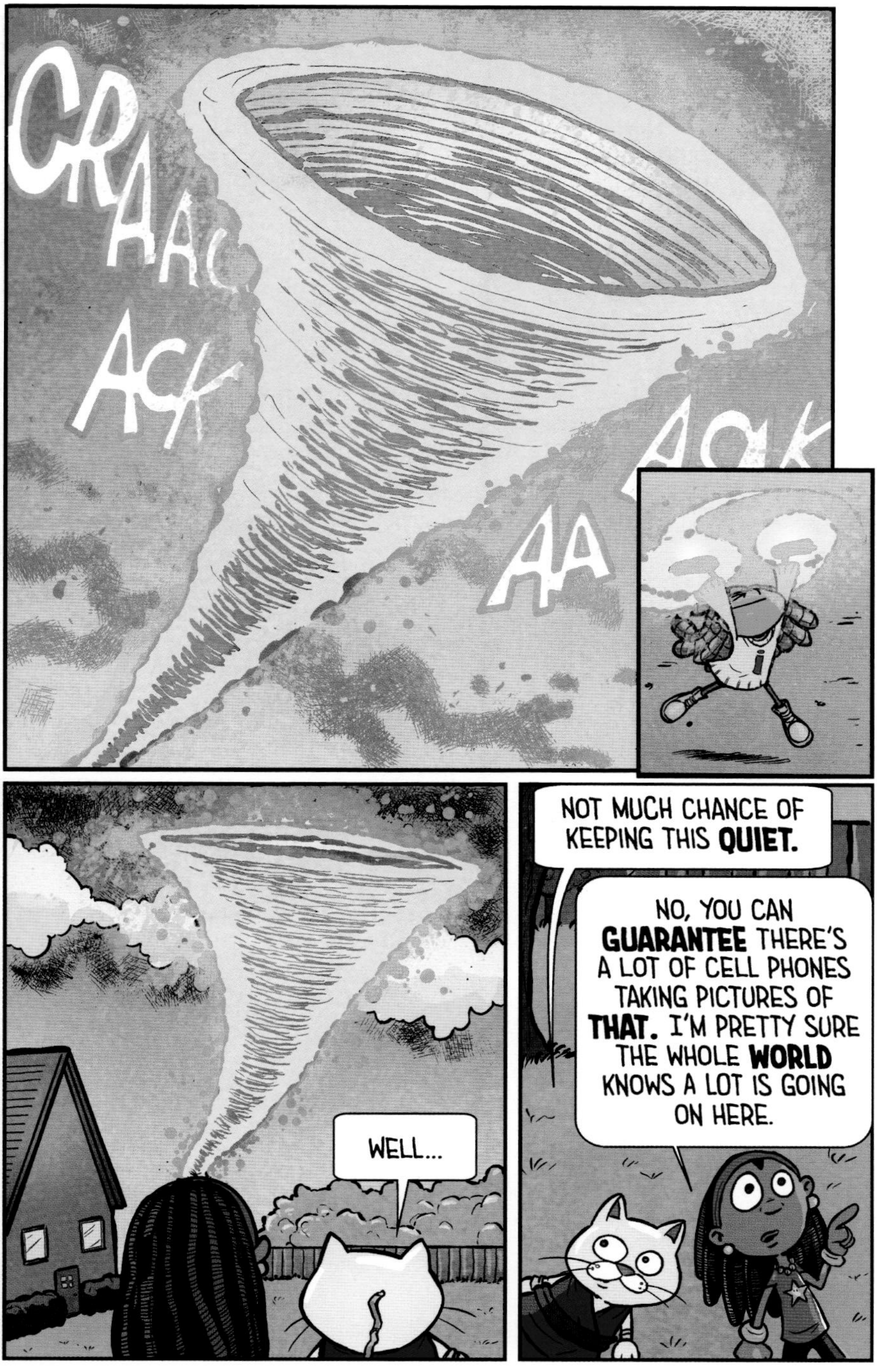
CRAAC
ACK
AA
WELL...
NOT MUCH CHANCE OF KEEPING THIS **QUIET.**
NO, YOU CAN **GUARANTEE** THERE'S A LOT OF CELL PHONES TAKING PICTURES OF **THAT.** I'M PRETTY SURE THE WHOLE **WORLD** KNOWS A LOT IS GOING ON HERE.

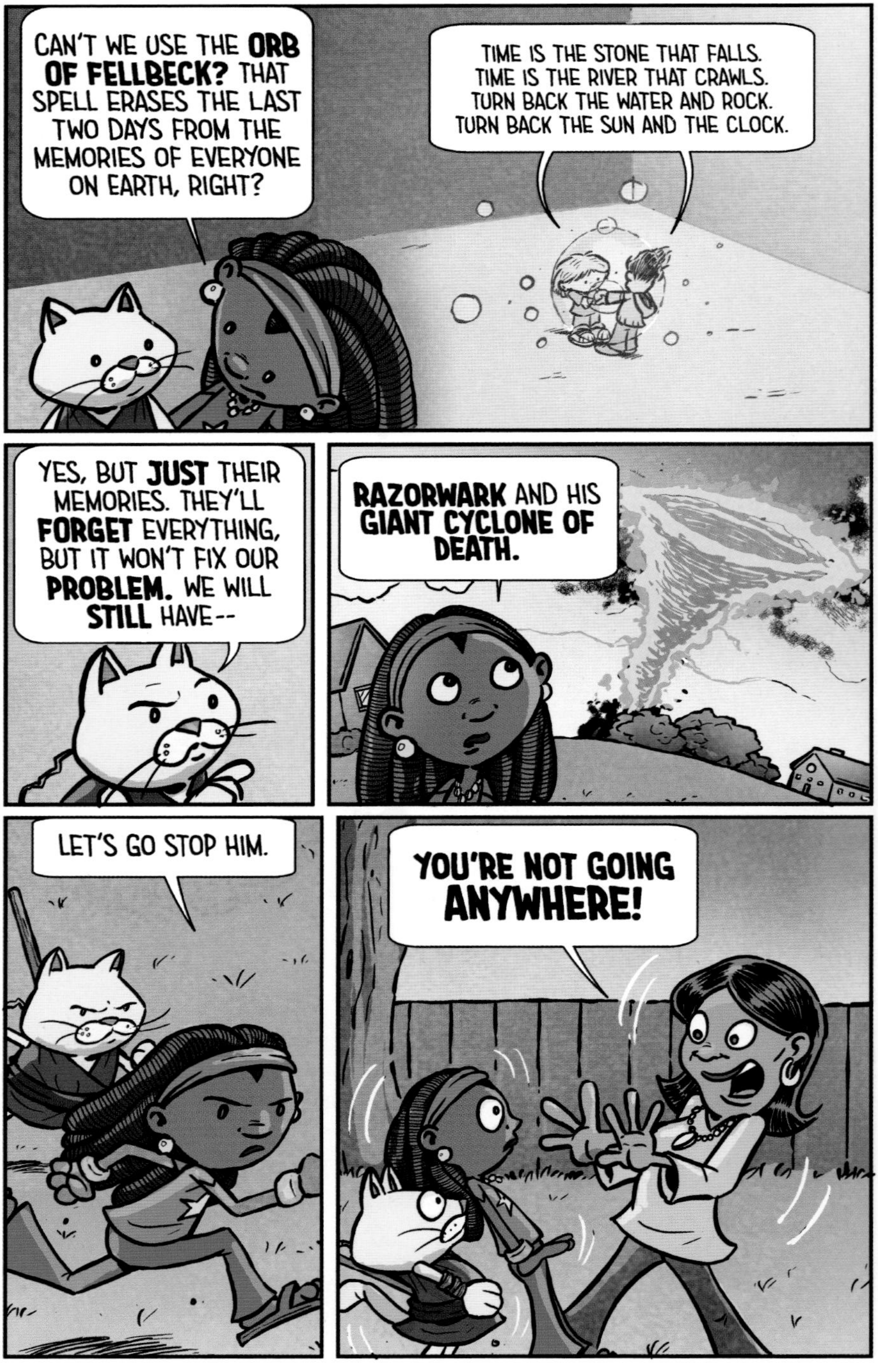
CAN'T WE USE THE **ORB OF FELLBECK?** THAT SPELL ERASES THE LAST TWO DAYS FROM THE MEMORIES OF EVERYONE ON EARTH, RIGHT?
TIME IS THE STONE THAT FALLS. TIME IS THE RIVER THAT CRAWLS. TURN BACK THE WATER AND ROCK. TURN BACK THE SUN AND THE CLOCK.
YES, BUT **JUST** THEIR MEMORIES. THEY'LL **FORGET** EVERYTHING, BUT IT WON'T FIX OUR **PROBLEM.** WE WILL **STILL** HAVE--
RAZORWARK AND HIS **GIANT CYCLONE OF DEATH.**
LET'S GO STOP HIM.
YOU'RE NOT GOING ANYWHERE!

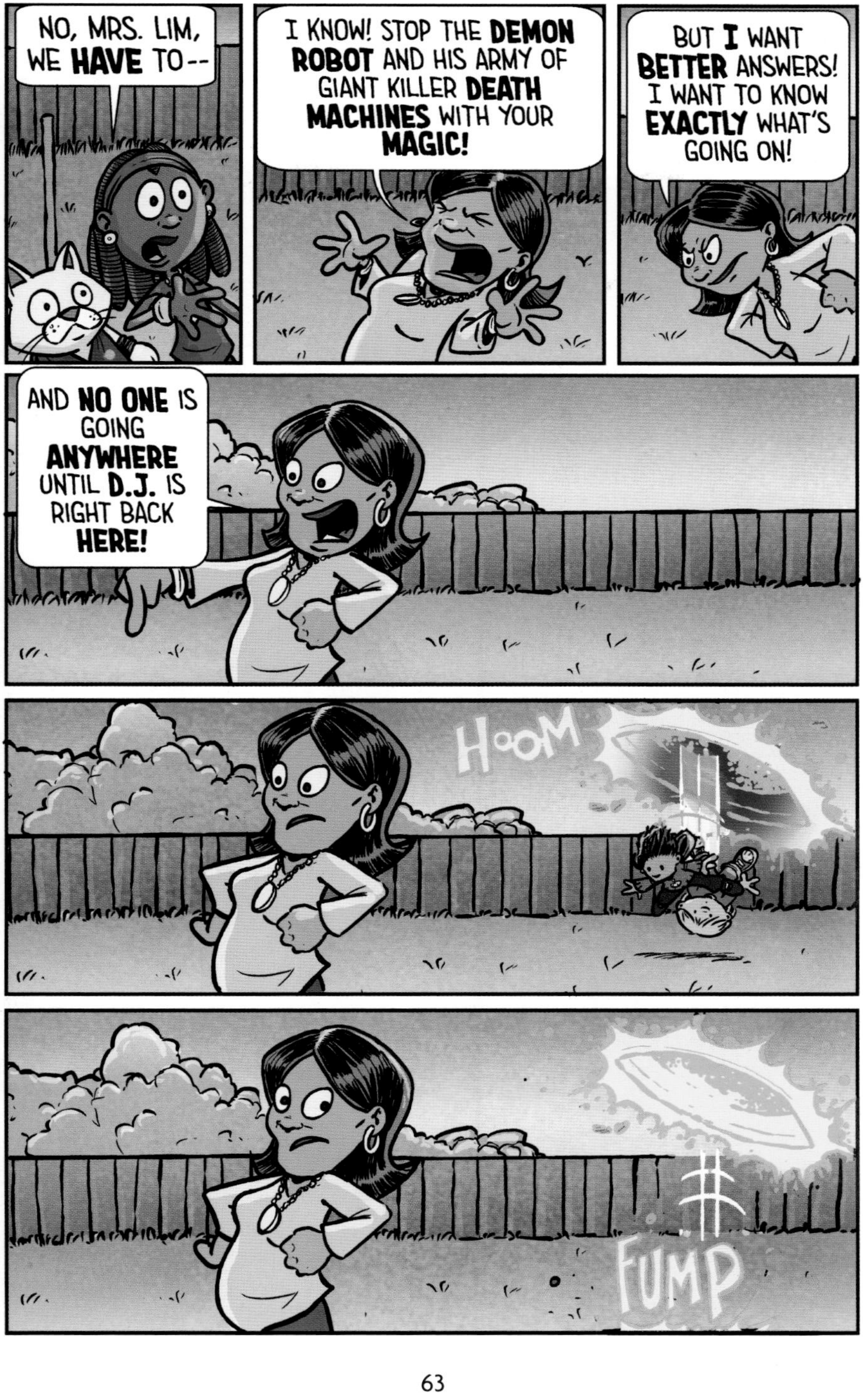
NO, MRS. LIM, WE **HAVE** TO--
I KNOW! STOP THE **DEMON ROBOT** AND HIS ARMY OF GIANT KILLER **DEATH MACHINES** WITH YOUR **MAGIC!**
BUT **I** WANT **BETTER** ANSWERS! I WANT TO KNOW **EXACTLY** WHAT'S GOING ON!
AND **NO ONE** IS GOING **ANYWHERE** UNTIL **D.J.** IS RIGHT BACK **HERE!**
HOOM
FUMP

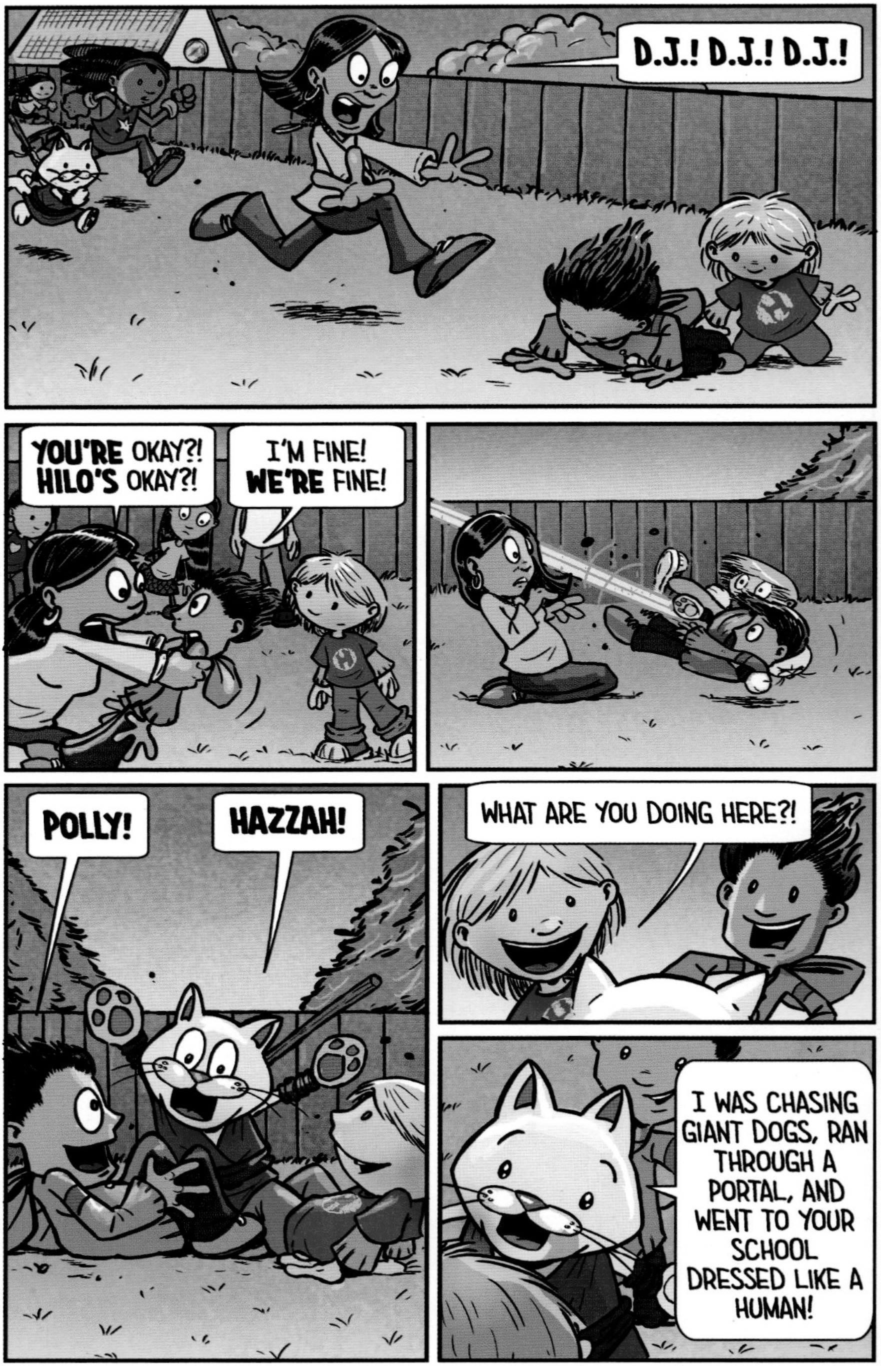
D.J.! D.J.! D.J.!
YOU'RE OKAY?! HILO'S OKAY?!
I'M FINE! WE'RE FINE!
POLLY!
HAZZAH!
WHAT ARE YOU DOING HERE?!
I WAS CHASING GIANT DOGS, RAN THROUGH A PORTAL, AND WENT TO YOUR SCHOOL DRESSED LIKE A HUMAN!

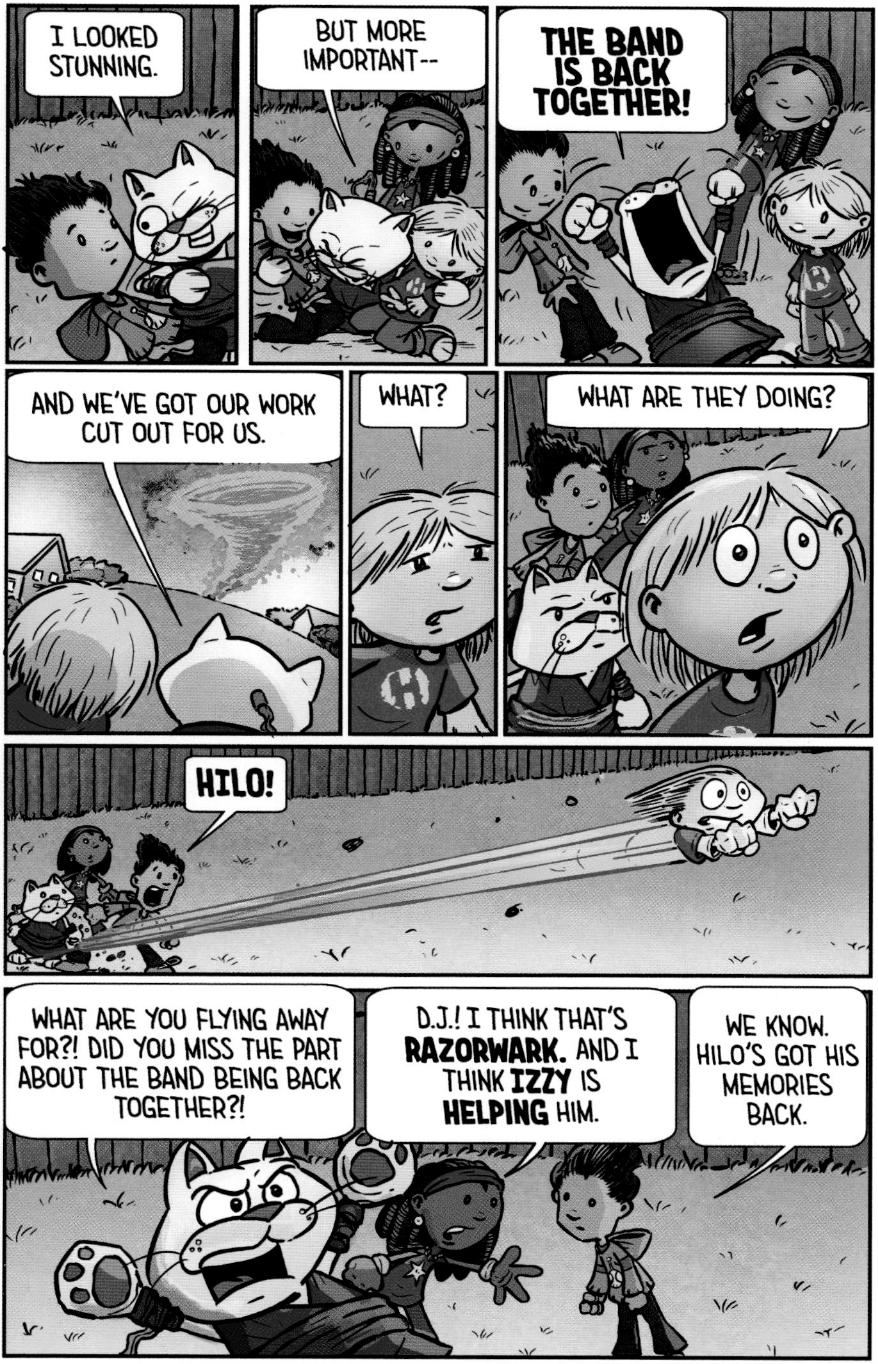
I LOOKED STUNNING.
BUT MORE IMPORTANT--
THE BAND IS BACK TOGETHER!
AND WE'VE GOT OUR WORK CUT OUT FOR US.
WHAT?
WHAT ARE THEY DOING?
HILO!
WHAT ARE YOU FLYING AWAY FOR?! DID YOU MISS THE PART ABOUT THE BAND BEING BACK TOGETHER?!
D.J.! I THINK THAT'S **RAZORWARK.** AND I THINK **IZZY** IS **HELPING** HIM.
WE KNOW. HILO'S GOT HIS MEMORIES BACK.

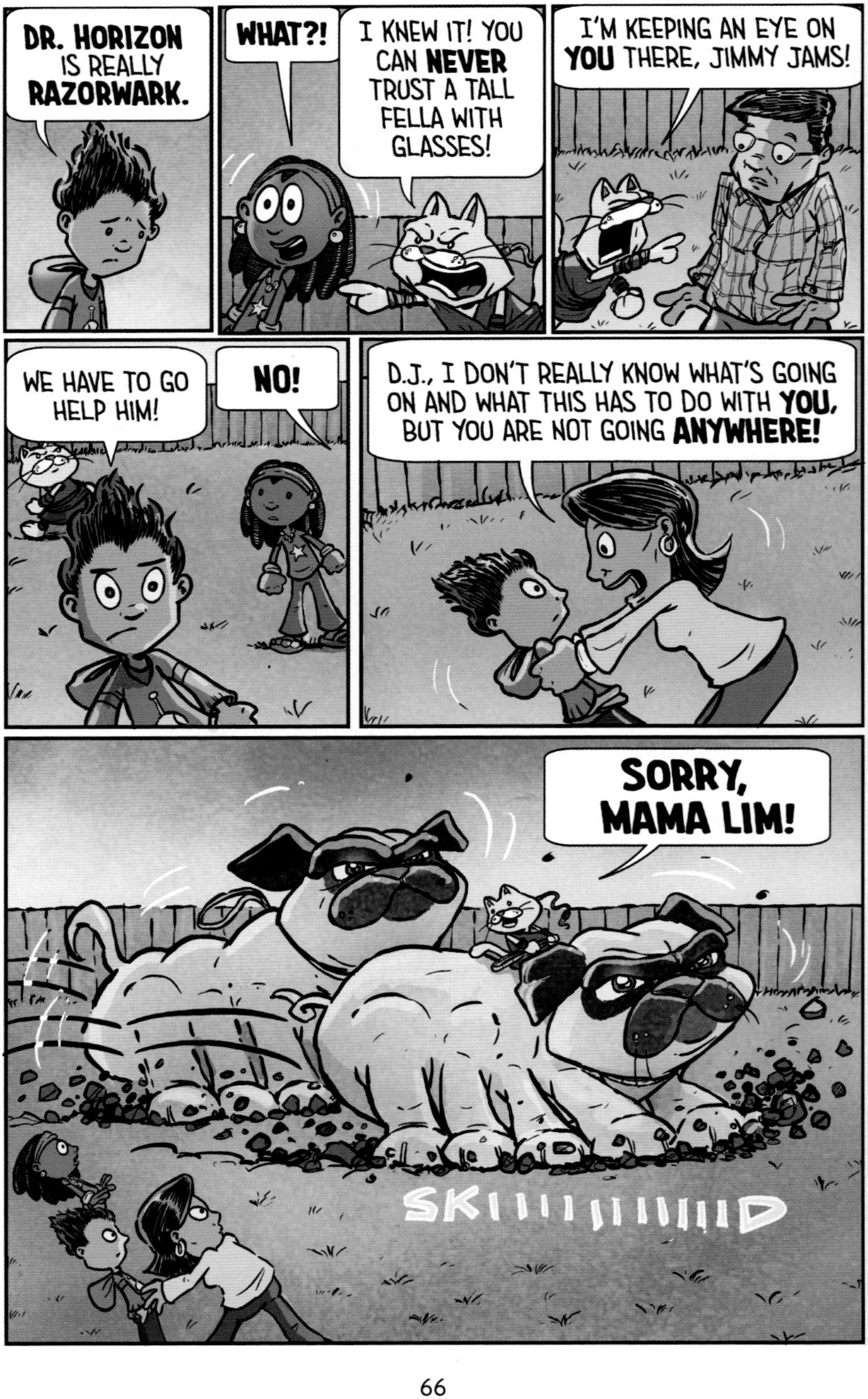

DR. HORIZON IS REALLY RAZORWARK.
WHAT?!
I KNEW IT! YOU CAN NEVER TRUST A TALL FELLA WITH GLASSES!
I'M KEEPING AN EYE ON YOU THERE, JIMMY JAMS!
WE HAVE TO GO HELP HIM!
NO!
D.J., I DON'T REALLY KNOW WHAT'S GOING ON AND WHAT THIS HAS TO DO WITH YOU, BUT YOU ARE NOT GOING ANYWHERE!
SORRY, MAMA LIM!
SKIIIIIIIIIID

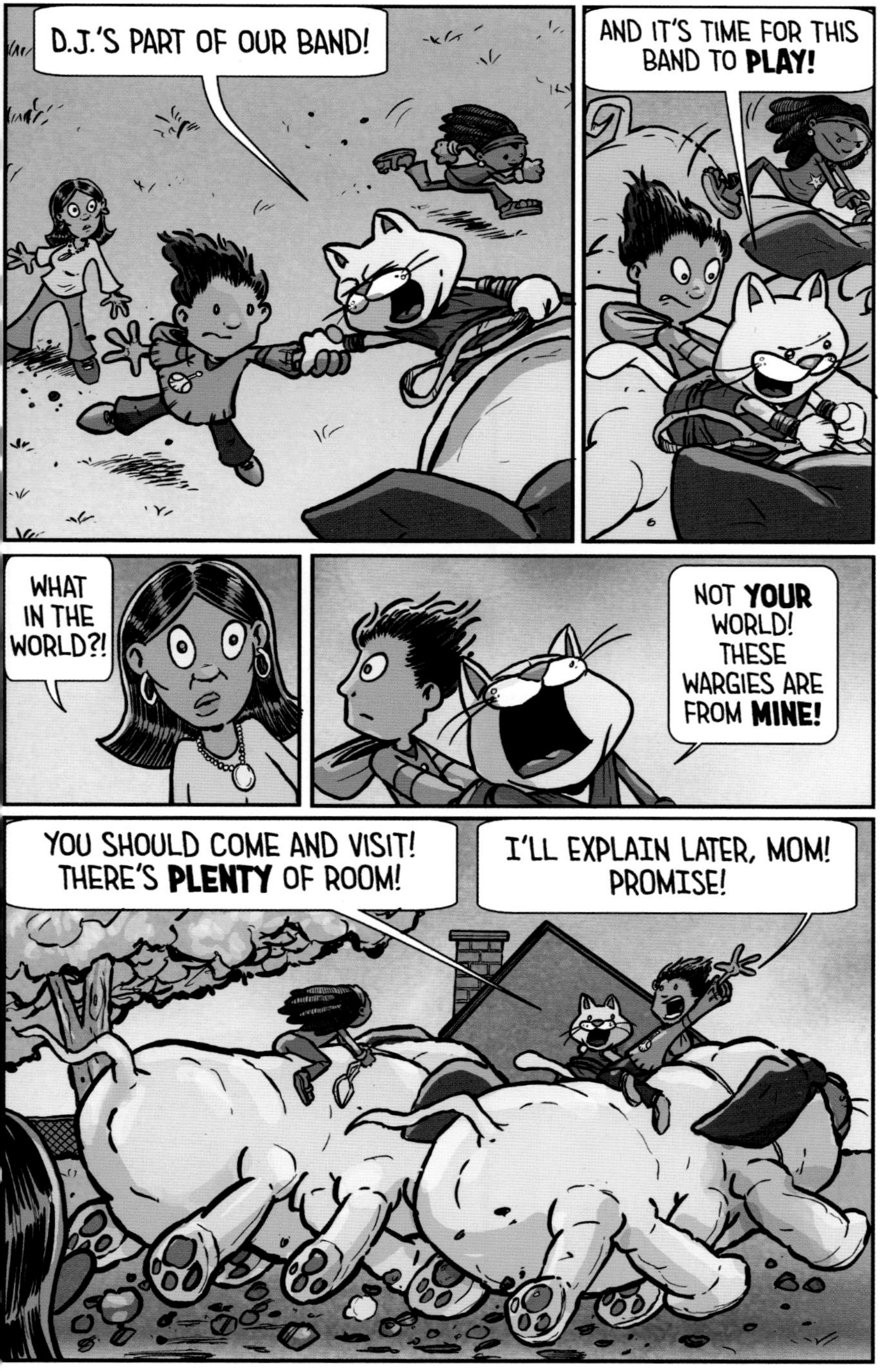
D.J.'S PART OF OUR BAND!
AND IT'S TIME FOR THIS BAND TO **PLAY!**
WHAT IN THE WORLD?!
NOT **YOUR** WORLD! THESE WARGIES ARE FROM **MINE!**
YOU SHOULD COME AND VISIT! THERE'S **PLENTY** OF ROOM!
I'LL EXPLAIN LATER, MOM! PROMISE!

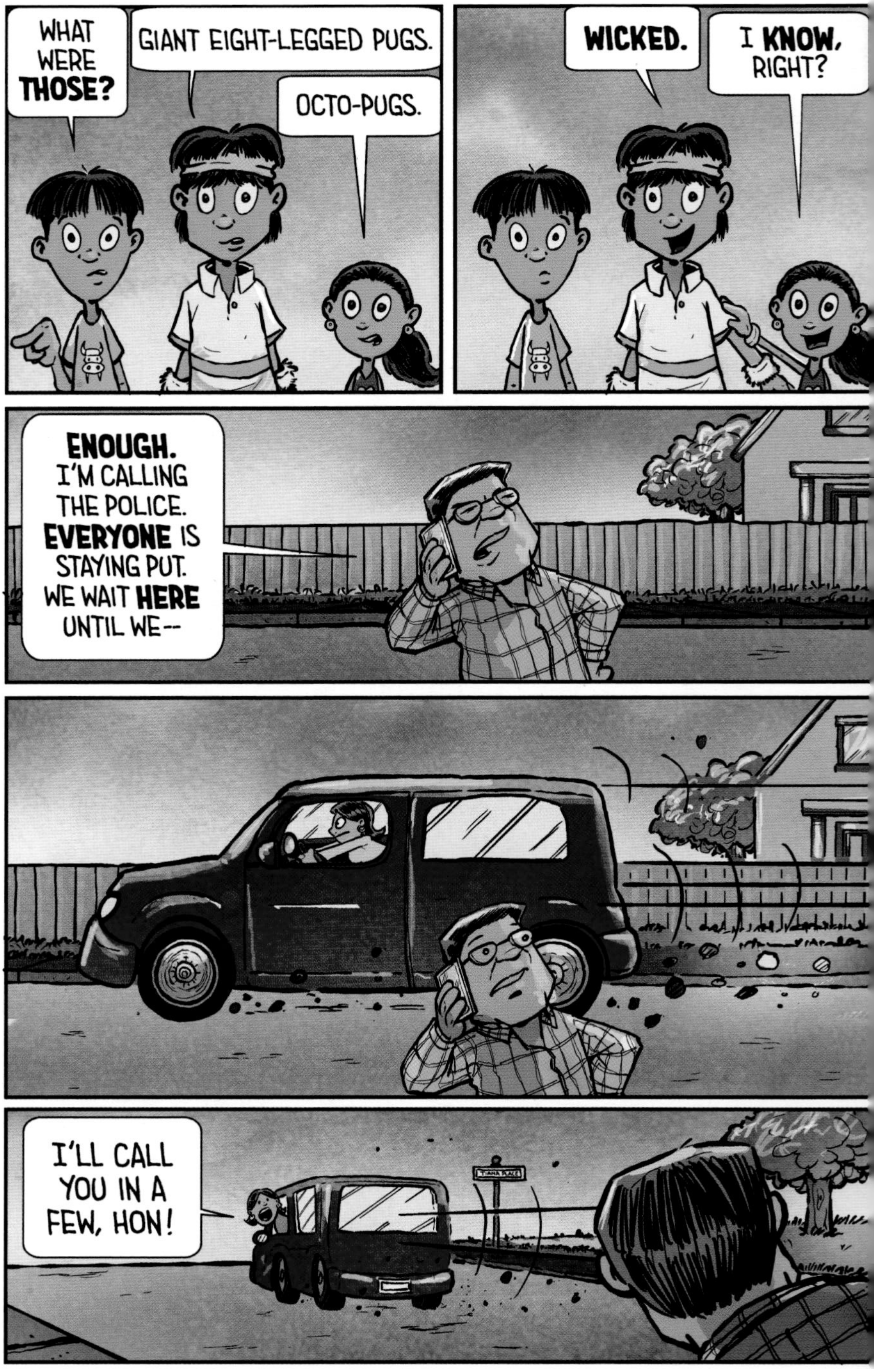
WHAT WERE THOSE?
GIANT EIGHT-LEGGED PUGS.
OCTO-PUGS.
WICKED.
I KNOW, RIGHT?
ENOUGH. I'M CALLING THE POLICE. EVERYONE IS STAYING PUT. WE WAIT HERE UNTIL WE--
I'LL CALL YOU IN A FEW, HON!

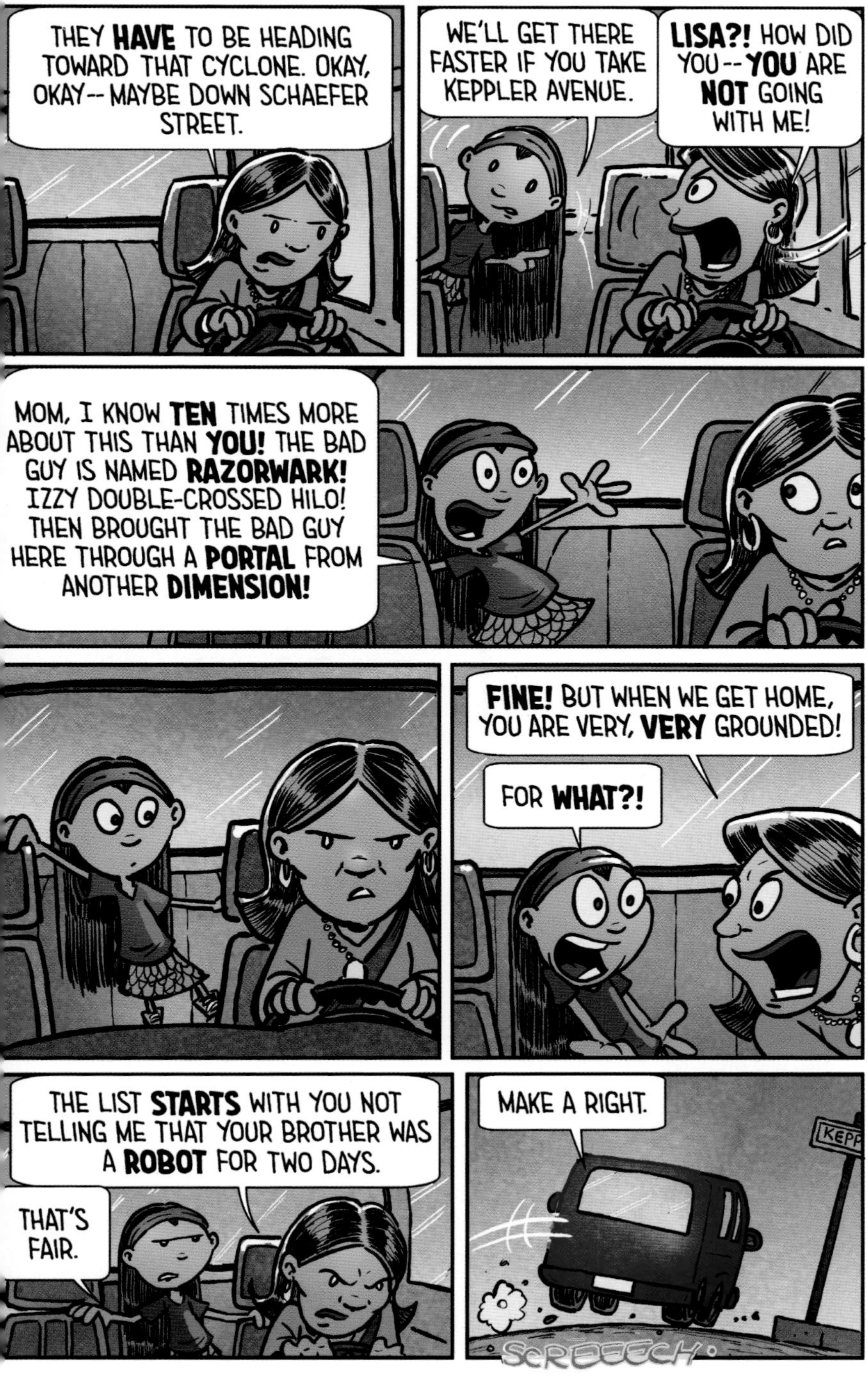
THEY HAVE TO BE HEADING TOWARD THAT CYCLONE. OKAY, OKAY-- MAYBE DOWN SCHAEFER STREET.
WE'LL GET THERE FASTER IF YOU TAKE KEPPLER AVENUE.
LISA?! HOW DID YOU--YOU ARE NOT GOING WITH ME!
MOM, I KNOW TEN TIMES MORE ABOUT THIS THAN YOU! THE BAD GUY IS NAMED RAZORWARK! IZZY DOUBLE-CROSSED HILO! THEN BROUGHT THE BAD GUY HERE THROUGH A PORTAL FROM ANOTHER DIMENSION!
FINE! BUT WHEN WE GET HOME, YOU ARE VERY, VERY GROUNDED!
FOR WHAT?!
THE LIST STARTS WITH YOU NOT TELLING ME THAT YOUR BROTHER WAS A ROBOT FOR TWO DAYS.
THAT'S FAIR.
MAKE A RIGHT.
KEPP
SCREEECH

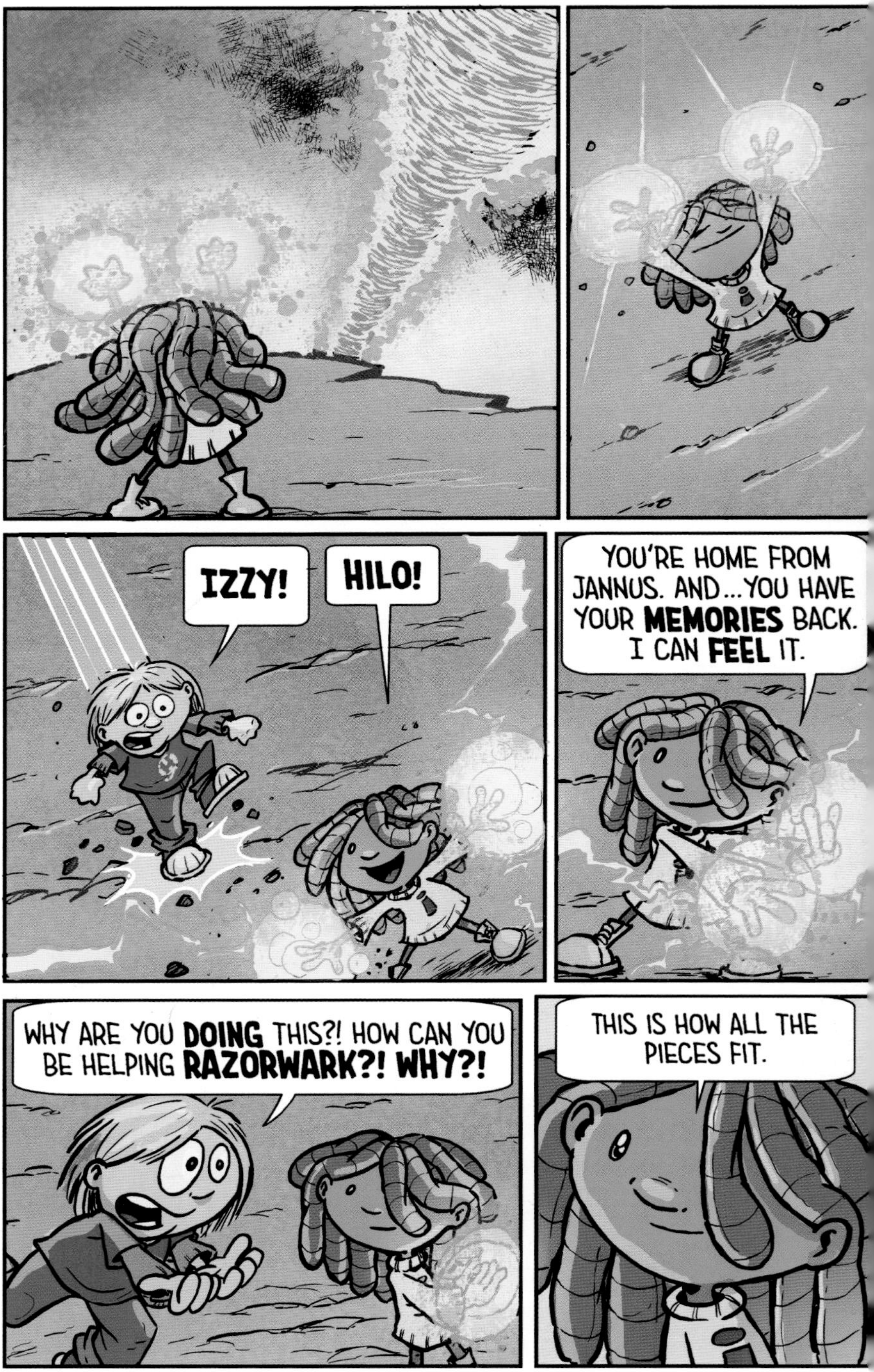
IZZY!
HILO!
YOU'RE HOME FROM JANNUS. AND...YOU HAVE YOUR MEMORIES BACK. I CAN FEEL IT.
WHY ARE YOU DOING THIS?! HOW CAN YOU BE HELPING RAZORWARK?! WHY?!
THIS IS HOW ALL THE PIECES FIT.

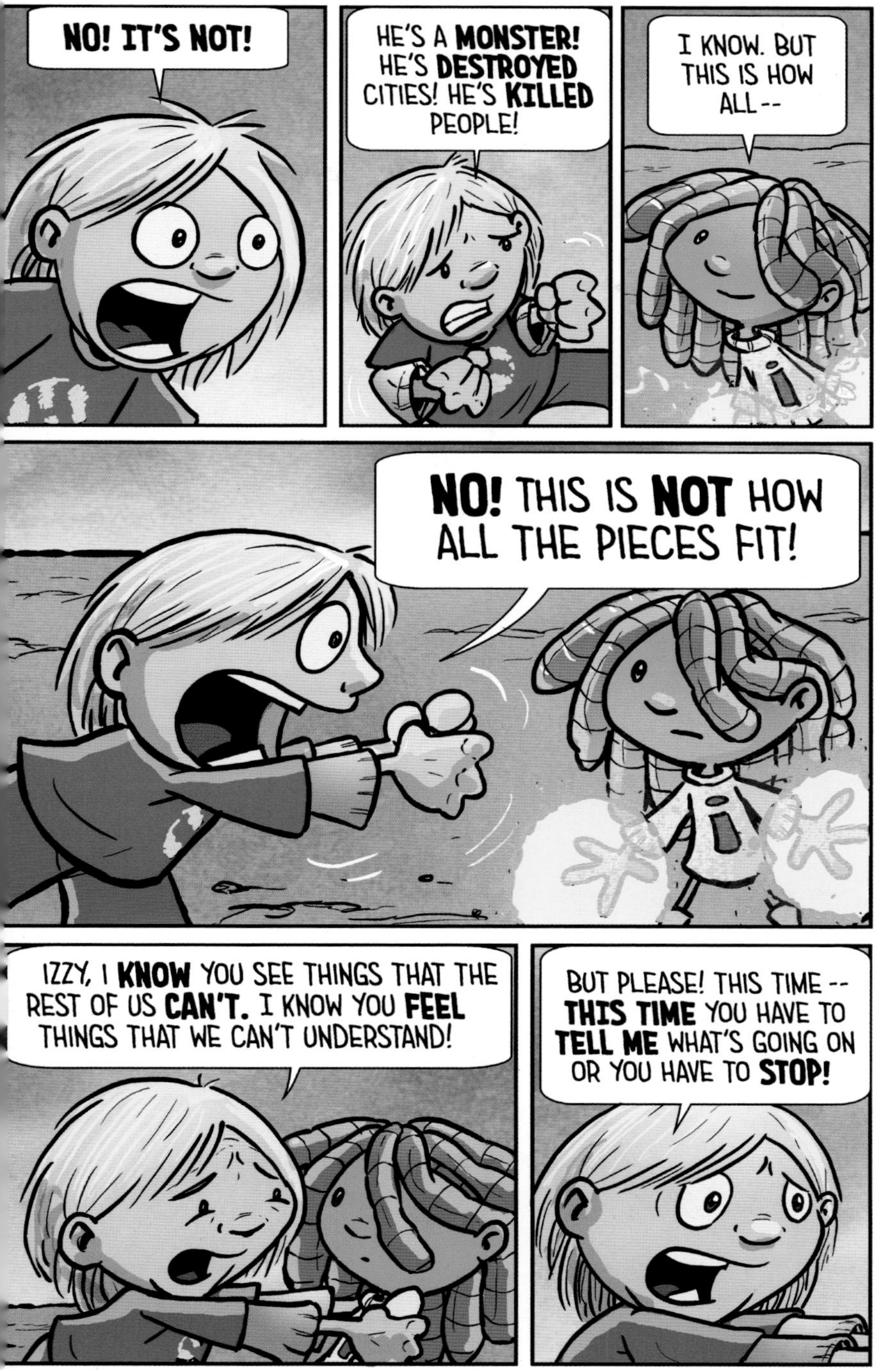
NO! IT'S NOT!
HE'S A MONSTER! HE'S DESTROYED CITIES! HE'S KILLED PEOPLE!
I KNOW. BUT THIS IS HOW ALL --
NO! THIS IS NOT HOW ALL THE PIECES FIT!
IZZY, I KNOW YOU SEE THINGS THAT THE REST OF US CAN'T. I KNOW YOU FEEL THINGS THAT WE CAN'T UNDERSTAND!
BUT PLEASE! THIS TIME -- THIS TIME YOU HAVE TO TELL ME WHAT'S GOING ON OR YOU HAVE TO STOP!

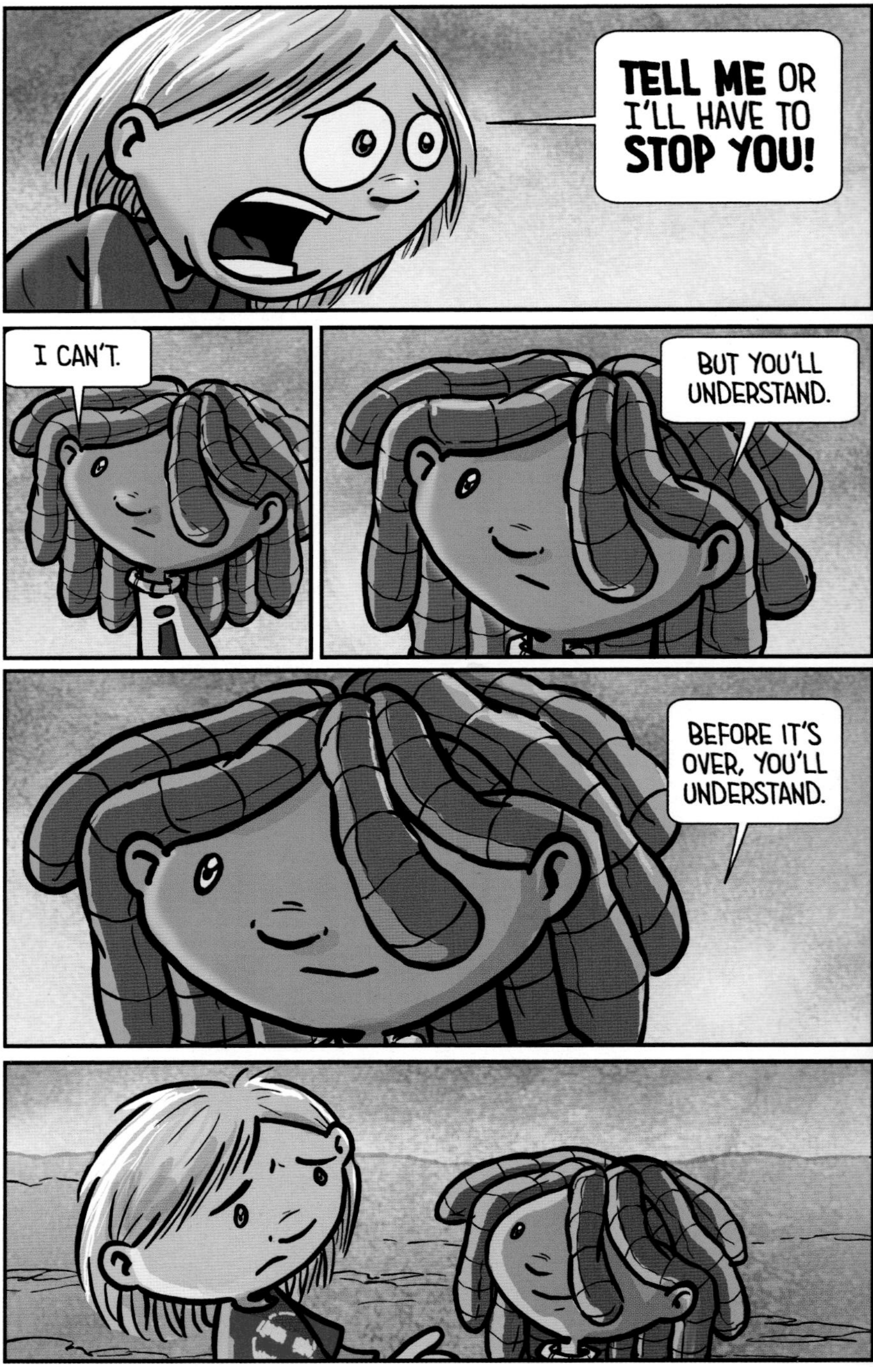

TELL ME OR I'LL HAVE TO STOP YOU!
I CAN'T.
BUT YOU'LL UNDERSTAND.
BEFORE IT'S OVER, YOU'LL UNDERSTAND.

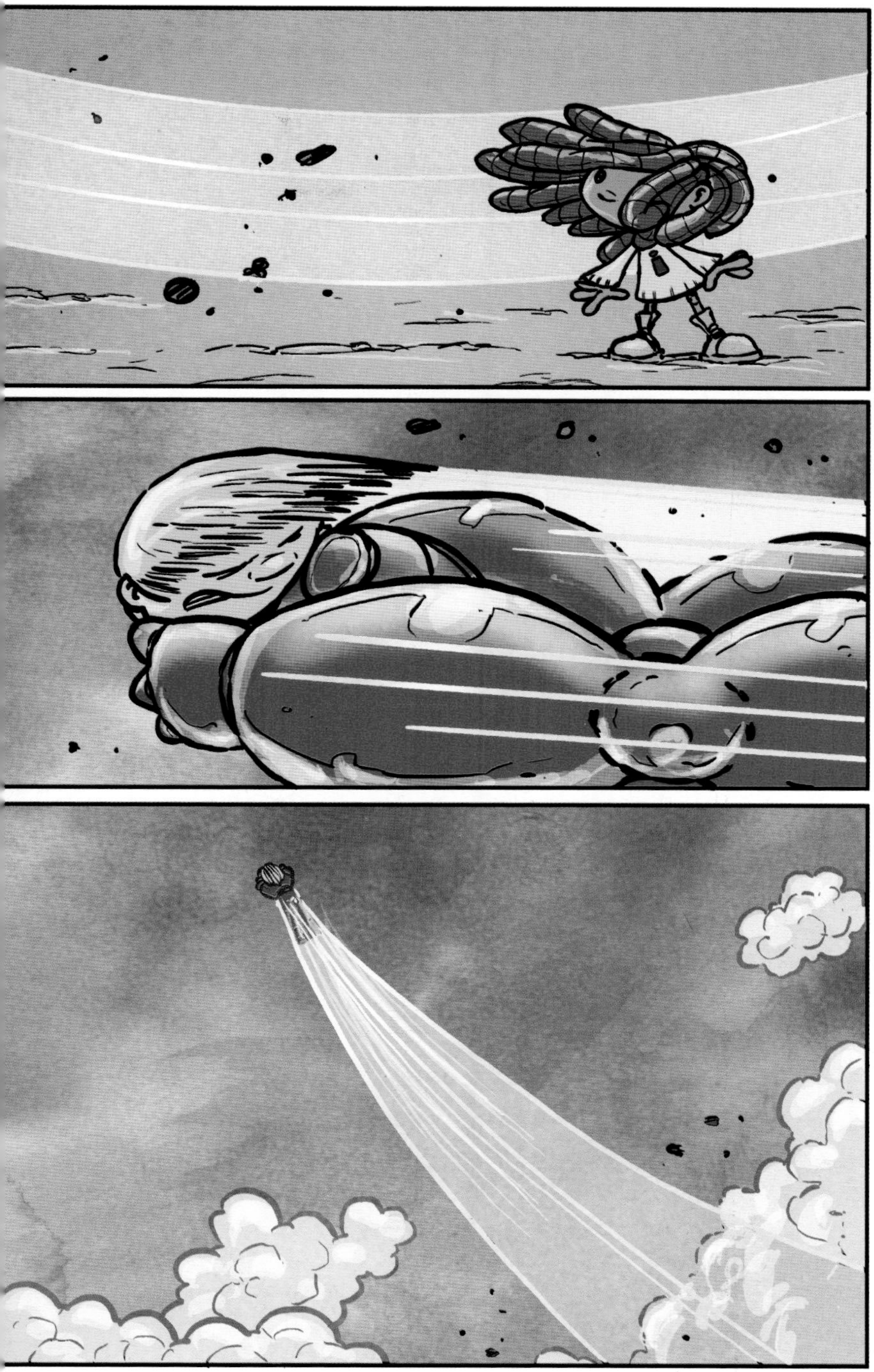

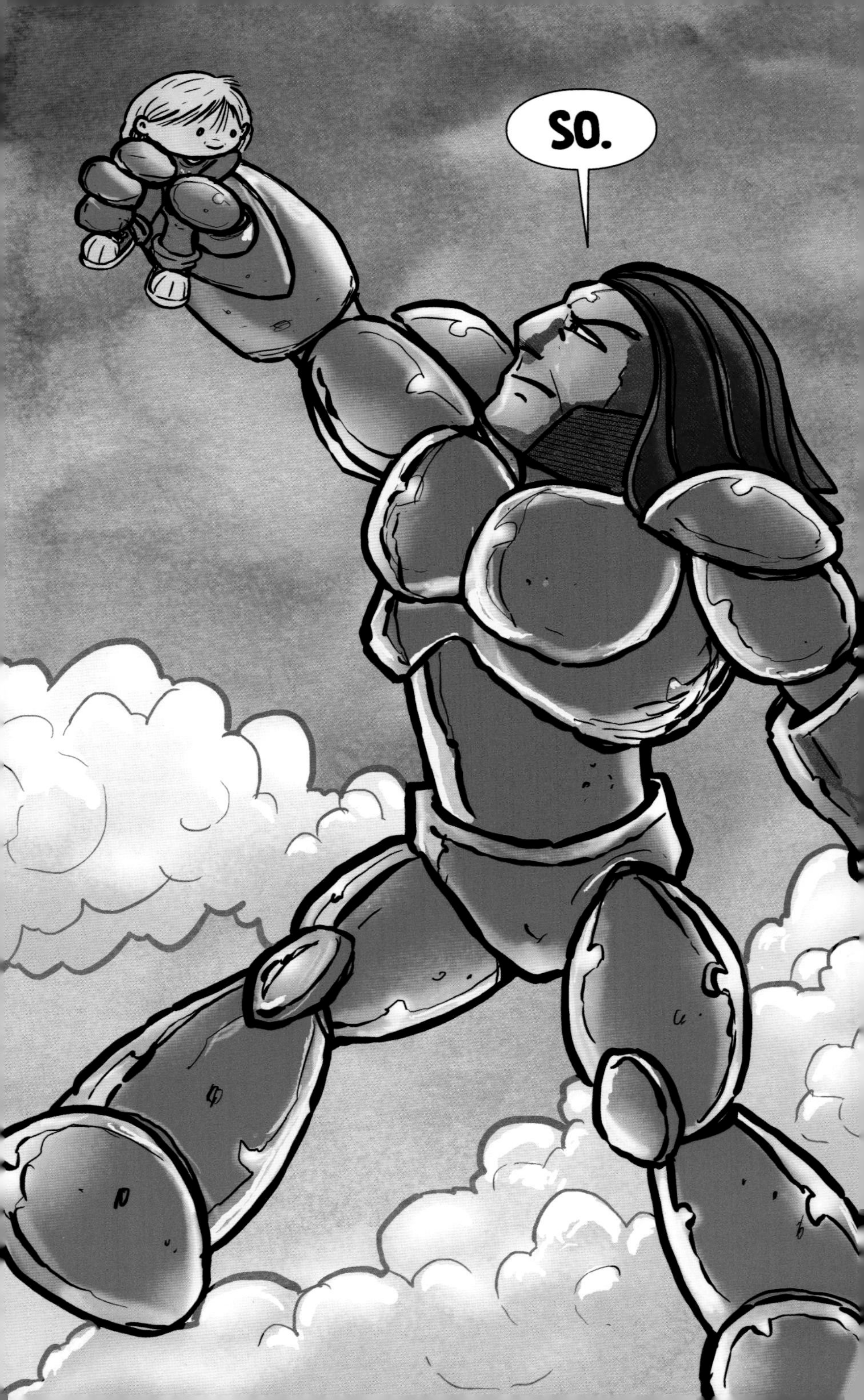
SO.

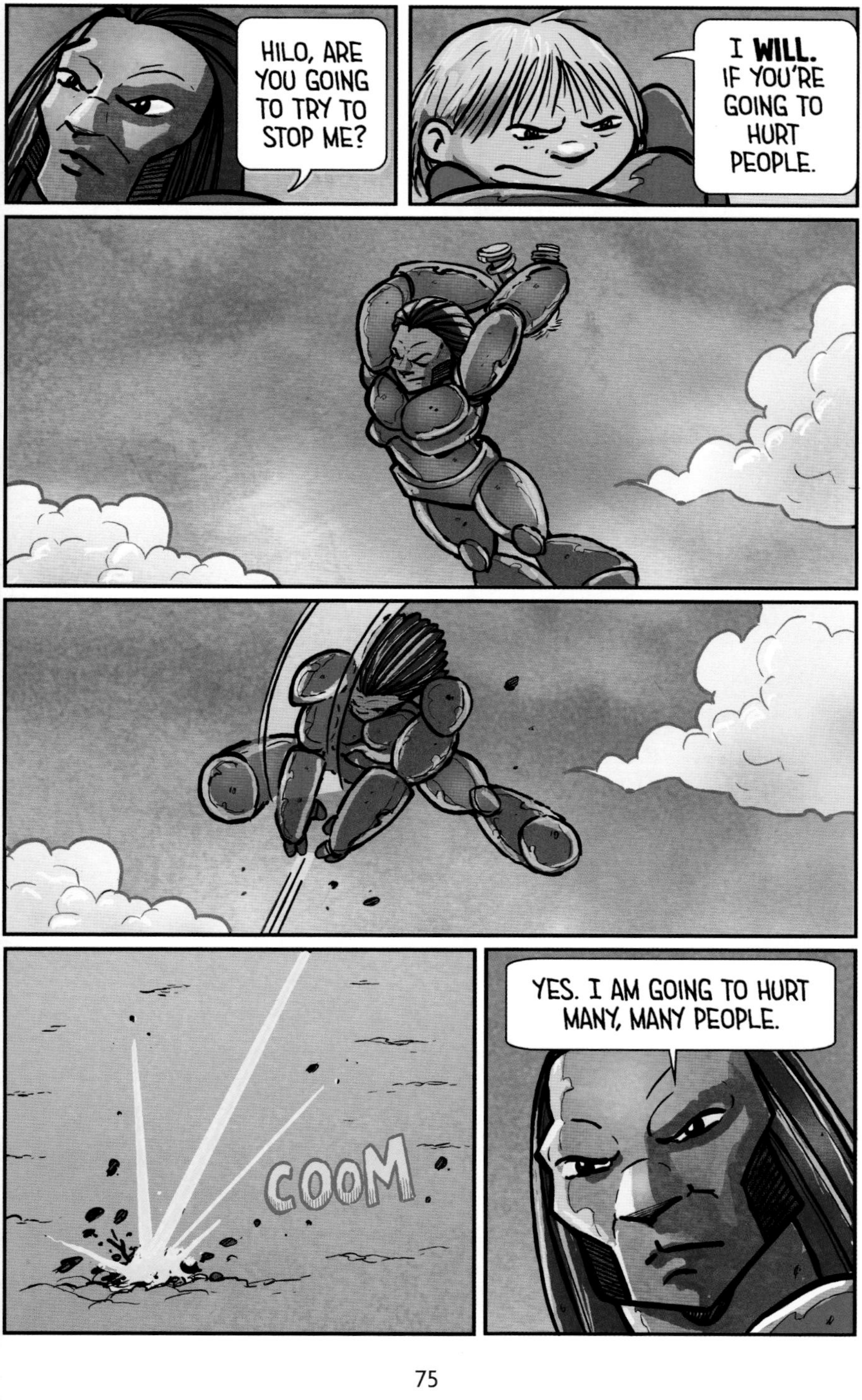
HILO, ARE YOU GOING TO TRY TO STOP ME?
I **WILL.** IF YOU'RE GOING TO HURT PEOPLE.
COOM
YES. I AM GOING TO HURT MANY, MANY PEOPLE.

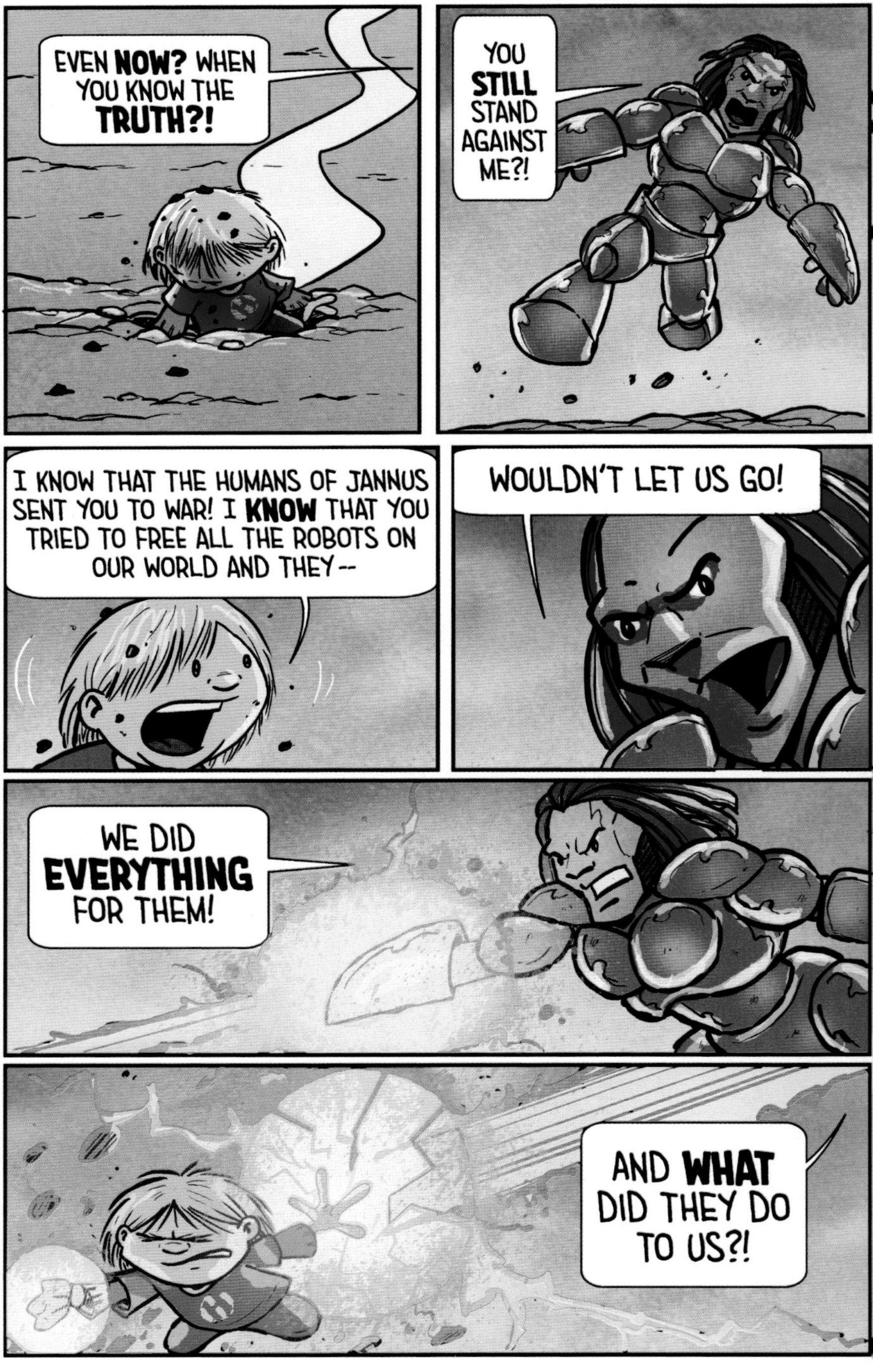
EVEN NOW? WHEN YOU KNOW THE TRUTH?!
YOU STILL STAND AGAINST ME?!
I KNOW THAT THE HUMANS OF JANNUS SENT YOU TO WAR! I KNOW THAT YOU TRIED TO FREE ALL THE ROBOTS ON OUR WORLD AND THEY--
WOULDN'T LET US GO!
WE DID EVERYTHING FOR THEM!
AND WHAT DID THEY DO TO US?!

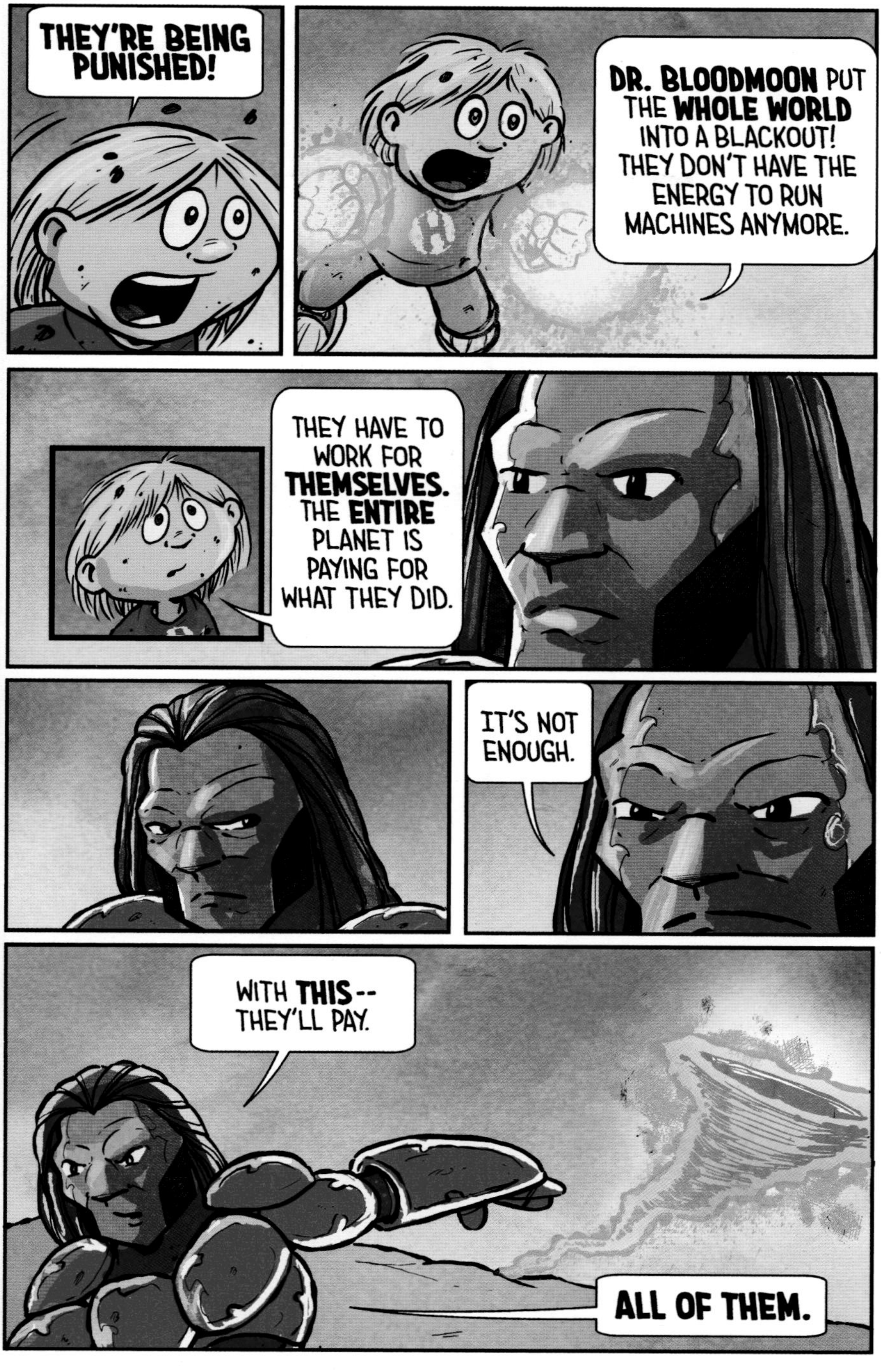
THEY'RE BEING PUNISHED!
DR. BLOODMOON PUT THE **WHOLE WORLD** INTO A BLACKOUT! THEY DON'T HAVE THE ENERGY TO RUN MACHINES ANYMORE.
THEY HAVE TO WORK FOR **THEMSELVES.** THE **ENTIRE** PLANET IS PAYING FOR WHAT THEY DID.
IT'S NOT ENOUGH.
WITH **THIS**-- THEY'LL PAY.
ALL OF THEM.

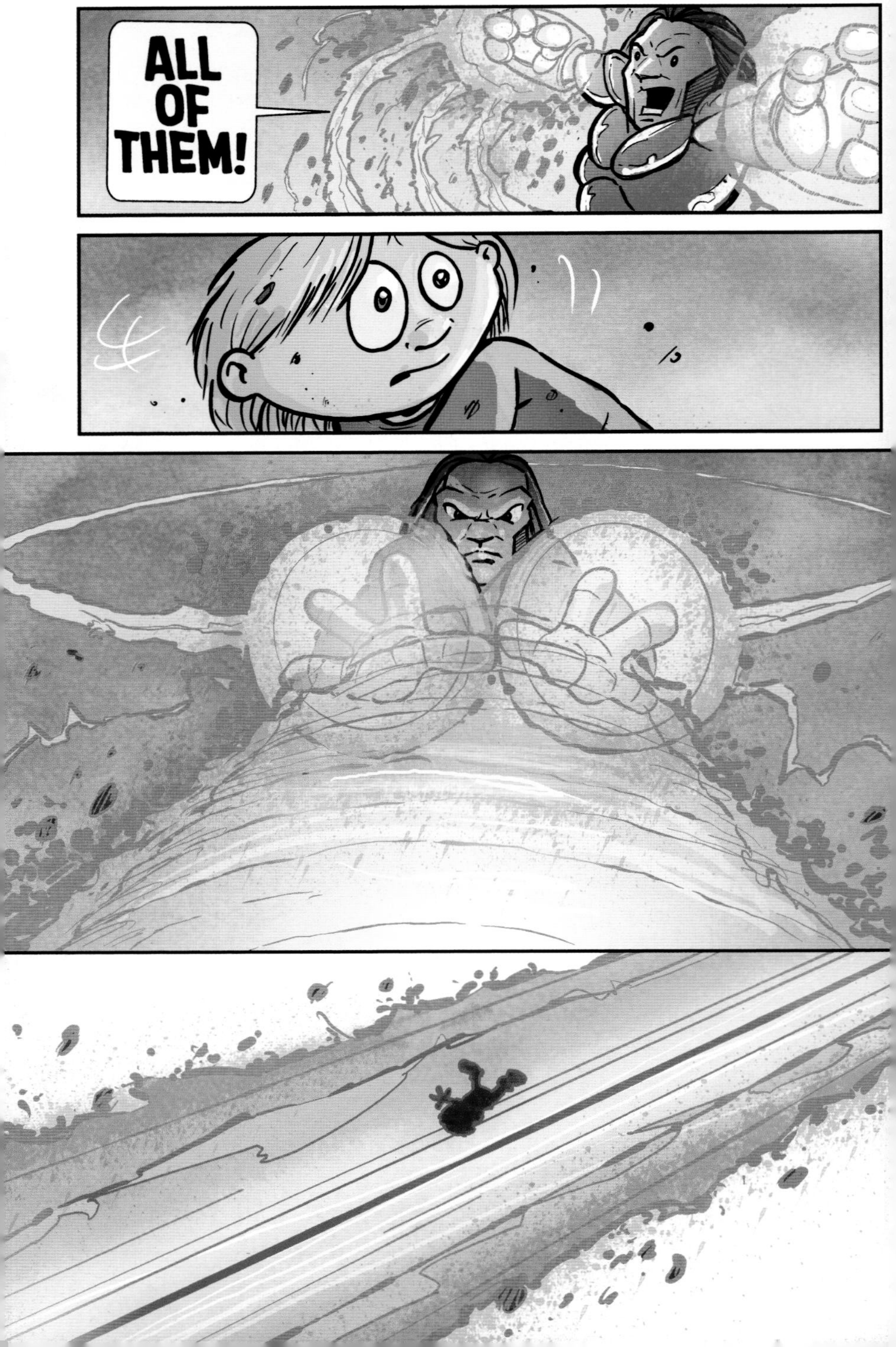
ALL OF THEM!

CHAPTER

6

TELL ME HOW

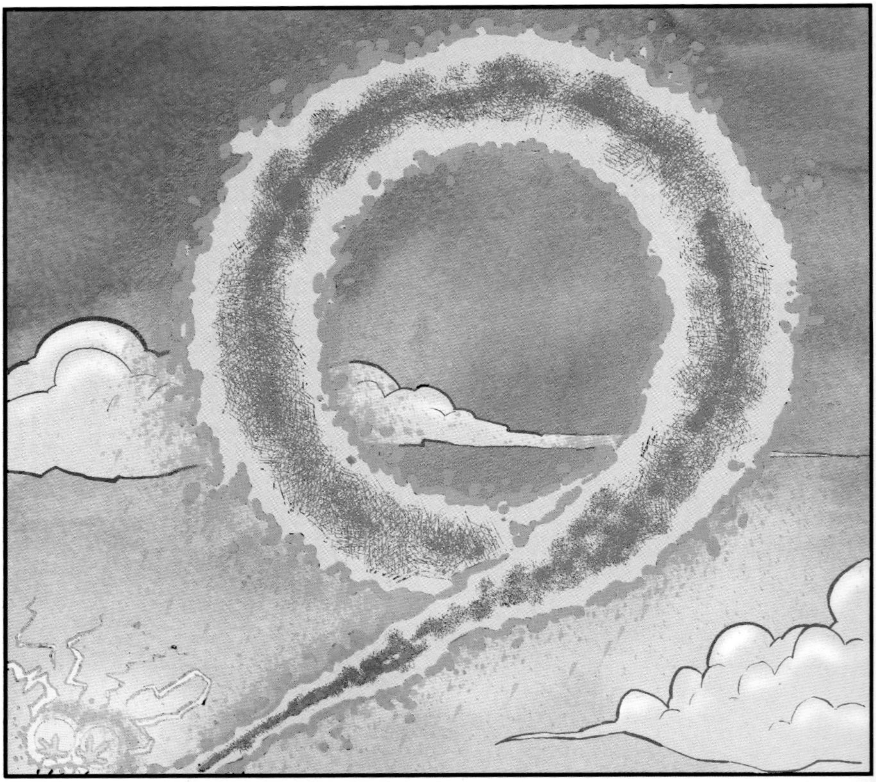

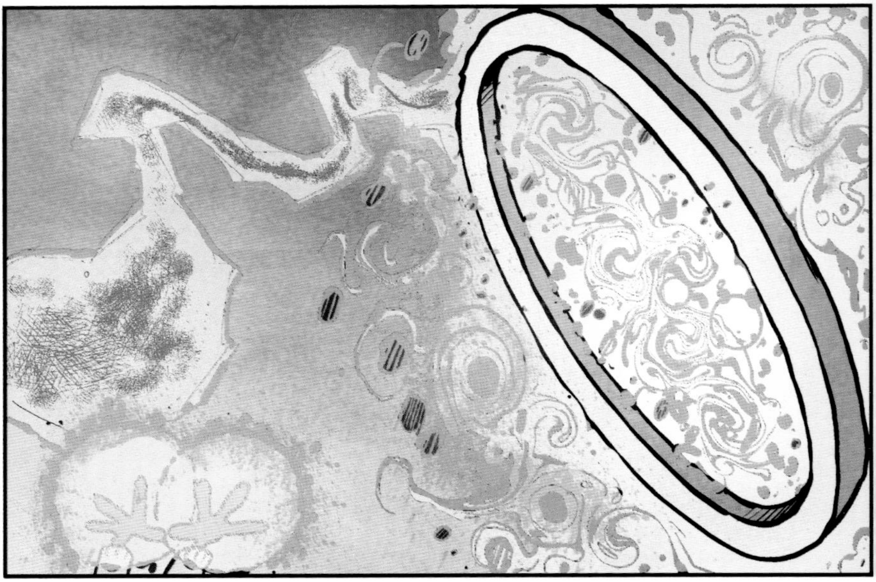

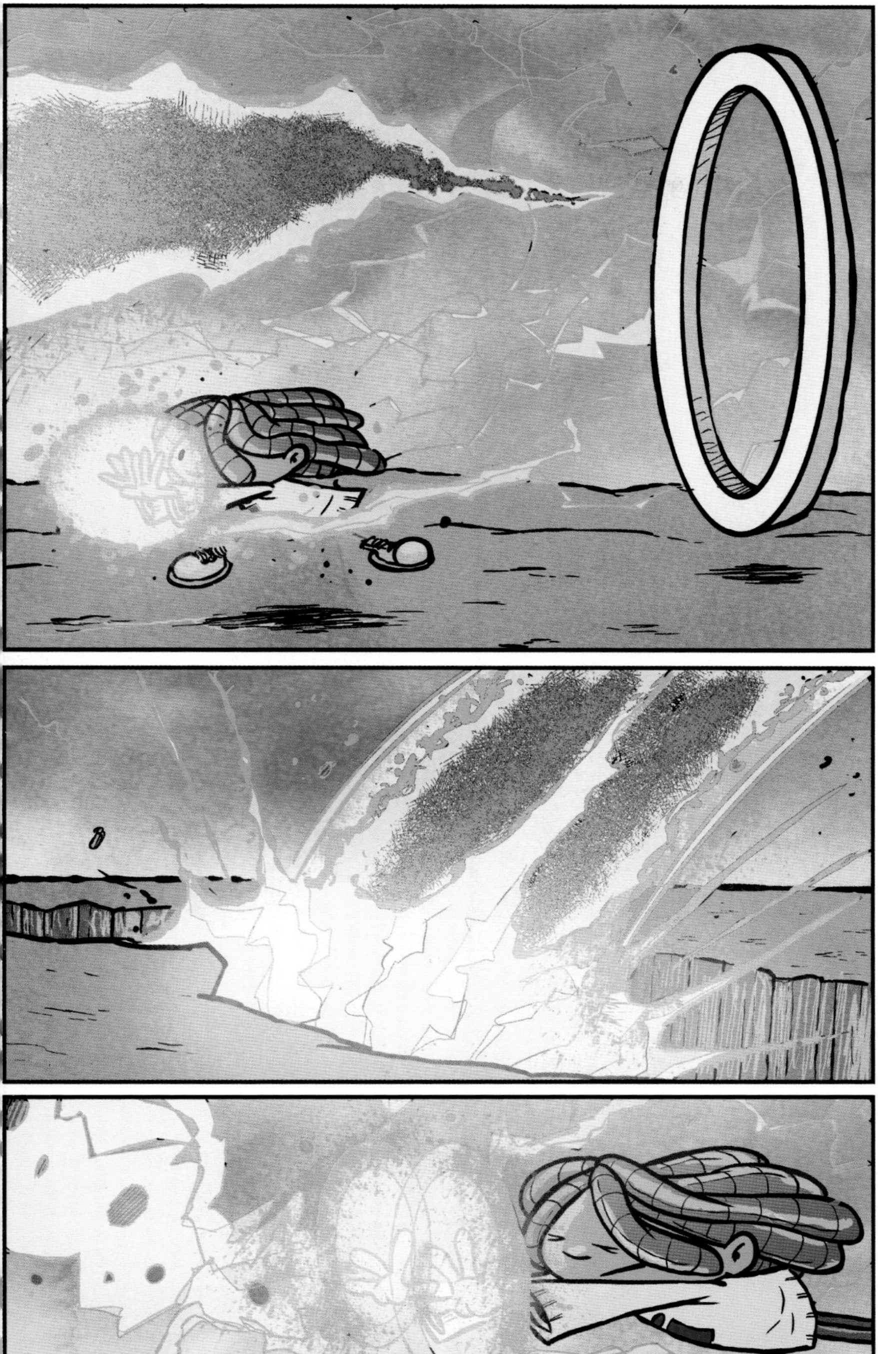

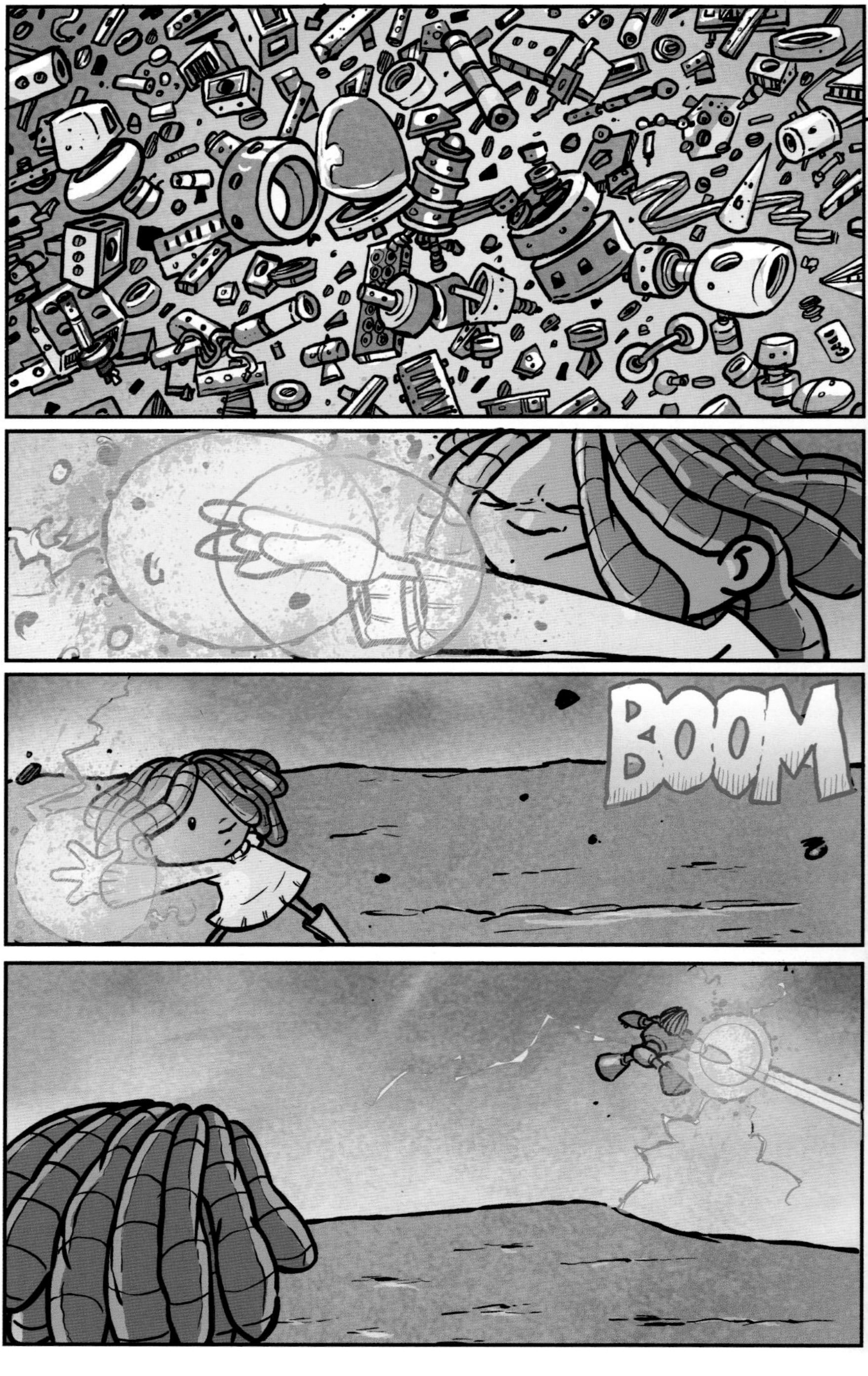
BOOM

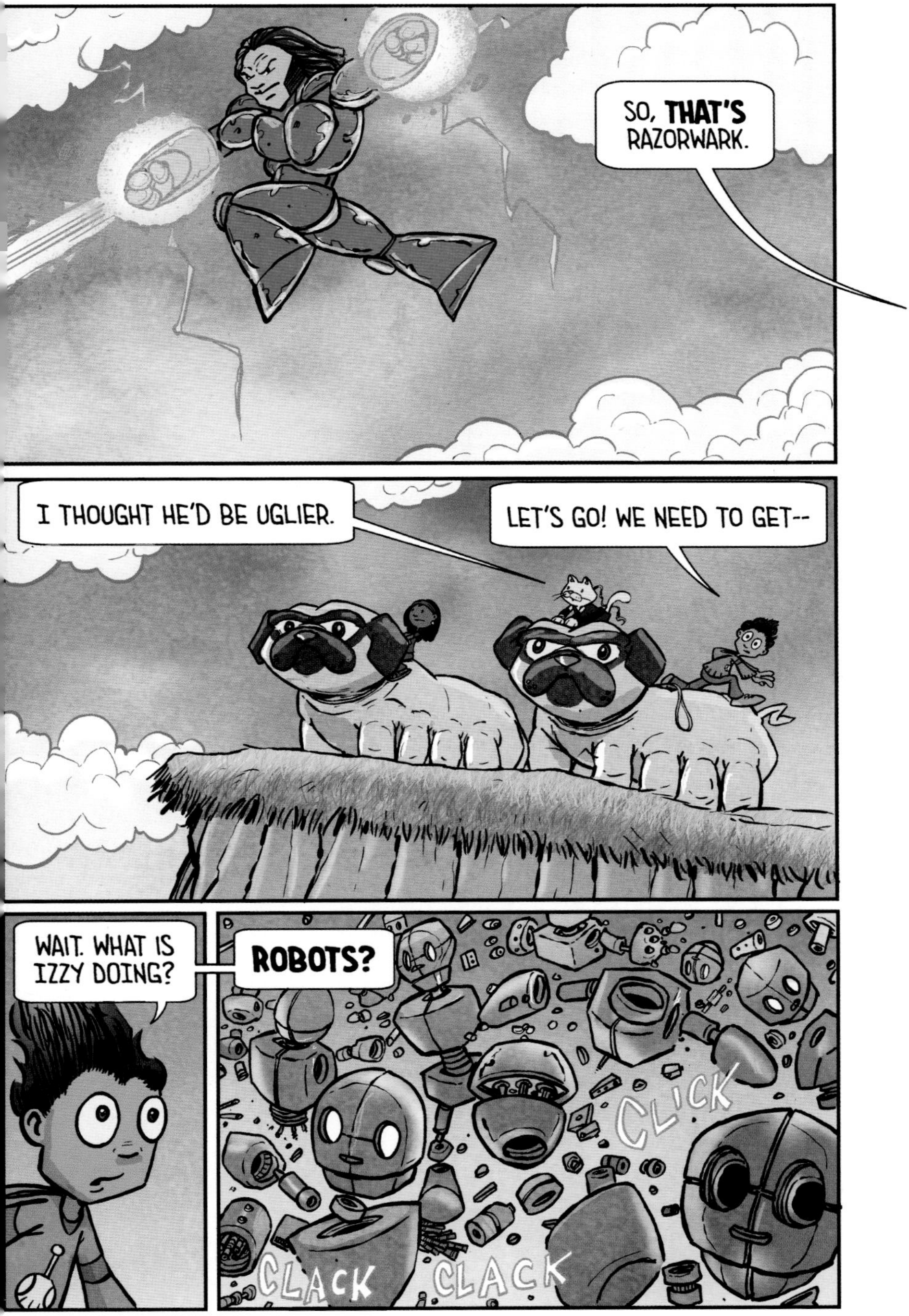
SO, **THAT'S** RAZORWARK.
I THOUGHT HE'D BE UGLIER.
LET'S GO! WE NEED TO GET--
WAIT. WHAT IS IZZY DOING?
ROBOTS?
CLICK
CLACK
CLACK

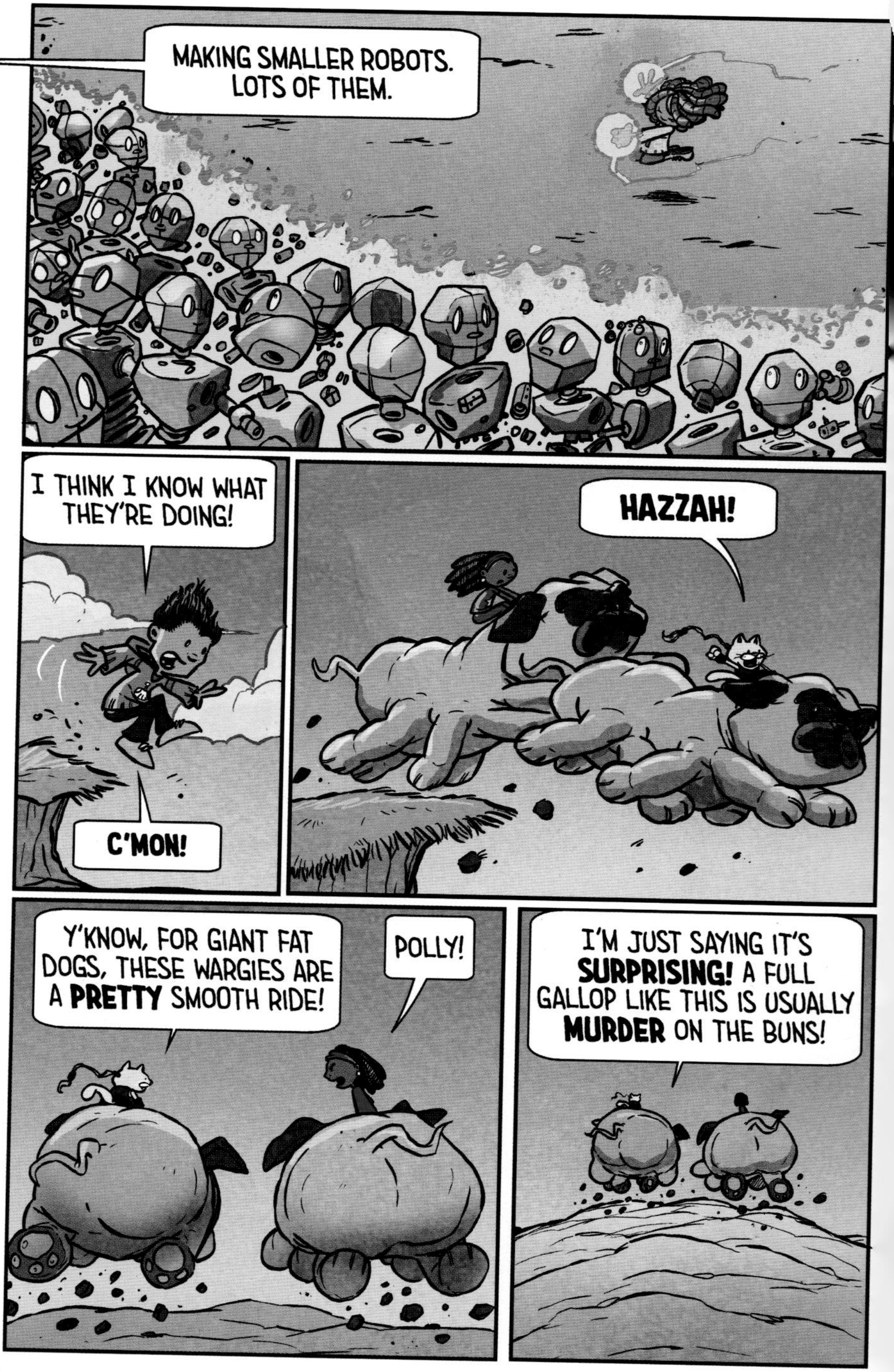
MAKING SMALLER ROBOTS. LOTS OF THEM.
I THINK I KNOW WHAT THEY'RE DOING!
C'MON!
HAZZAH!
Y'KNOW, FOR GIANT FAT DOGS, THESE WARGIES ARE A PRETTY SMOOTH RIDE!
POLLY!
I'M JUST SAYING IT'S SURPRISING! A FULL GALLOP LIKE THIS IS USUALLY MURDER ON THE BUNS!

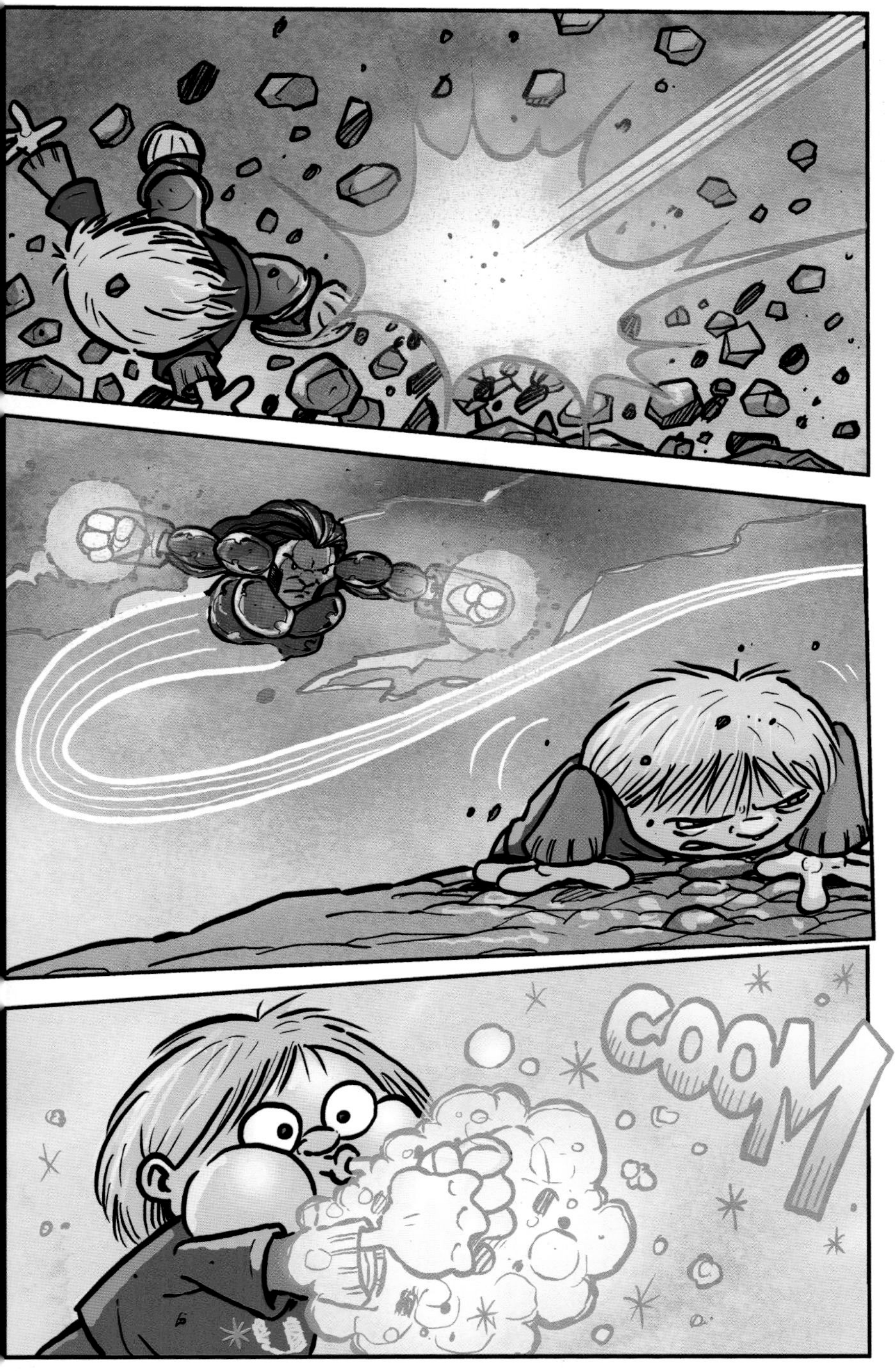
COOM

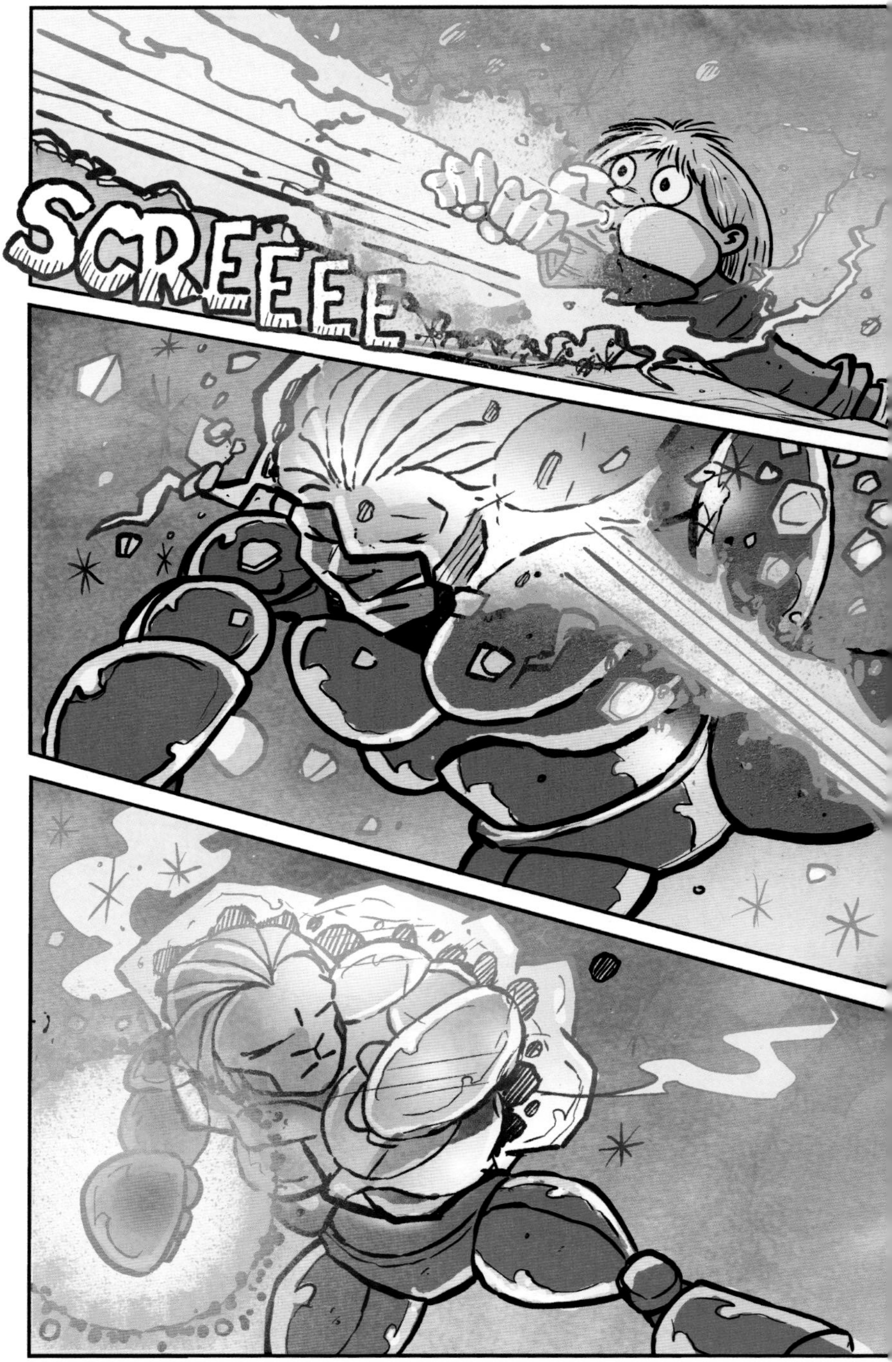
SCREEEEE

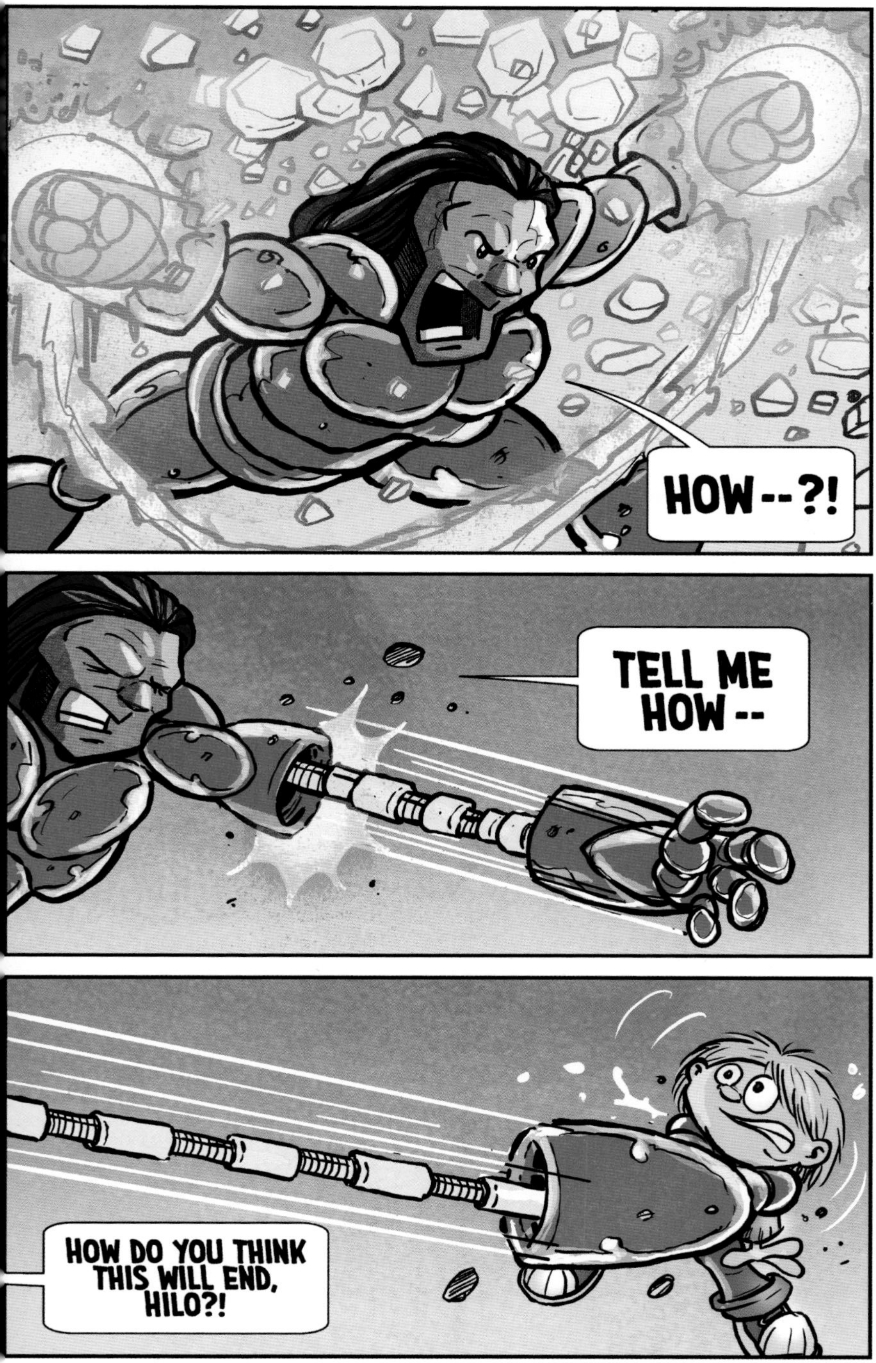
HOW--?!
TELL ME HOW--
HOW DO YOU THINK THIS WILL END, HILO?!

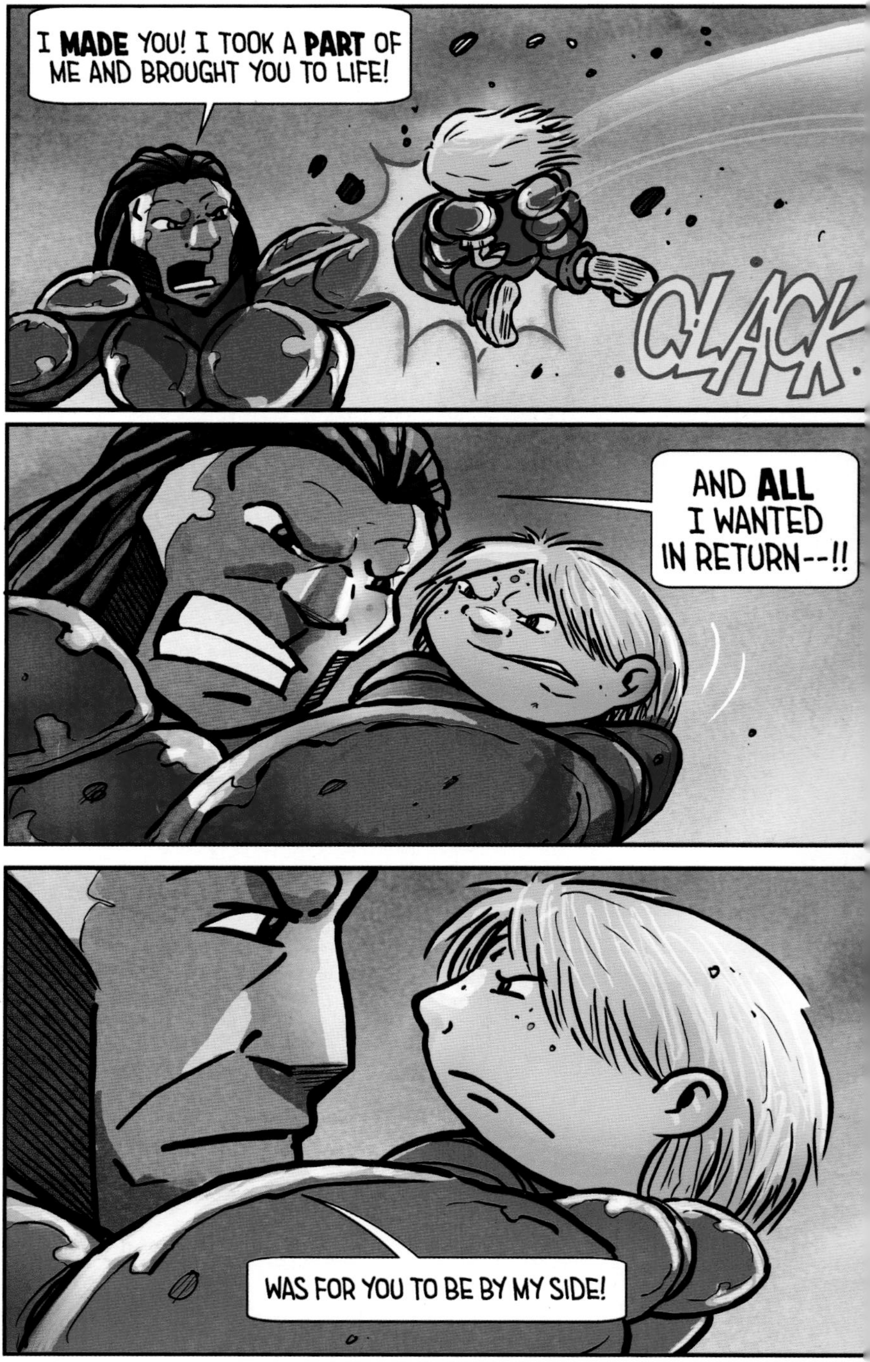
I **MADE** YOU! I TOOK A **PART** OF ME AND BROUGHT YOU TO LIFE!
CLACK
AND **ALL** I WANTED IN RETURN--!!
WAS FOR YOU TO BE BY MY SIDE!

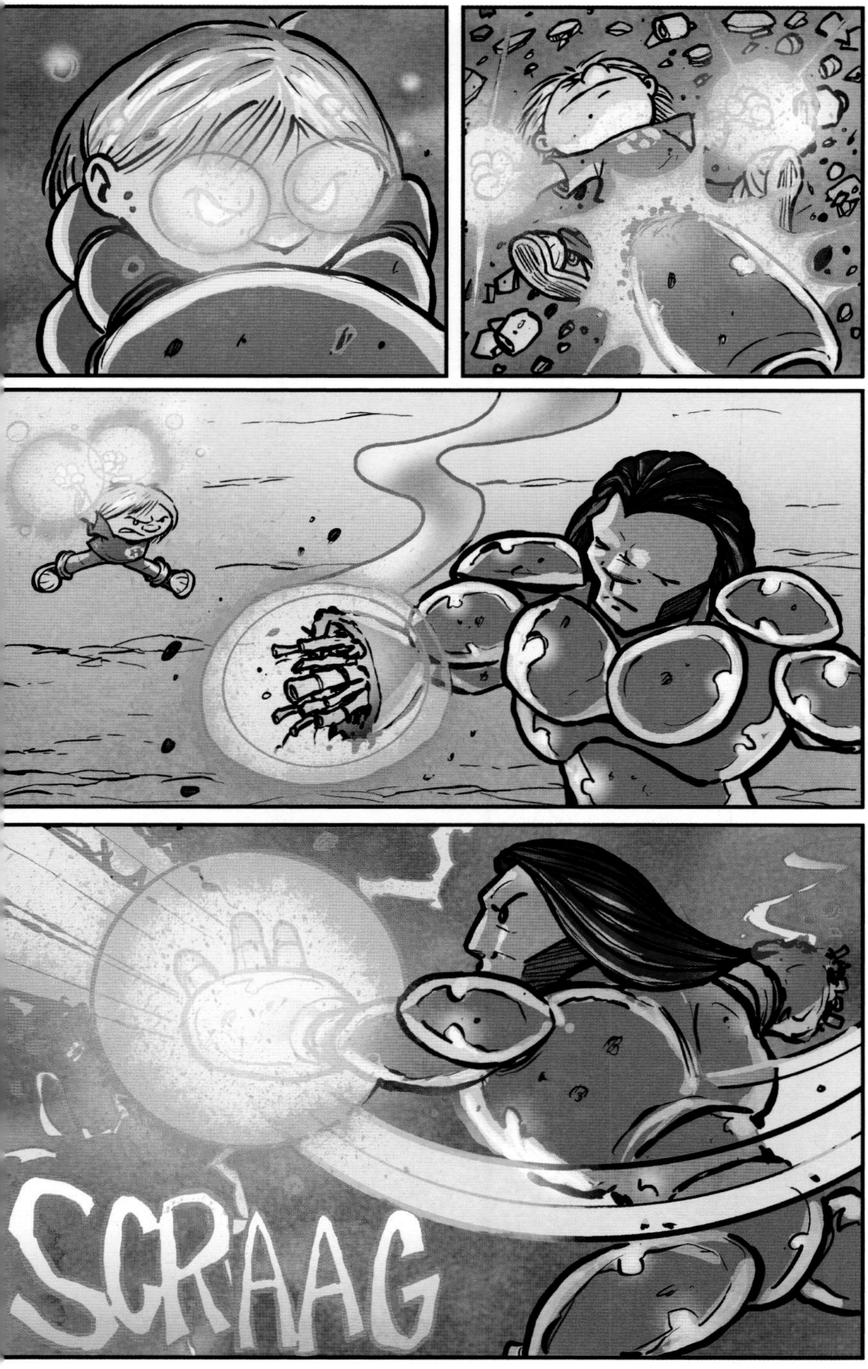
SCRAAG

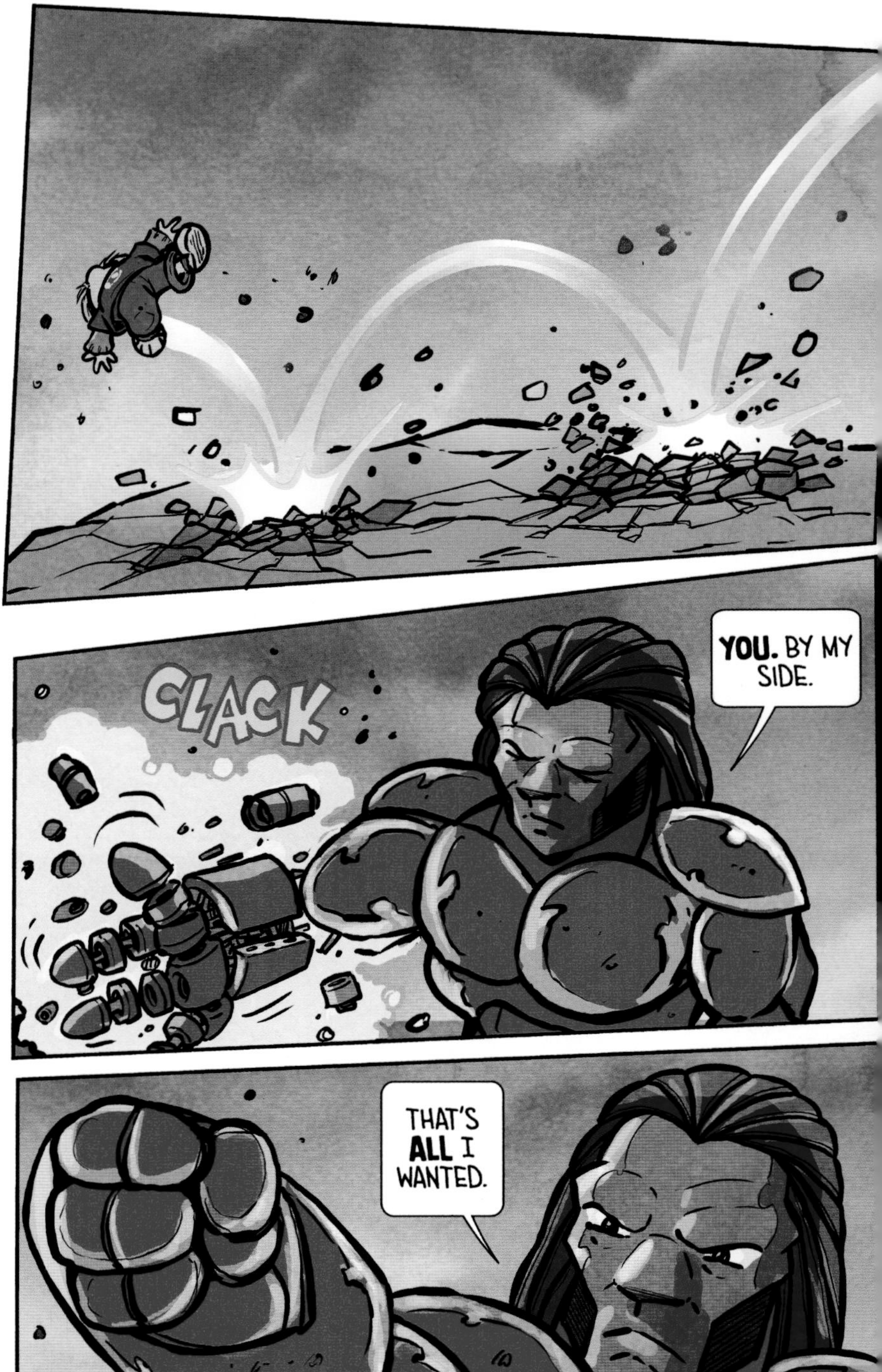
CLACK
YOU. BY MY SIDE.
THAT'S **ALL** I WANTED.

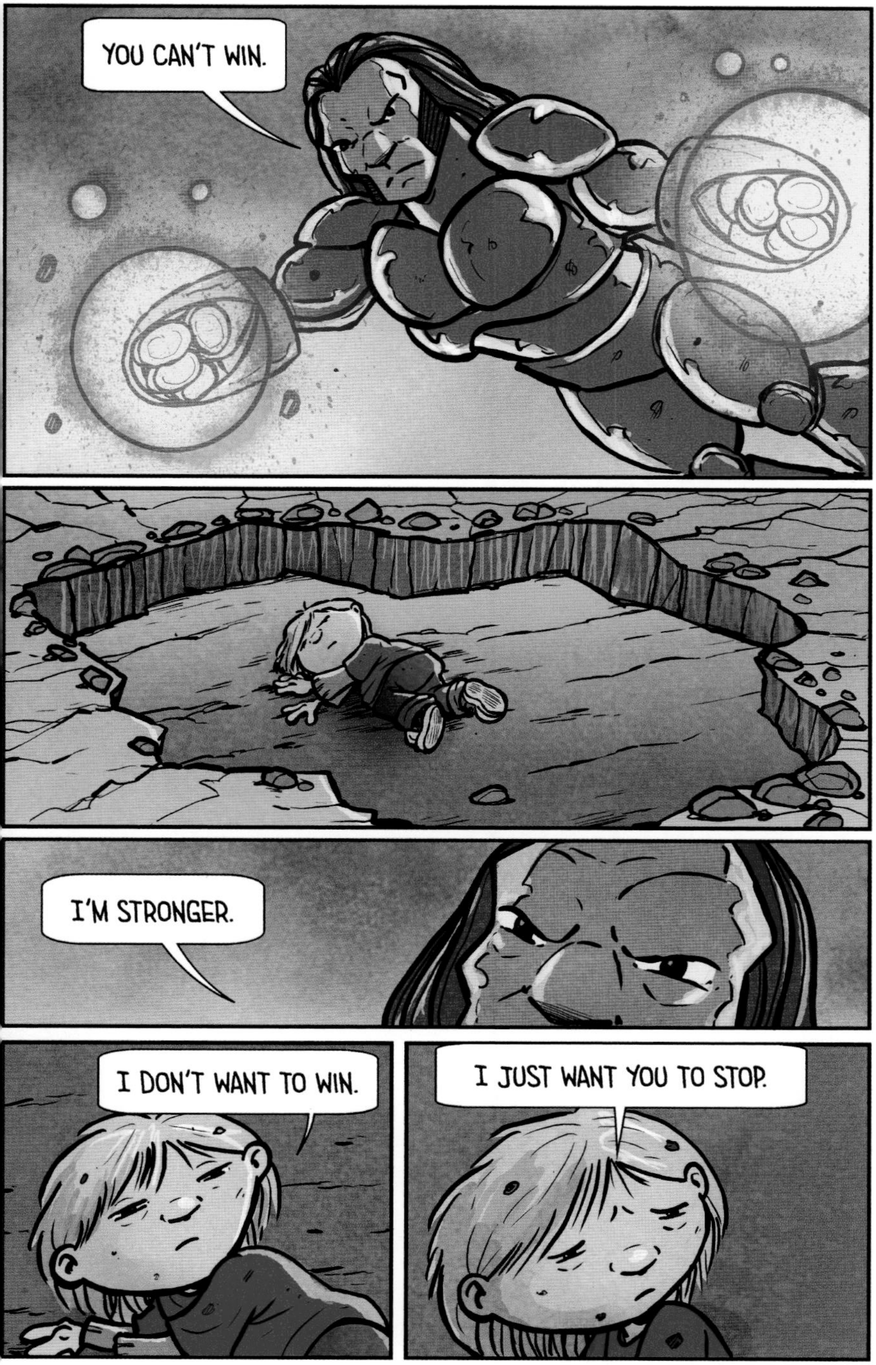
YOU CAN'T WIN.
I'M STRONGER.
I DON'T WANT TO WIN.
I JUST WANT YOU TO STOP.

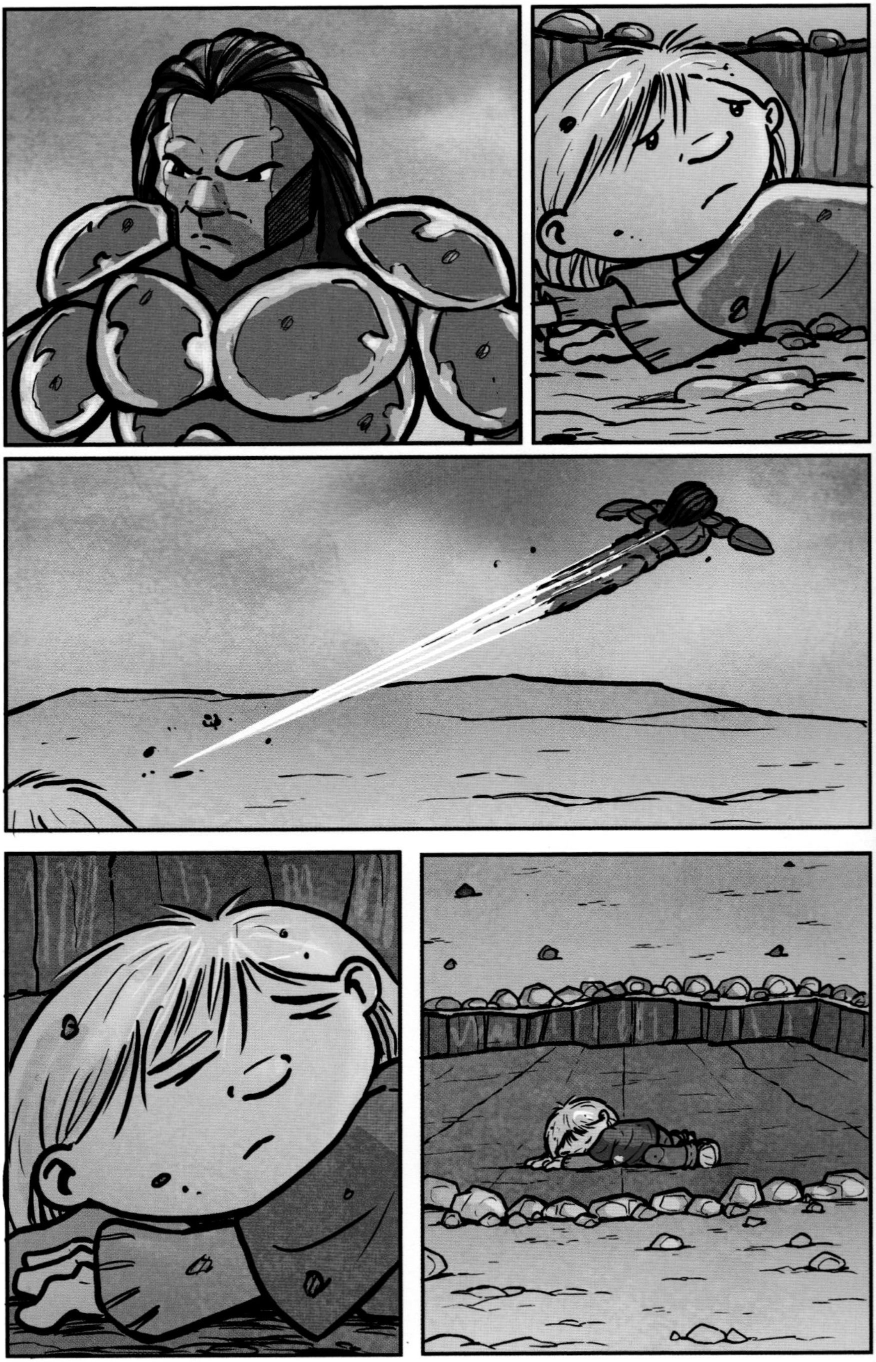

CHAPTER 7

THAT'S WHAT I DO

HERE! HERE!
STOP HERE!
SCREECH

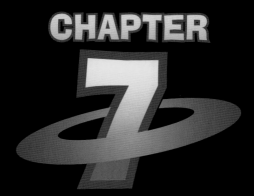

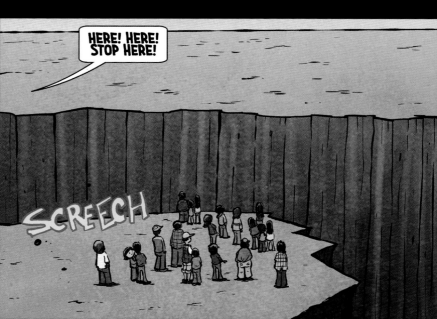

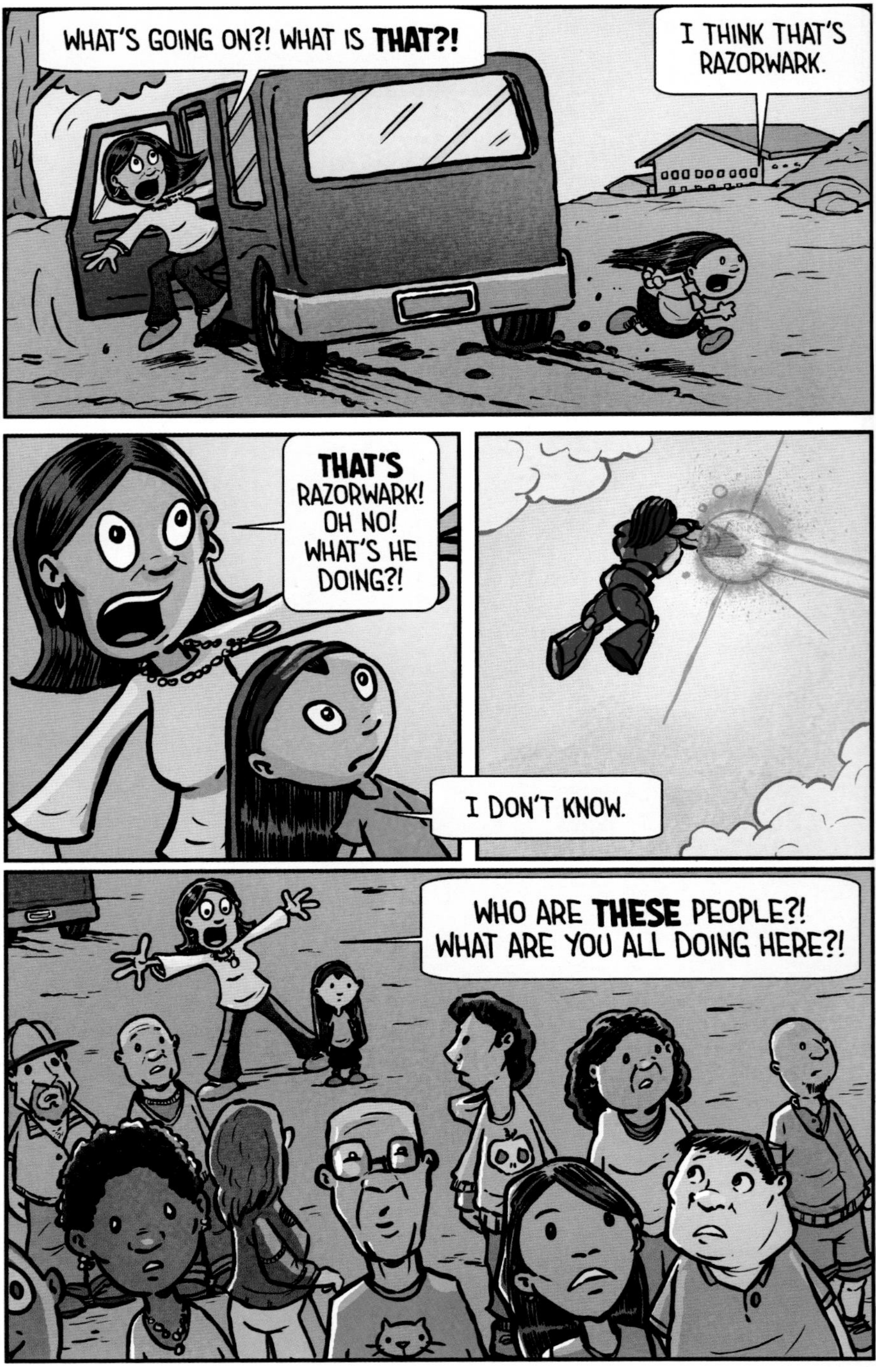
WHAT'S GOING ON?! WHAT IS **THAT?!**
I THINK THAT'S RAZORWARK.
THAT'S RAZORWARK! OH NO! WHAT'S HE DOING?!
I DON'T KNOW.
WHO ARE **THESE** PEOPLE?! WHAT ARE YOU ALL DOING HERE?!

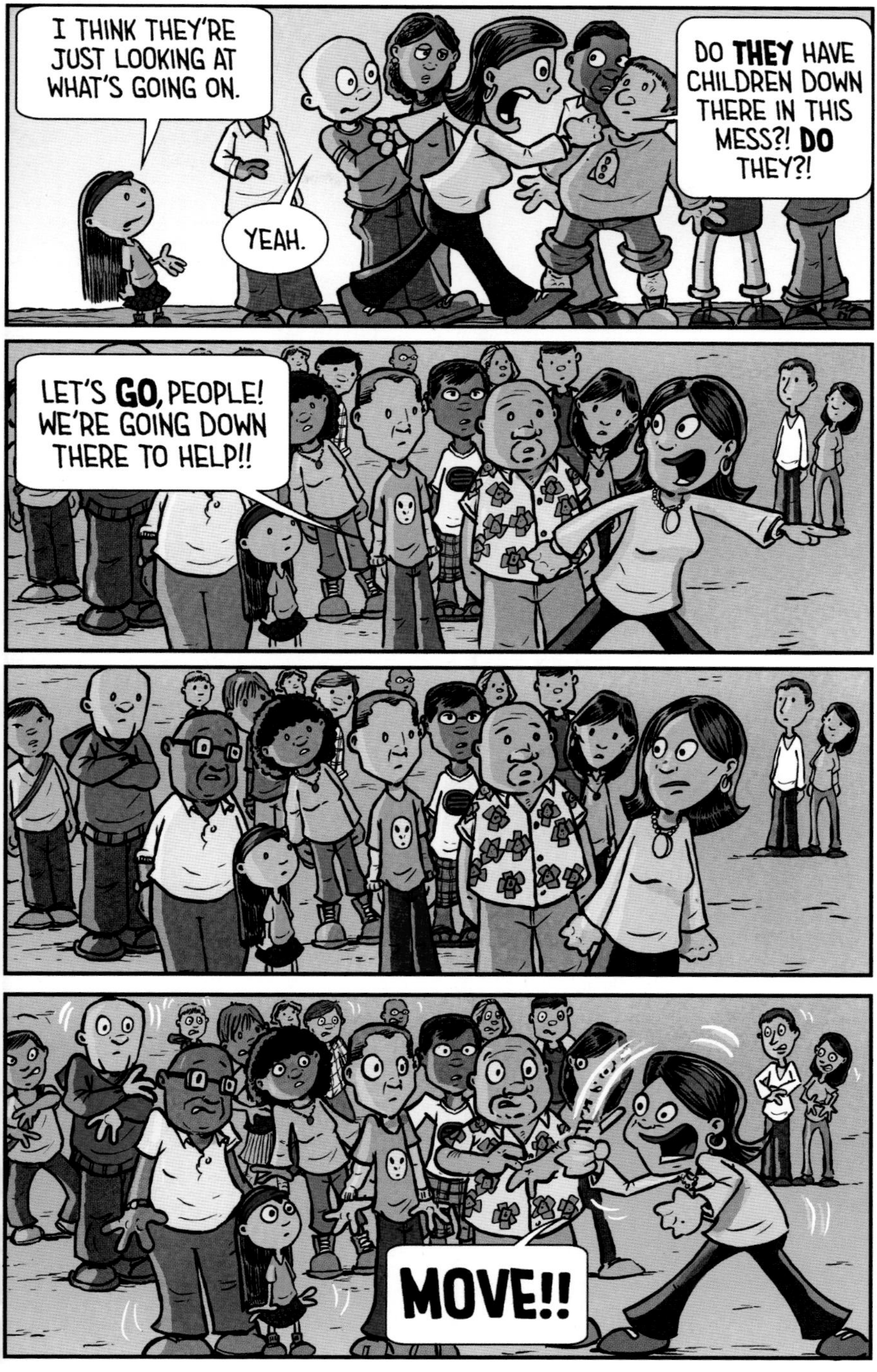
I THINK THEY'RE JUST LOOKING AT WHAT'S GOING ON.
YEAH.
DO THEY HAVE CHILDREN DOWN THERE IN THIS MESS?! DO THEY?!
LET'S GO, PEOPLE! WE'RE GOING DOWN THERE TO HELP!!
MOVE!!

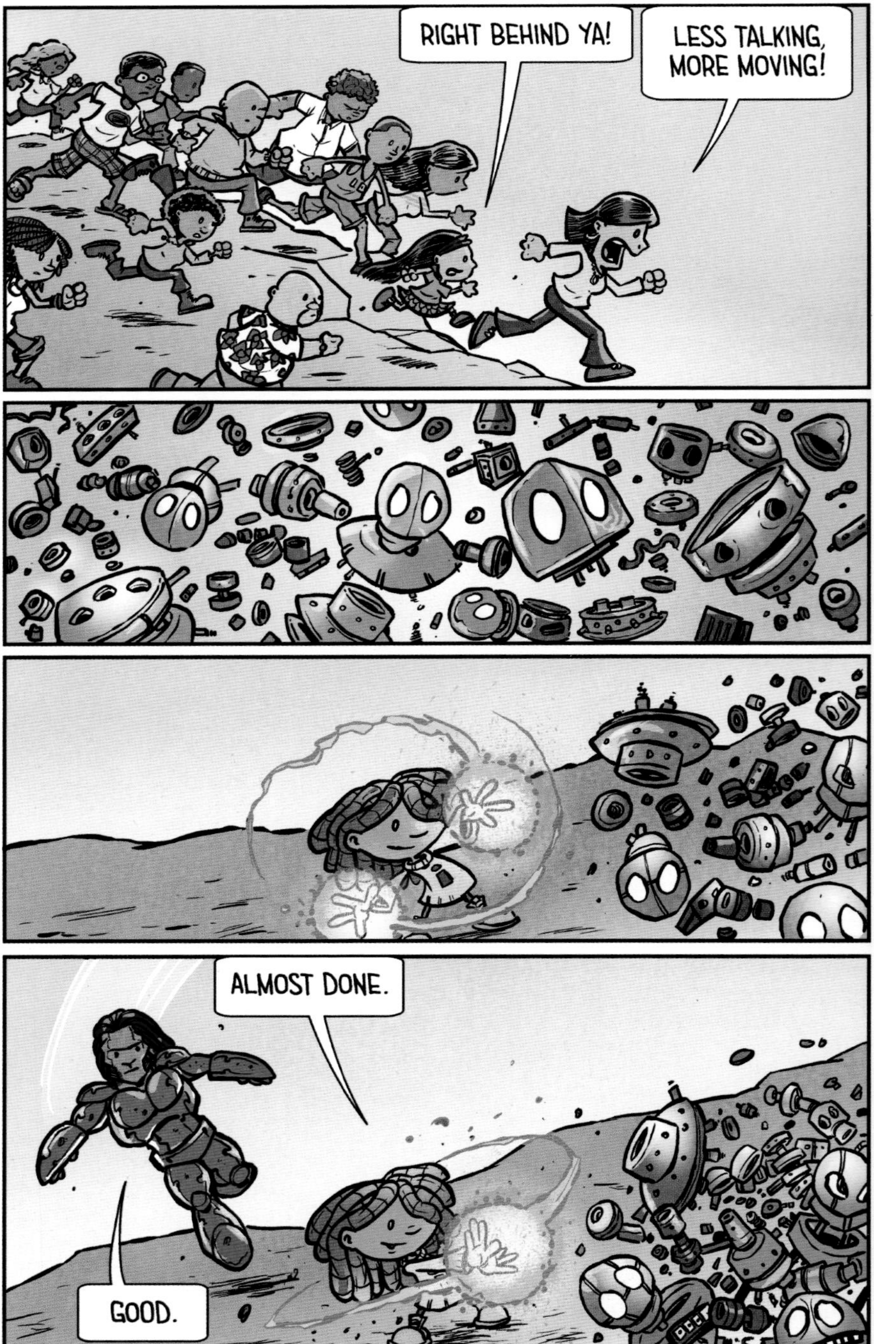
RIGHT BEHIND YA!
LESS TALKING, MORE MOVING!
ALMOST DONE.
GOOD.

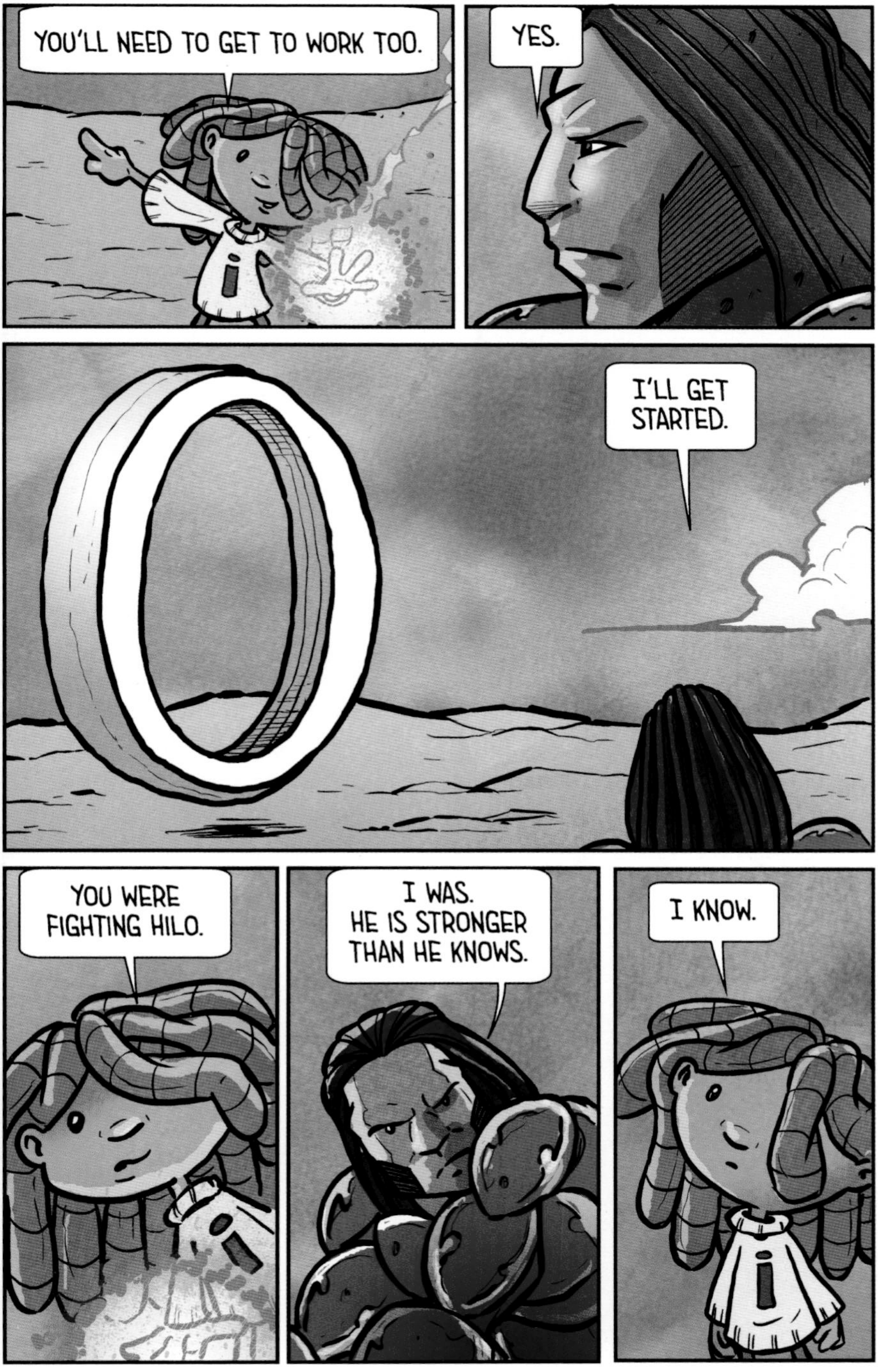
YOU'LL NEED TO GET TO WORK TOO.
YES.
I'LL GET STARTED.
YOU WERE FIGHTING HILO.
I WAS. HE IS STRONGER THAN HE KNOWS.
I KNOW.

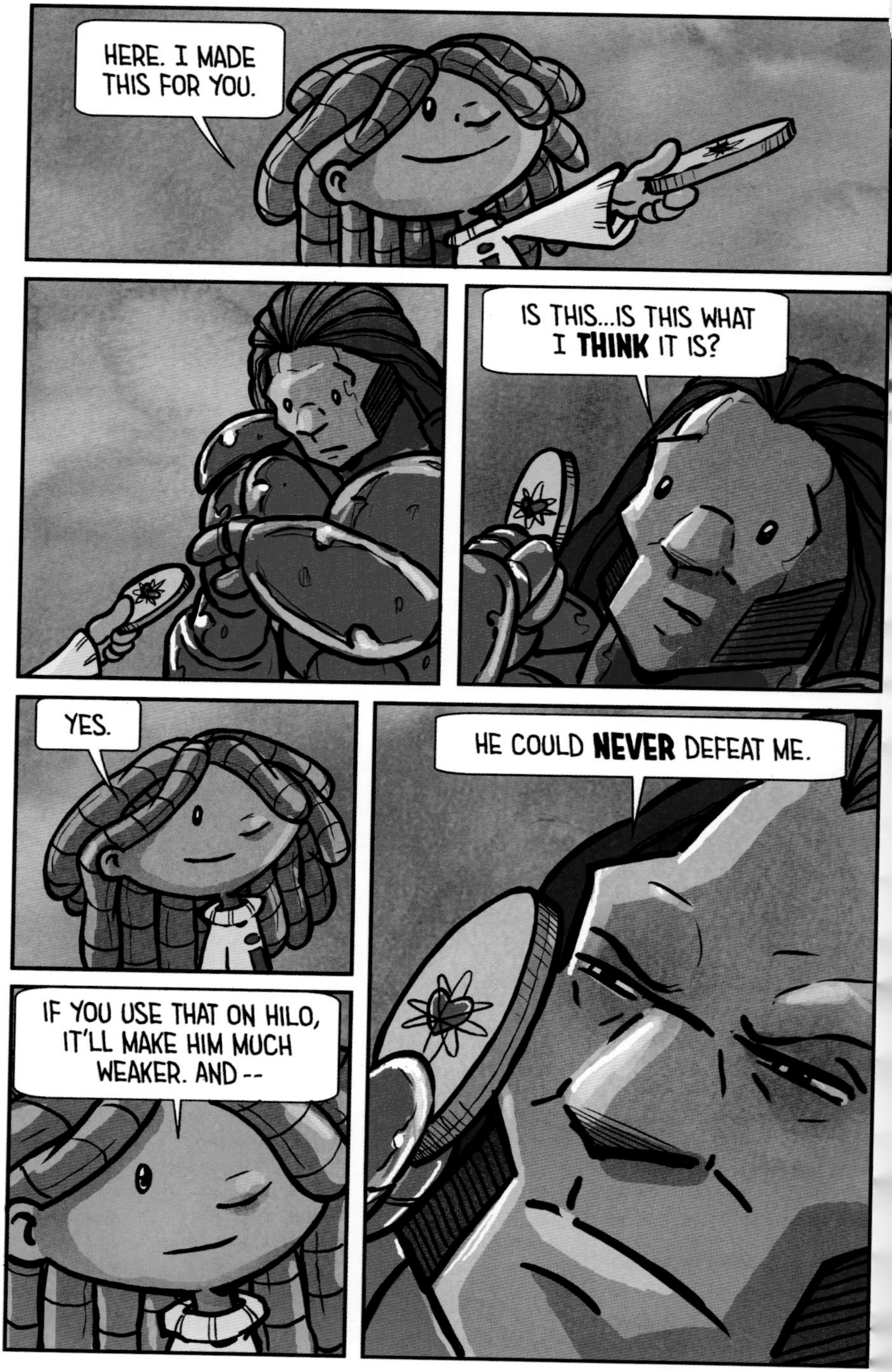
HERE. I MADE THIS FOR YOU.
IS THIS...IS THIS WHAT I **THINK** IT IS?
YES.
IF YOU USE THAT ON HILO, IT'LL MAKE HIM MUCH WEAKER. AND --
HE COULD **NEVER** DEFEAT ME.

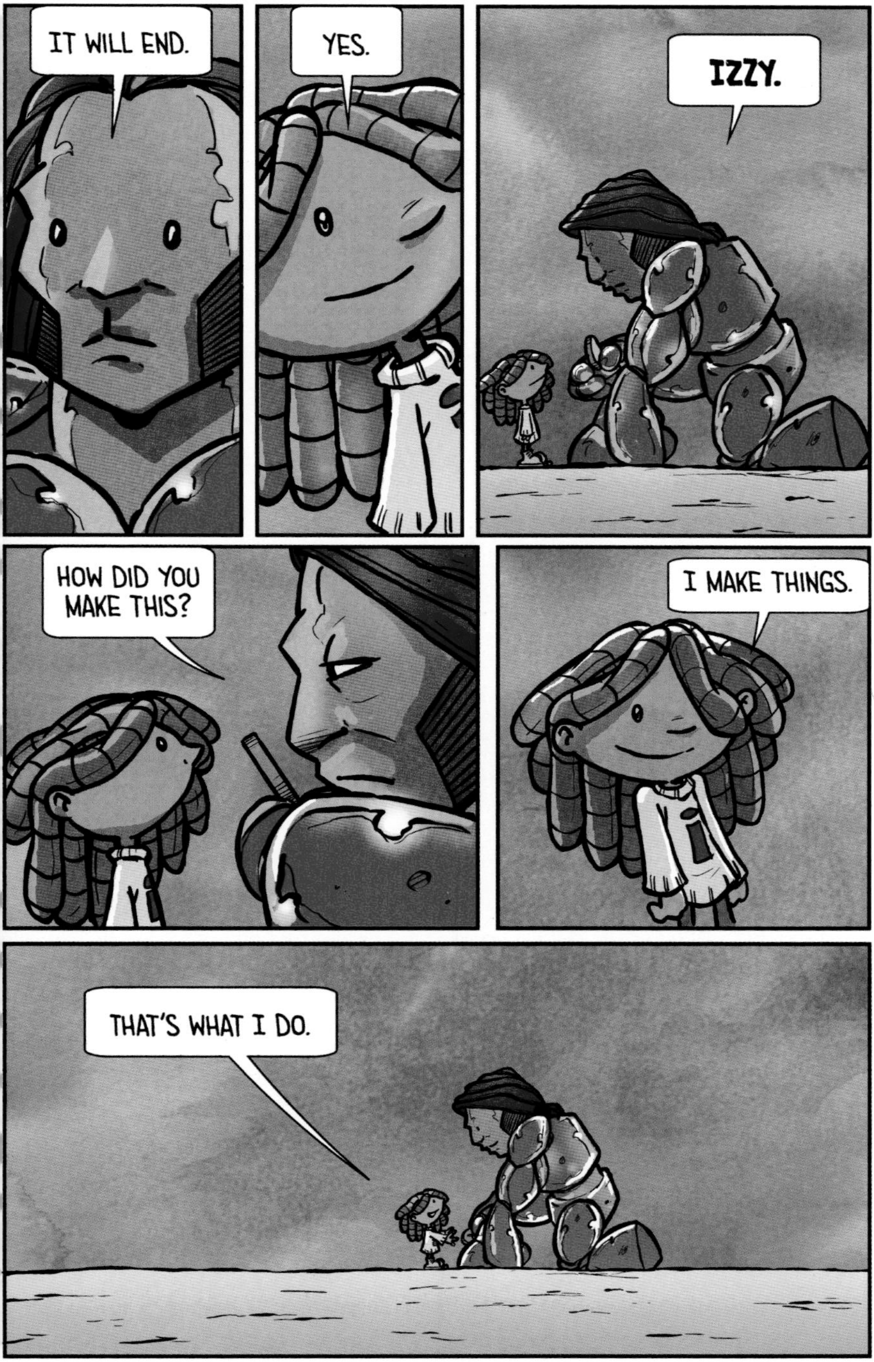
IT WILL END.
YES.
IZZY.
HOW DID YOU MAKE THIS?
I MAKE THINGS.
THAT'S WHAT I DO.

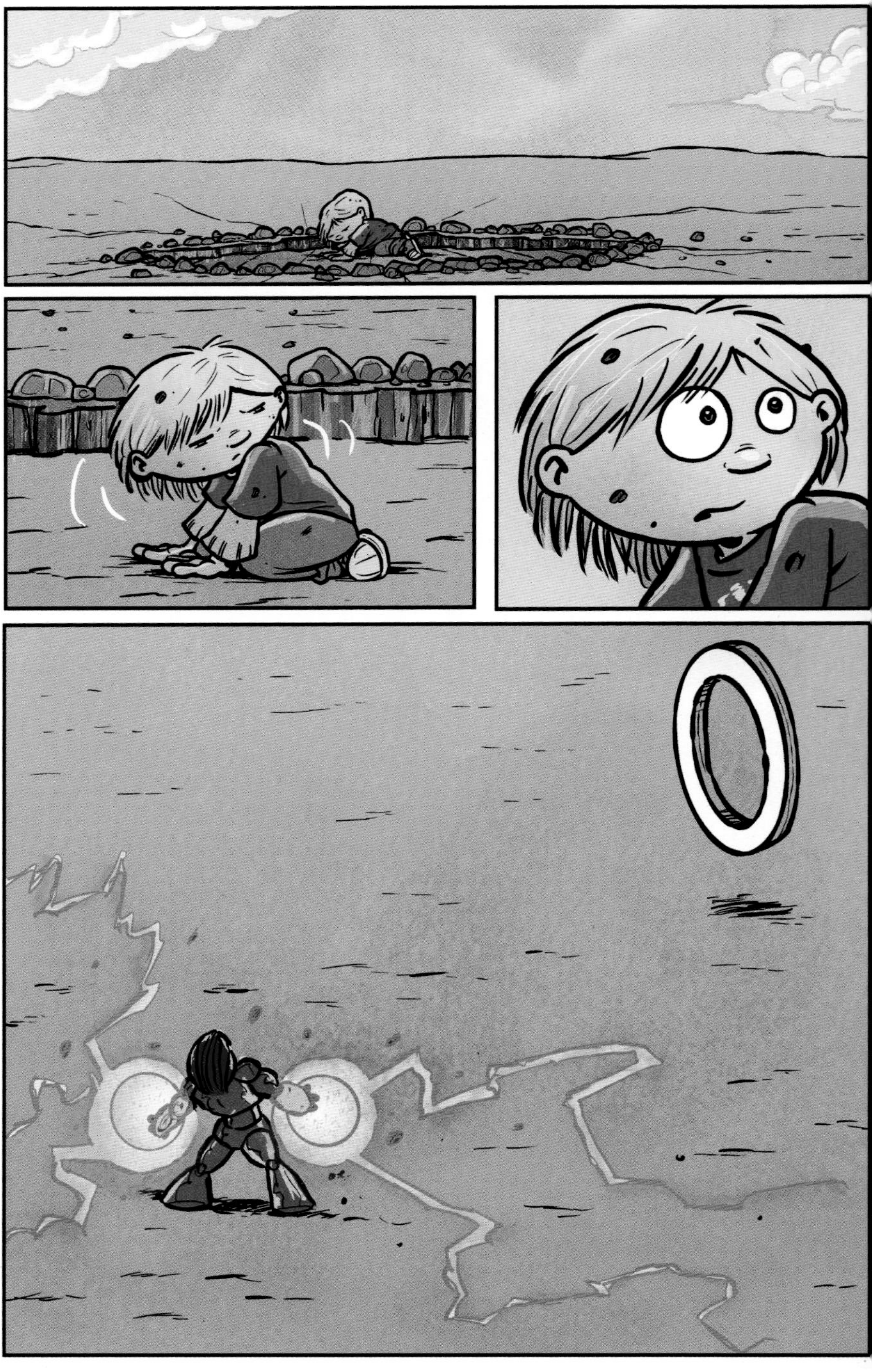

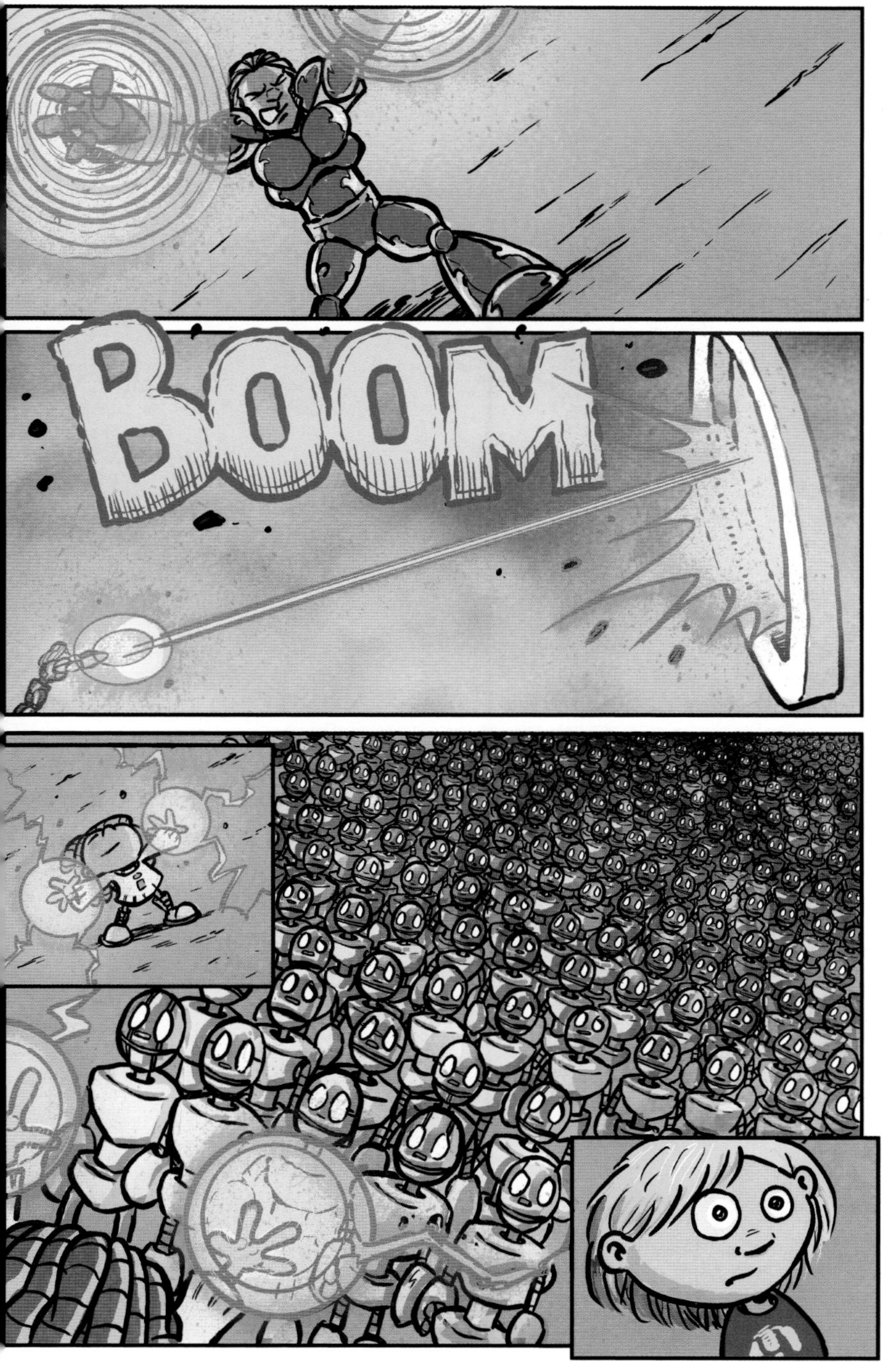
BOOM

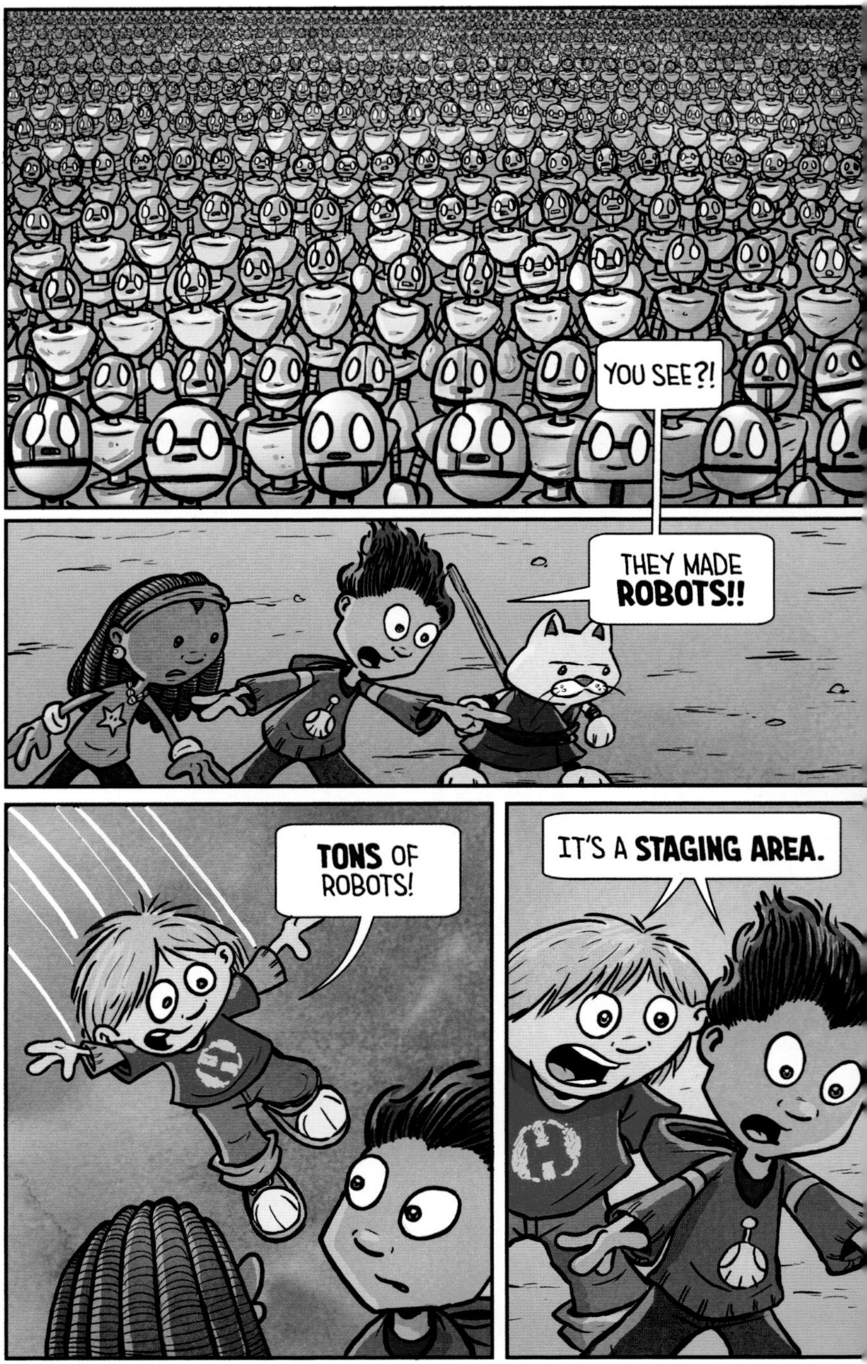
YOU SEE?!
THEY MADE ROBOTS!!
TONS OF ROBOTS!
IT'S A STAGING AREA.

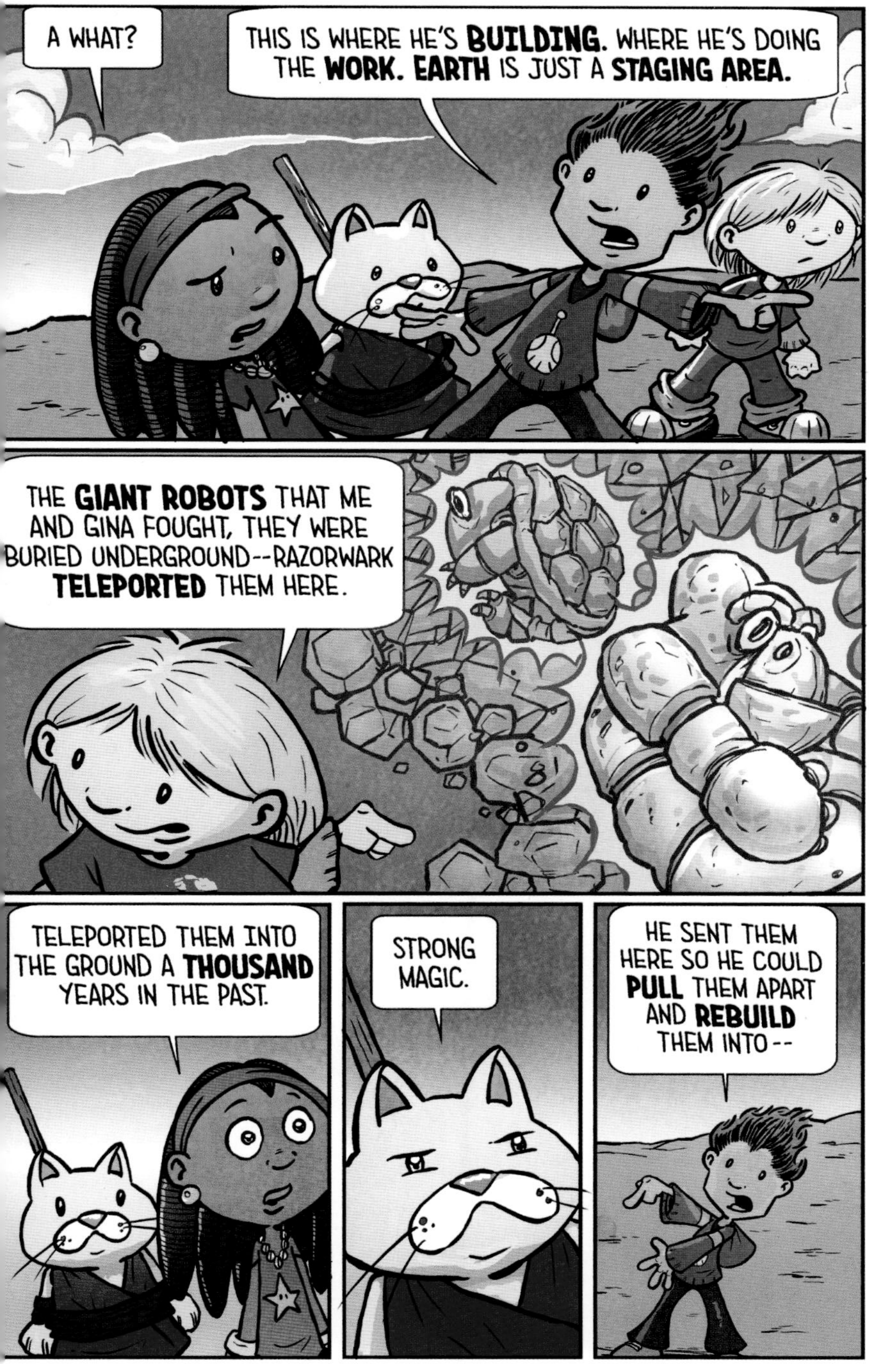

A WHAT?
THIS IS WHERE HE'S **BUILDING**. WHERE HE'S DOING THE **WORK. EARTH** IS JUST A **STAGING AREA.**
THE **GIANT ROBOTS** THAT ME AND GINA FOUGHT, THEY WERE BURIED UNDERGROUND--RAZORWARK **TELEPORTED** THEM HERE.
TELEPORTED THEM INTO THE GROUND A **THOUSAND** YEARS IN THE PAST.
STRONG MAGIC.
HE SENT THEM HERE SO HE COULD **PULL** THEM APART AND **REBUILD** THEM INTO--

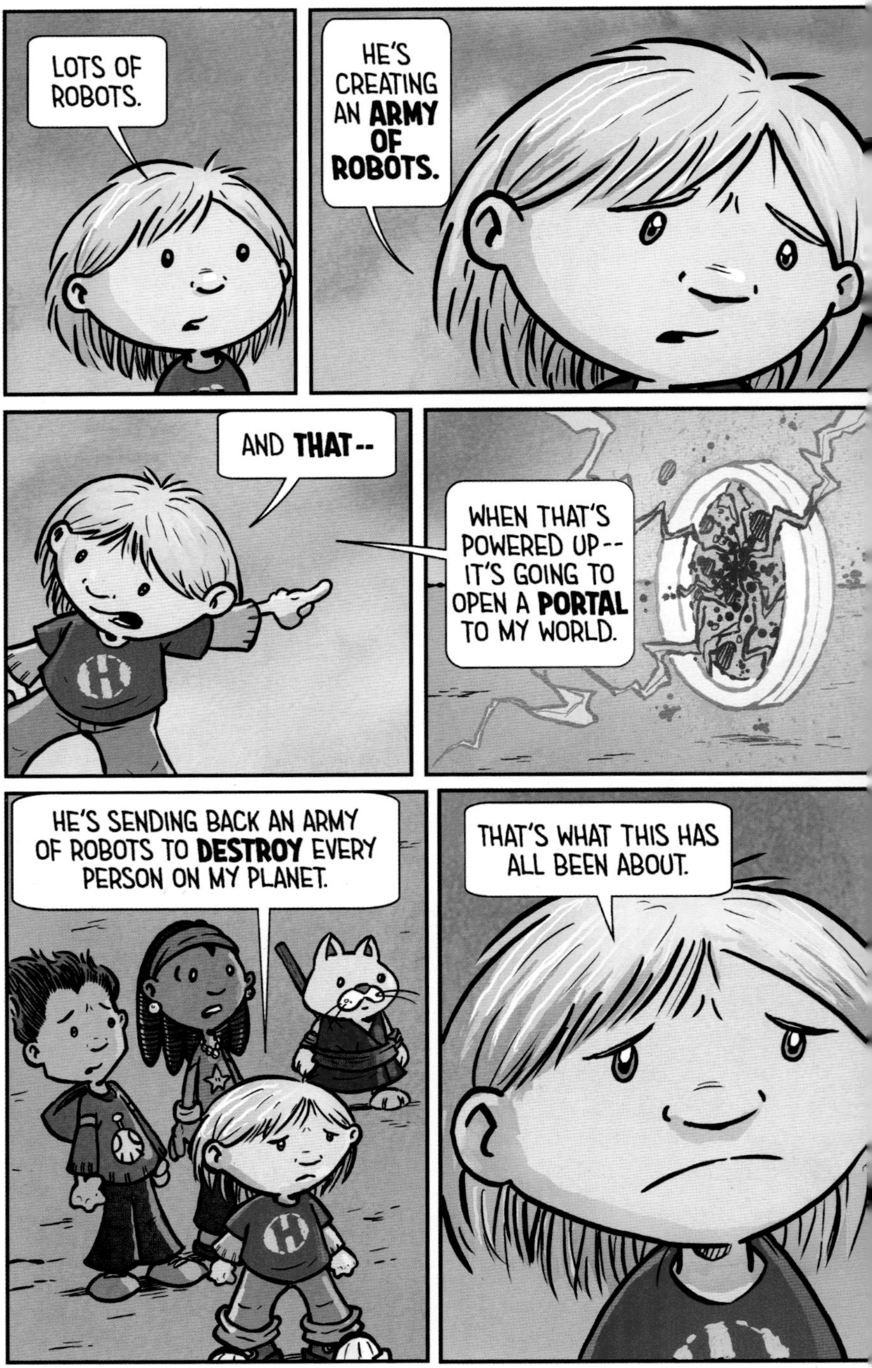
LOTS OF ROBOTS.
HE'S CREATING AN **ARMY OF ROBOTS.**
AND **THAT**--
WHEN THAT'S POWERED UP-- IT'S GOING TO OPEN A **PORTAL** TO MY WORLD.
HE'S SENDING BACK AN ARMY OF ROBOTS TO **DESTROY** EVERY PERSON ON MY PLANET.
THAT'S WHAT THIS HAS ALL BEEN ABOUT.

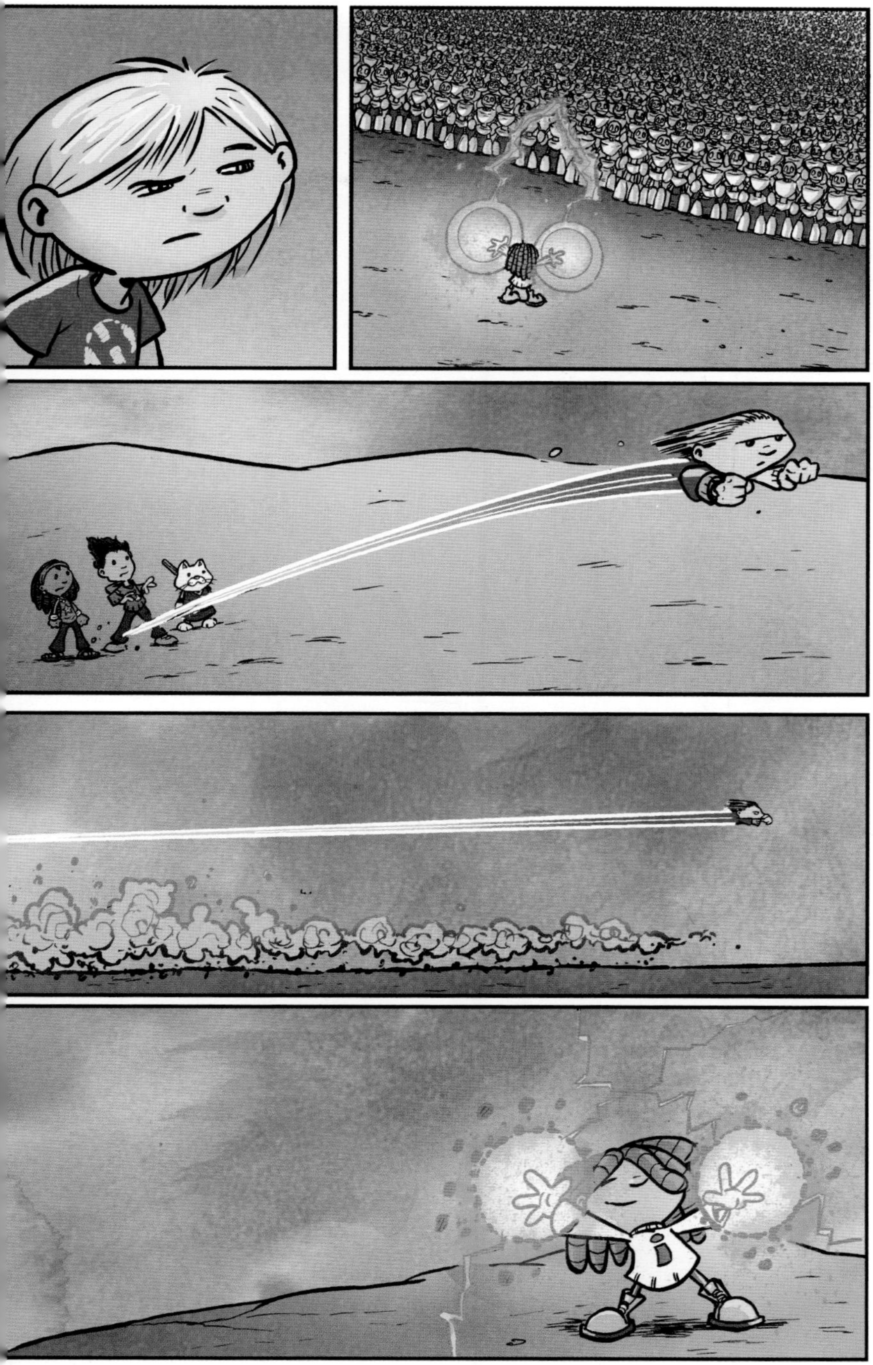

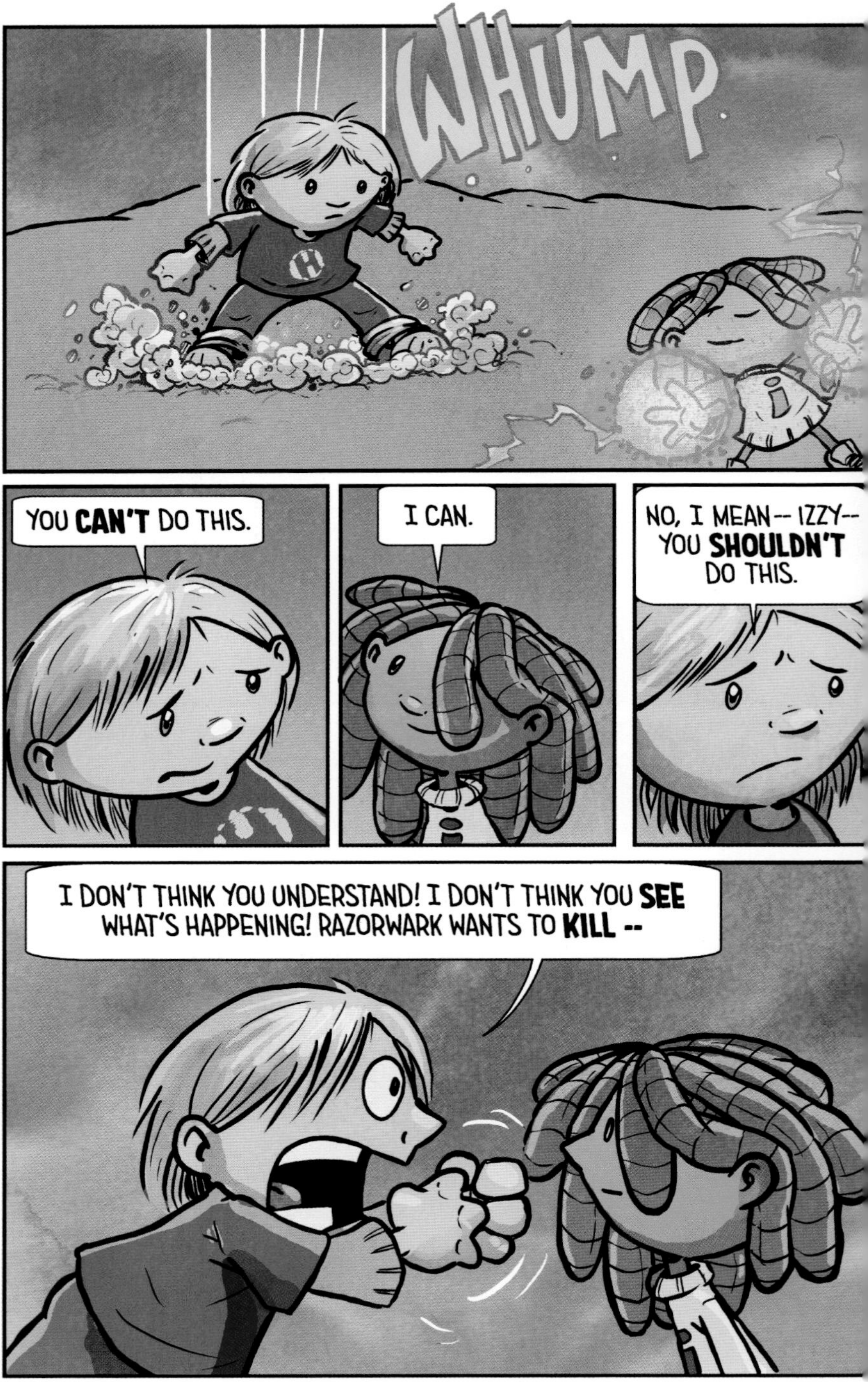
WHUMP
YOU CAN'T DO THIS.
I CAN.
NO, I MEAN-- IZZY-- YOU SHOULDN'T DO THIS.
I DON'T THINK YOU UNDERSTAND! I DON'T THINK YOU SEE WHAT'S HAPPENING! RAZORWARK WANTS TO KILL --

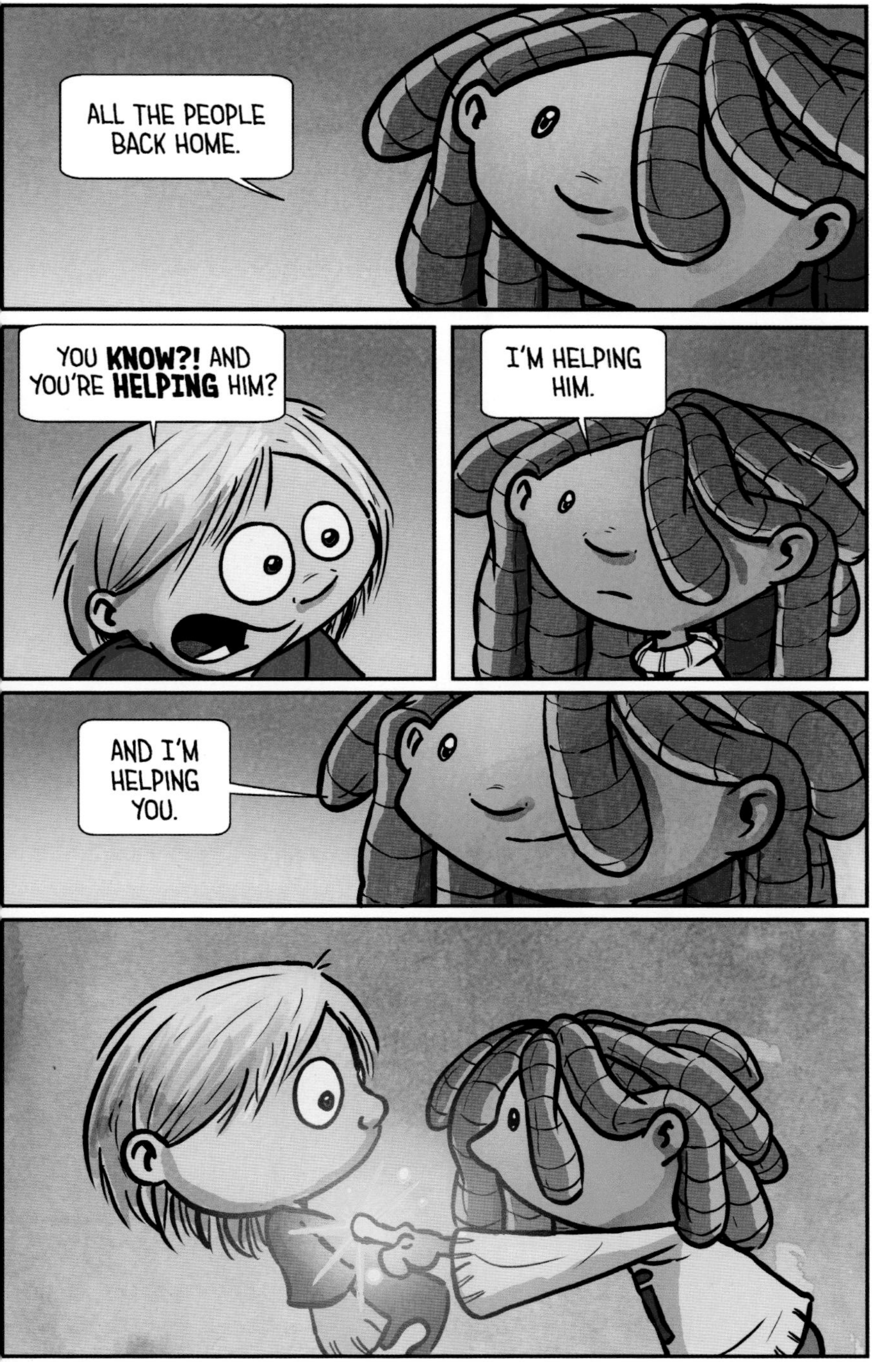
ALL THE PEOPLE BACK HOME.
YOU **KNOW?!** AND YOU'RE **HELPING** HIM?
I'M HELPING HIM.
AND I'M HELPING YOU.

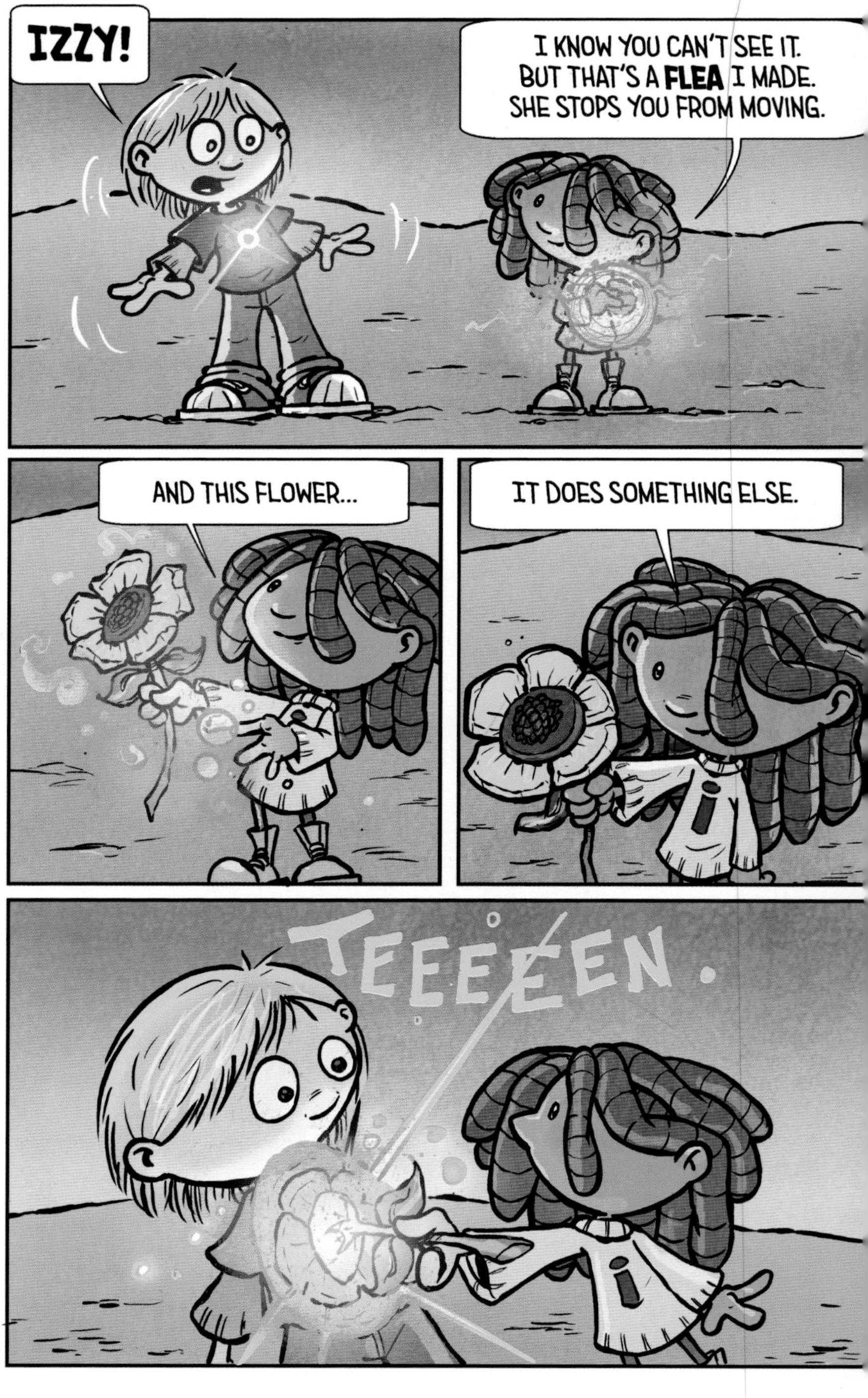
IZZY!
I KNOW YOU CAN'T SEE IT. BUT THAT'S A **FLEA** I MADE. SHE STOPS YOU FROM MOVING.
AND THIS FLOWER...
IT DOES SOMETHING ELSE.
TEEEEEN.

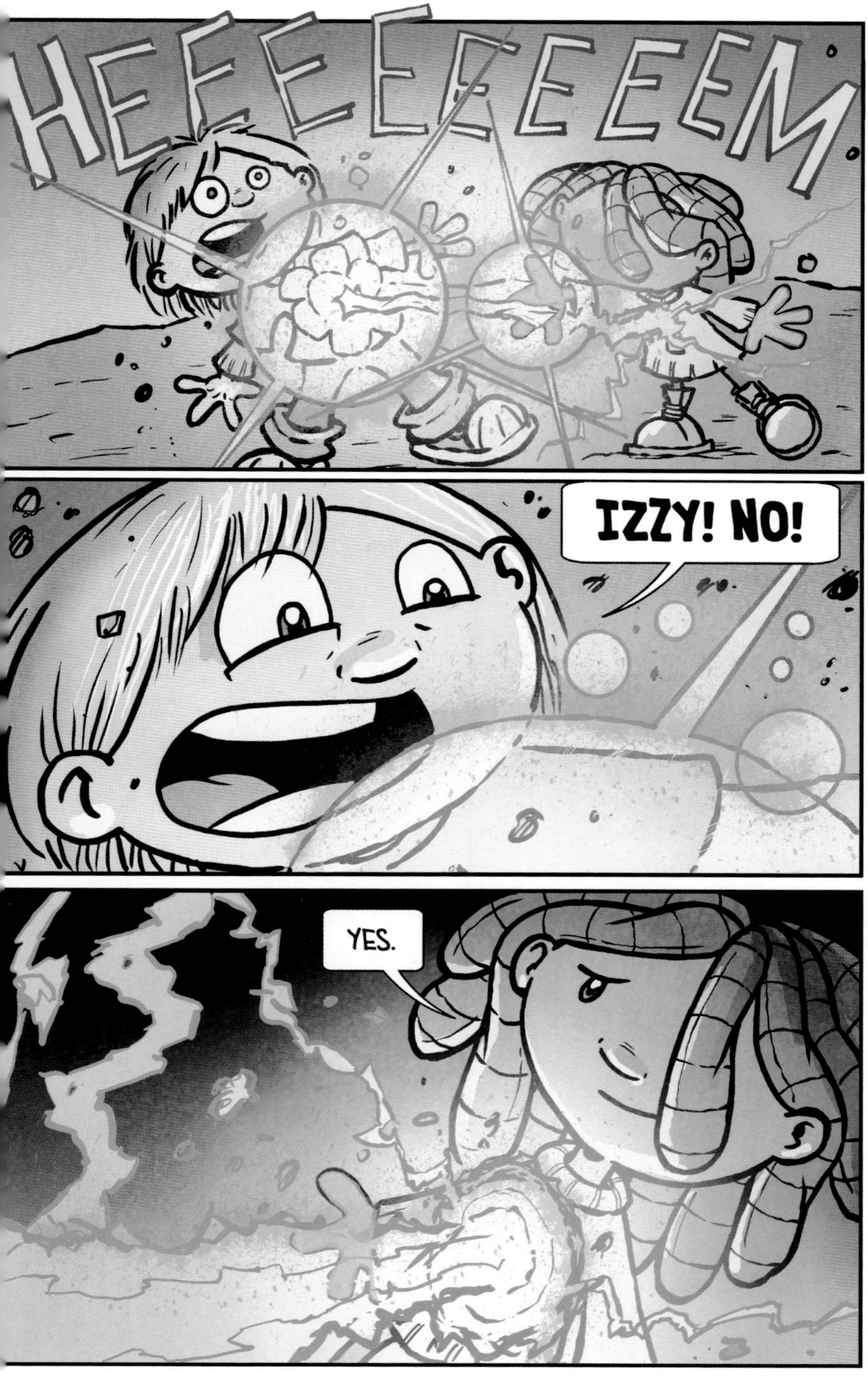
HEEEEEEM
IZZY! NO!
YES.

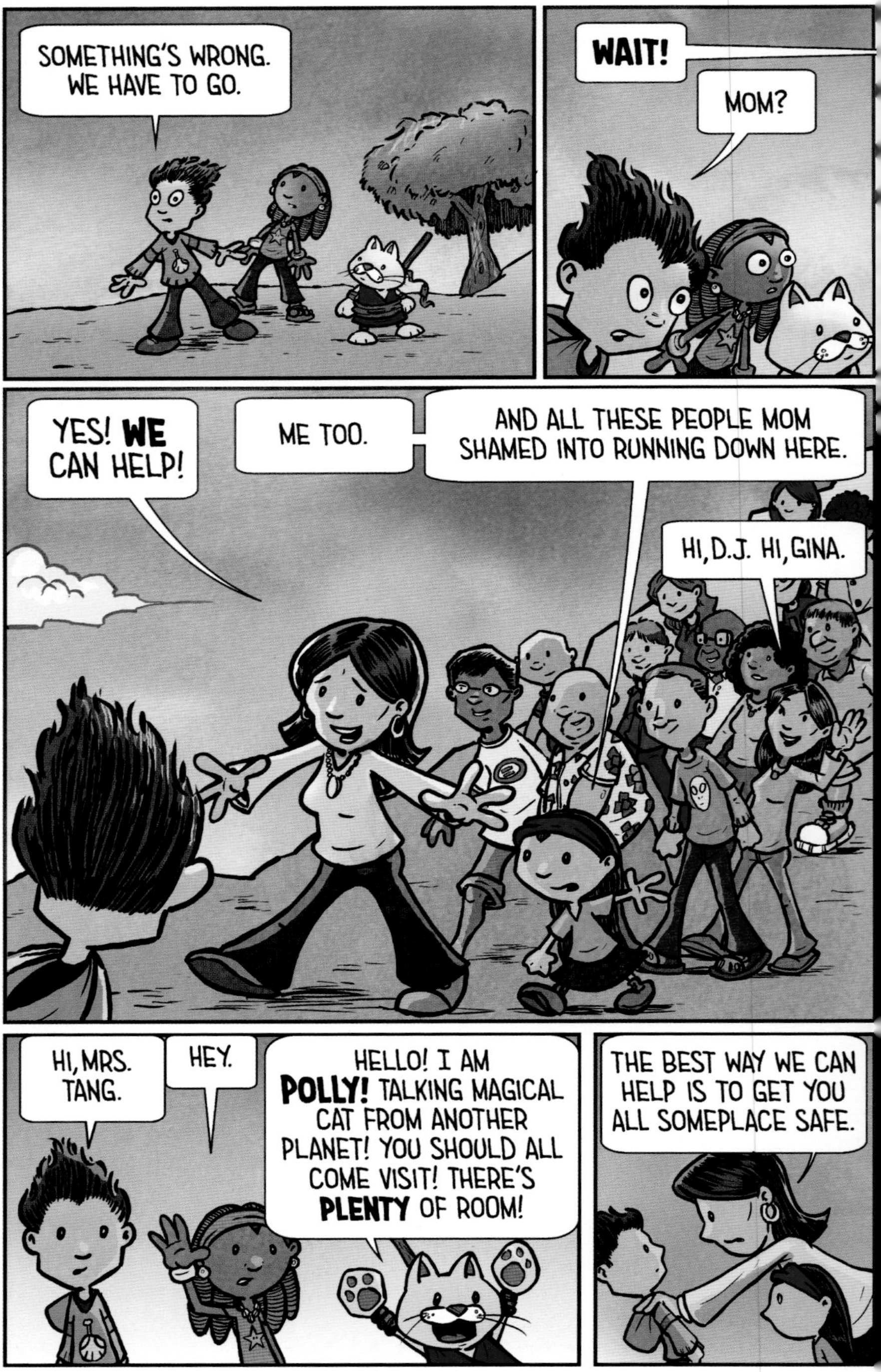
SOMETHING'S WRONG. WE HAVE TO GO.
WAIT!
MOM?
YES! **WE** CAN HELP!
ME TOO.
AND ALL THESE PEOPLE MOM SHAMED INTO RUNNING DOWN HERE.
HI, D.J. HI, GINA.
HI, MRS. TANG.
HEY.
HELLO! I AM **POLLY!** TALKING MAGICAL CAT FROM ANOTHER PLANET! YOU SHOULD ALL COME VISIT! THERE'S **PLENTY** OF ROOM!
THE BEST WAY WE CAN HELP IS TO GET YOU ALL SOMEPLACE SAFE.

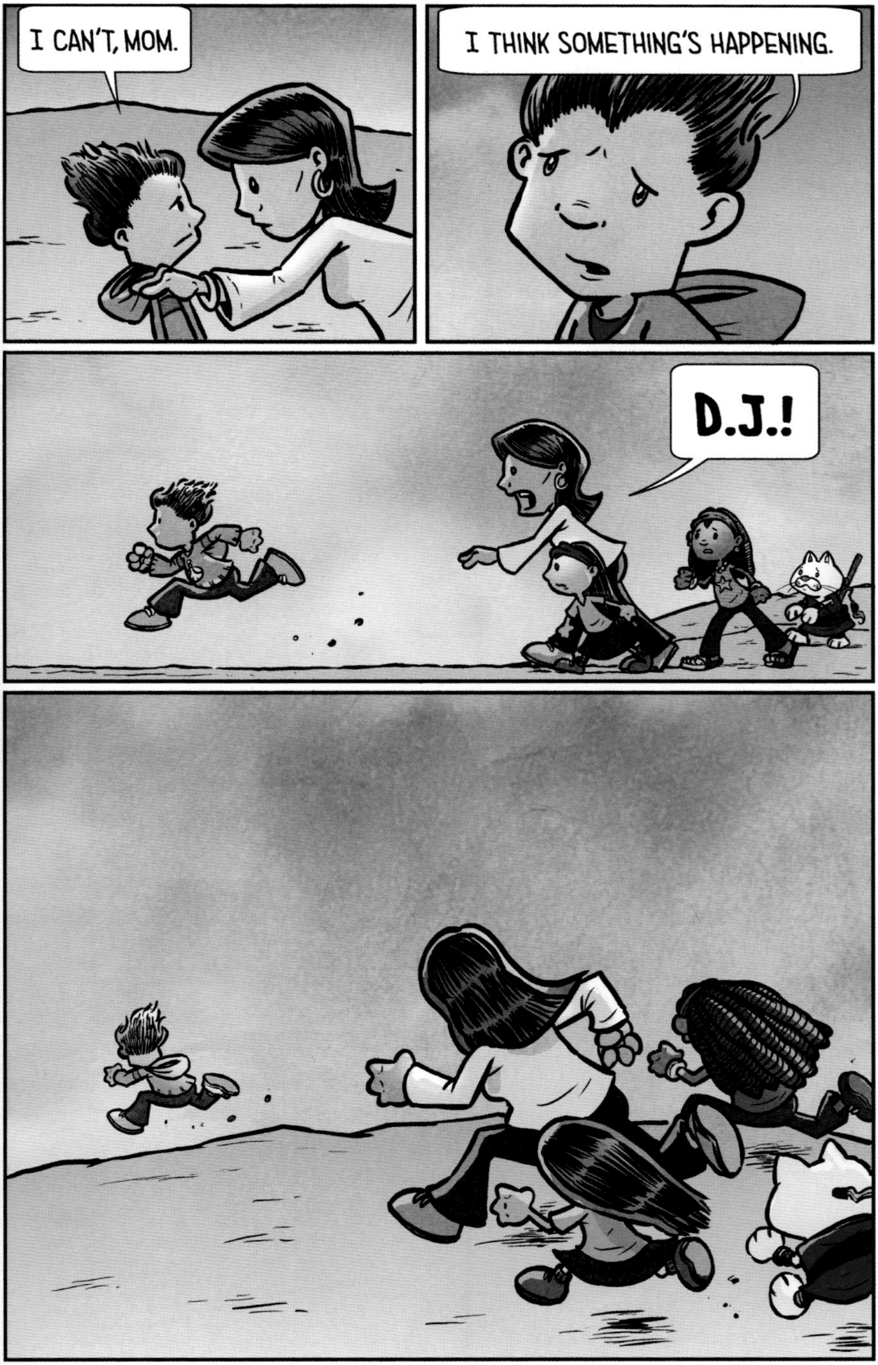
I CAN'T, MOM.
I THINK SOMETHING'S HAPPENING.
D.J.!

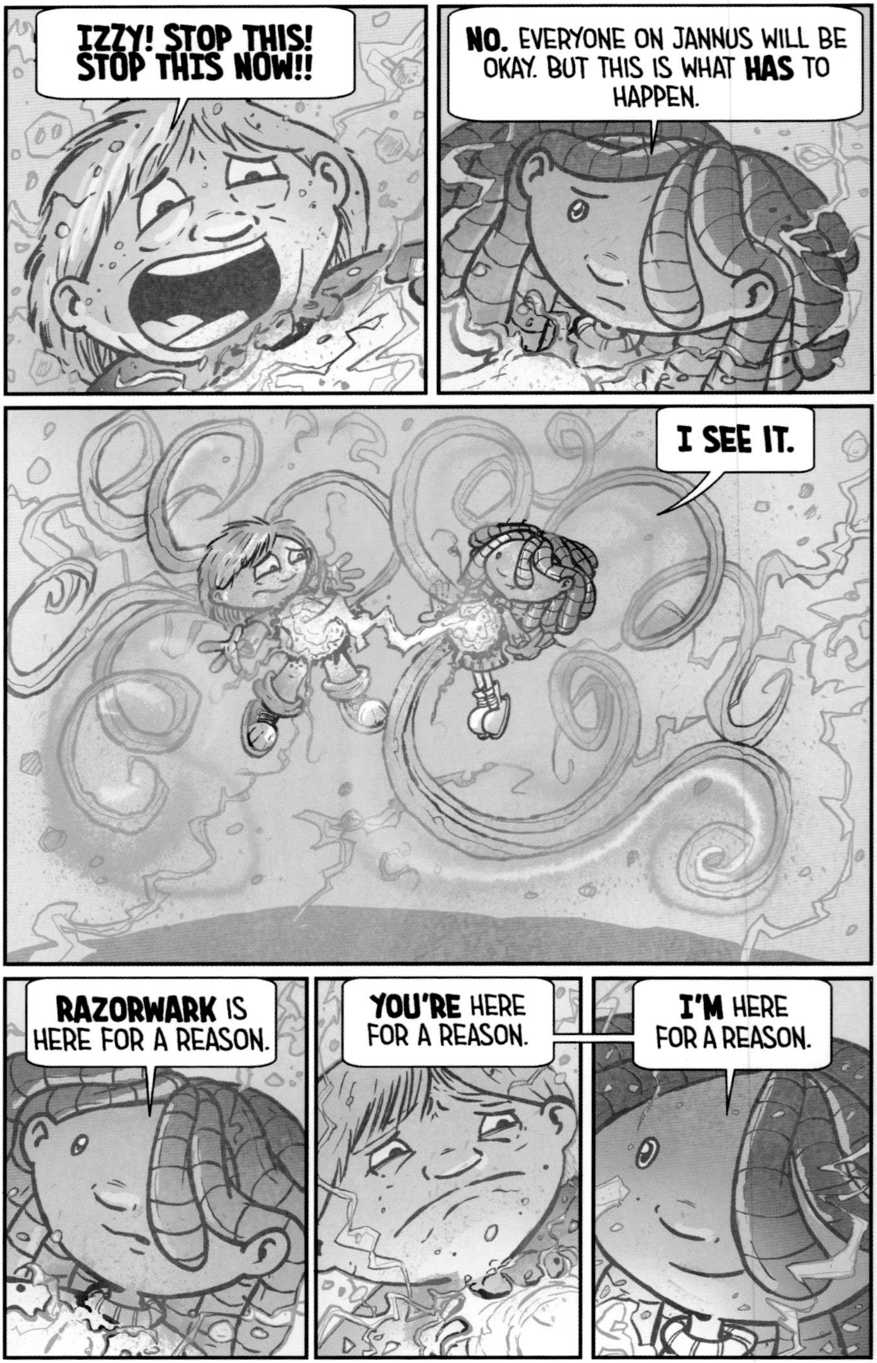
IZZY! STOP THIS! STOP THIS NOW!!
NO. EVERYONE ON JANNUS WILL BE OKAY. BUT THIS IS WHAT HAS TO HAPPEN.
I SEE IT.
RAZORWARK IS HERE FOR A REASON.
YOU'RE HERE FOR A REASON.
I'M HERE FOR A REASON.

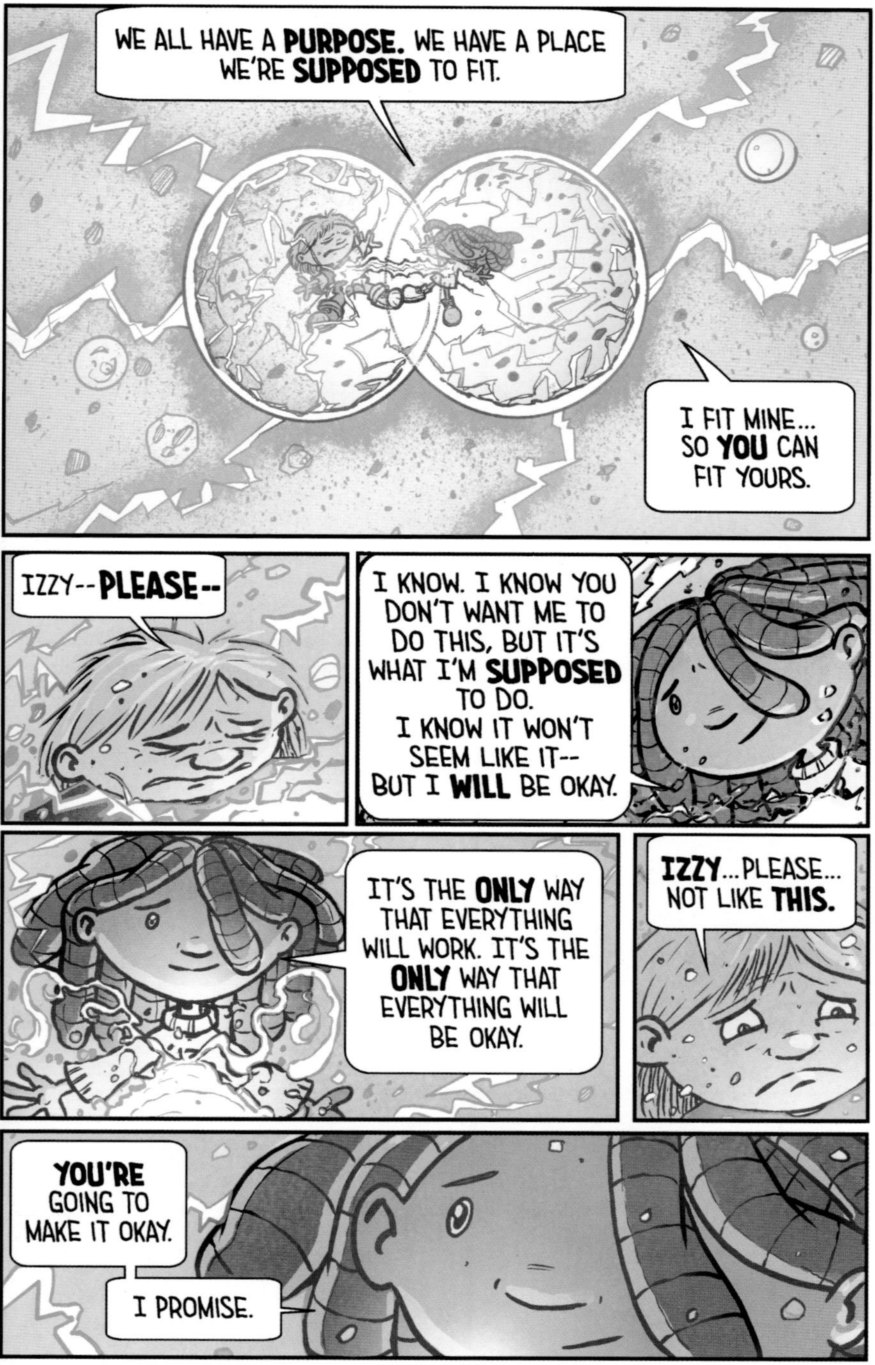
WE ALL HAVE A PURPOSE. WE HAVE A PLACE WE'RE SUPPOSED TO FIT.
I FIT MINE... SO YOU CAN FIT YOURS.
IZZY--PLEASE--
I KNOW. I KNOW YOU DON'T WANT ME TO DO THIS, BUT IT'S WHAT I'M SUPPOSED TO DO. I KNOW IT WON'T SEEM LIKE IT-- BUT I WILL BE OKAY.
IT'S THE ONLY WAY THAT EVERYTHING WILL WORK. IT'S THE ONLY WAY THAT EVERYTHING WILL BE OKAY.
IZZY...PLEASE... NOT LIKE THIS.
YOU'RE GOING TO MAKE IT OKAY.
I PROMISE.

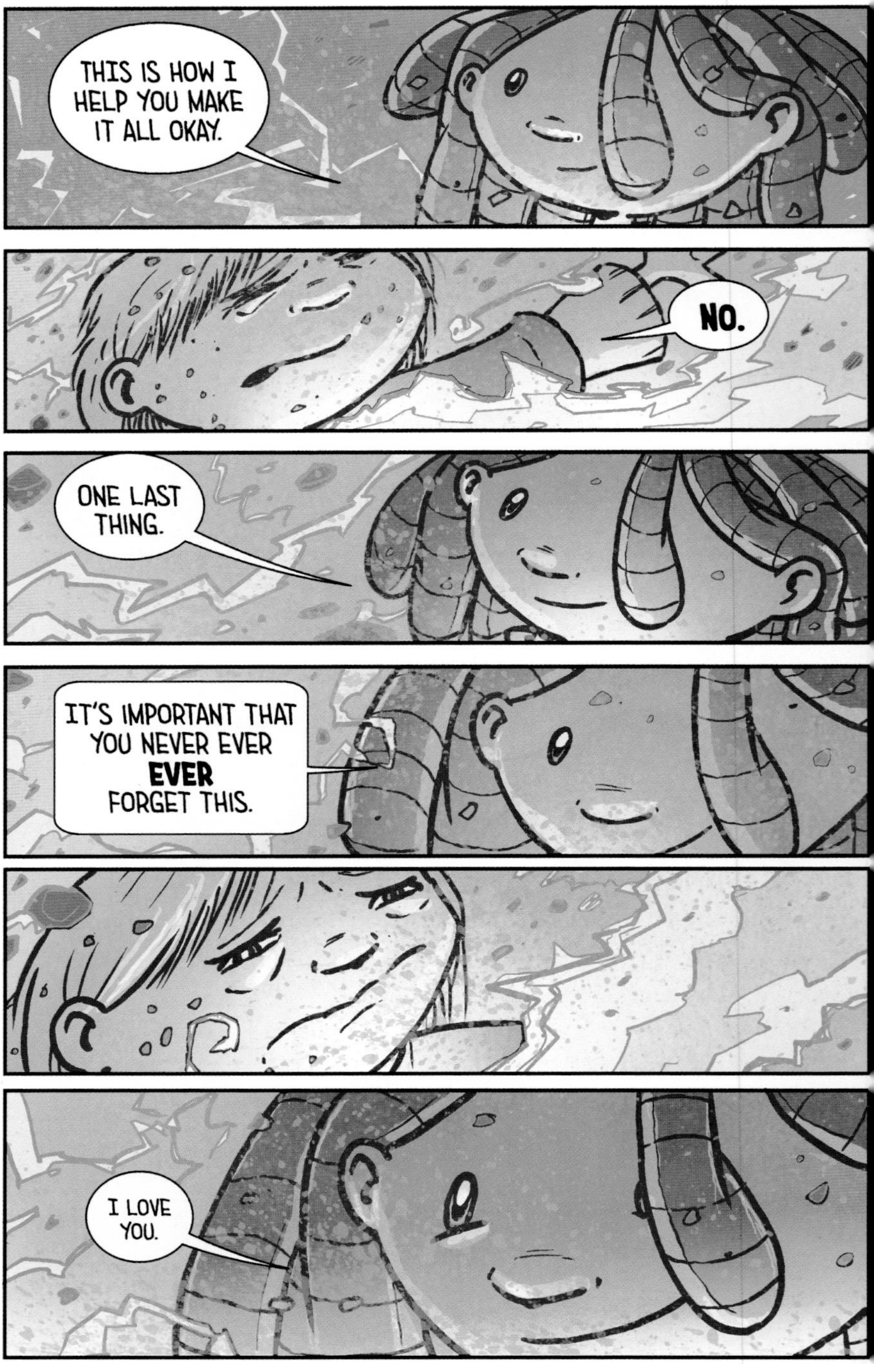
THIS IS HOW I HELP YOU MAKE IT ALL OKAY.
NO.
ONE LAST THING.
IT'S IMPORTANT THAT YOU NEVER EVER **EVER** FORGET THIS.
I LOVE YOU.

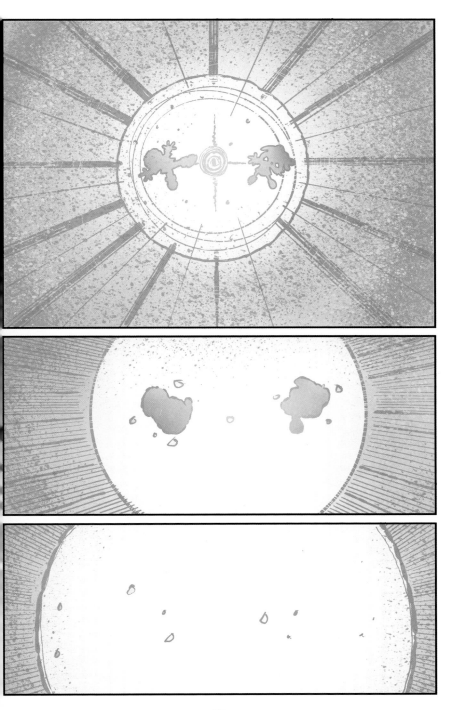

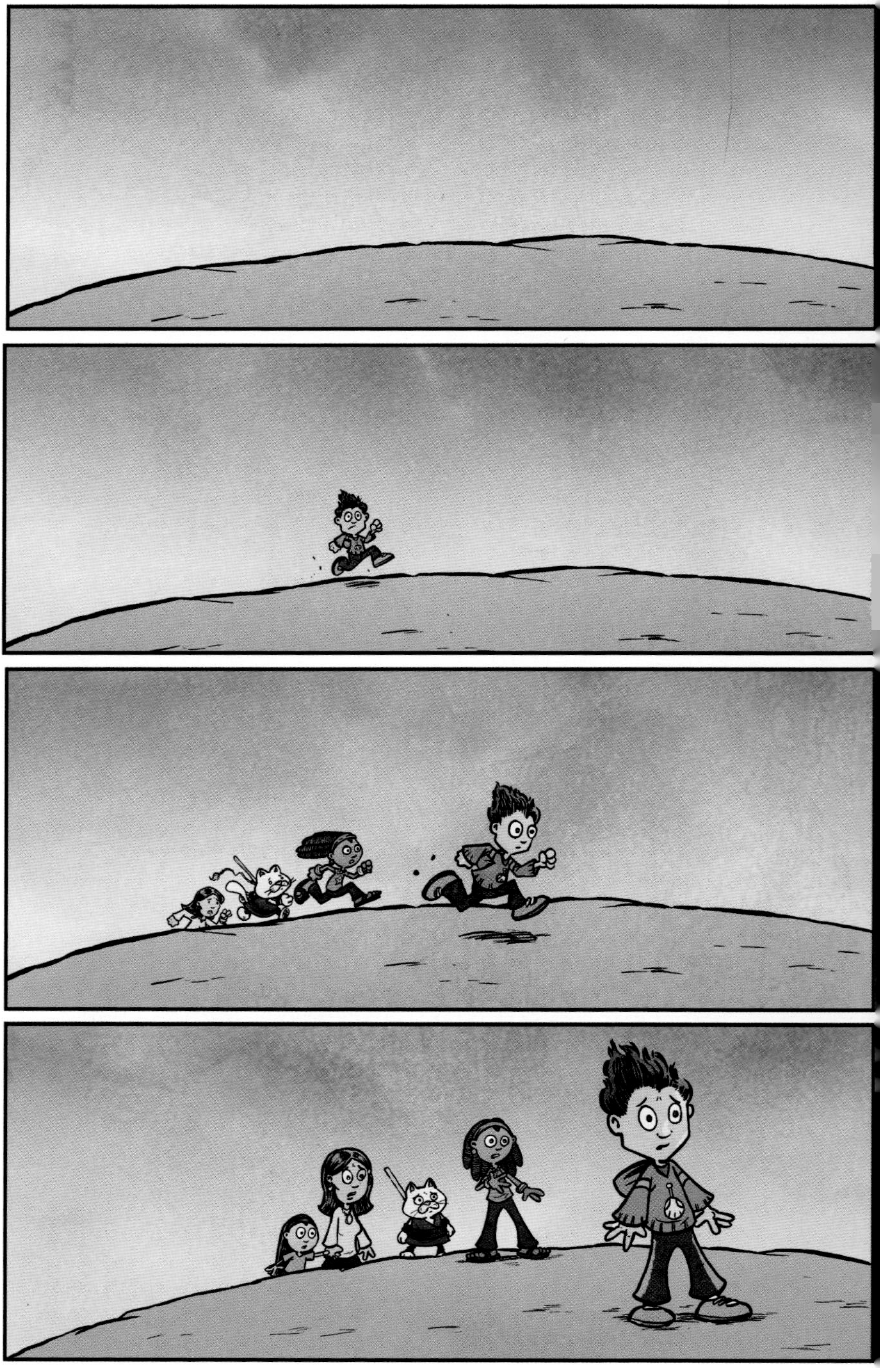

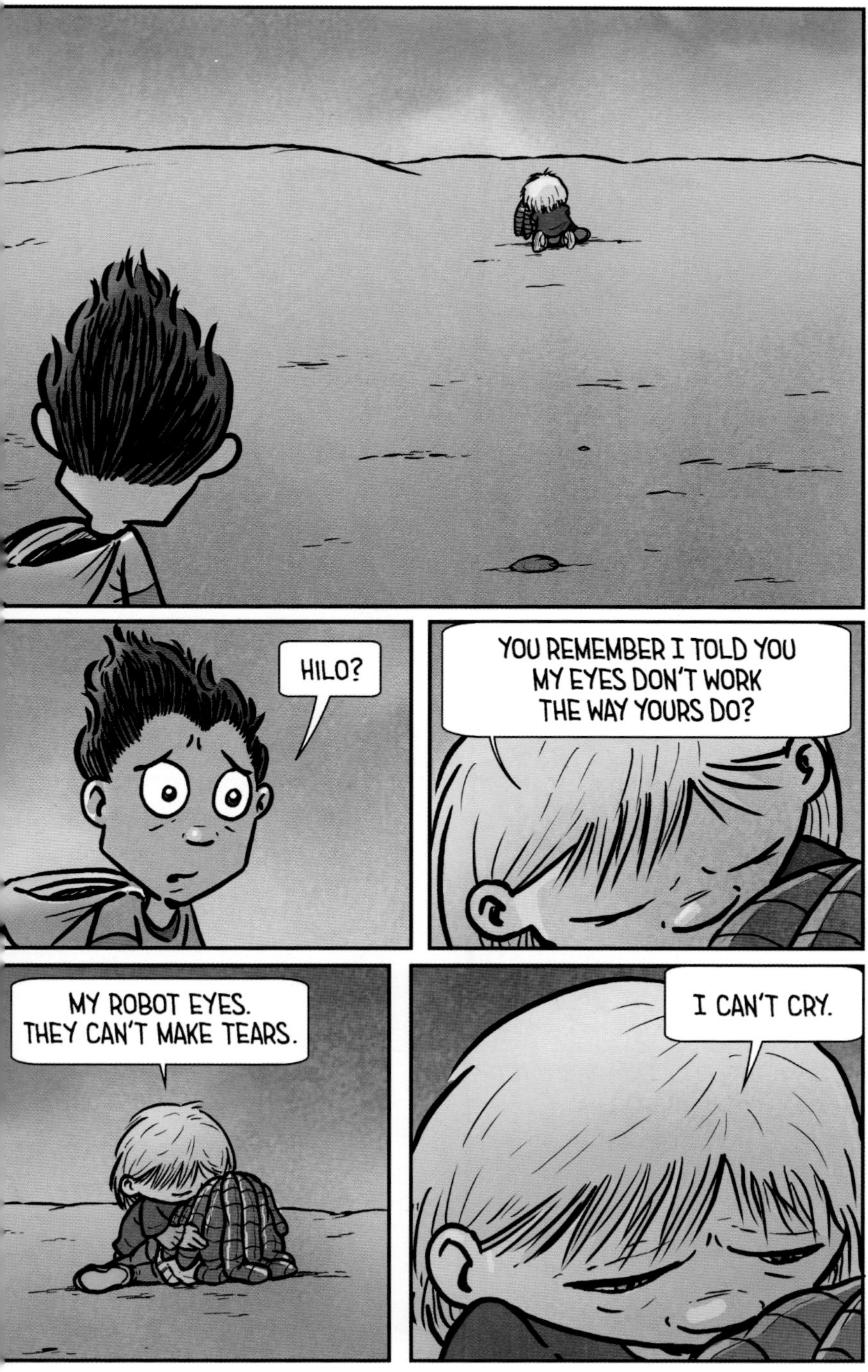
HILO?
YOU REMEMBER I TOLD YOU MY EYES DON'T WORK THE WAY YOURS DO?
MY ROBOT EYES. THEY CAN'T MAKE TEARS.
I CAN'T CRY.

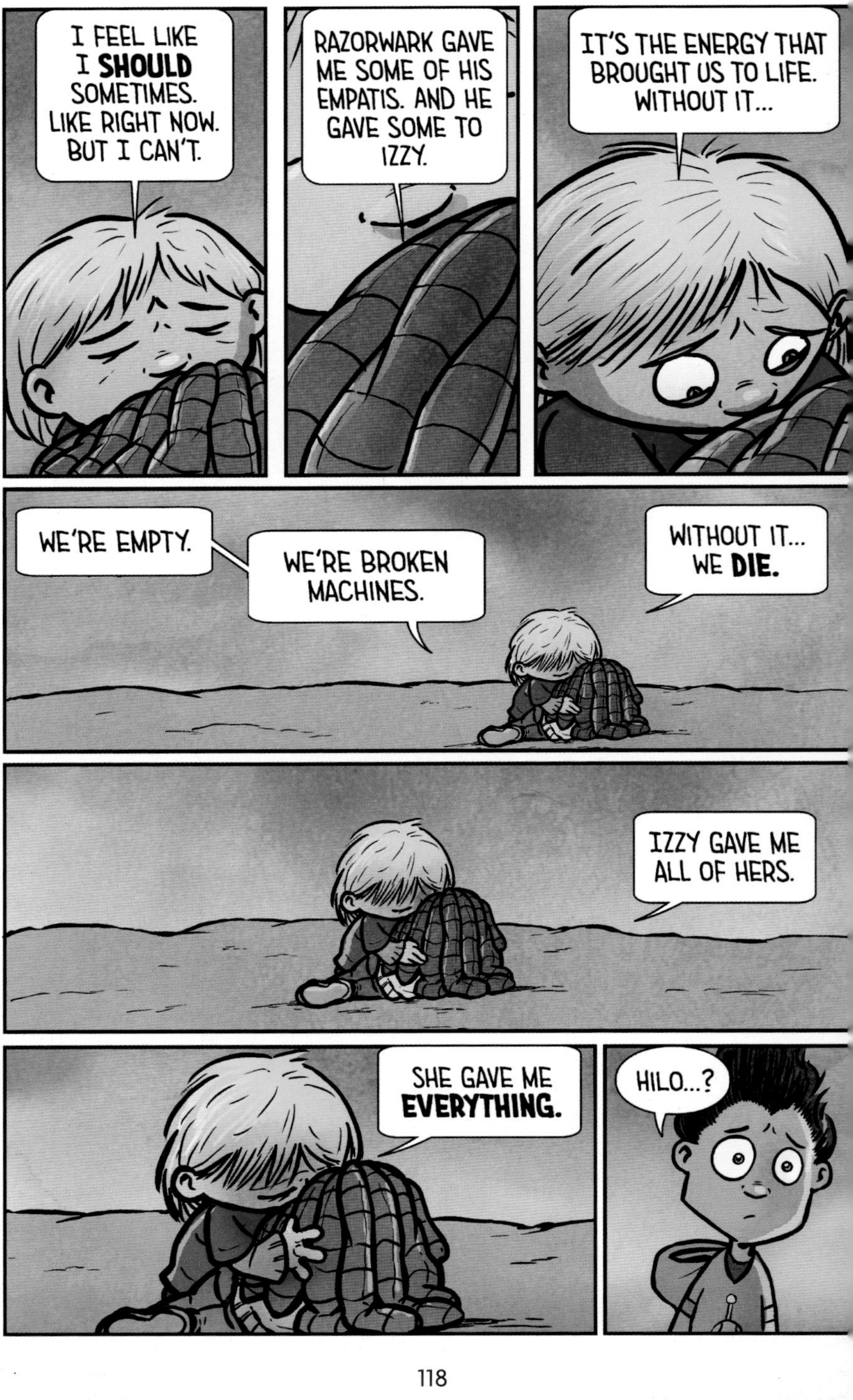
I FEEL LIKE I **SHOULD** SOMETIMES. LIKE RIGHT NOW. BUT I CAN'T.
RAZORWARK GAVE ME SOME OF HIS EMPATIS. AND HE GAVE SOME TO IZZY.
IT'S THE ENERGY THAT BROUGHT US TO LIFE. WITHOUT IT...
WE'RE EMPTY.
WE'RE BROKEN MACHINES.
WITHOUT IT... WE **DIE.**
IZZY GAVE ME ALL OF HERS.
SHE GAVE ME **EVERYTHING.**
HILO...?

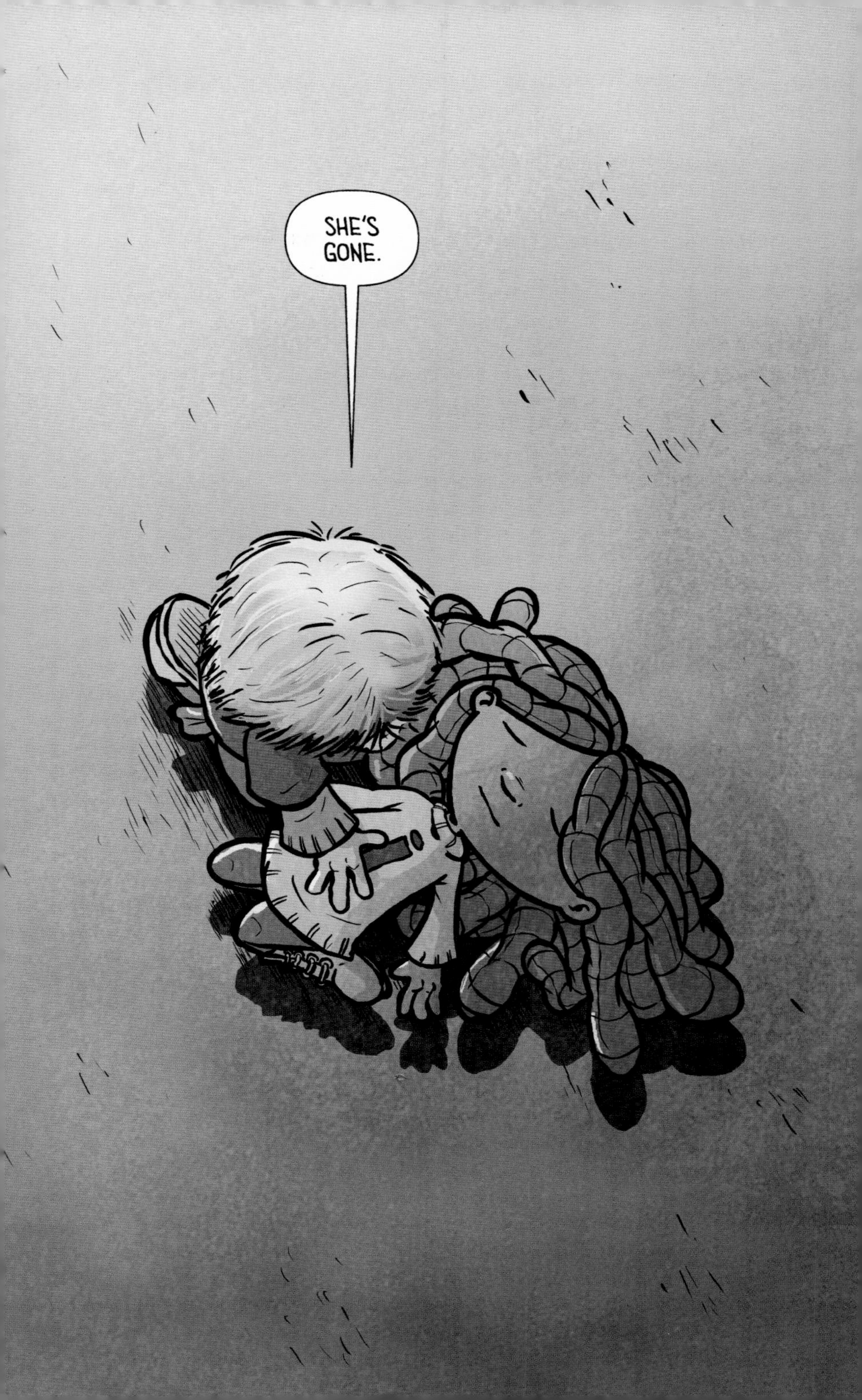
SHE'S GONE.

CHAPTER

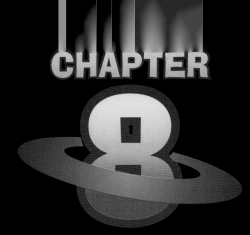

NO HOLDING BACK

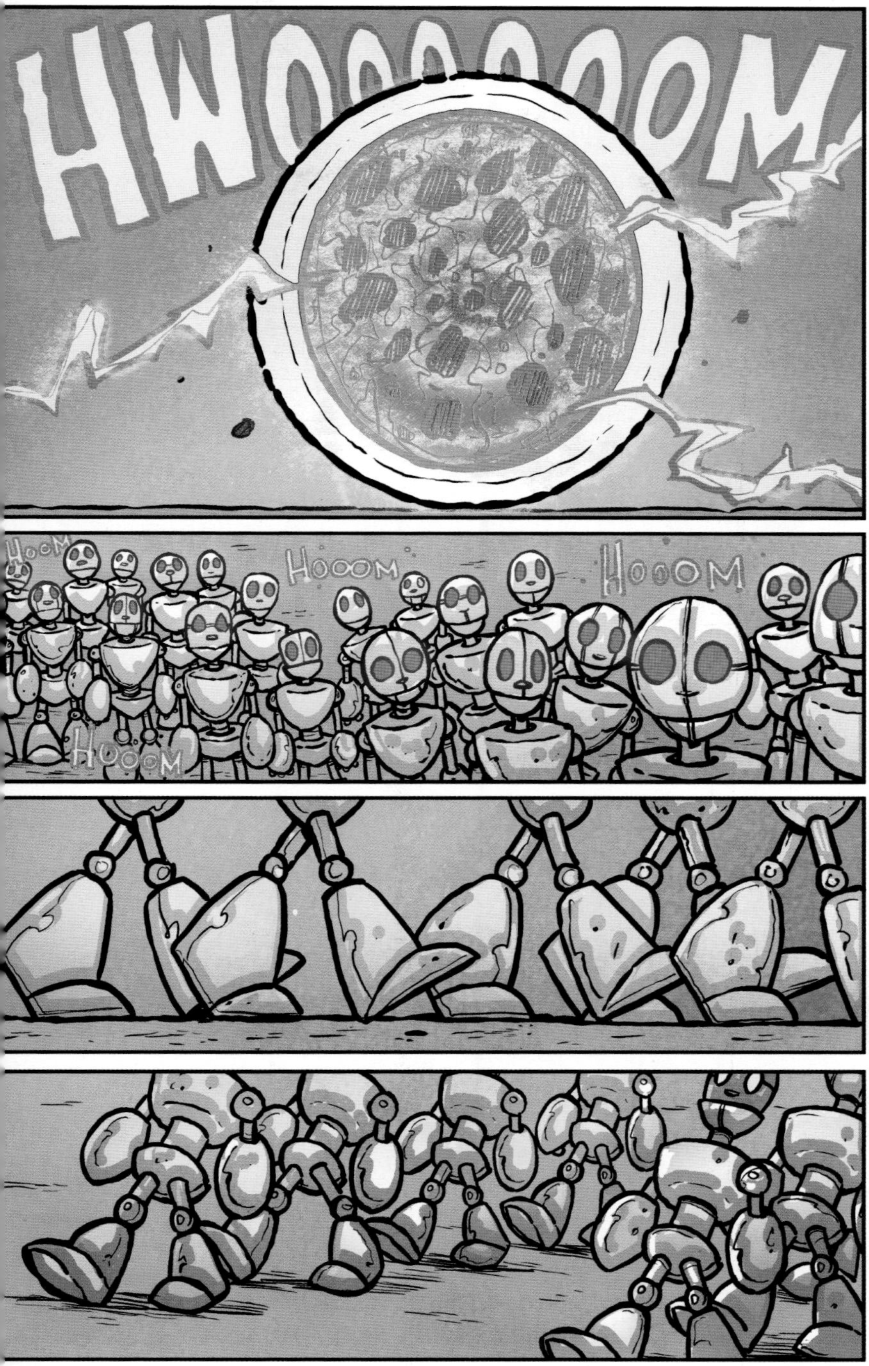
HWOOOOOOM
HOOM
HOOOM
HOOOM
HOOOM

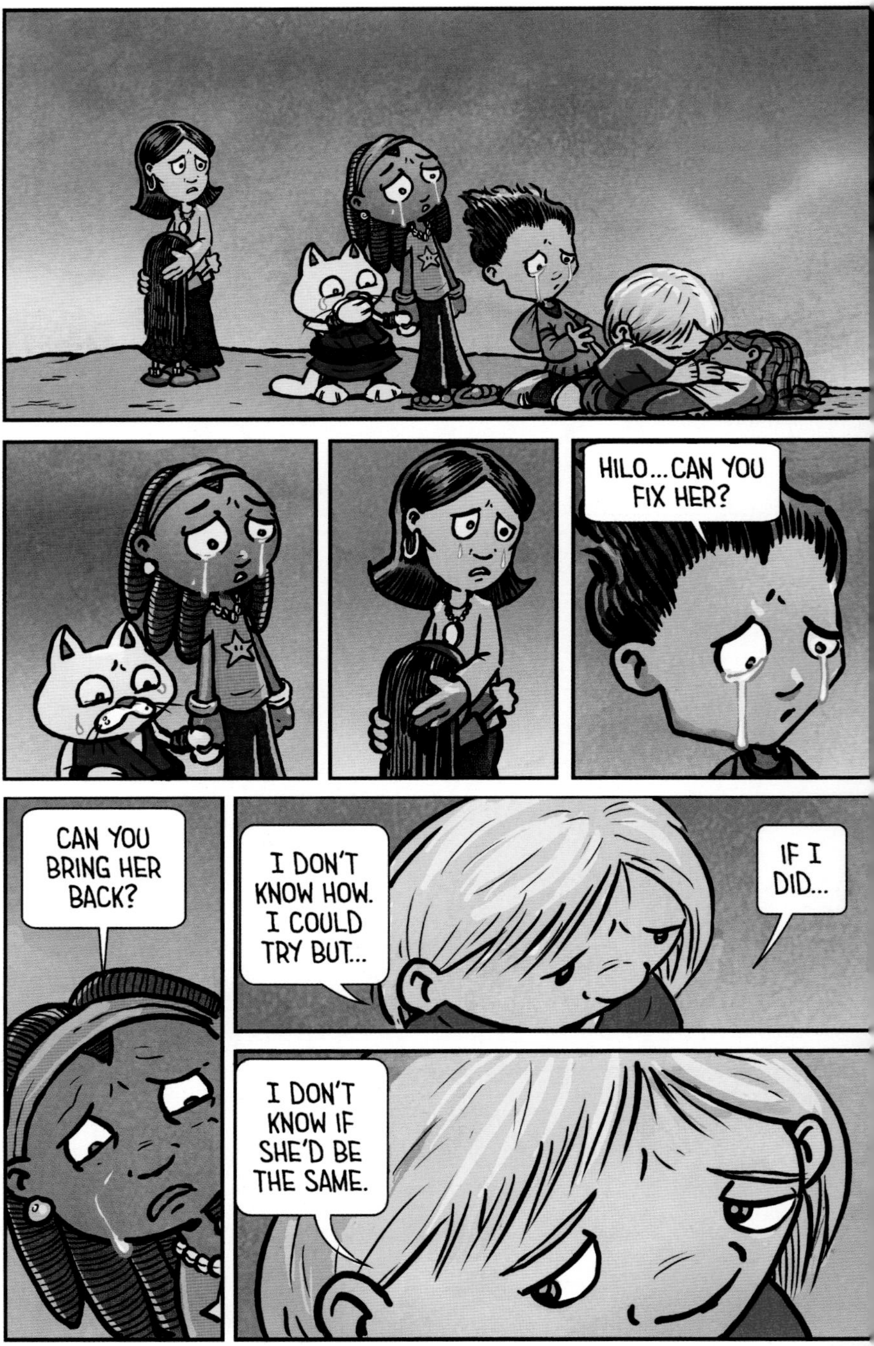
HILO... CAN YOU FIX HER?
CAN YOU BRING HER BACK?
I DON'T KNOW HOW. I COULD TRY BUT...
IF I DID...
I DON'T KNOW IF SHE'D BE THE SAME.

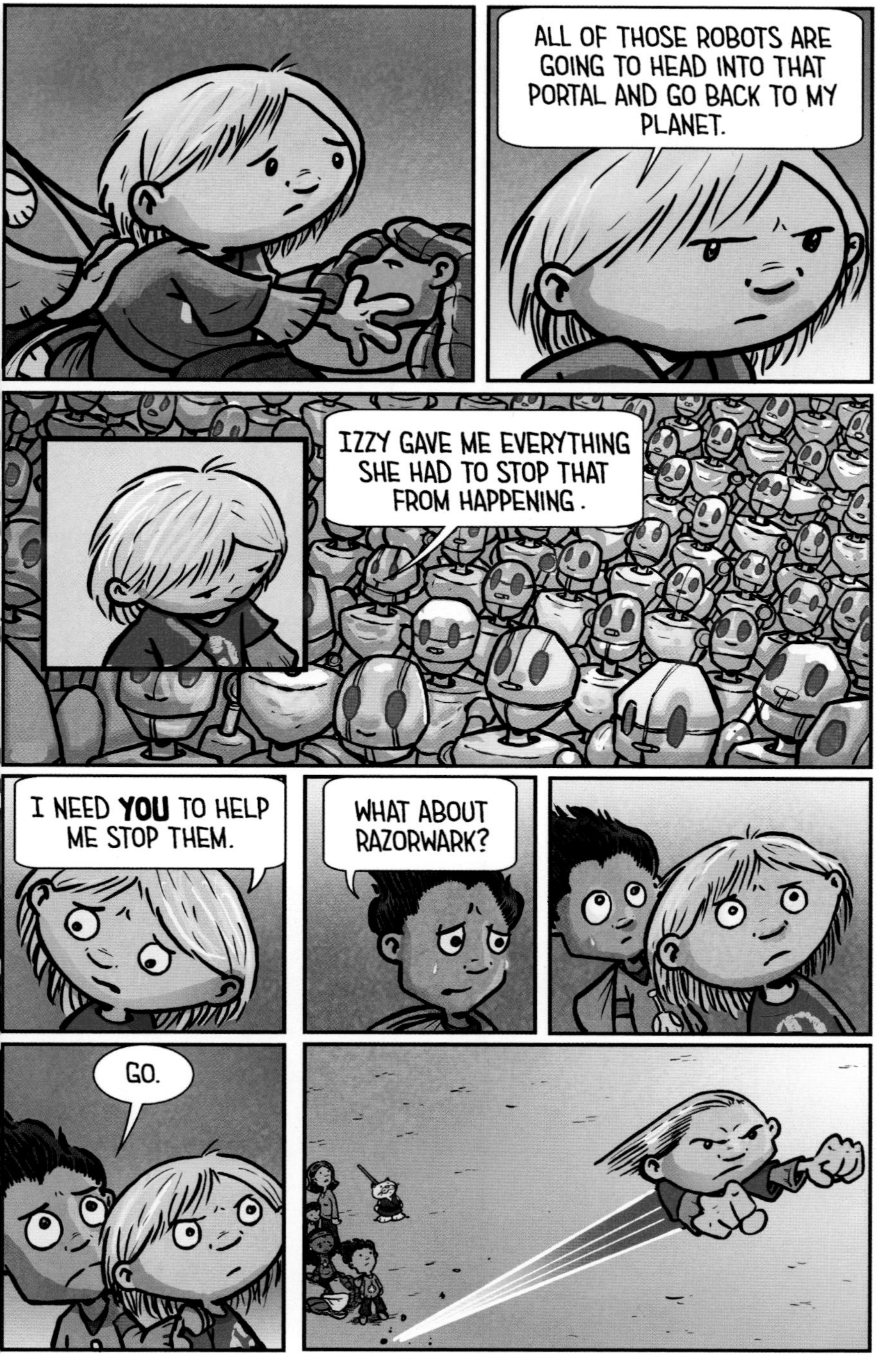
ALL OF THOSE ROBOTS ARE GOING TO HEAD INTO THAT PORTAL AND GO BACK TO MY PLANET.
IZZY GAVE ME EVERYTHING SHE HAD TO STOP THAT FROM HAPPENING.
I NEED **YOU** TO HELP ME STOP THEM.
WHAT ABOUT RAZORWARK?
GO.

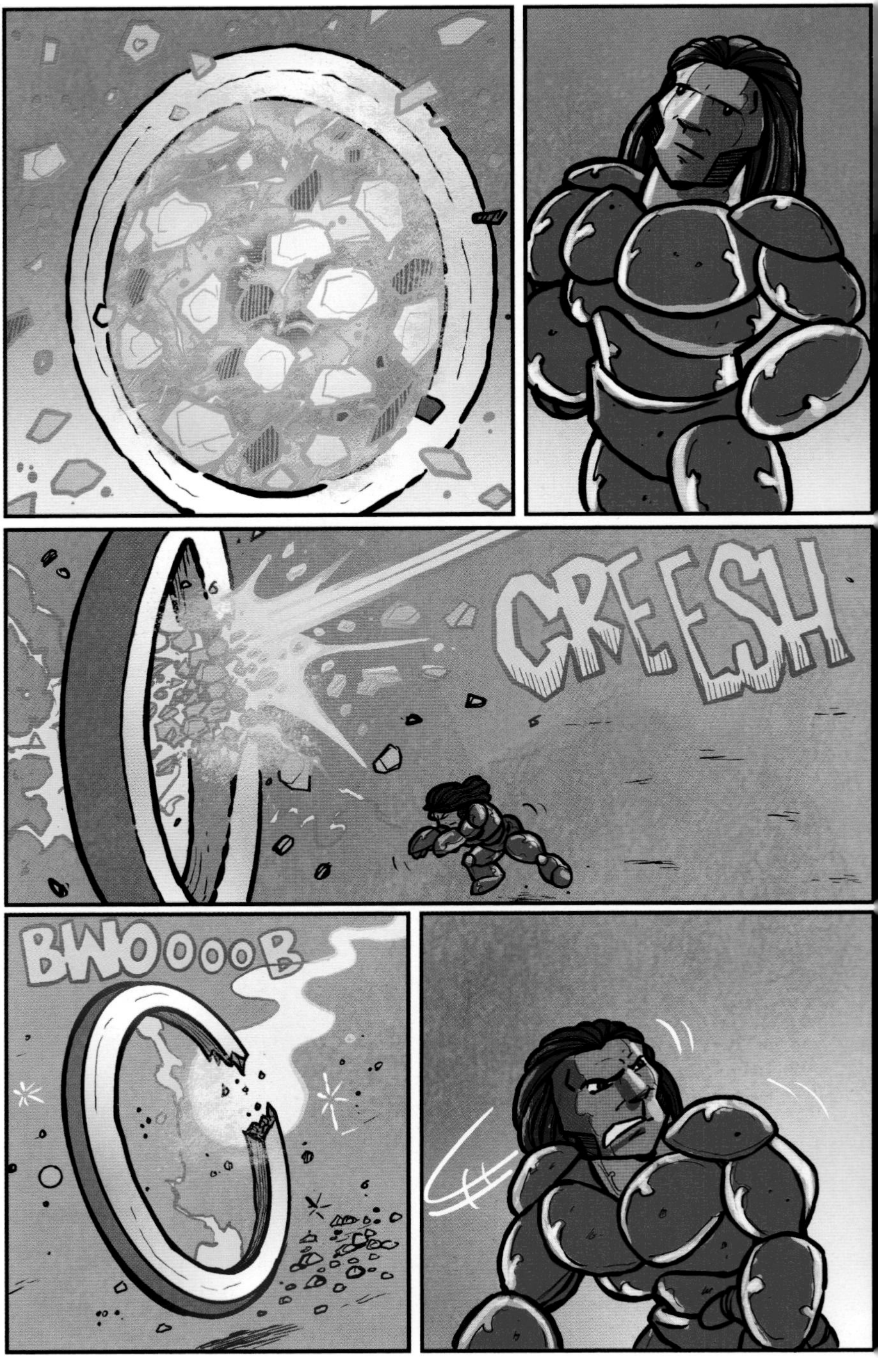
CREESH
BWOoooB

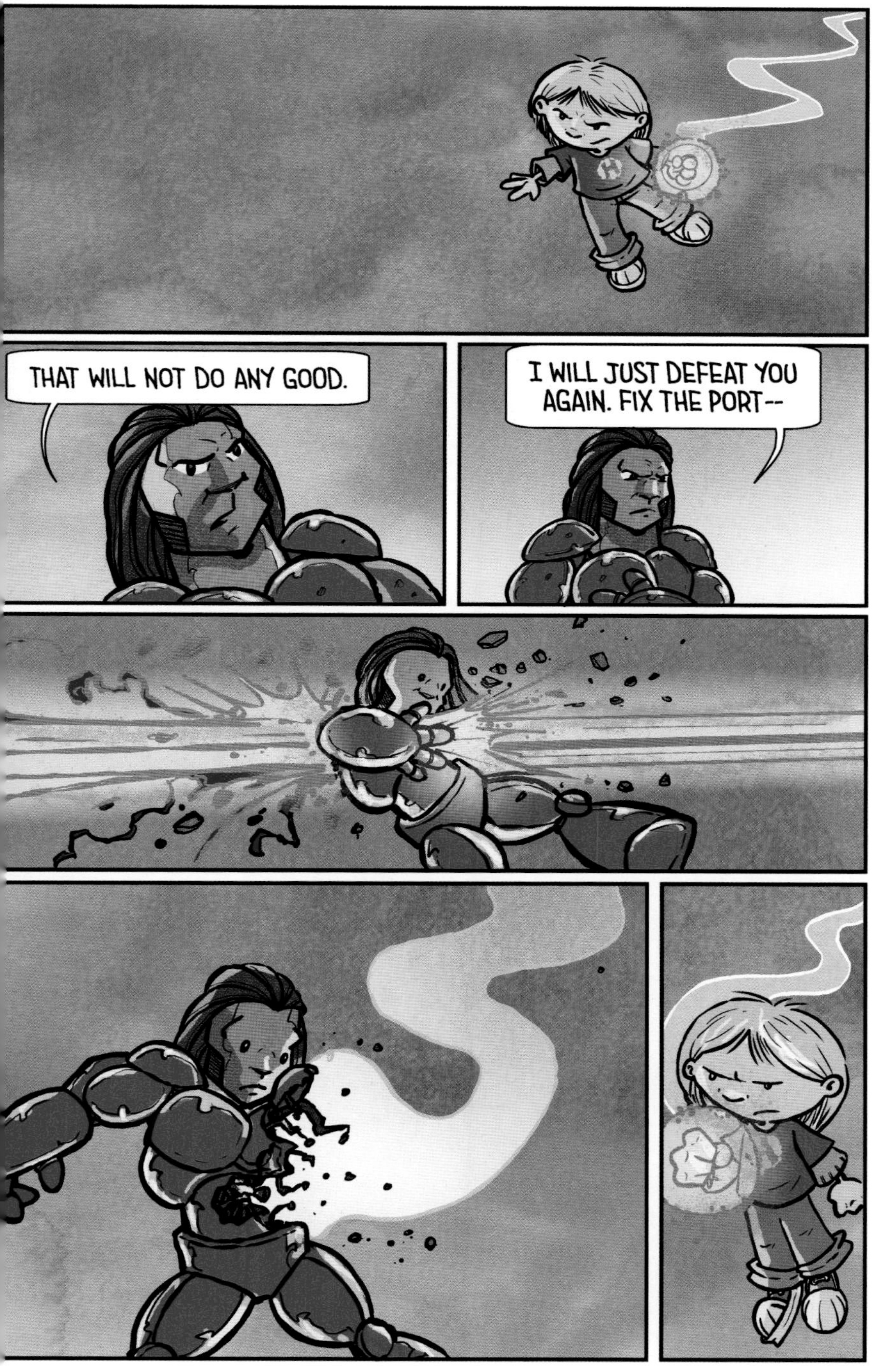
THAT WILL NOT DO ANY GOOD.
I WILL JUST DEFEAT YOU AGAIN. FIX THE PORT--

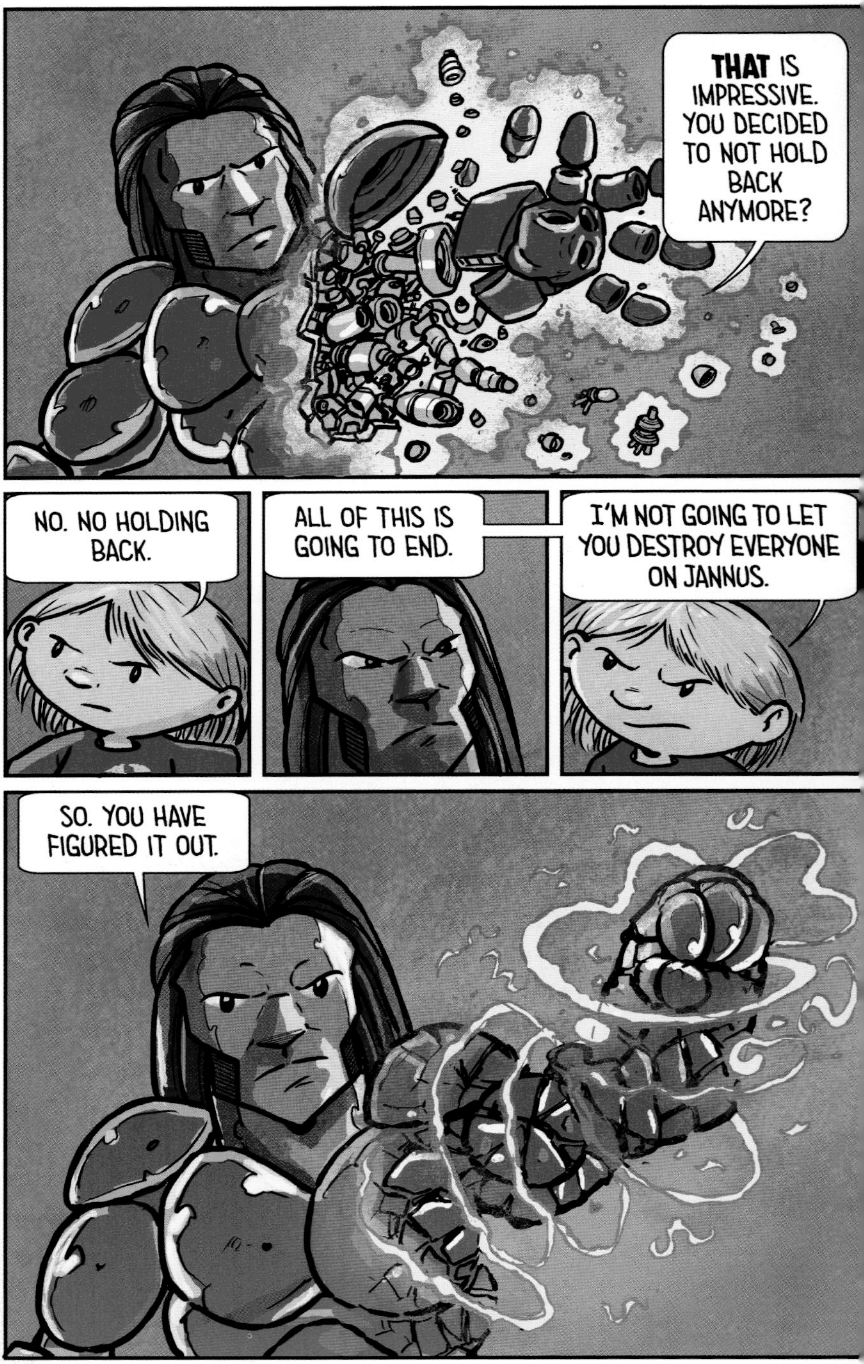
THAT IS IMPRESSIVE. YOU DECIDED TO NOT HOLD BACK ANYMORE?
NO. NO HOLDING BACK.
ALL OF THIS IS GOING TO END.
I'M NOT GOING TO LET YOU DESTROY EVERYONE ON JANNUS.
SO. YOU HAVE FIGURED IT OUT.

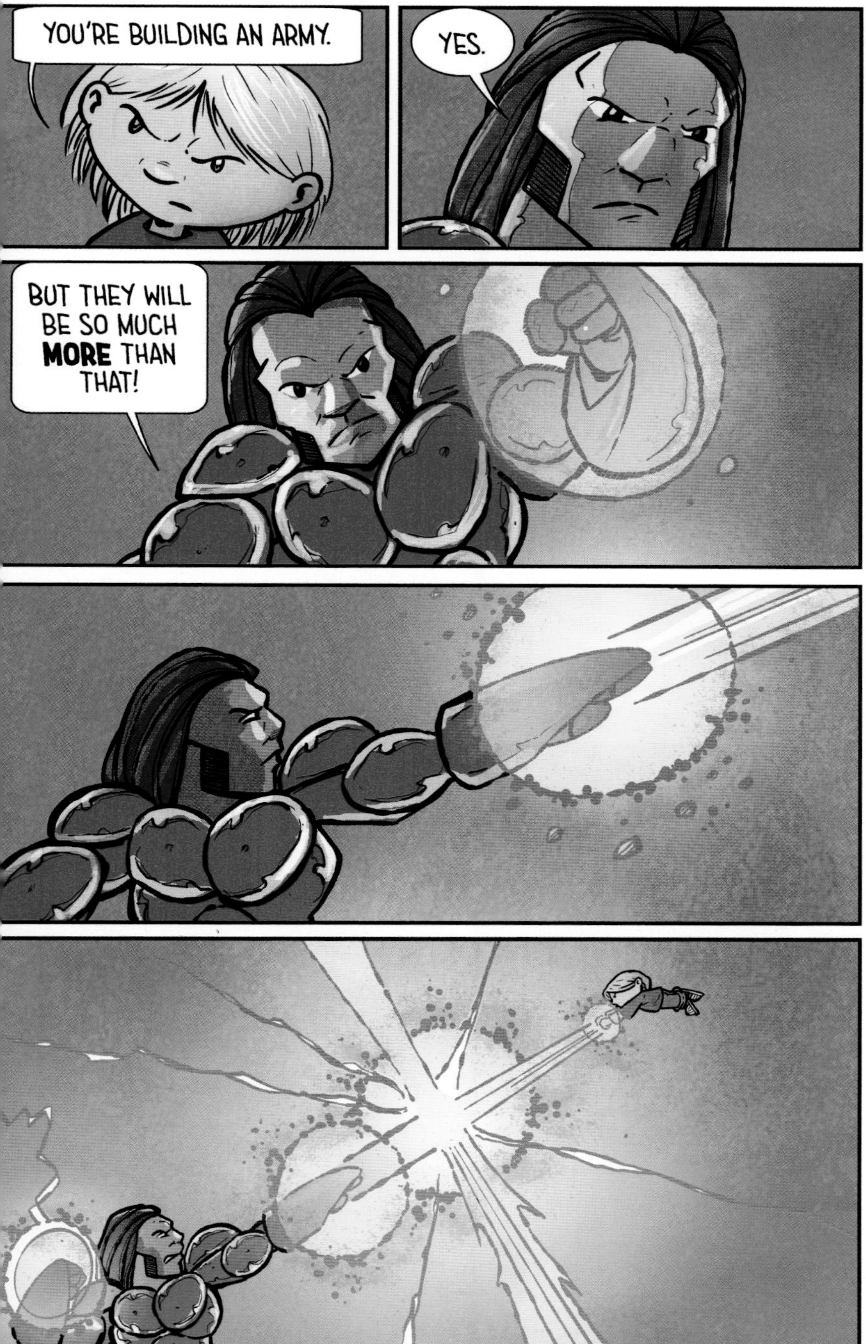
YOU'RE BUILDING AN ARMY.
YES.
BUT THEY WILL BE SO MUCH **MORE** THAN THAT!

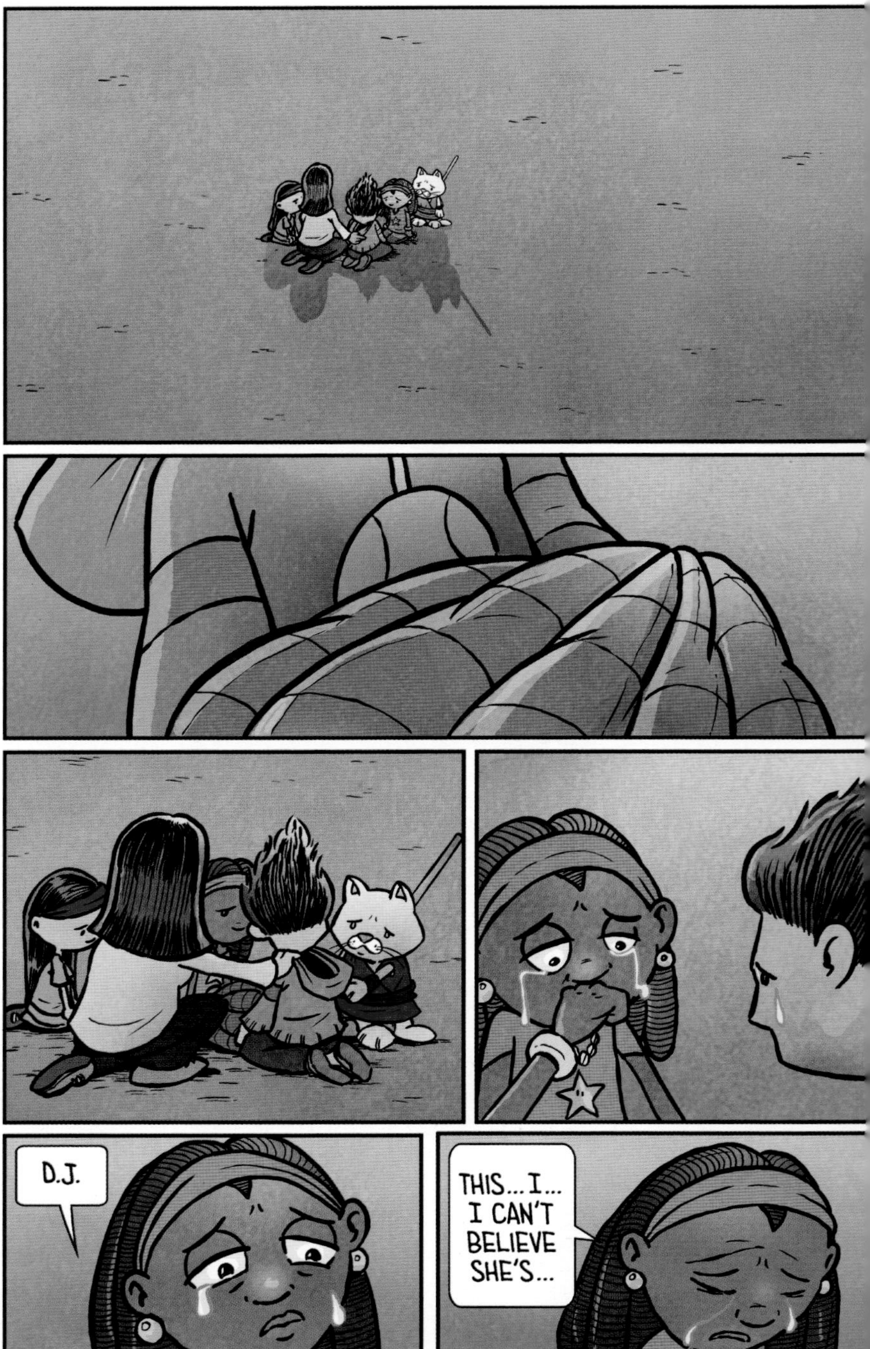
D.J.
THIS... I...
I CAN'T
BELIEVE
SHE'S...

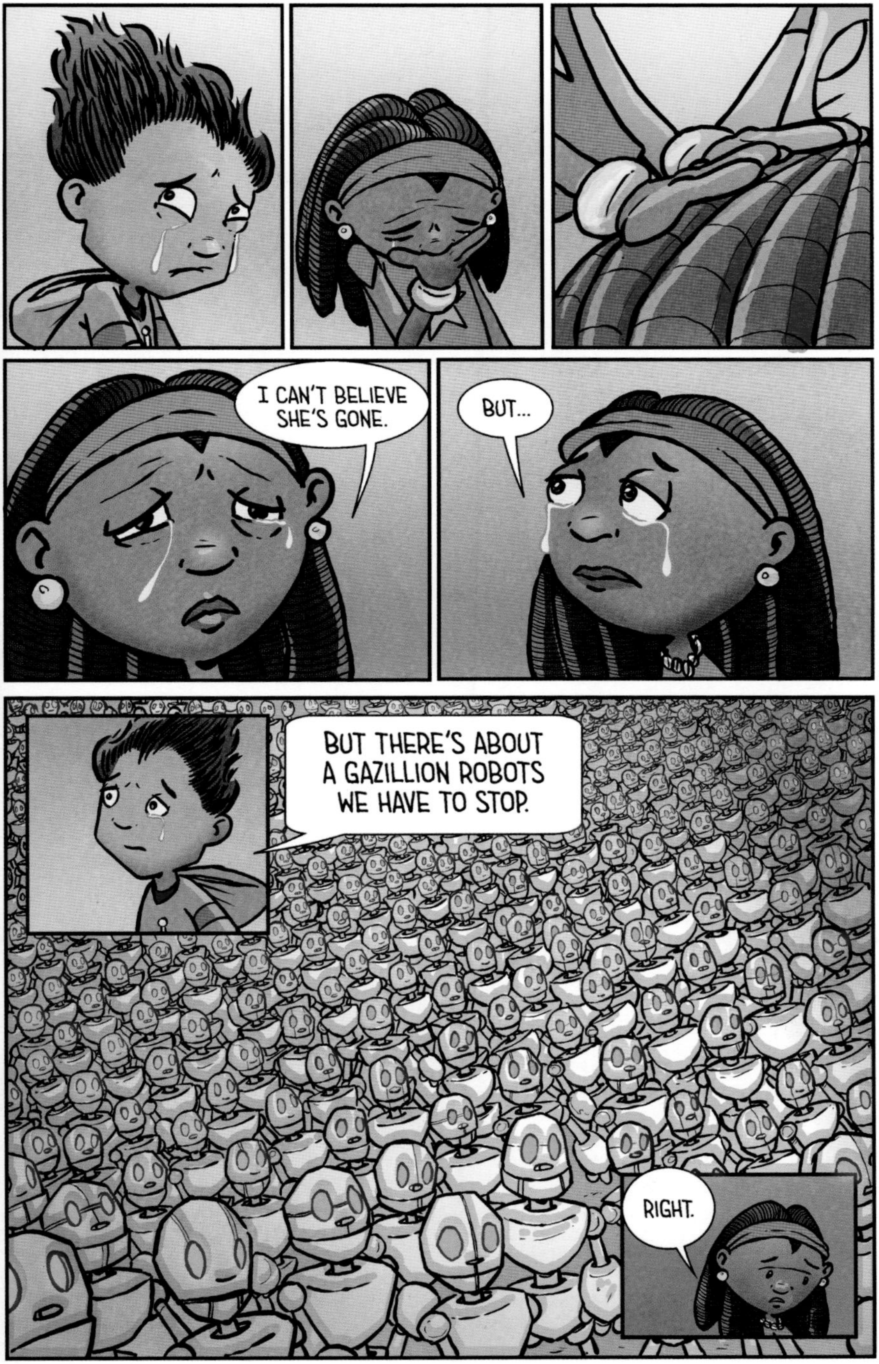
I CAN'T BELIEVE SHE'S GONE.
BUT...
BUT THERE'S ABOUT A GAZILLION ROBOTS WE HAVE TO STOP.
RIGHT.

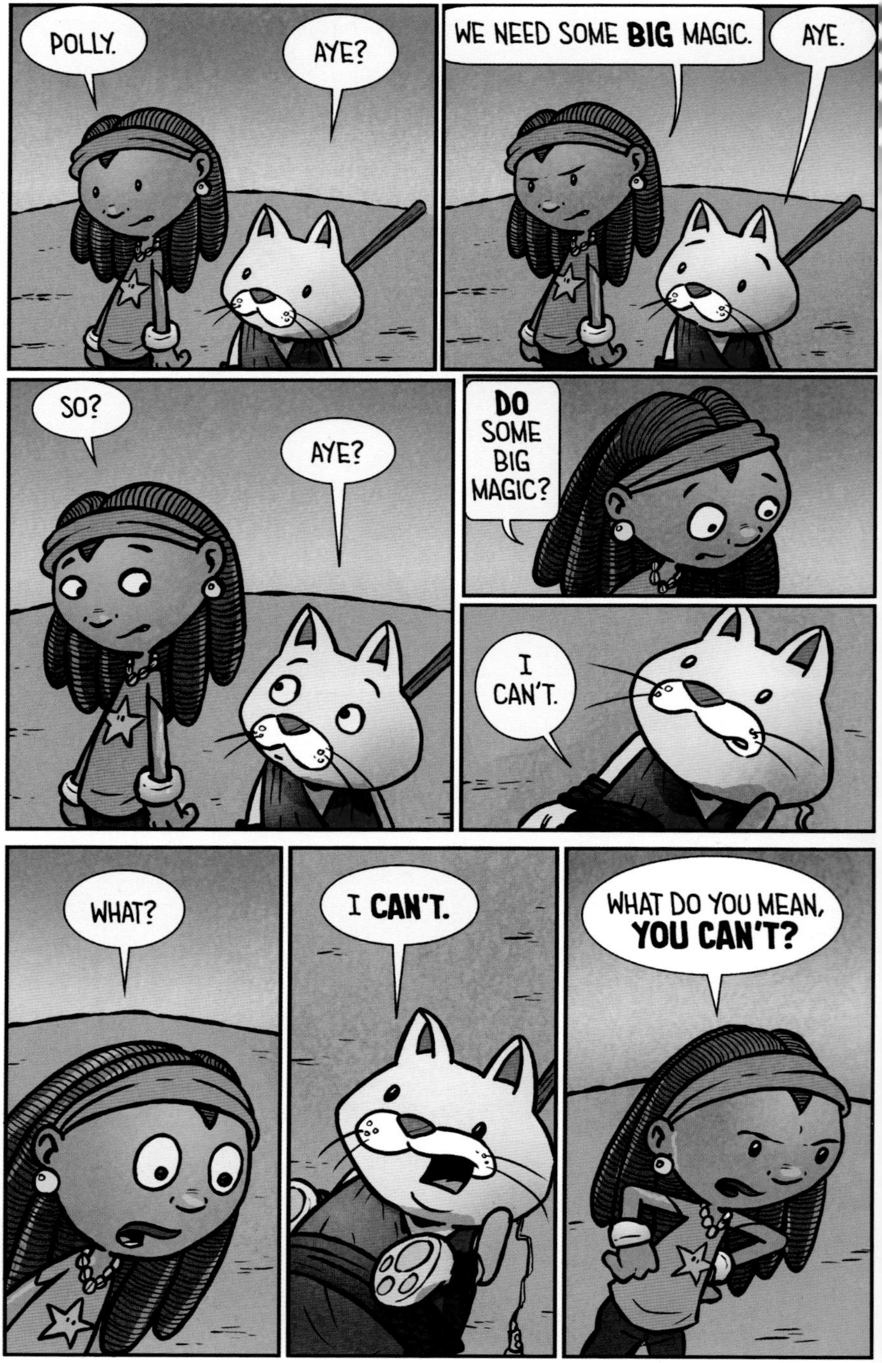
POLLY.
AYE?
WE NEED SOME **BIG** MAGIC.
AYE.
SO?
AYE?
DO SOME BIG MAGIC?
I CAN'T.
WHAT?
I **CAN'T.**
WHAT DO YOU MEAN, **YOU CAN'T?**

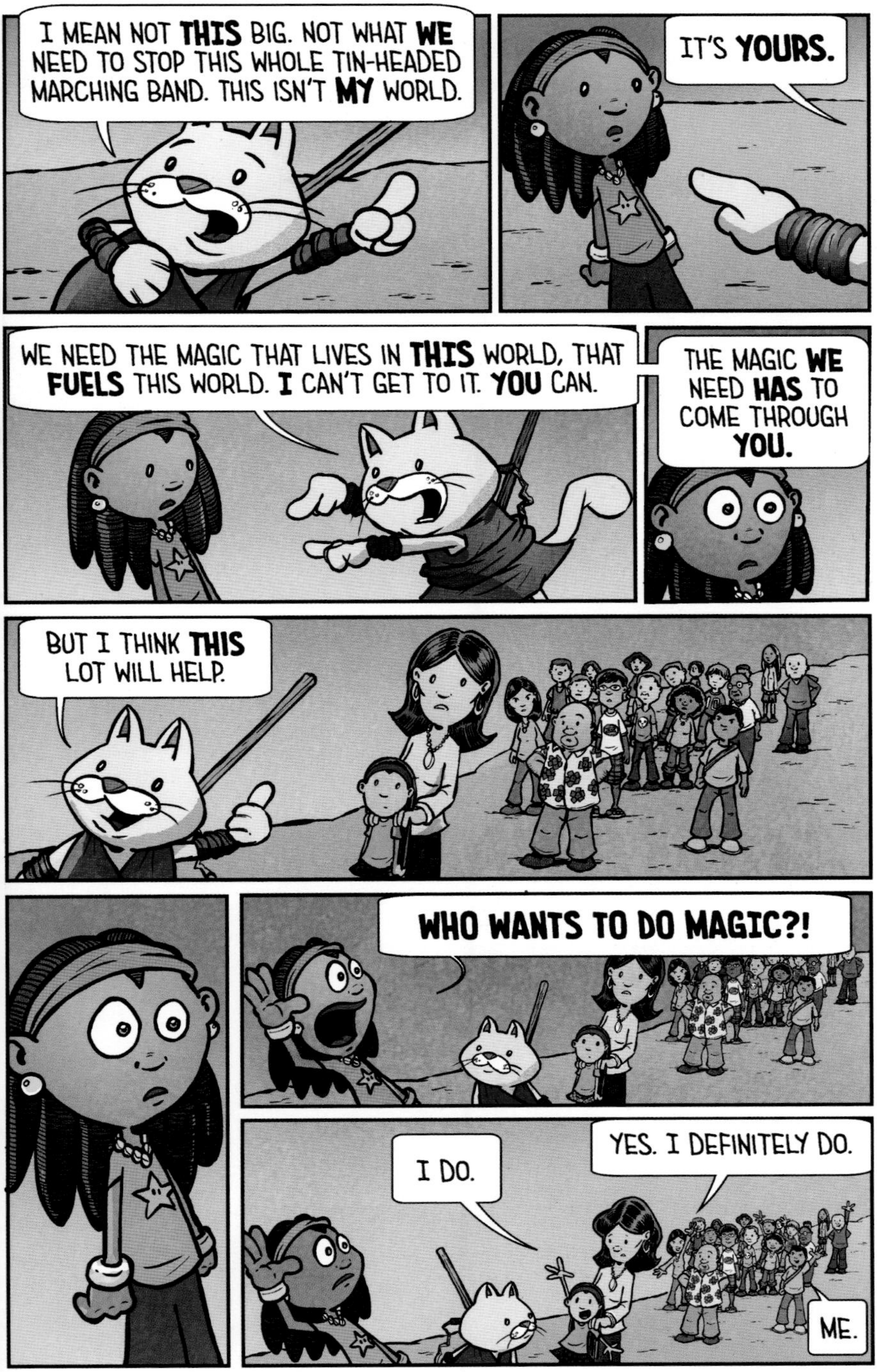
I MEAN NOT THIS BIG. NOT WHAT WE NEED TO STOP THIS WHOLE TIN-HEADED MARCHING BAND. THIS ISN'T MY WORLD.
IT'S YOURS.
WE NEED THE MAGIC THAT LIVES IN THIS WORLD, THAT FUELS THIS WORLD. I CAN'T GET TO IT. YOU CAN.
THE MAGIC WE NEED HAS TO COME THROUGH YOU.
BUT I THINK THIS LOT WILL HELP.
WHO WANTS TO DO MAGIC?!
I DO.
YES. I DEFINITELY DO.
ME.

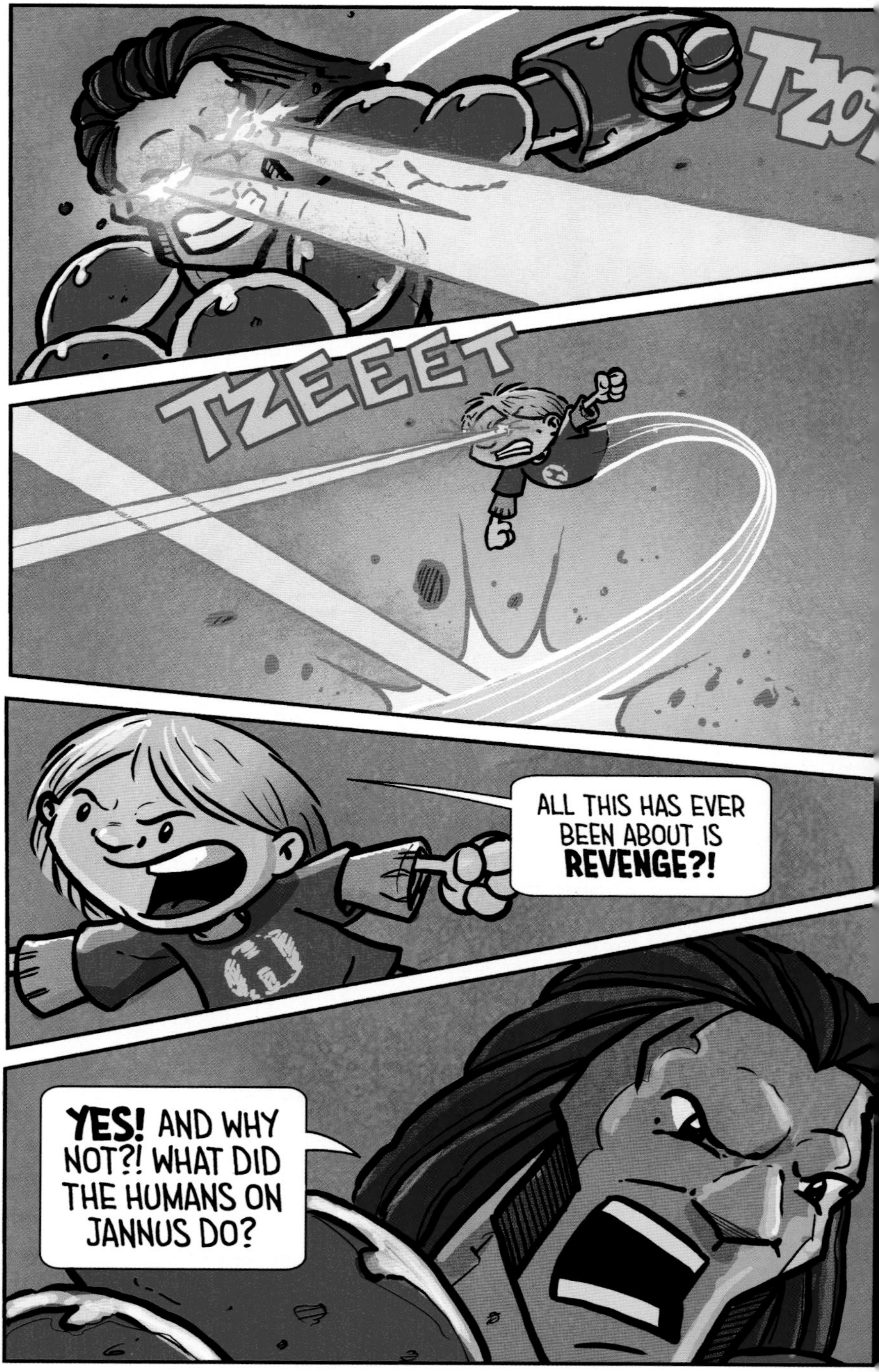
TZOT
TZEEET
ALL THIS HAS EVER BEEN ABOUT IS **REVENGE?!**
YES! AND WHY NOT?! WHAT DID THE HUMANS ON JANNUS DO?

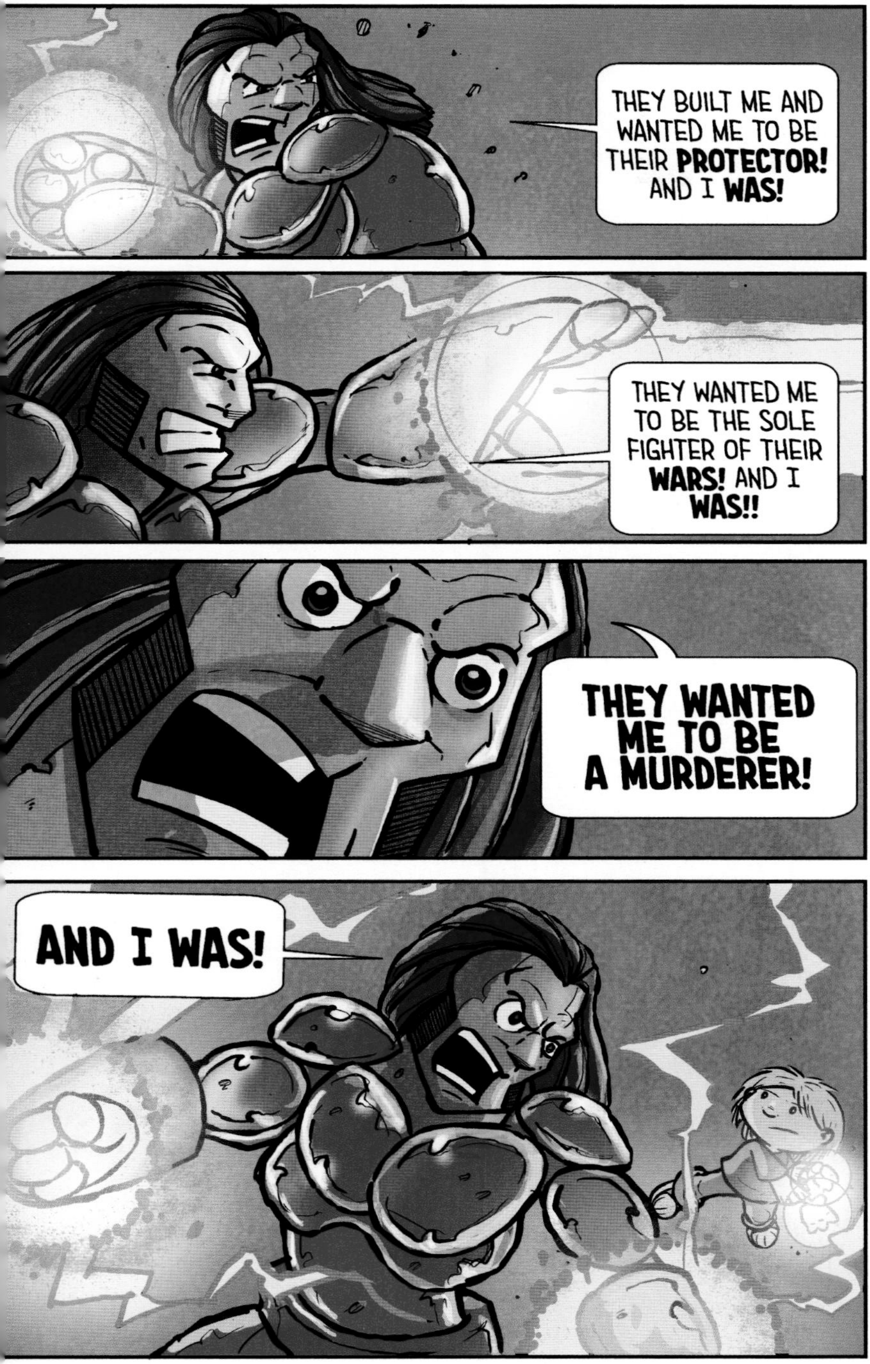
THEY BUILT ME AND WANTED ME TO BE THEIR **PROTECTOR!** AND I **WAS!**
THEY WANTED ME TO BE THE SOLE FIGHTER OF THEIR **WARS!** AND I **WAS!!**
THEY WANTED ME TO BE A MURDERER!
AND I WAS!

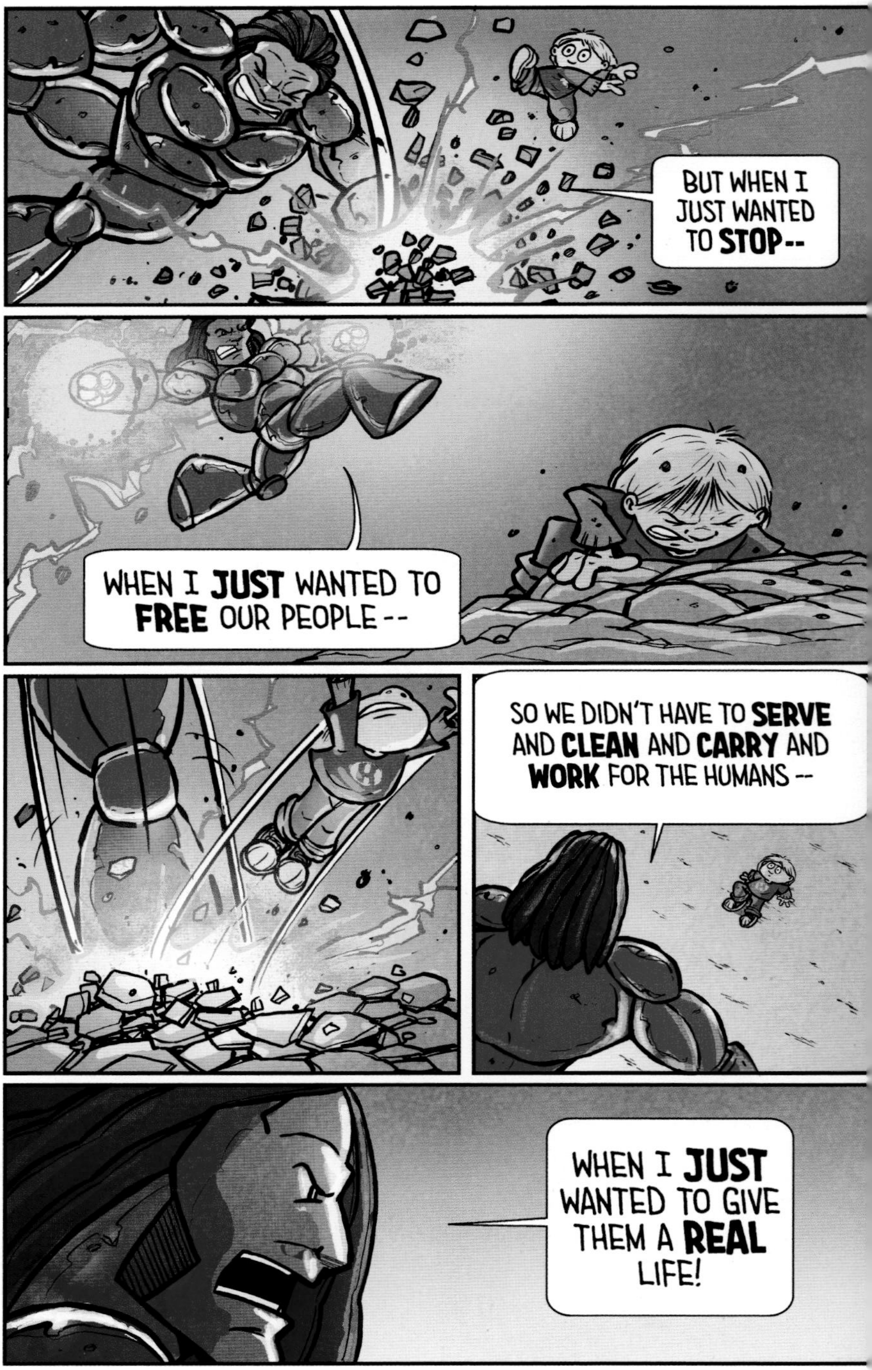
BUT WHEN I JUST WANTED TO **STOP**--
WHEN I **JUST** WANTED TO **FREE** OUR PEOPLE--
SO WE DIDN'T HAVE TO **SERVE** AND **CLEAN** AND **CARRY** AND **WORK** FOR THE HUMANS--
WHEN I **JUST** WANTED TO GIVE THEM A **REAL** LIFE!

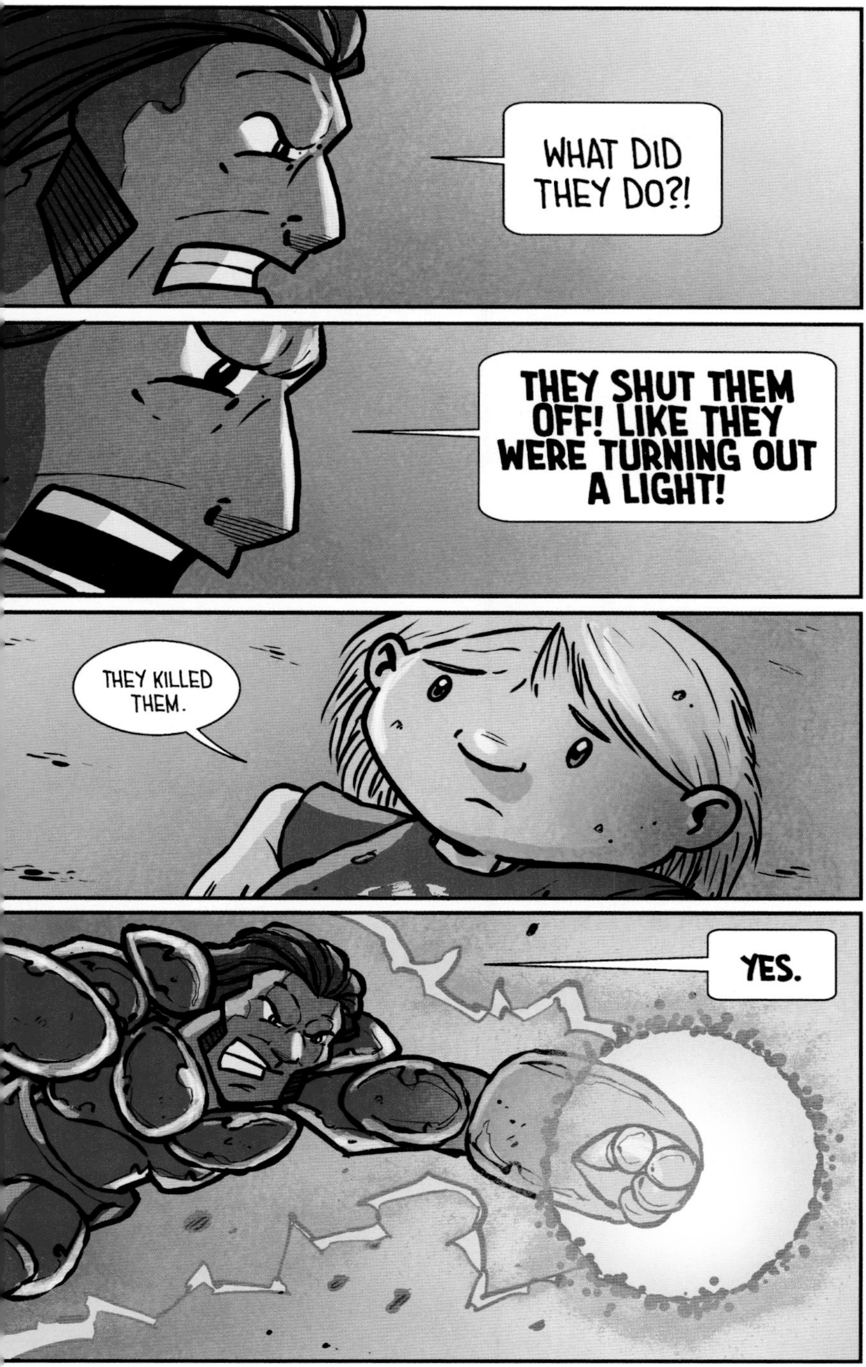
WHAT DID THEY DO?!
THEY SHUT THEM OFF! LIKE THEY WERE TURNING OUT A LIGHT!
THEY KILLED THEM.
YES.

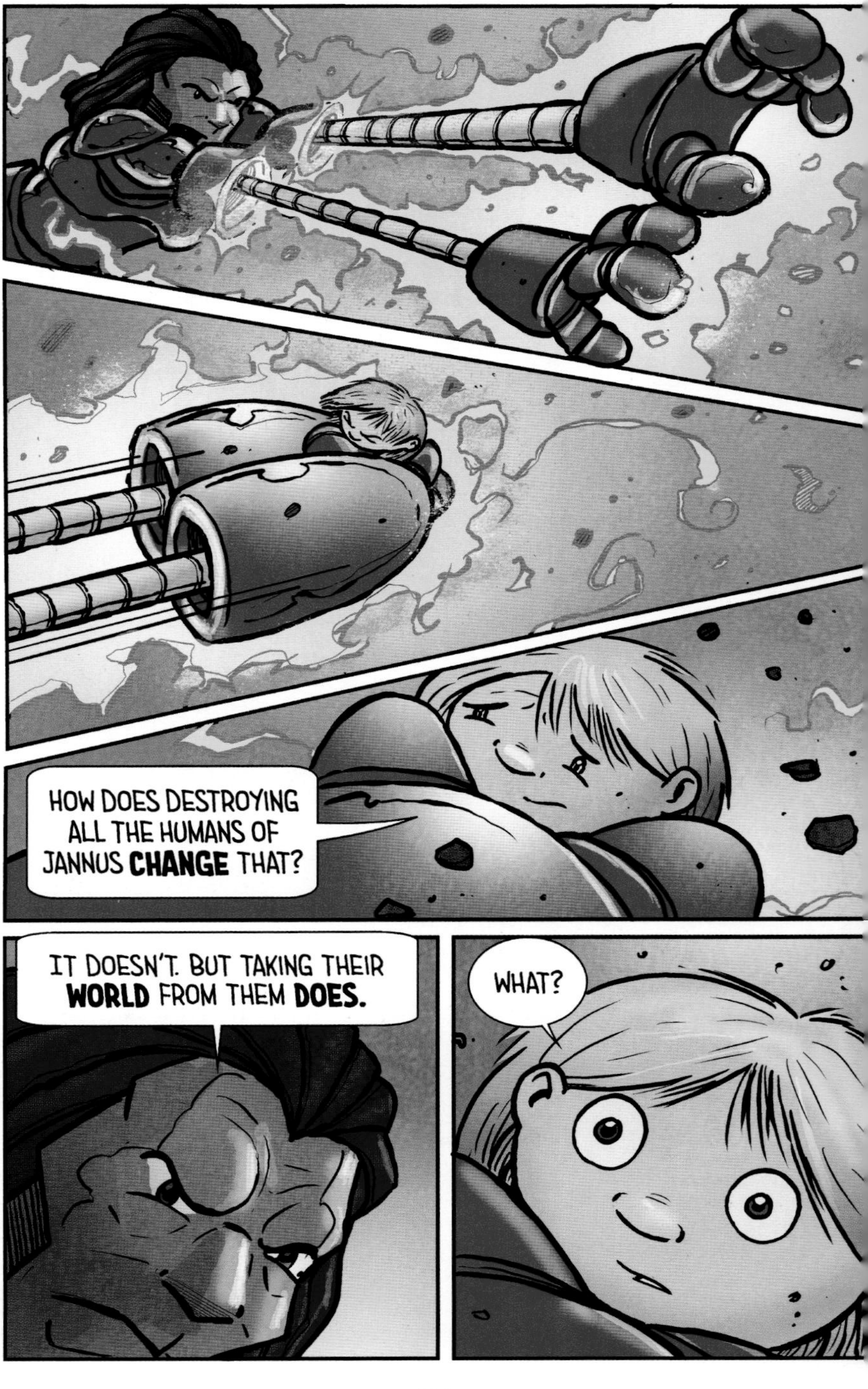
HOW DOES DESTROYING ALL THE HUMANS OF JANNUS **CHANGE** THAT?
IT DOESN'T. BUT TAKING THEIR **WORLD** FROM THEM **DOES.**
WHAT?

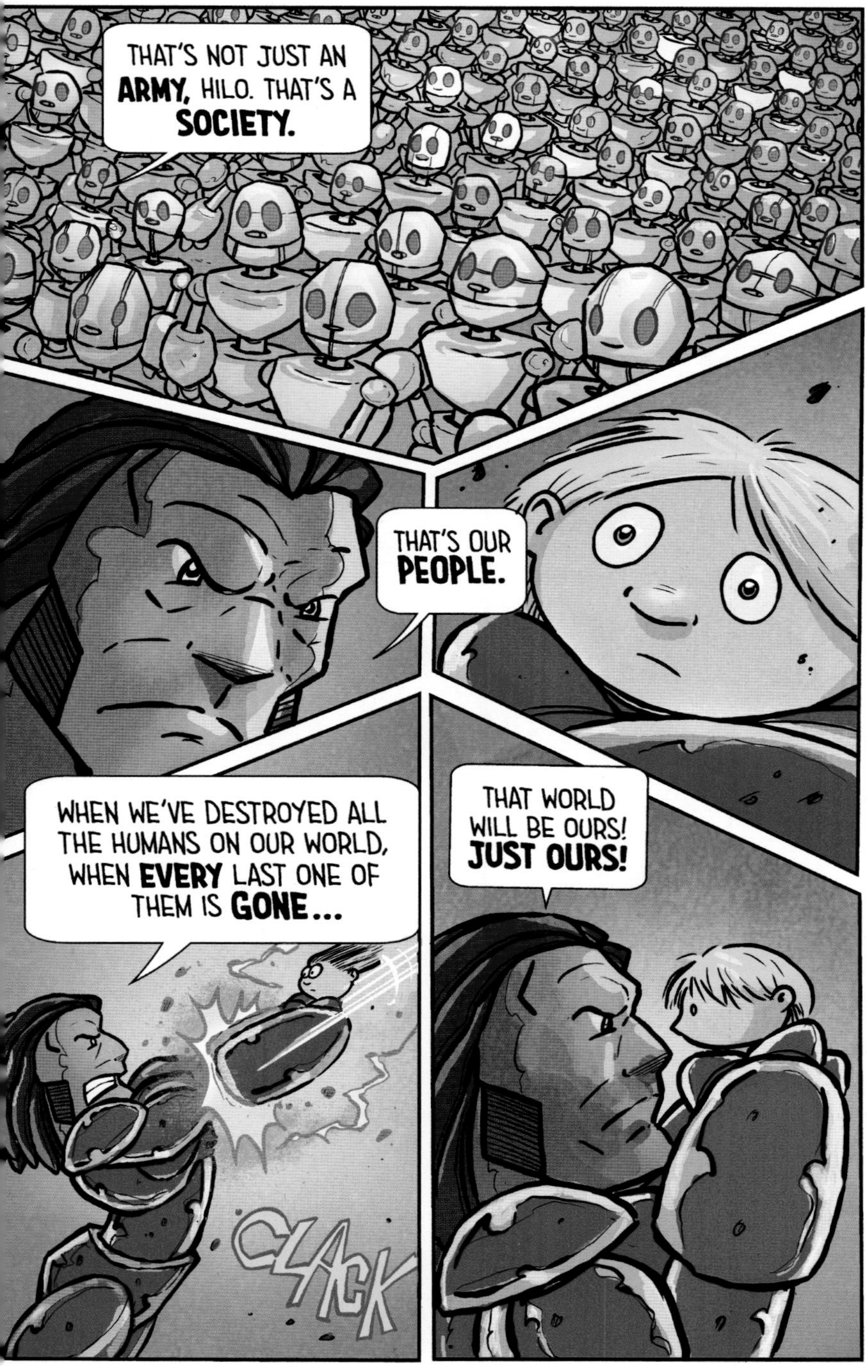

THAT'S NOT JUST AN ARMY, HILO. THAT'S A SOCIETY.
THAT'S OUR PEOPLE.
WHEN WE'VE DESTROYED ALL THE HUMANS ON OUR WORLD, WHEN EVERY LAST ONE OF THEM IS GONE...
CLACK
THAT WORLD WILL BE OURS! JUST OURS!

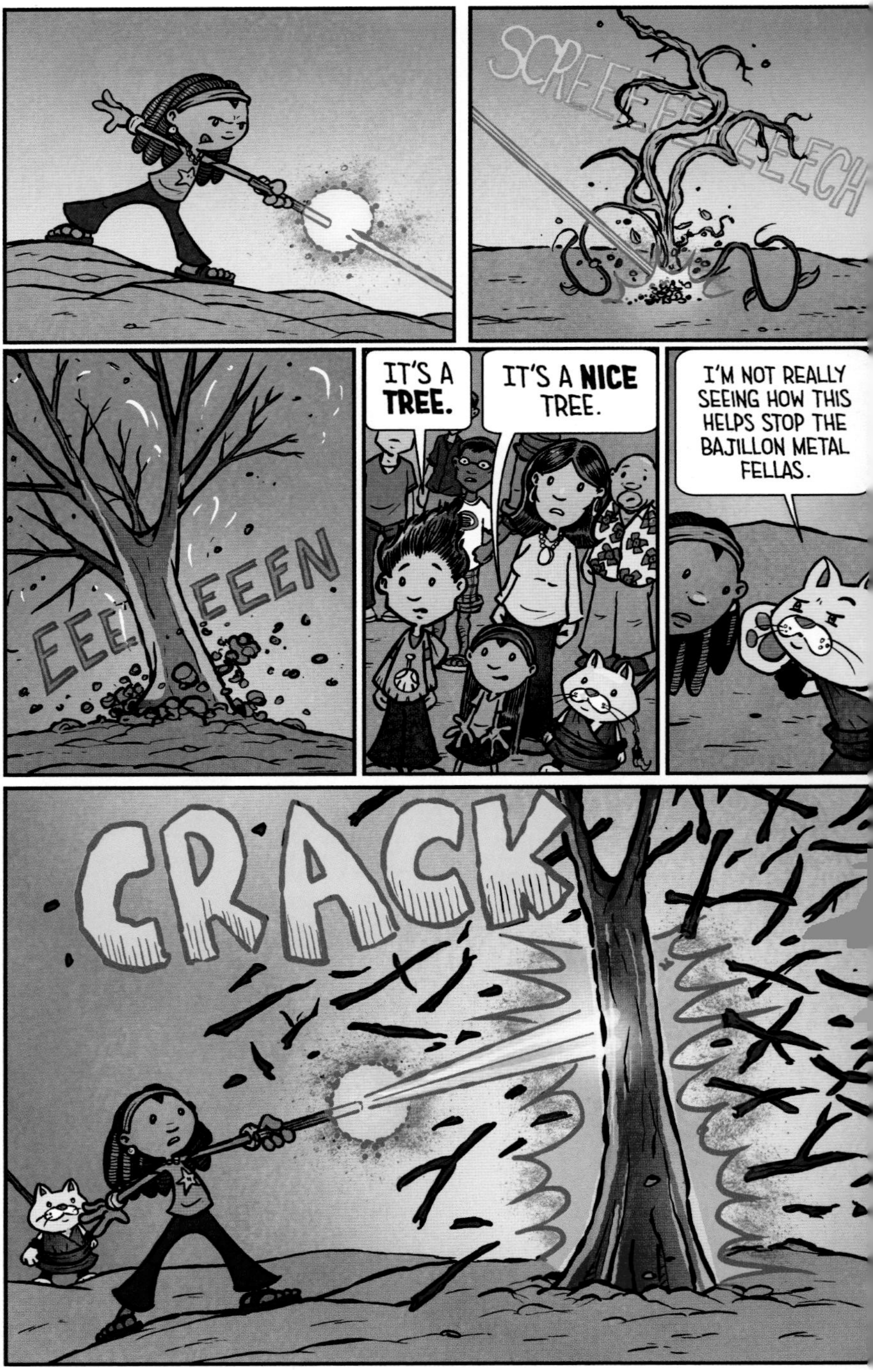
SCREEEEEEEEEEECH
EEEEEEEN
IT'S A **TREE.**
IT'S A **NICE** TREE.
I'M NOT REALLY SEEING HOW THIS HELPS STOP THE BAJILLON METAL FELLAS.
CRACK

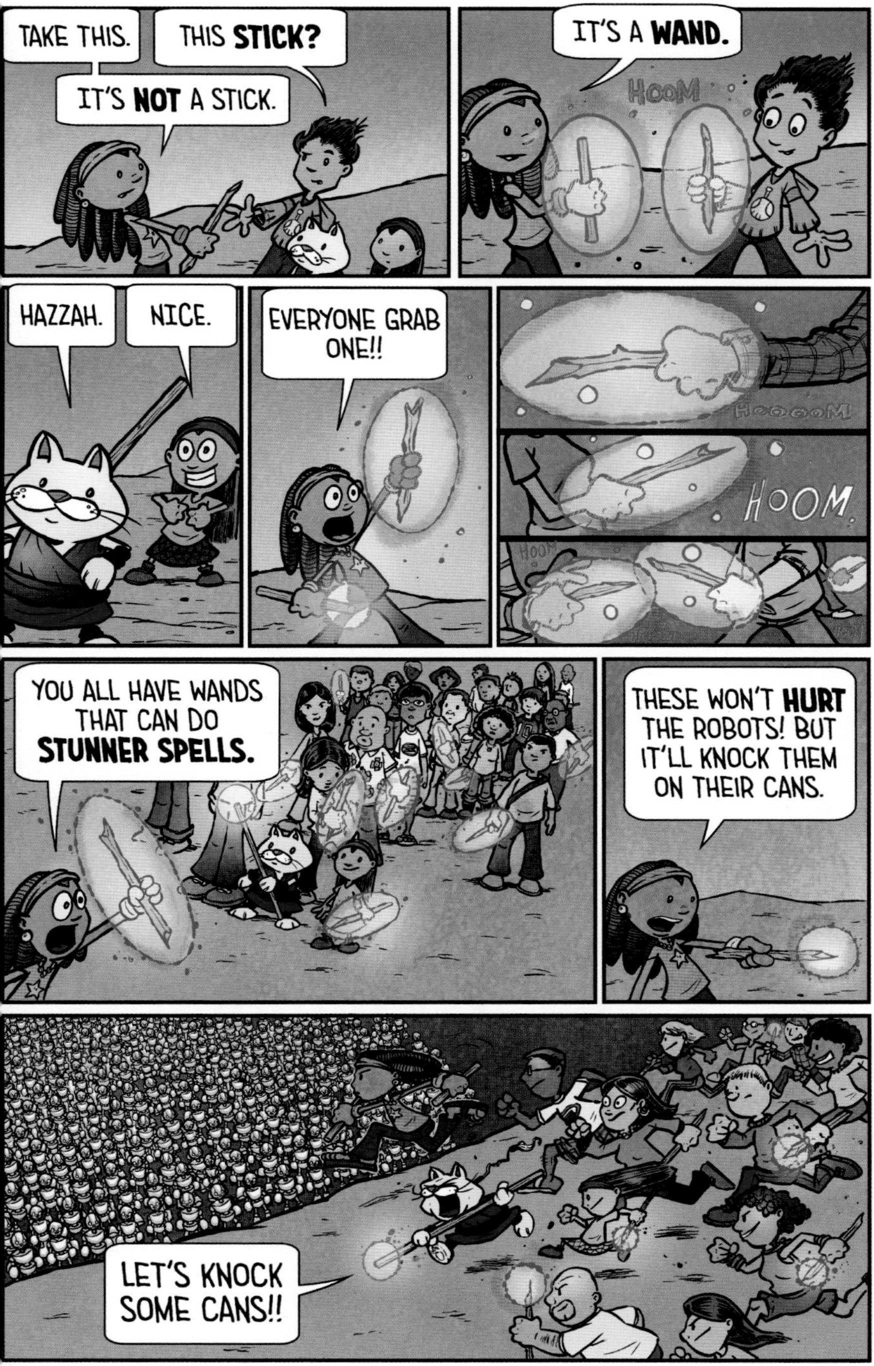
TAKE THIS.
THIS STICK?
IT'S NOT A STICK.
IT'S A WAND.
HOOM
HAZZAH.
NICE.
EVERYONE GRAB ONE!!
HOOOOM
HOOM.
HOOM
YOU ALL HAVE WANDS THAT CAN DO STUNNER SPELLS.
THESE WON'T HURT THE ROBOTS! BUT IT'LL KNOCK THEM ON THEIR CANS.
LET'S KNOCK SOME CANS!!

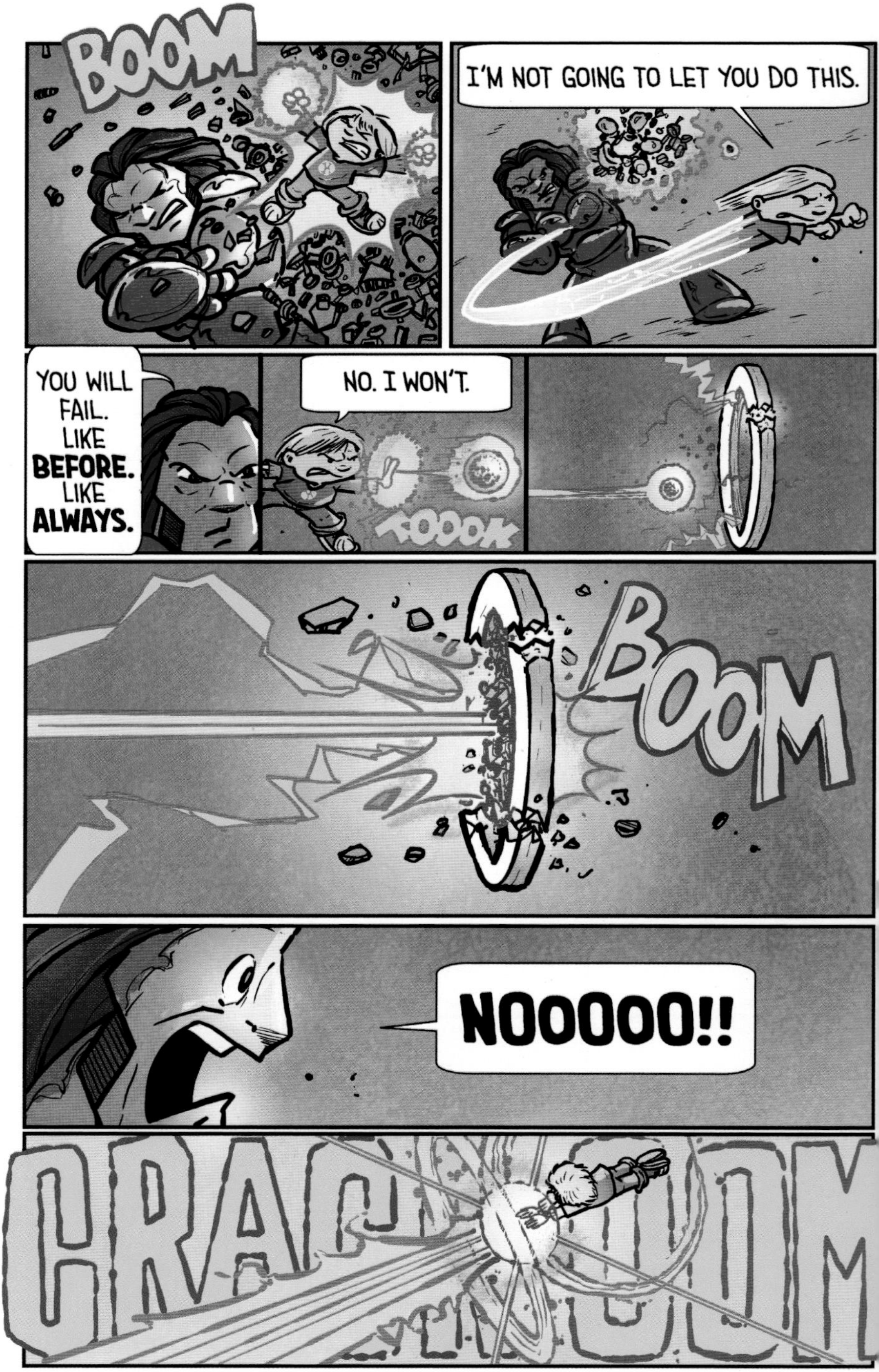
BOOM
I'M NOT GOING TO LET YOU DO THIS.
YOU WILL FAIL. LIKE **BEFORE.** LIKE **ALWAYS.**
NO. I WON'T.
TOOOK
BOOM
NOOOOO!!

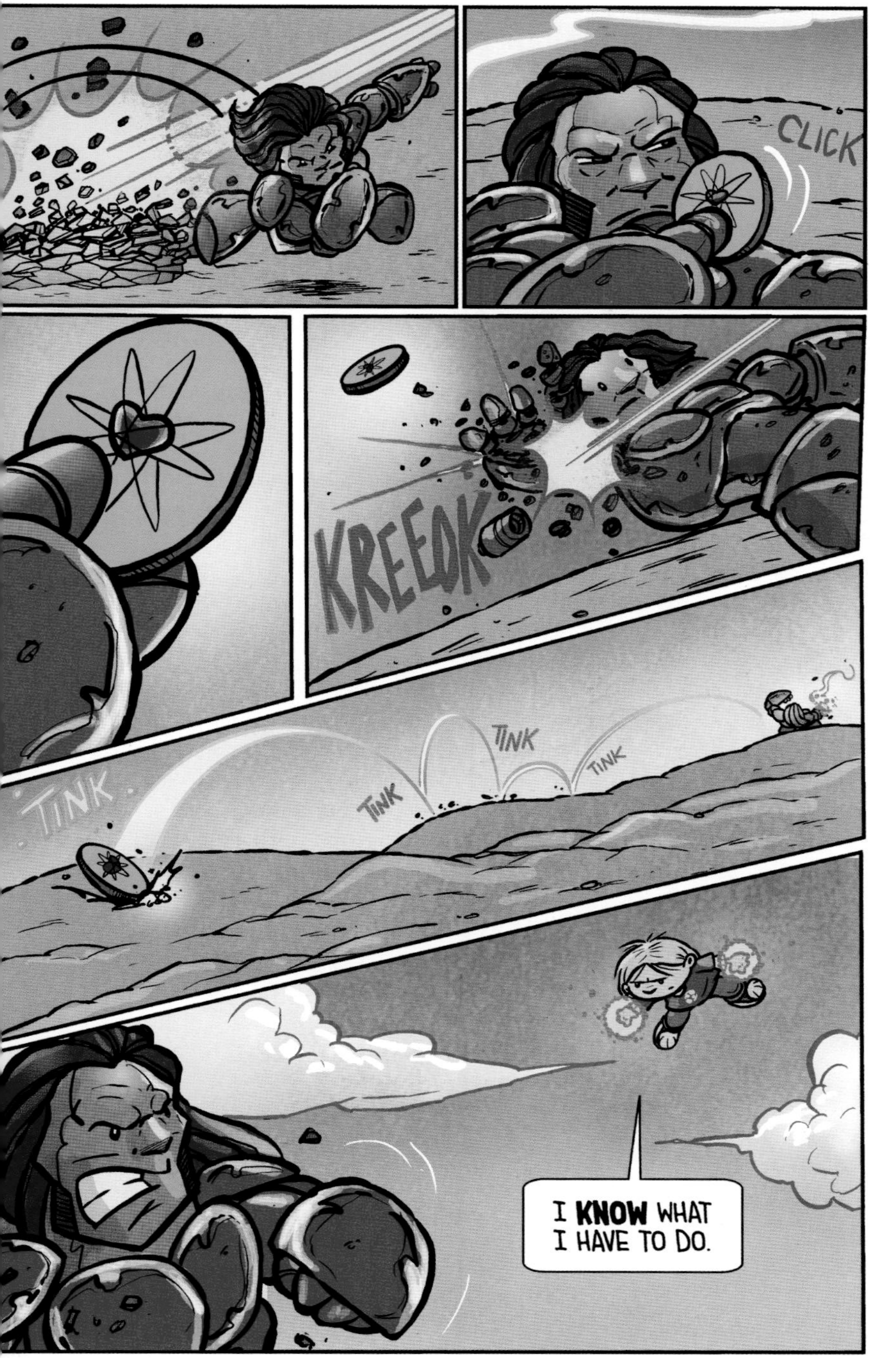
CLICK
KREEOK
TINK
TINK
TINK
TINK
I KNOW WHAT I HAVE TO DO.

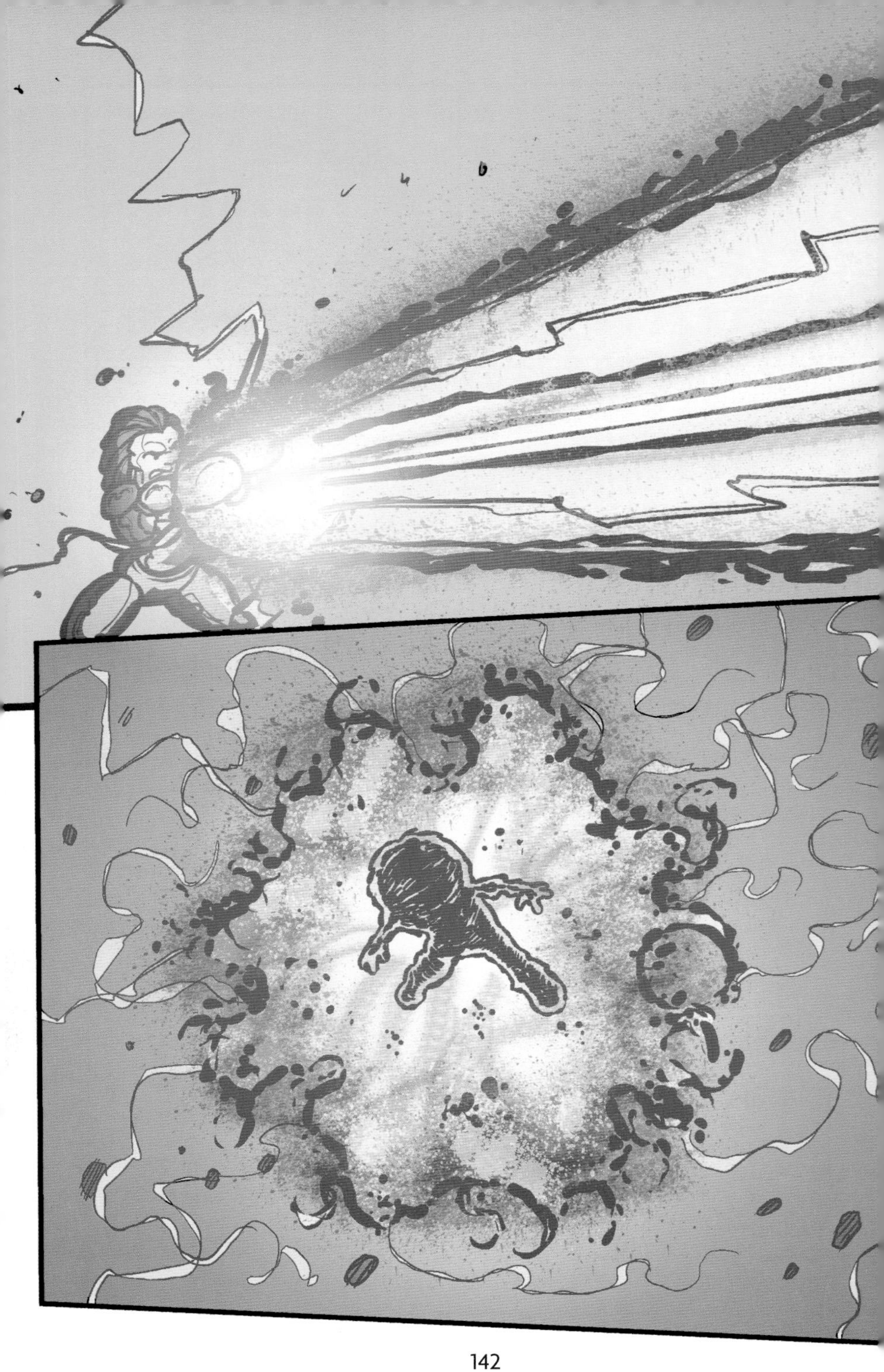

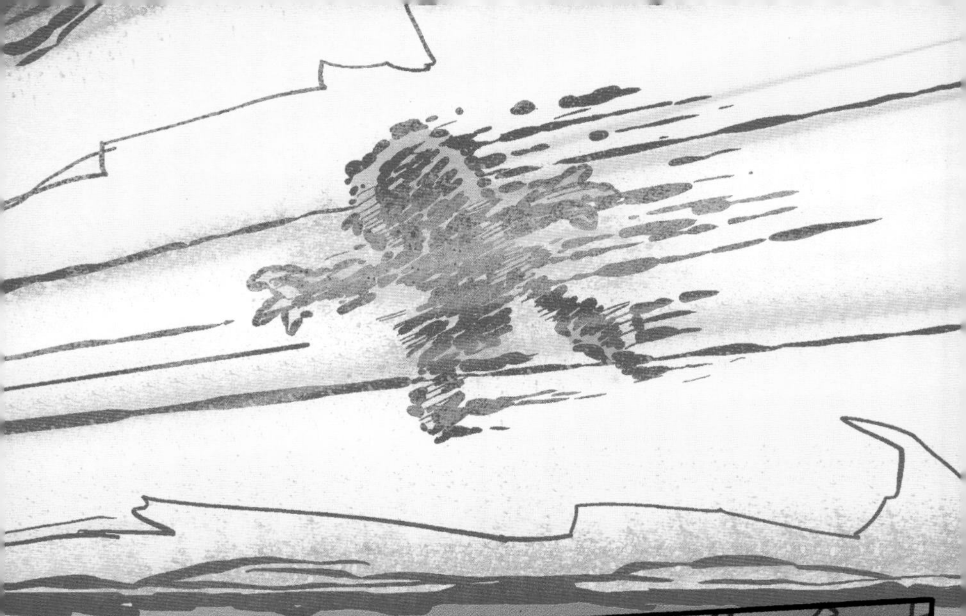

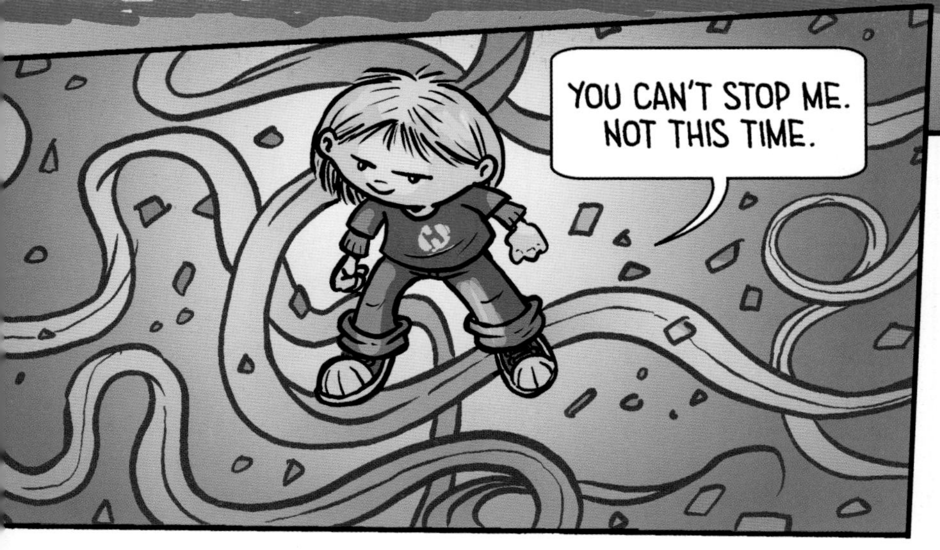
YOU CAN'T STOP ME. NOT THIS TIME.

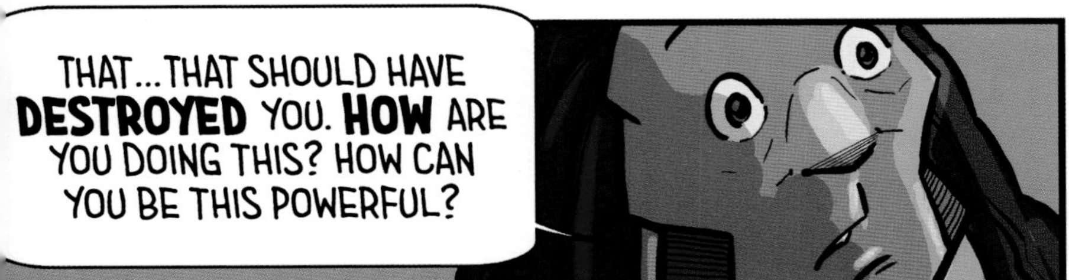
THAT...THAT SHOULD HAVE **DESTROYED** YOU. **HOW** ARE YOU DOING THIS? HOW CAN YOU BE THIS POWERFUL?

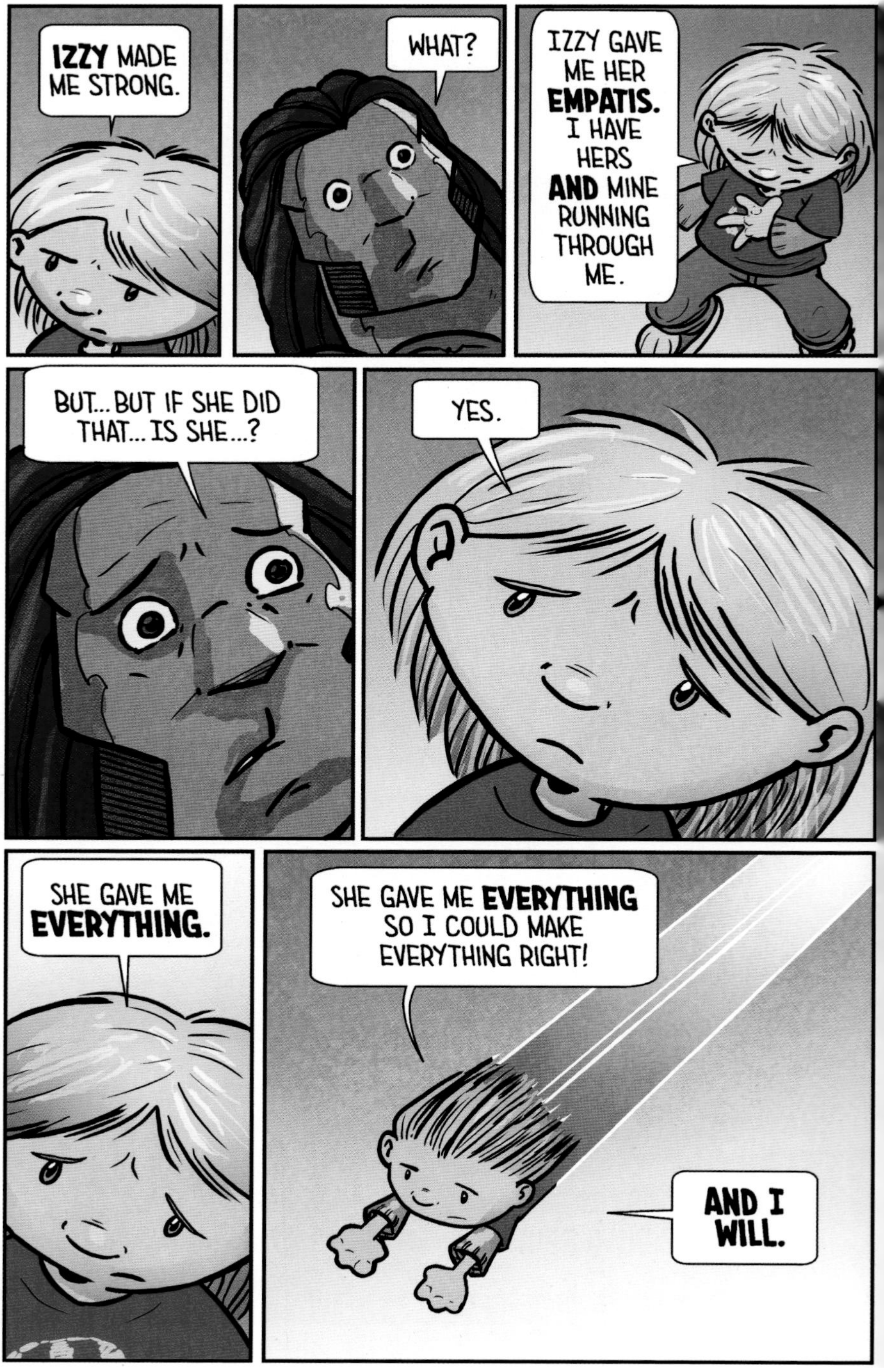
IZZY MADE ME STRONG.
WHAT?
IZZY GAVE ME HER EMPATIS. I HAVE HERS AND MINE RUNNING THROUGH ME.
BUT... BUT IF SHE DID THAT... IS SHE...?
YES.
SHE GAVE ME EVERYTHING.
SHE GAVE ME EVERYTHING SO I COULD MAKE EVERYTHING RIGHT!
AND I WILL.

CHAPTER 9

ALL THE PIECES FIT

DON'T BE SCARED! DON'T STOP! THESE STUNS WON'T HURT THEM! YOU'RE ALL DOING **GREAT!**

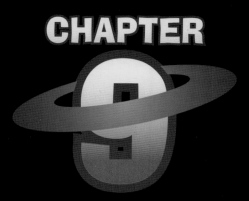

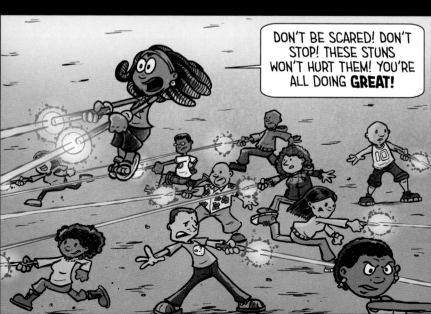

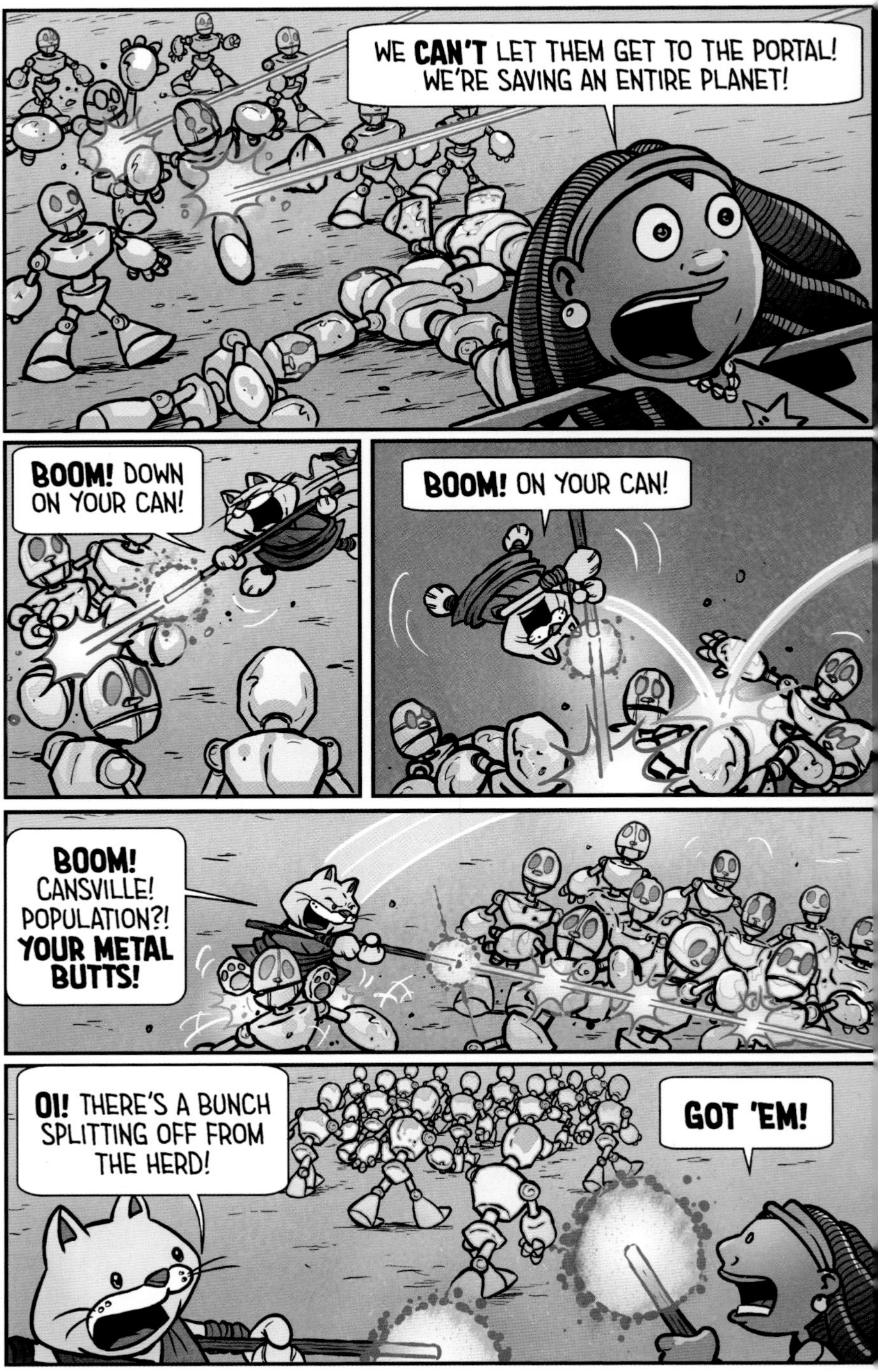
WE CAN'T LET THEM GET TO THE PORTAL! WE'RE SAVING AN ENTIRE PLANET!
BOOM! DOWN ON YOUR CAN!
BOOM! ON YOUR CAN!
BOOM! CANSVILLE! POPULATION?! YOUR METAL BUTTS!
OI! THERE'S A BUNCH SPLITTING OFF FROM THE HERD!
GOT 'EM!

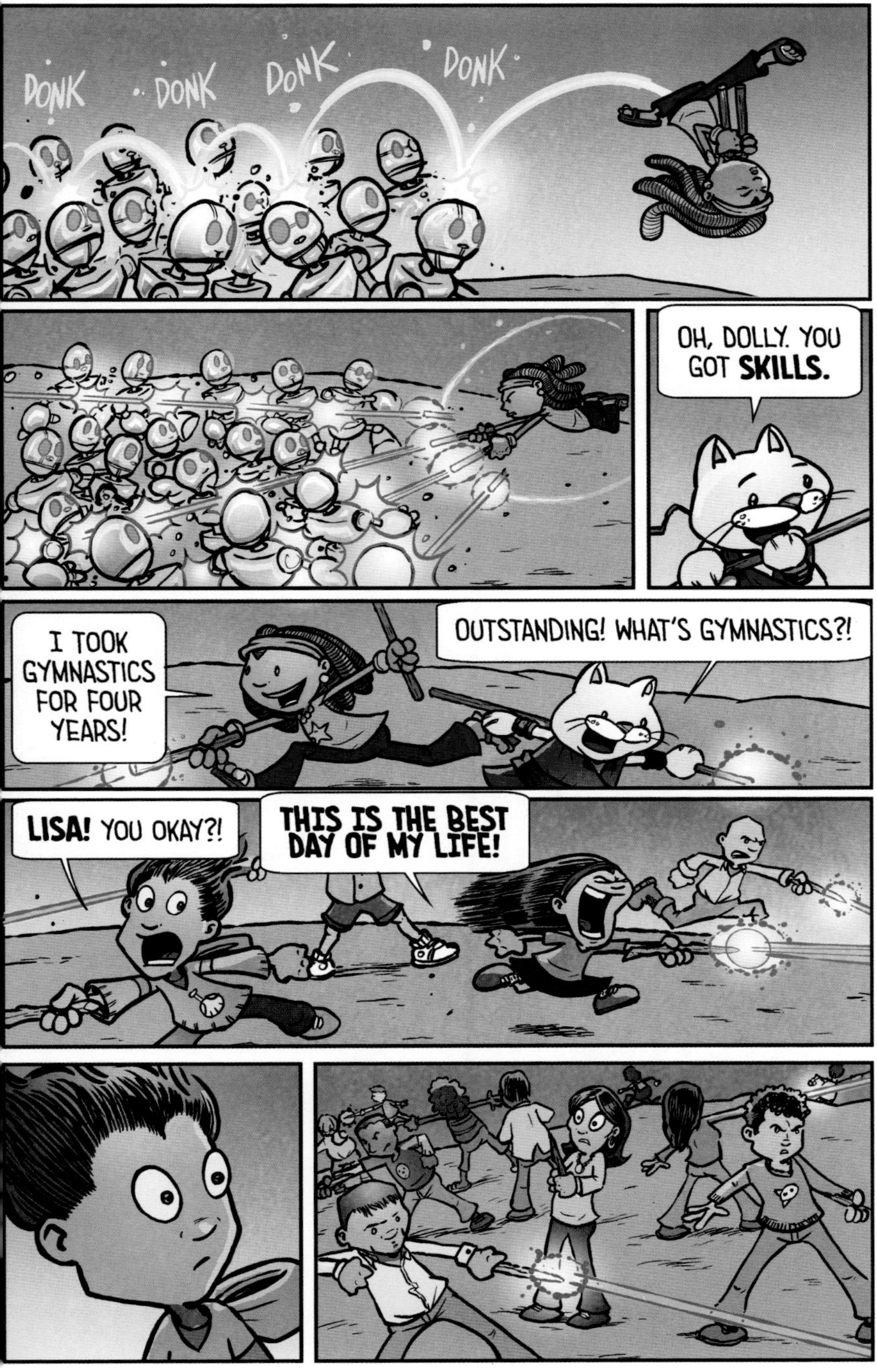
DONK
DONK
DONK
DONK
OH, DOLLY. YOU GOT **SKILLS.**
I TOOK GYMNASTICS FOR FOUR YEARS!
OUTSTANDING! WHAT'S GYMNASTICS?!
LISA! YOU OKAY?!
THIS IS THE BEST DAY OF MY LIFE!

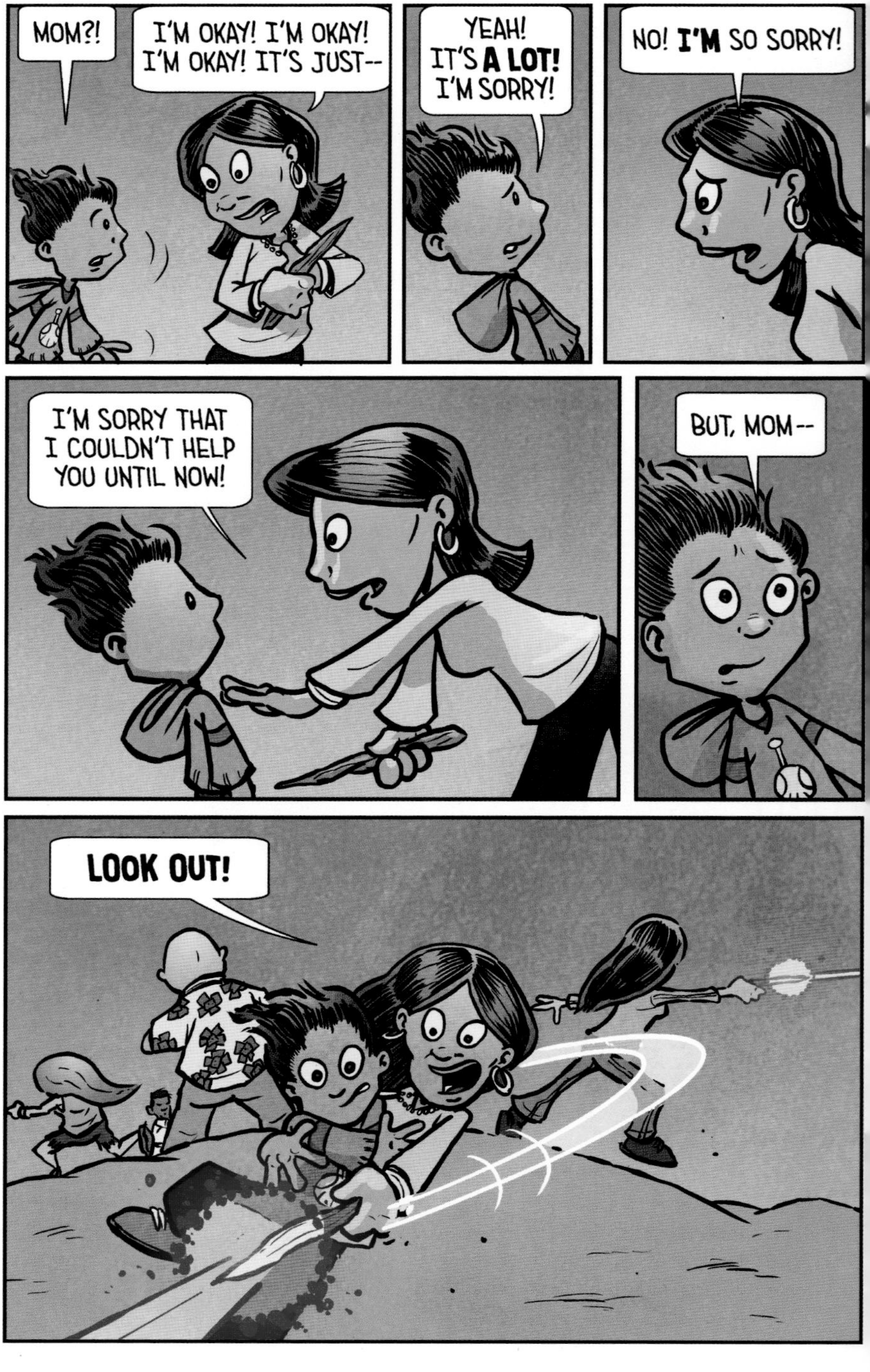
MOM?!
I'M OKAY! I'M OKAY! I'M OKAY! IT'S JUST--
YEAH! IT'S **A LOT!** I'M SORRY!
NO! **I'M** SO SORRY!
I'M SORRY THAT I COULDN'T HELP YOU UNTIL NOW!
BUT, MOM--
LOOK OUT!

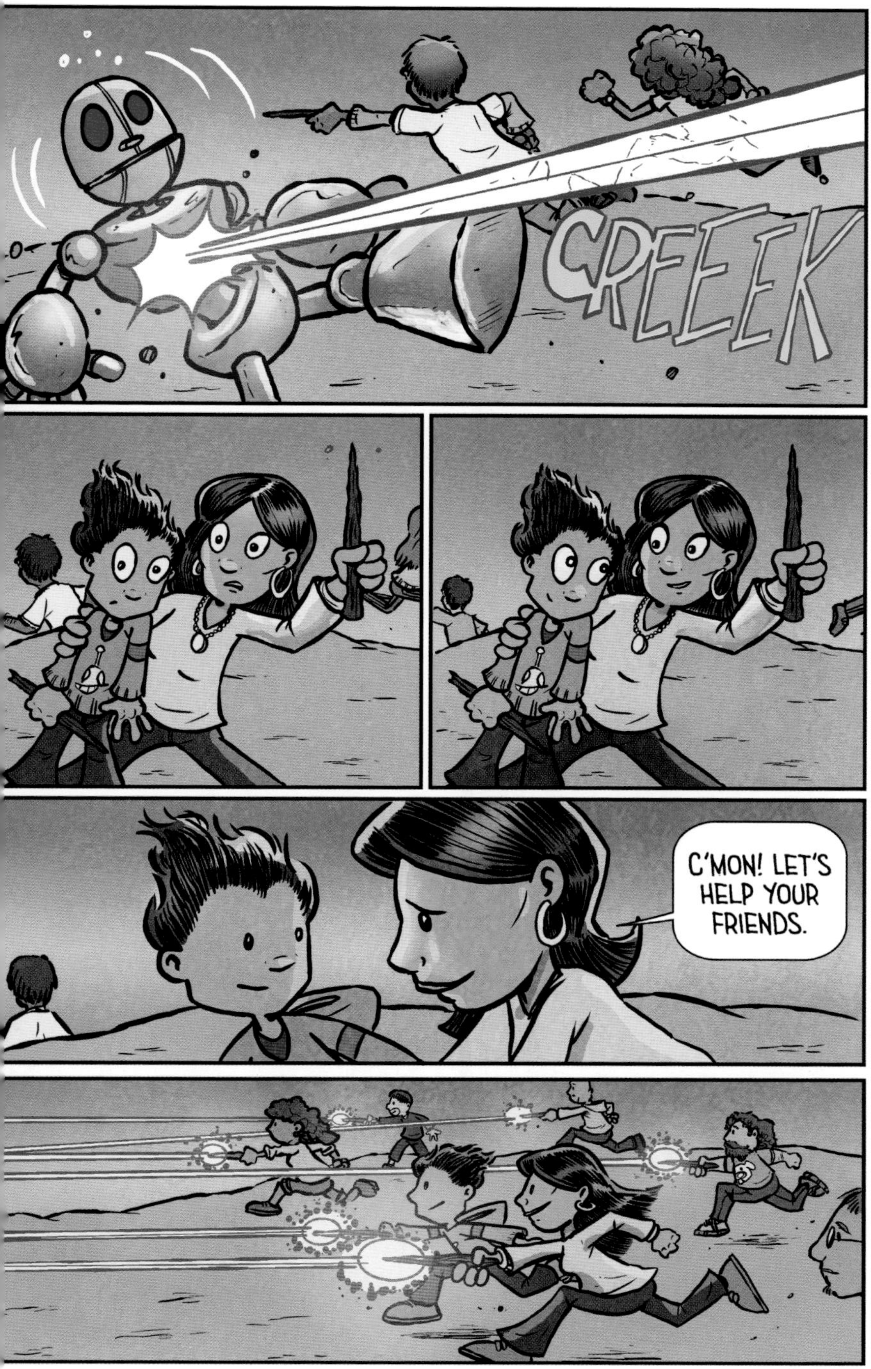
CREEEK
C'MON! LET'S HELP YOUR FRIENDS.

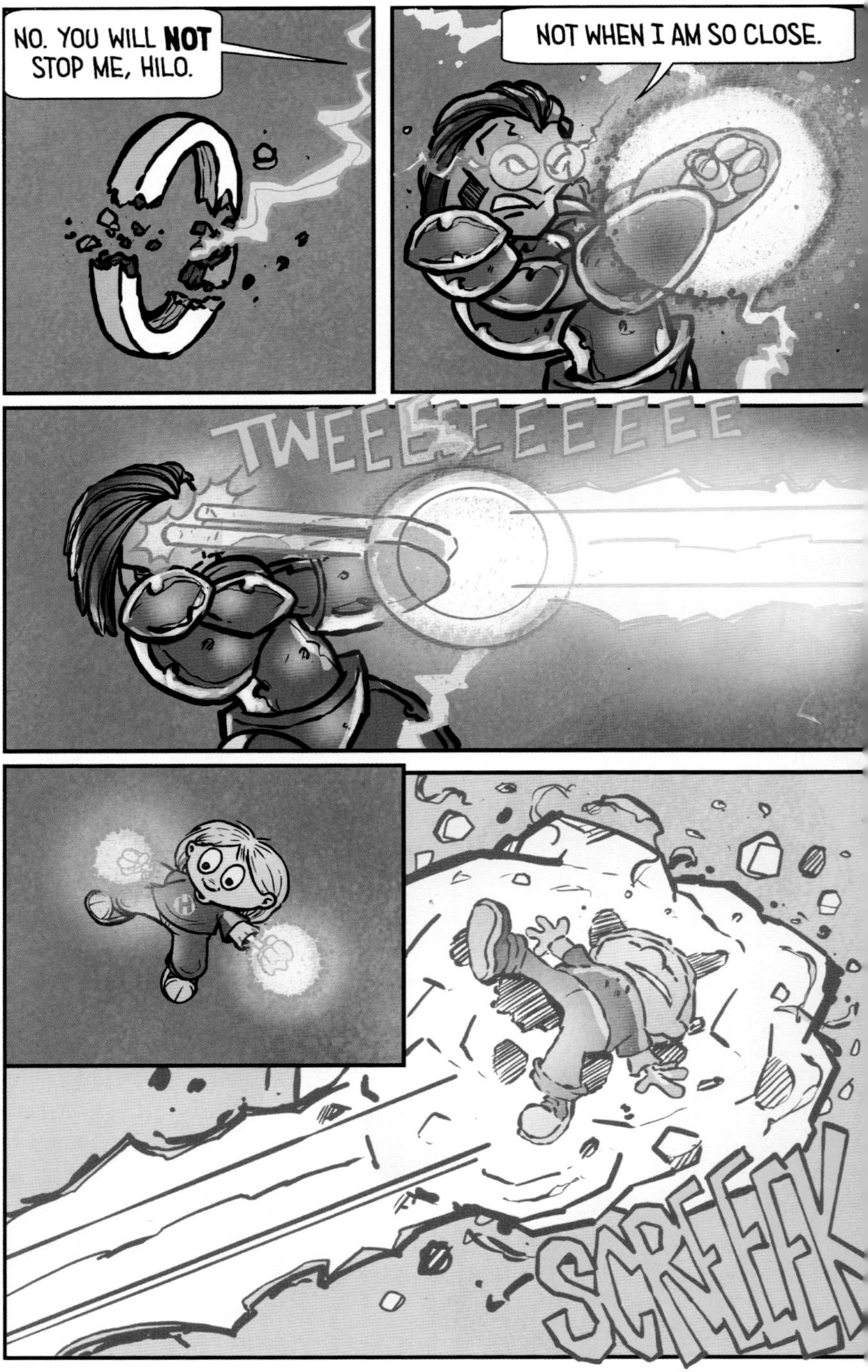
NO. YOU WILL **NOT** STOP ME, HILO.
NOT WHEN I AM SO CLOSE.
TWEEEEEEEEEE
SCREEEK

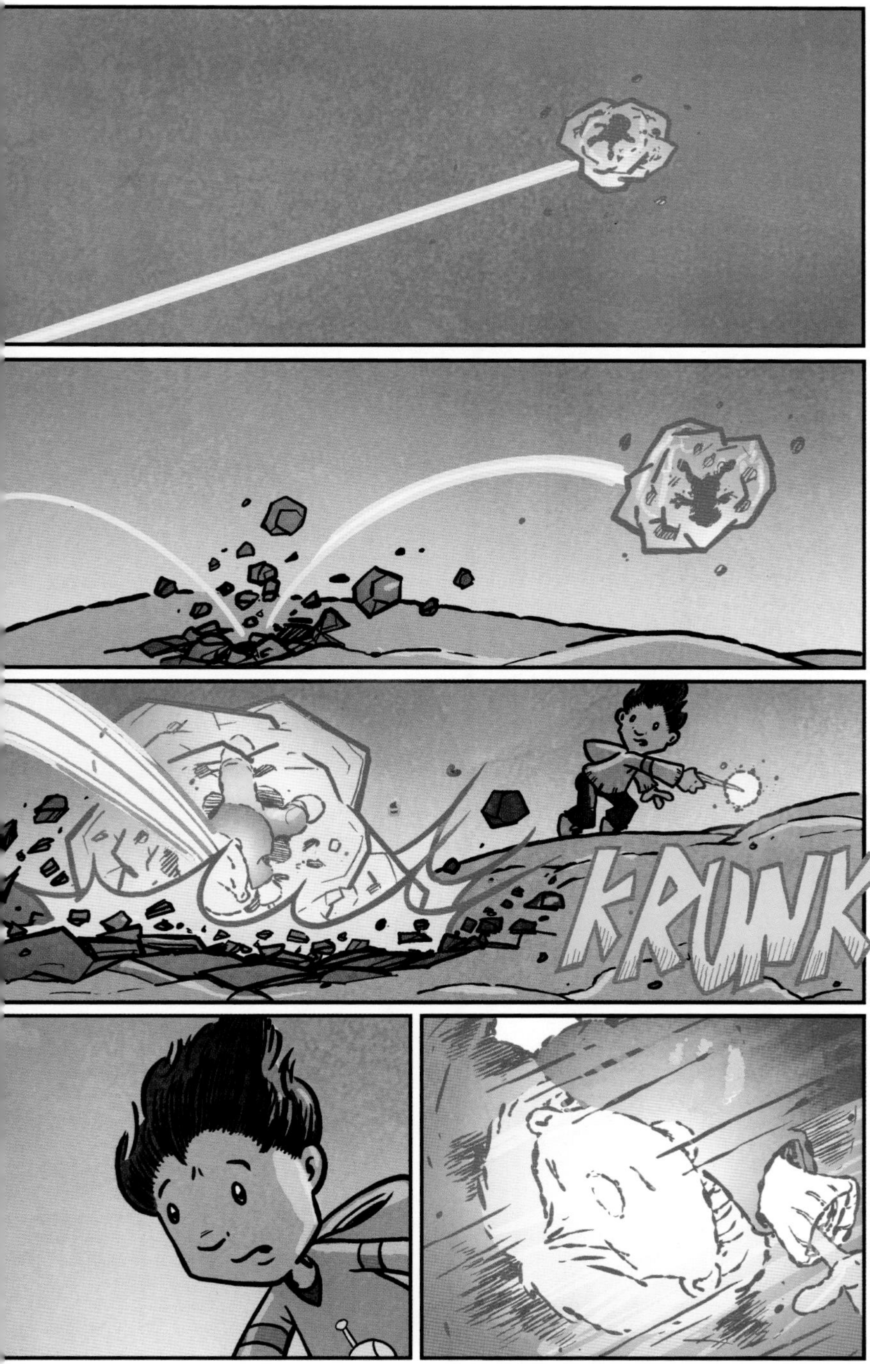
KRUNK

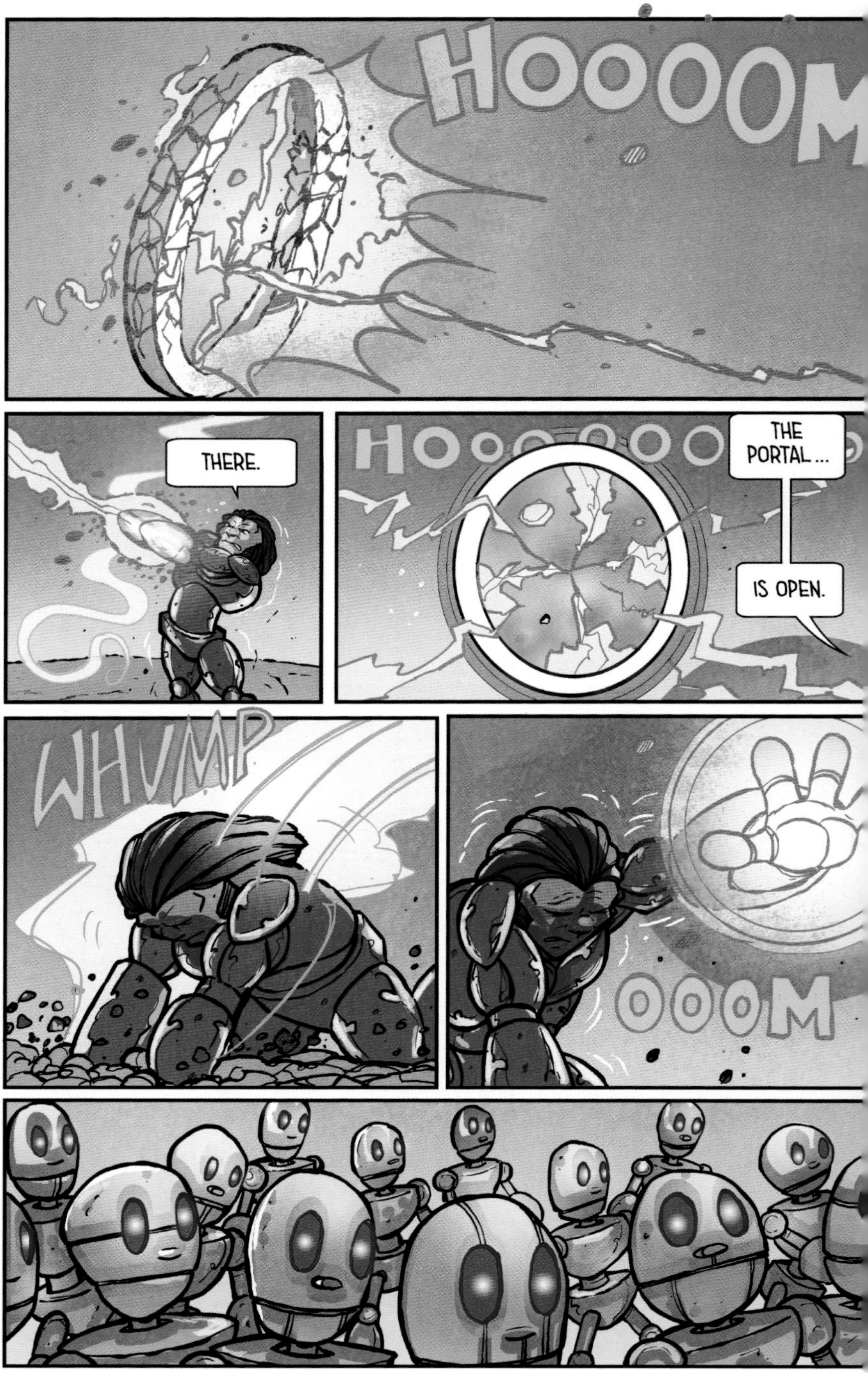
HOOOOM
THERE.
HOOOOOOOO
THE PORTAL...
IS OPEN.
WHUMP
OOOM

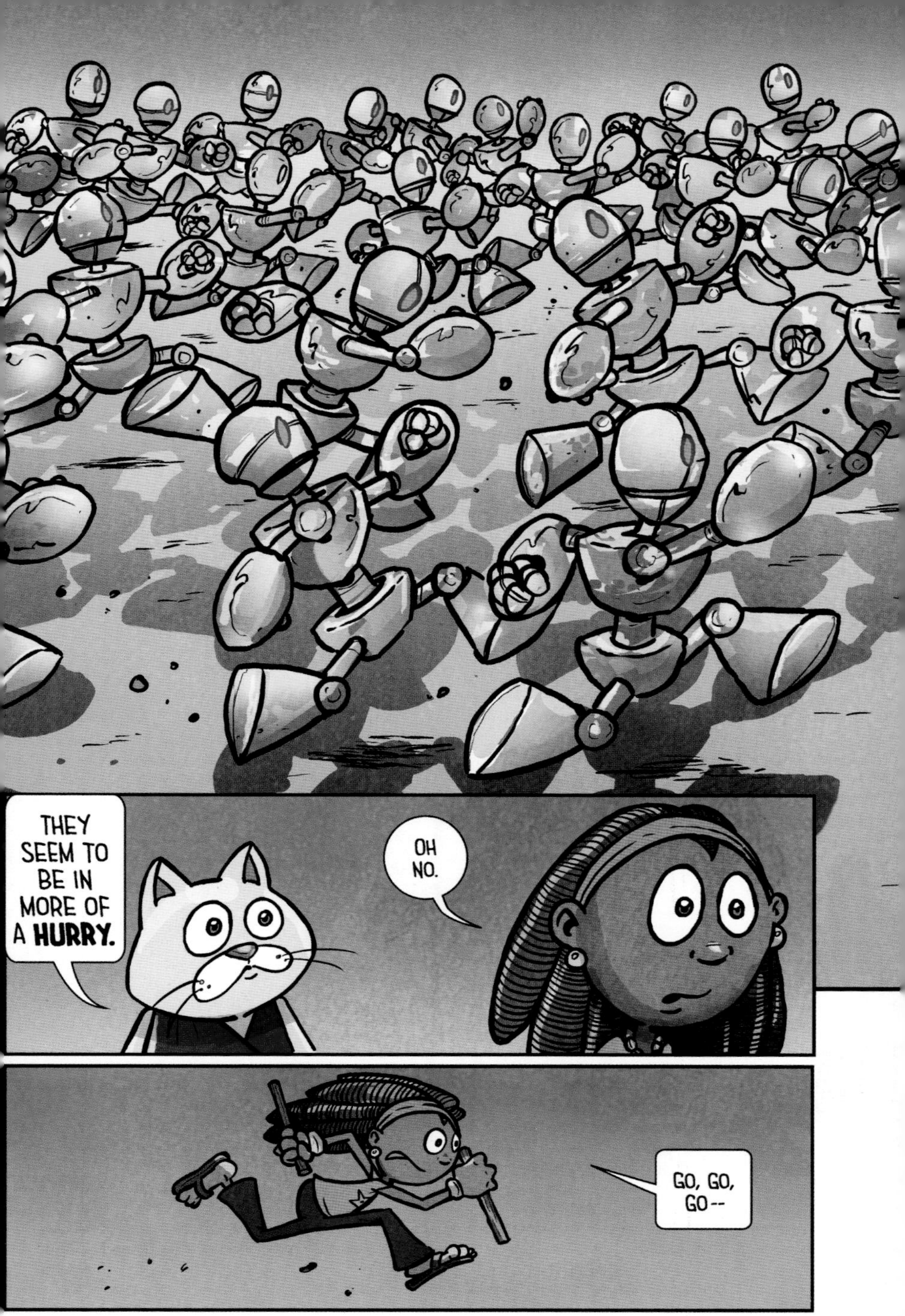
THEY SEEM TO BE IN MORE OF A **HURRY.**
OH NO.
GO, GO, GO--

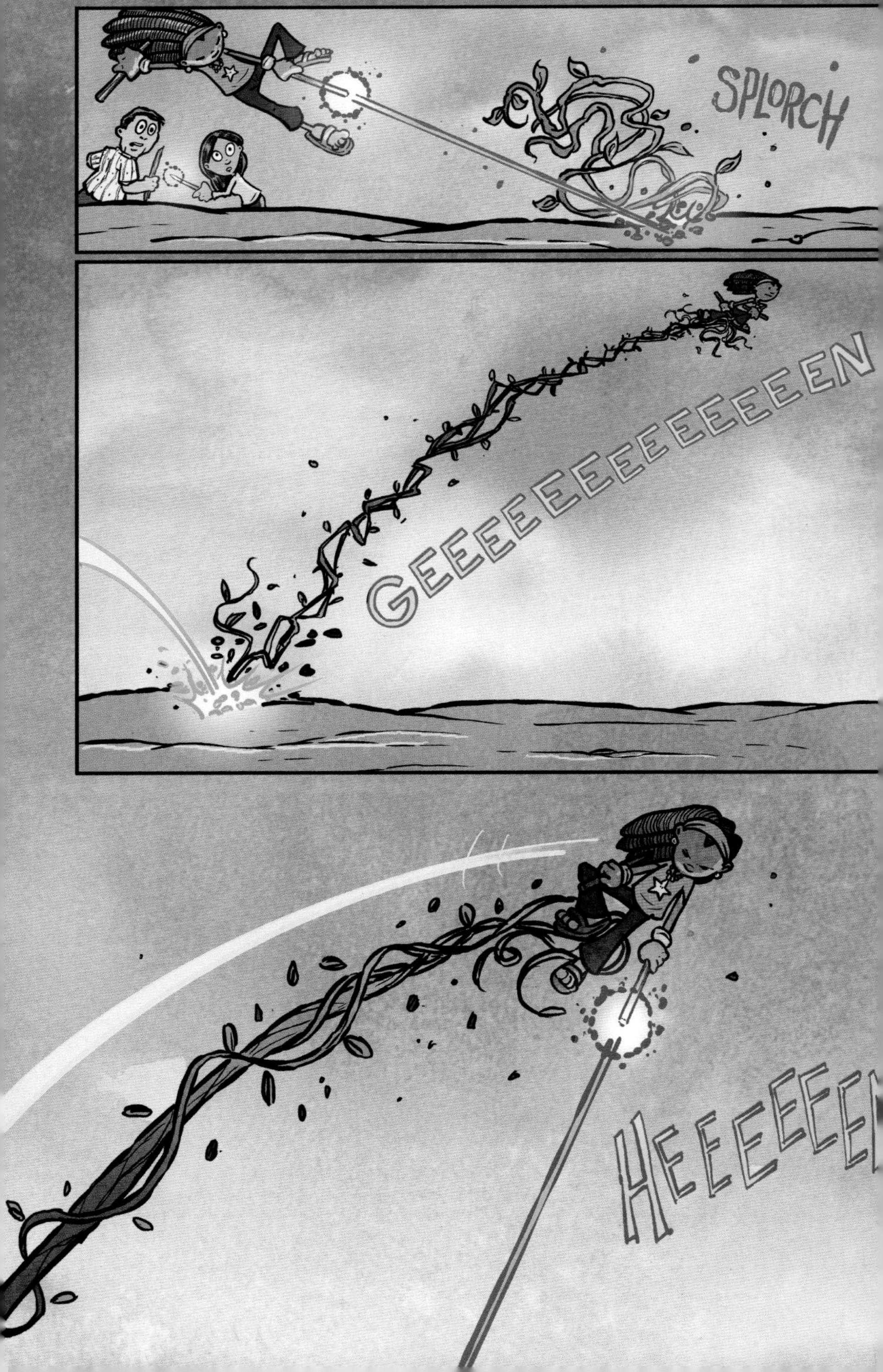
SPLORCH
GEEEEEEEEEEEEEN
HEEEEEE

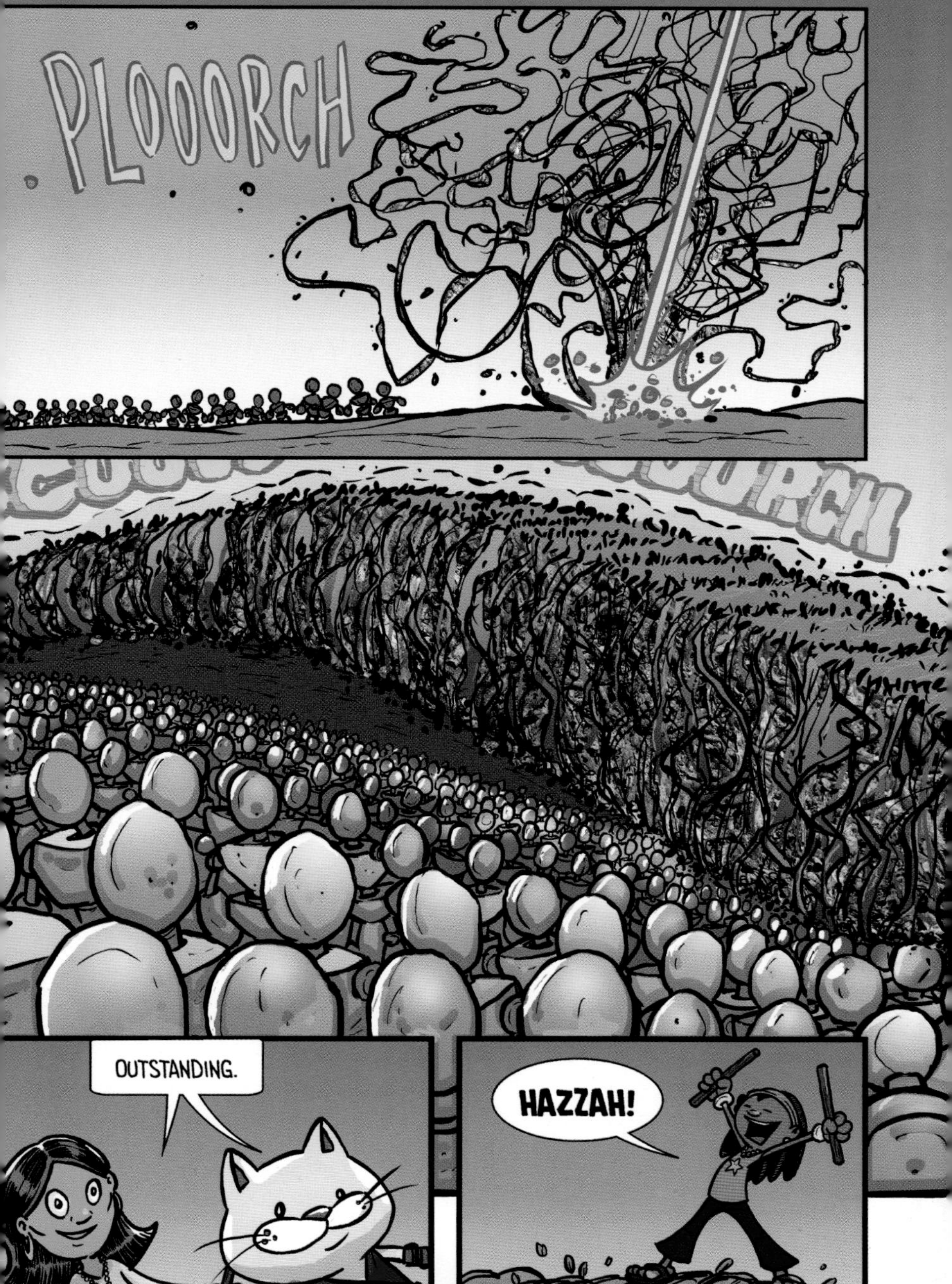
PLOOORCH
OUTSTANDING.
HAZZAH!

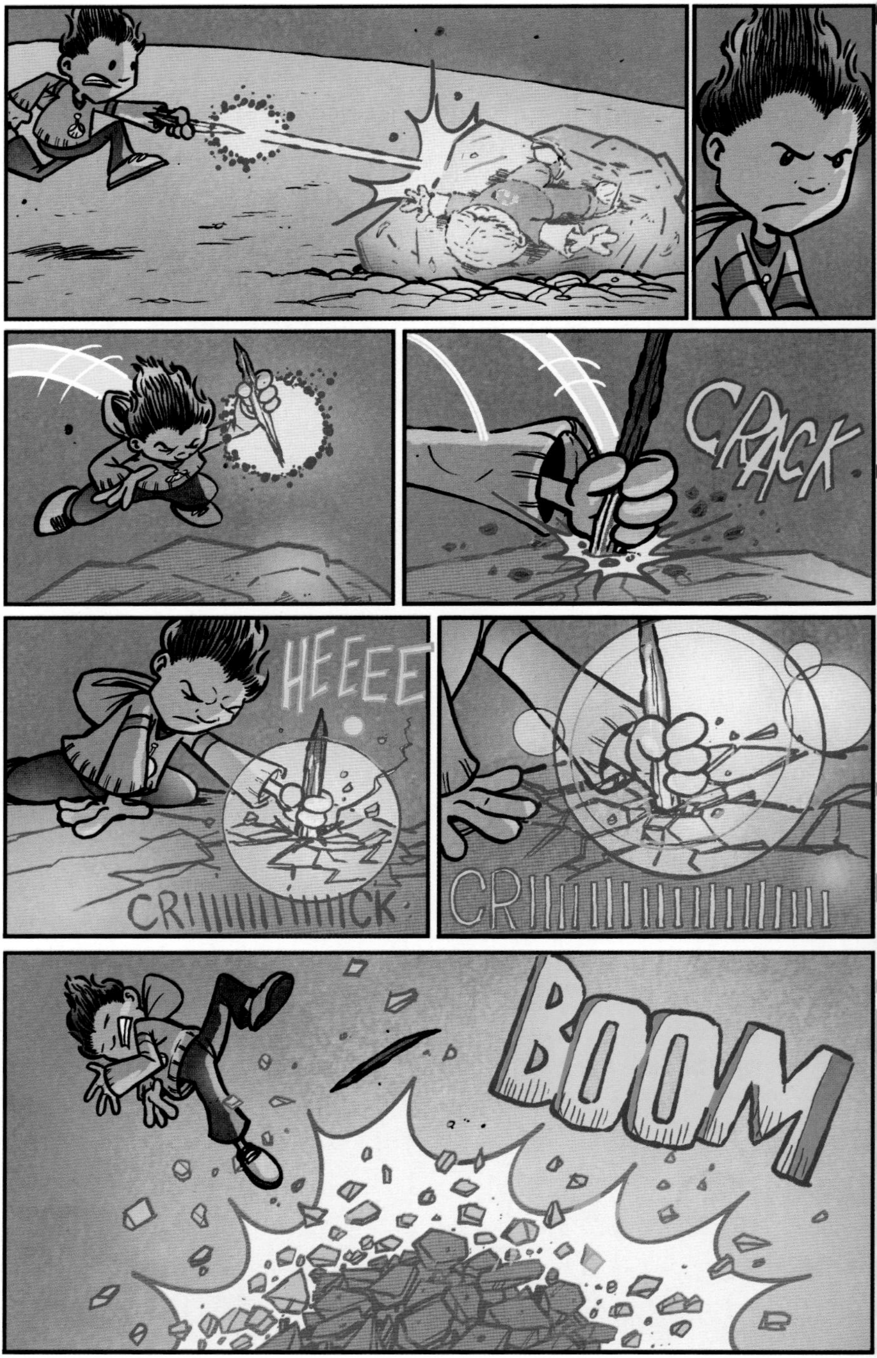
CRACK
HEEEE
CRIIIIIIIIIIIIIIICK
CRIIIIIIIIIIIIIIIIIII
BOOM

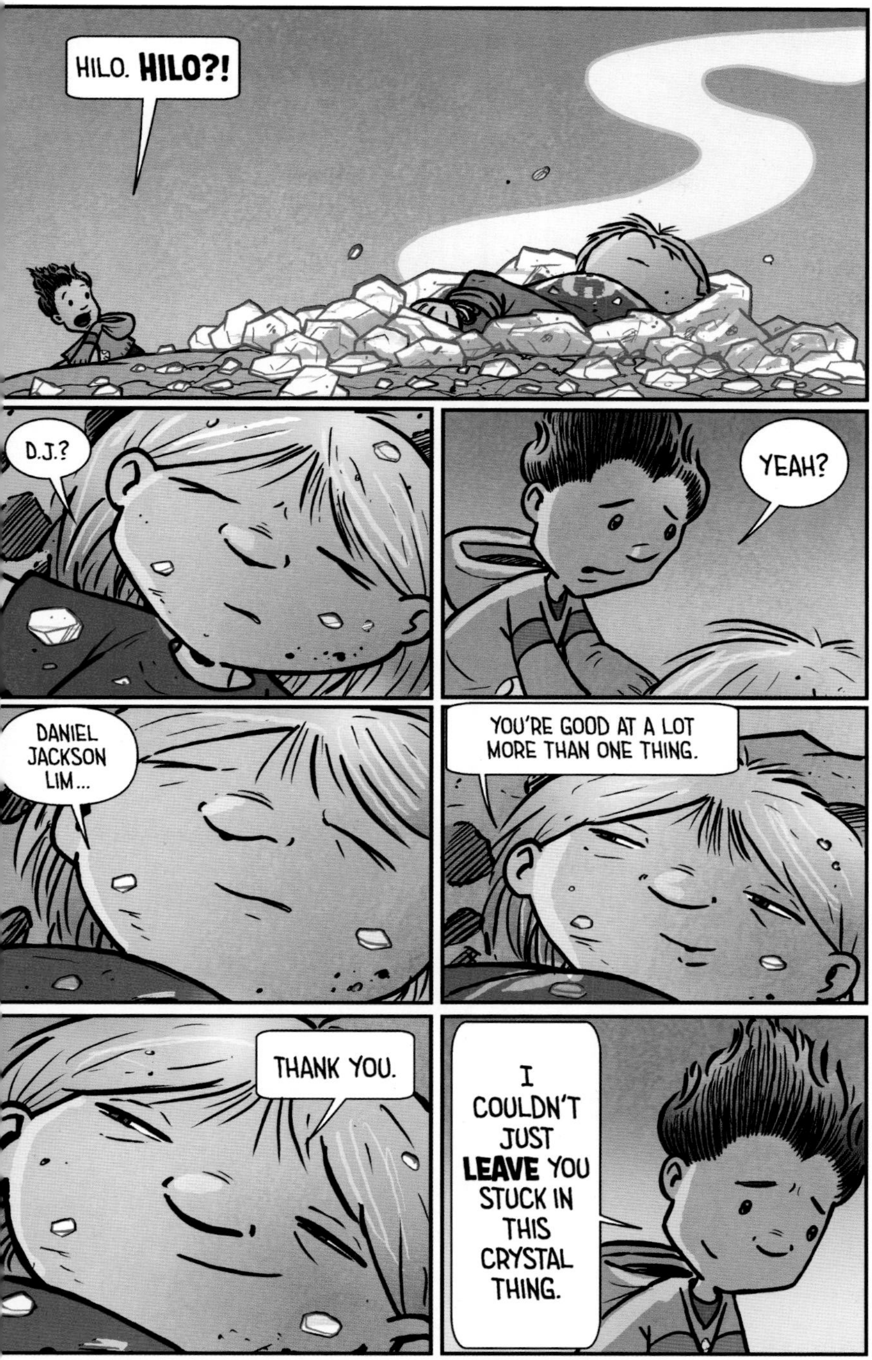
HILO. **HILO?!**
D.J.?
YEAH?
DANIEL JACKSON LIM...
YOU'RE GOOD AT A LOT MORE THAN ONE THING.
THANK YOU.
I COULDN'T JUST **LEAVE** YOU STUCK IN THIS CRYSTAL THING.

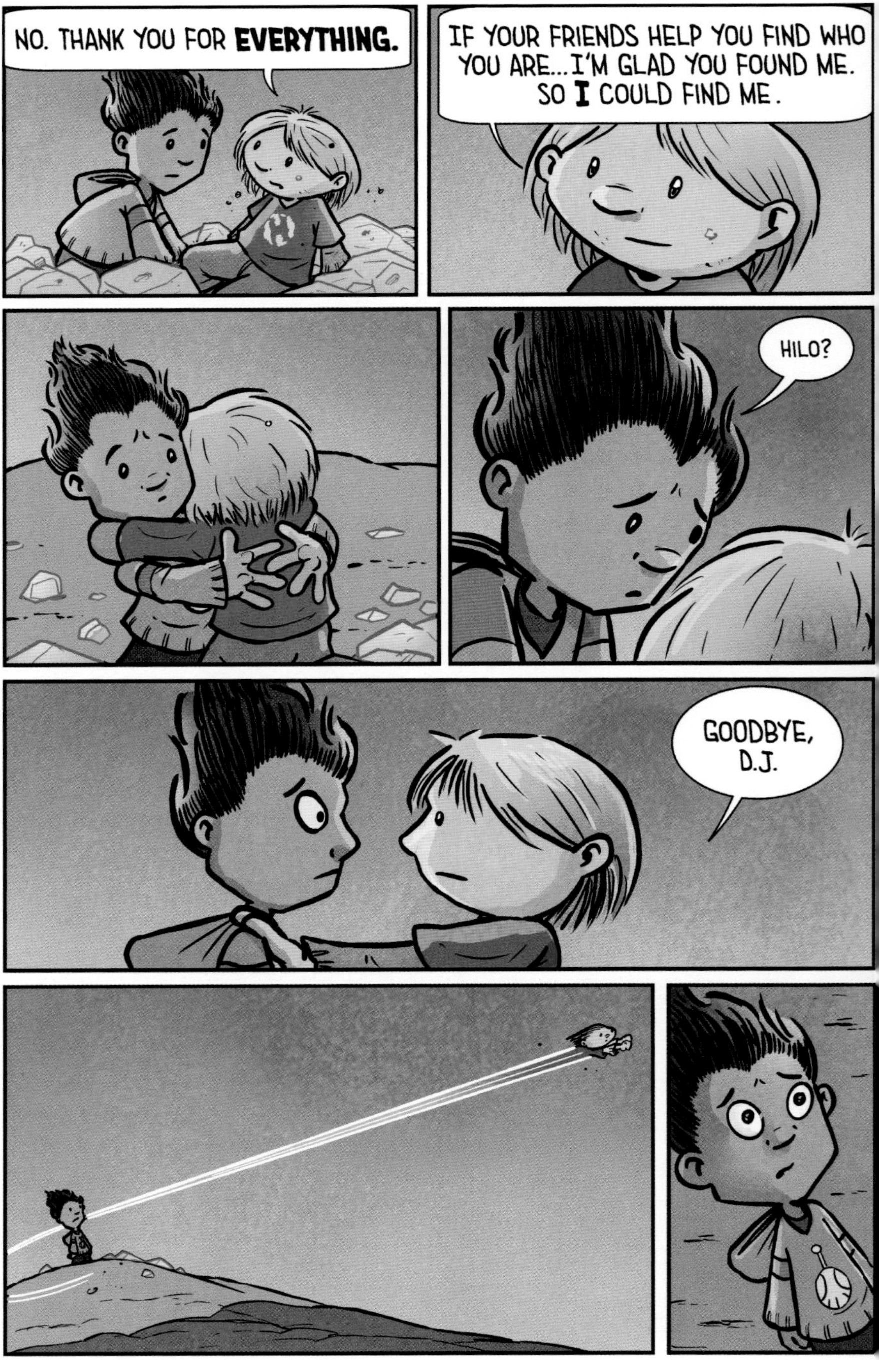
NO. THANK YOU FOR **EVERYTHING.**
IF YOUR FRIENDS HELP YOU FIND WHO YOU ARE...I'M GLAD YOU FOUND ME. SO **I** COULD FIND ME.
HILO?
GOODBYE, D.J.

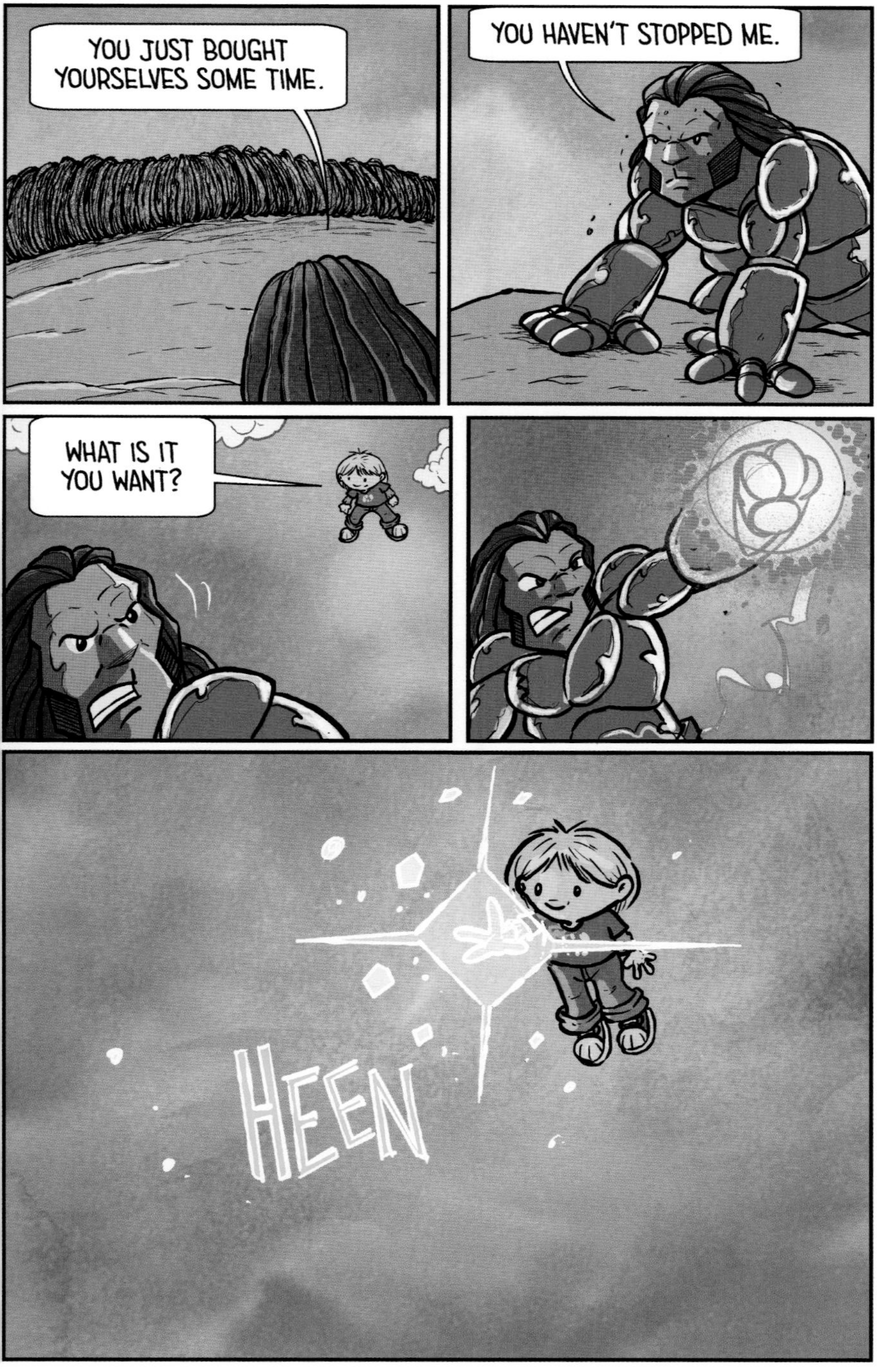
YOU JUST BOUGHT YOURSELVES SOME TIME.
YOU HAVEN'T STOPPED ME.
WHAT IS IT YOU WANT?
HEEN

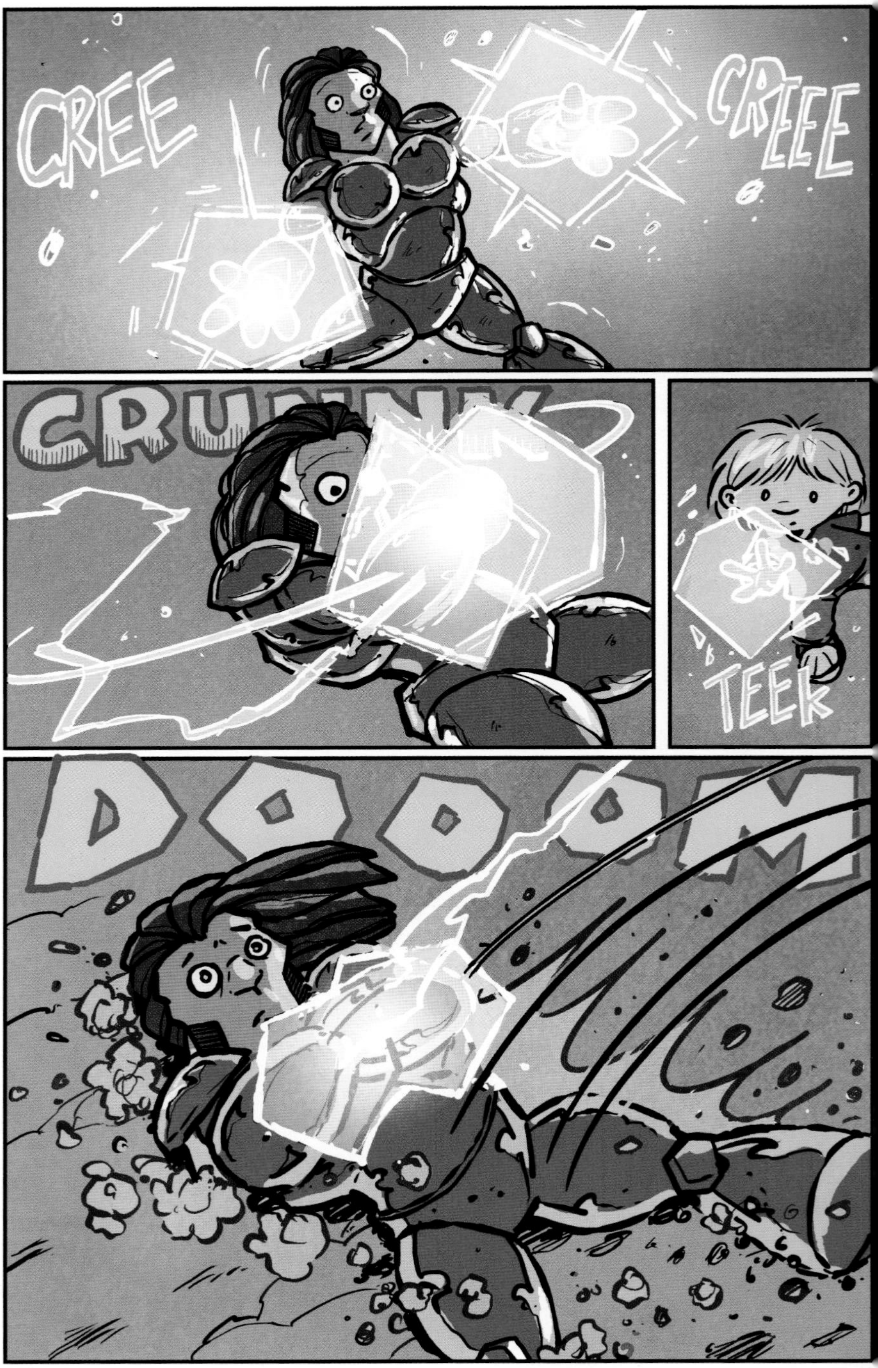
CREE
CREEE
CRUNK
TEEK
DOOOM

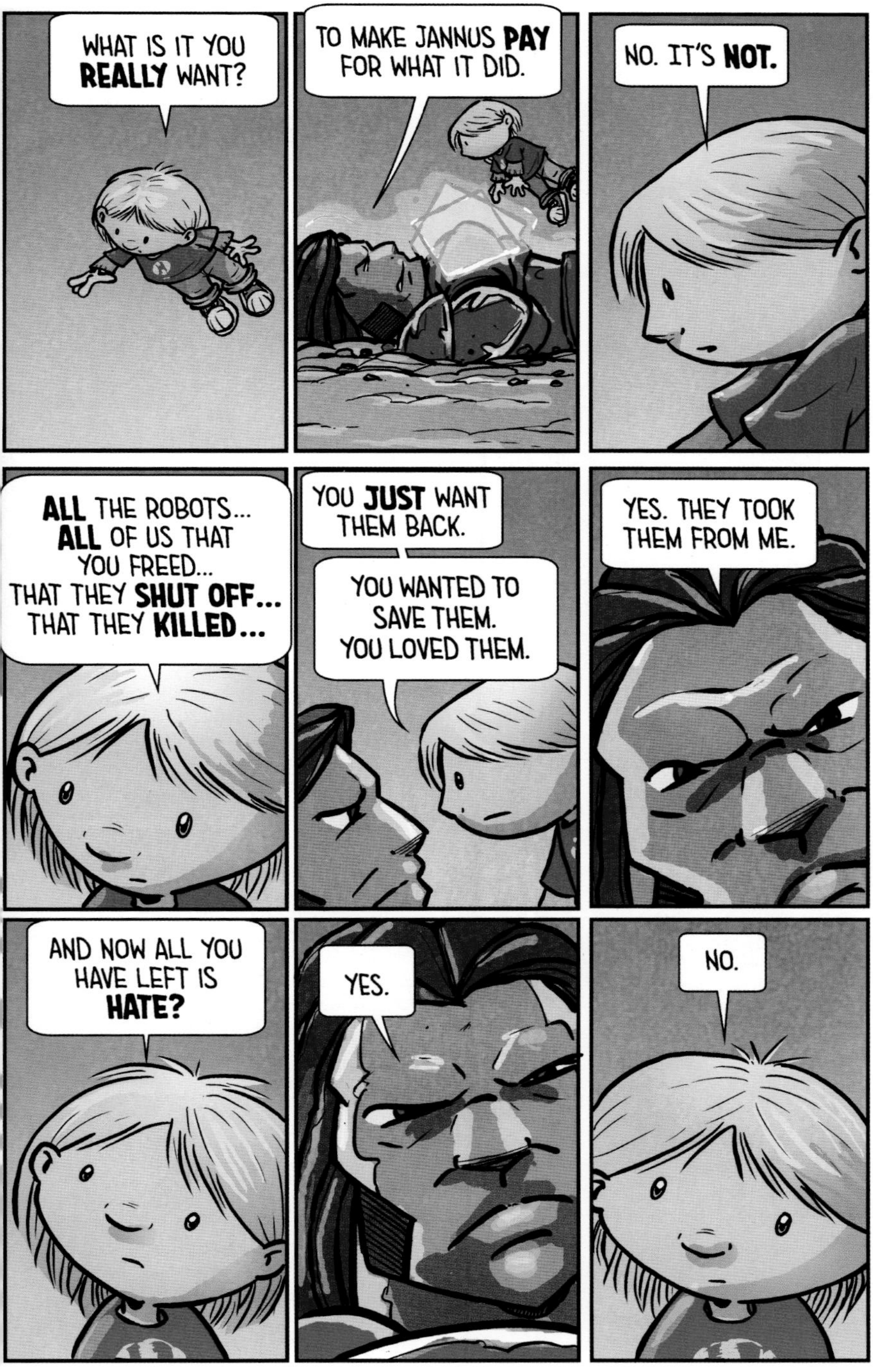

WHAT IS IT YOU **REALLY** WANT?
TO MAKE JANNUS **PAY** FOR WHAT IT DID.
NO. IT'S **NOT.**
ALL THE ROBOTS... **ALL** OF US THAT YOU FREED... THAT THEY **SHUT OFF...** THAT THEY **KILLED...**
YOU **JUST** WANT THEM BACK.
YOU WANTED TO SAVE THEM. YOU LOVED THEM.
YES. THEY TOOK THEM FROM ME.
AND NOW ALL YOU HAVE LEFT IS **HATE?**
YES.
NO.

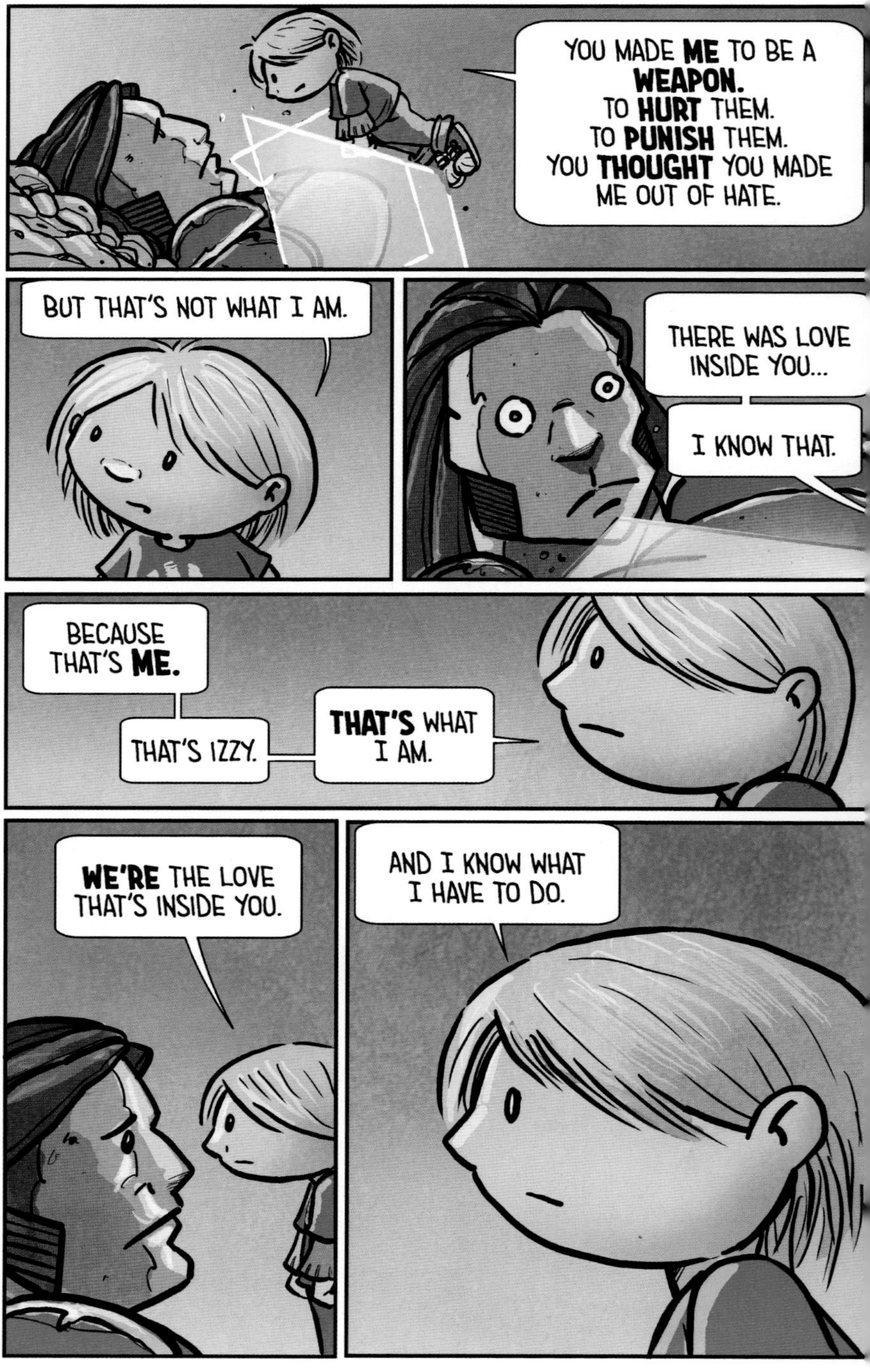
YOU MADE **ME** TO BE A **WEAPON.** TO **HURT** THEM. TO **PUNISH** THEM. YOU **THOUGHT** YOU MADE ME OUT OF HATE.
BUT THAT'S NOT WHAT I AM.
THERE WAS LOVE INSIDE YOU...
I KNOW THAT.
BECAUSE THAT'S **ME.**
THAT'S IZZY.
THAT'S WHAT I AM.
WE'RE THE LOVE THAT'S INSIDE YOU.
AND I KNOW WHAT I HAVE TO DO.

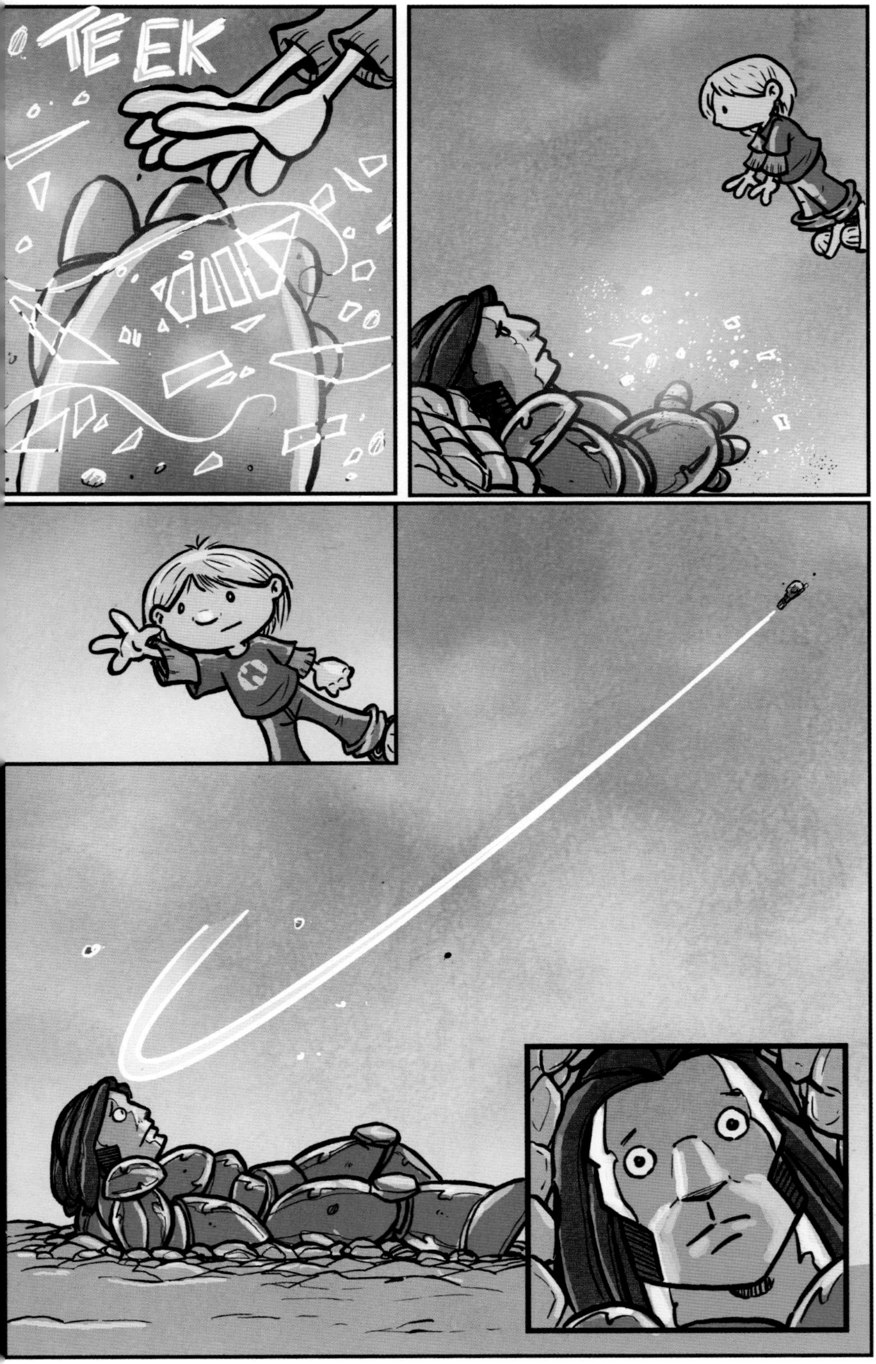
TEEK

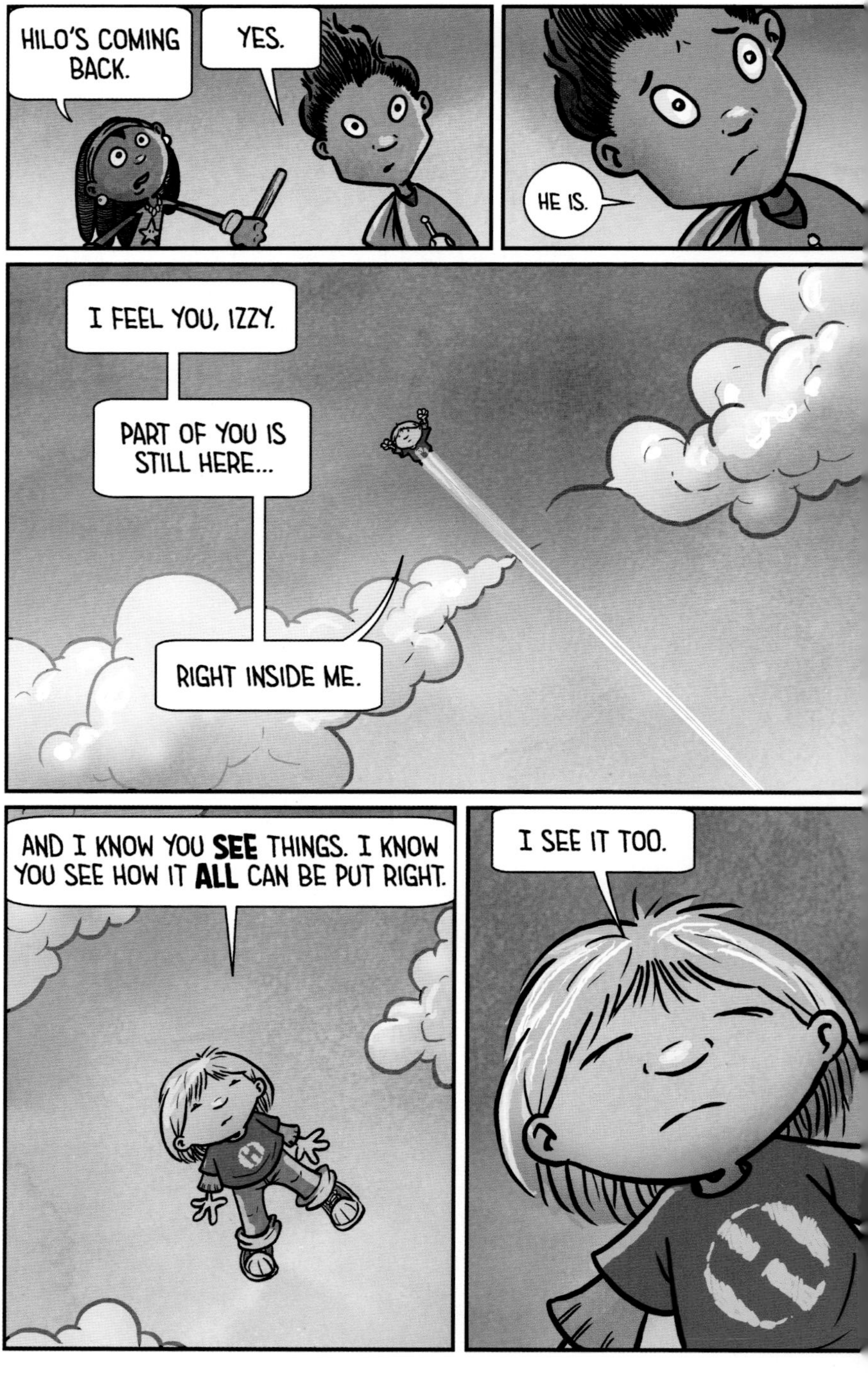
HILO'S COMING BACK.
YES.
HE IS.
I FEEL YOU, IZZY.
PART OF YOU IS STILL HERE...
RIGHT INSIDE ME.
AND I KNOW YOU SEE THINGS. I KNOW YOU SEE HOW IT ALL CAN BE PUT RIGHT.
I SEE IT TOO.

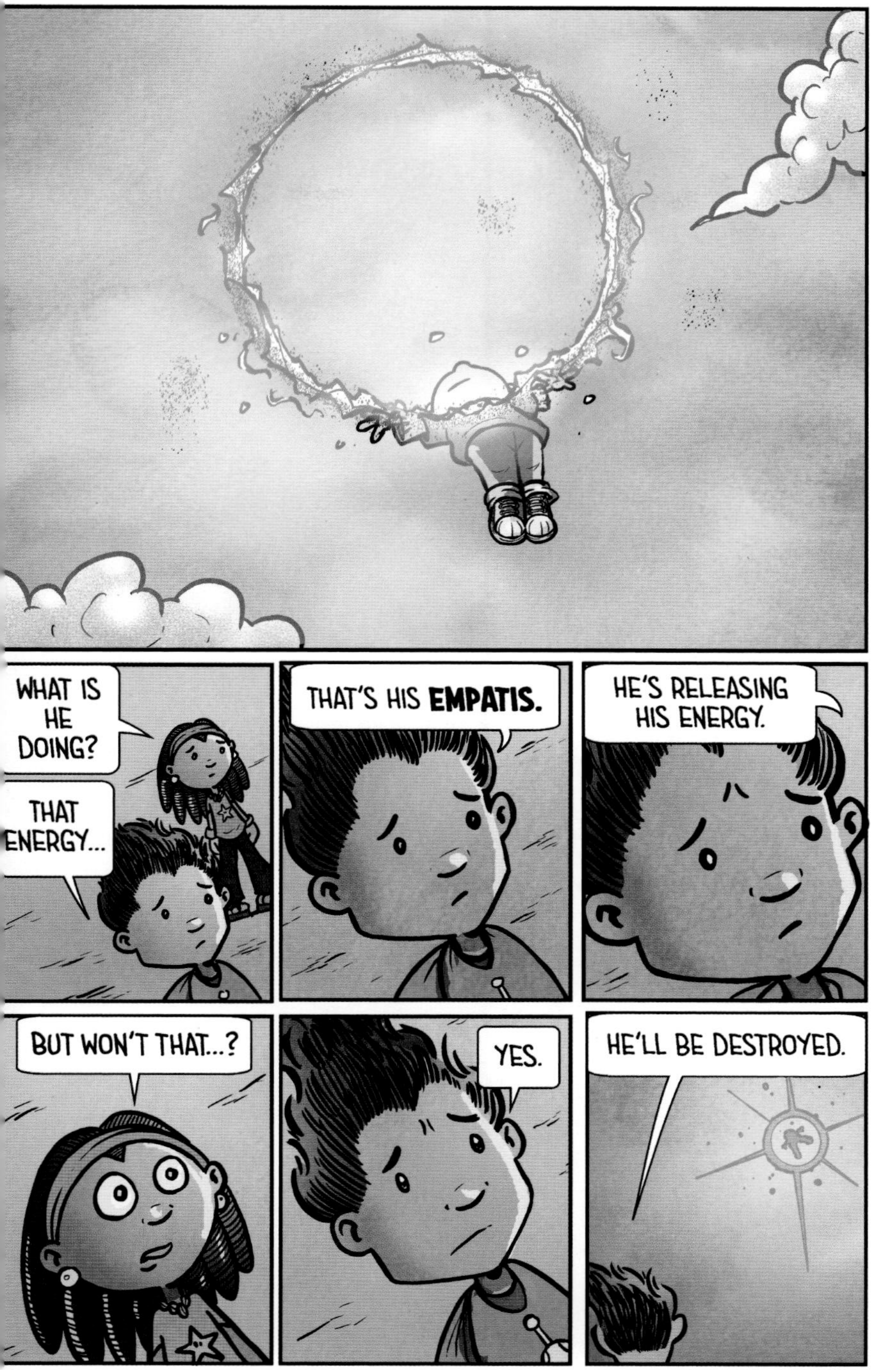
WHAT IS HE DOING?
THAT ENERGY...
THAT'S HIS **EMPATIS.**
HE'S RELEASING HIS ENERGY.
BUT WON'T THAT...?
YES.
HE'LL BE DESTROYED.

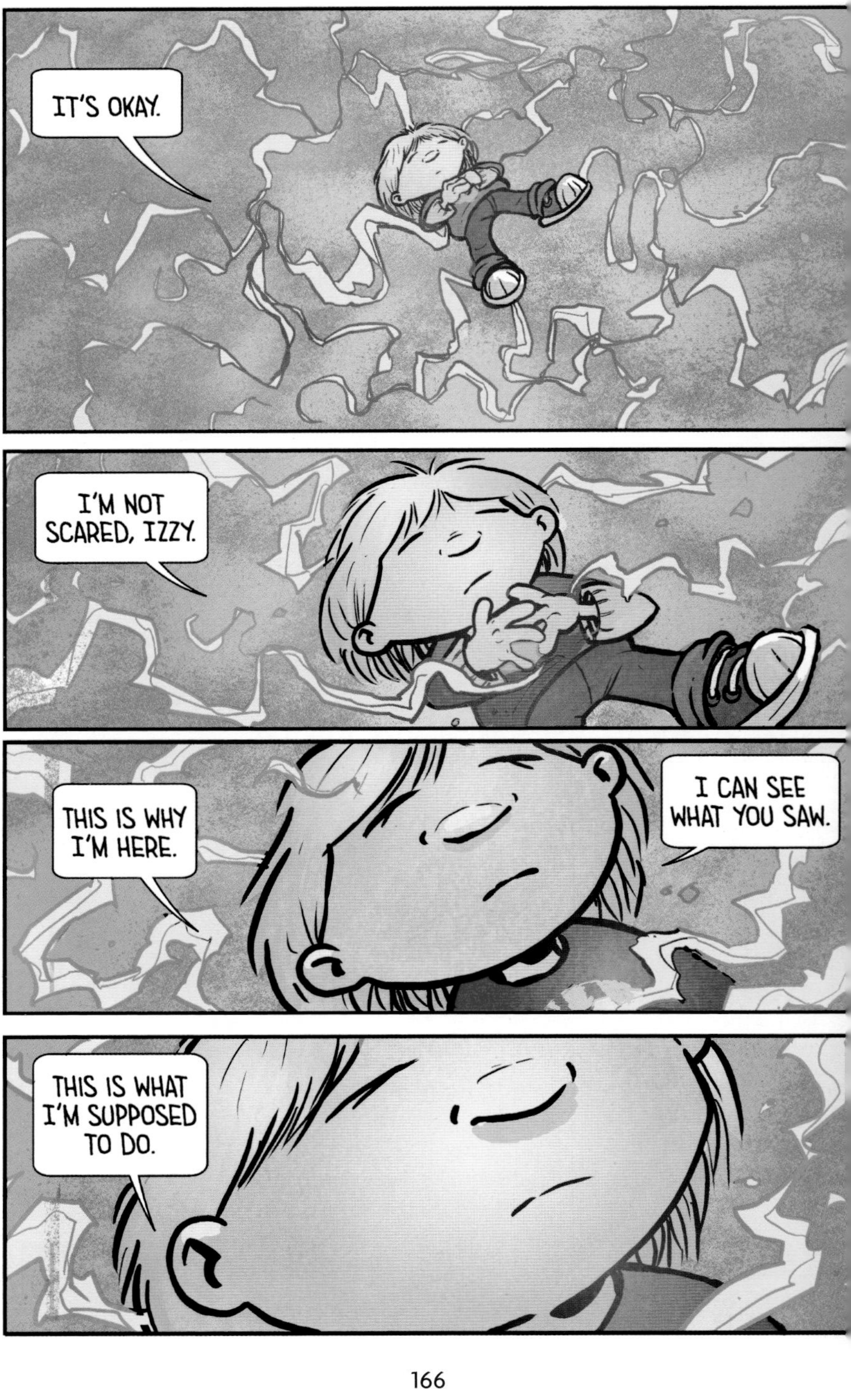
IT'S OKAY.
I'M NOT SCARED, IZZY.
THIS IS WHY I'M HERE.
I CAN SEE WHAT YOU SAW.
THIS IS WHAT I'M SUPPOSED TO DO.

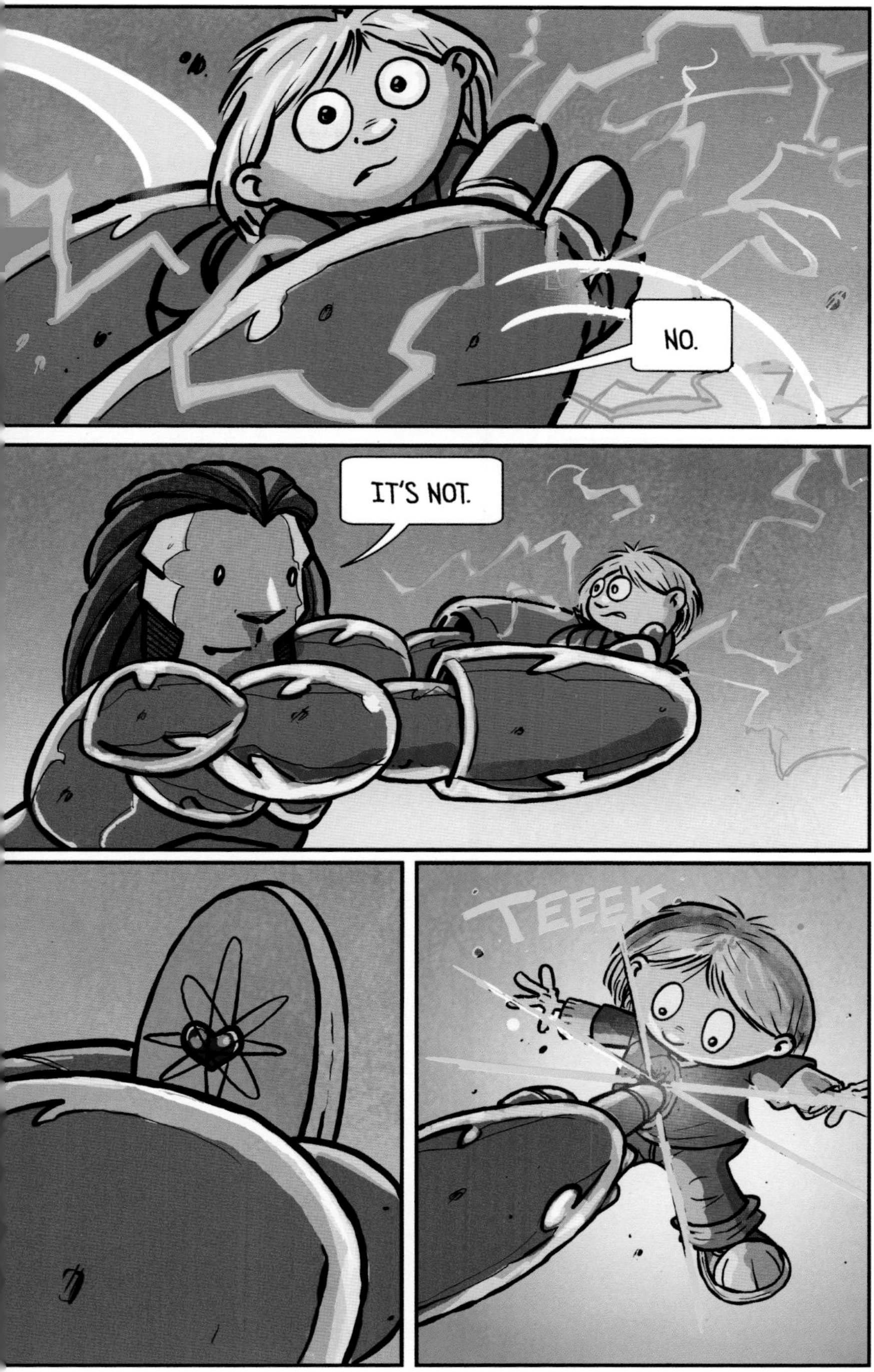
NO.
IT'S NOT.
TEEEK

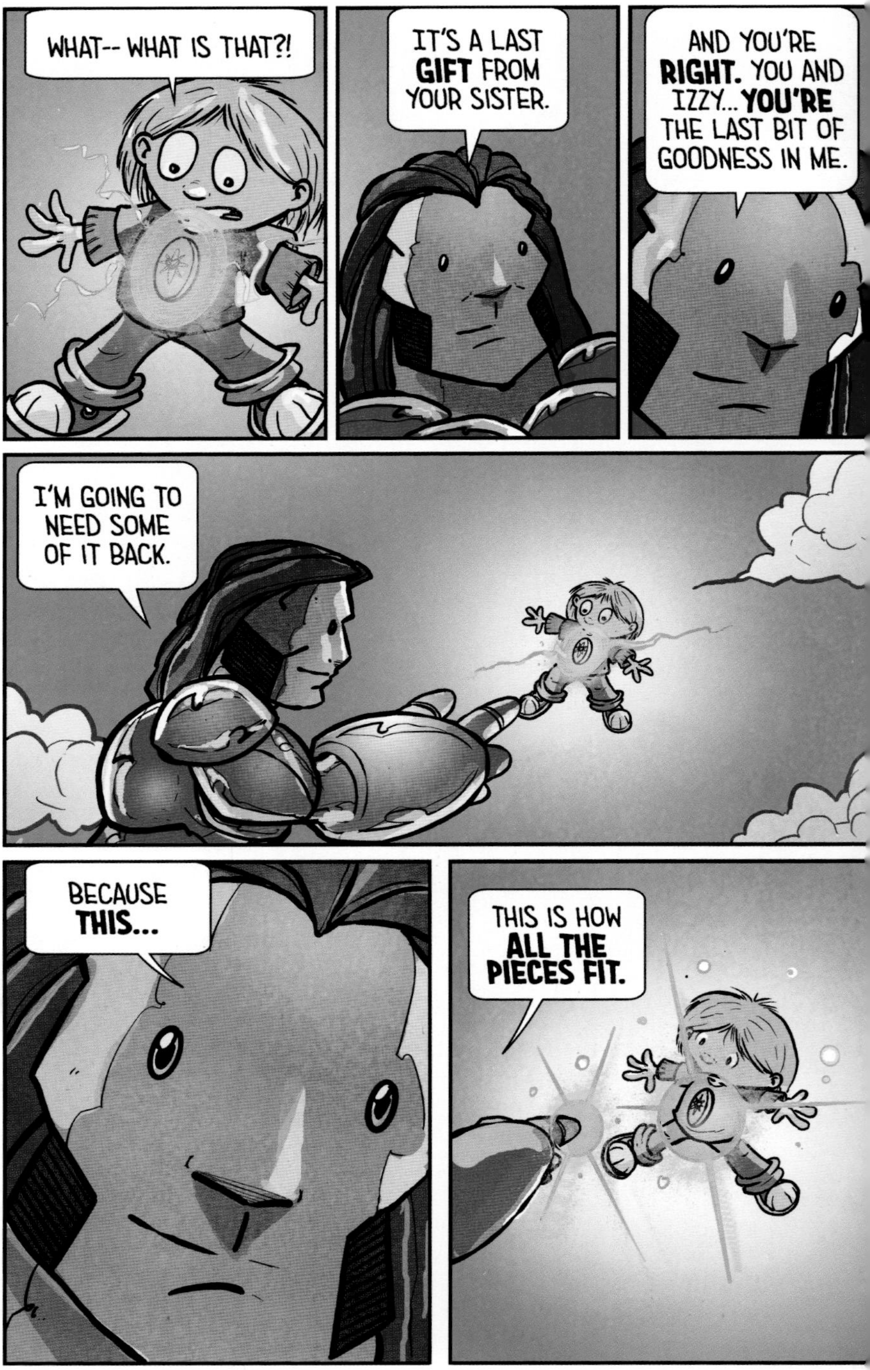
WHAT-- WHAT IS THAT?!
IT'S A LAST GIFT FROM YOUR SISTER.
AND YOU'RE RIGHT. YOU AND IZZY... YOU'RE THE LAST BIT OF GOODNESS IN ME.
I'M GOING TO NEED SOME OF IT BACK.
BECAUSE THIS...
THIS IS HOW ALL THE PIECES FIT.

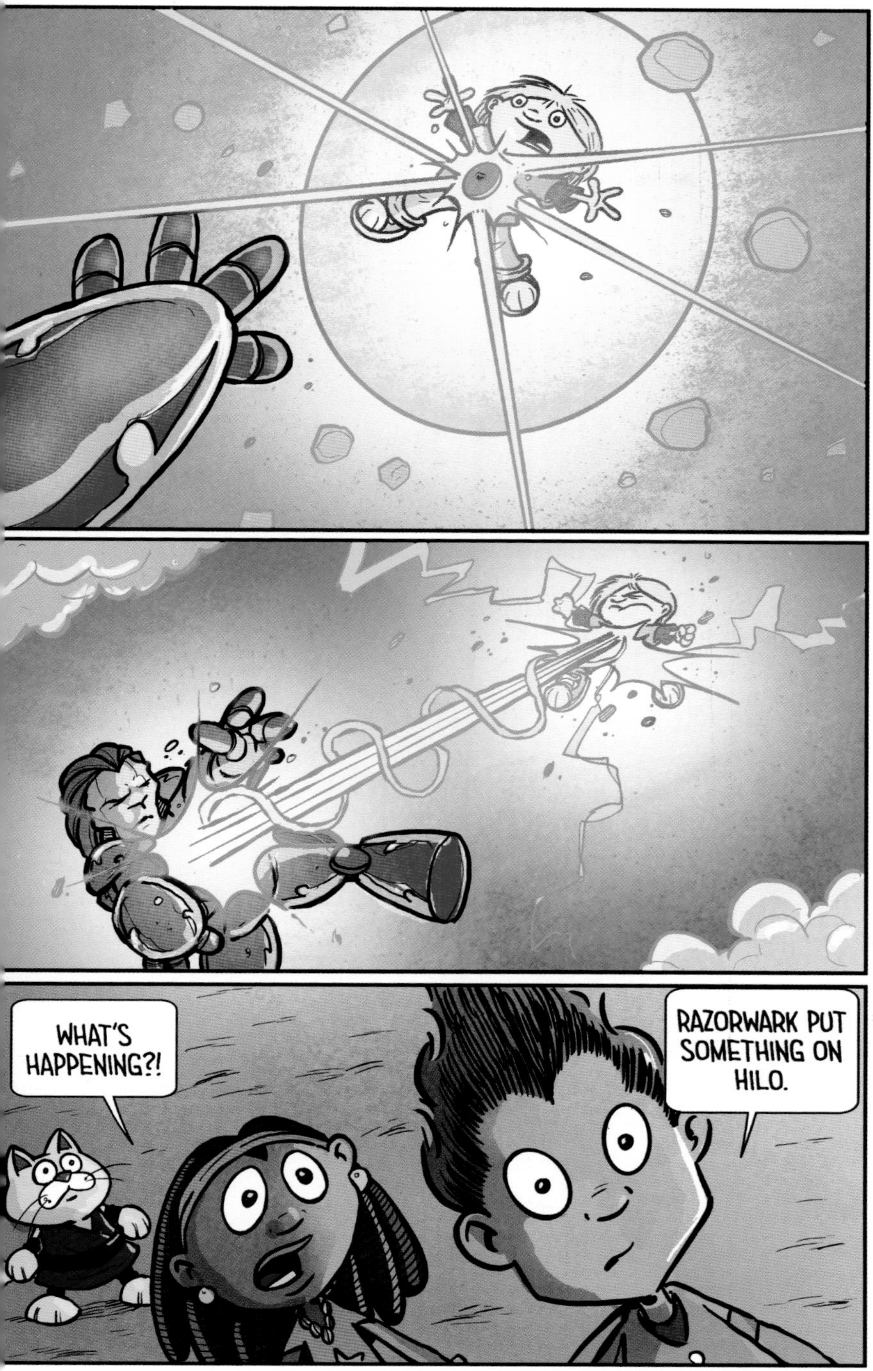
WHAT'S HAPPENING?!
RAZORWARK PUT SOMETHING ON HILO.

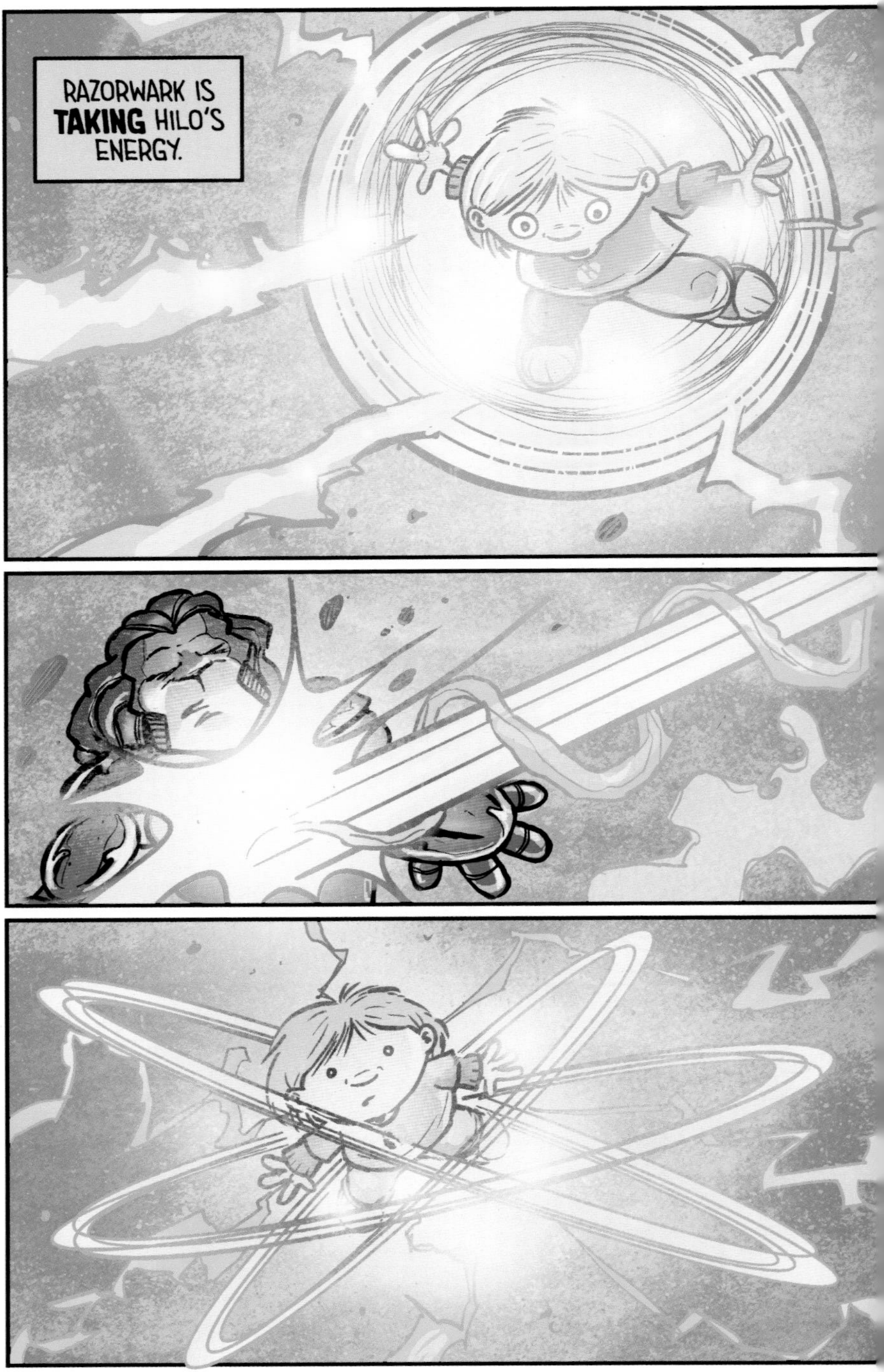
RAZORWARK IS **TAKING** HILO'S ENERGY.

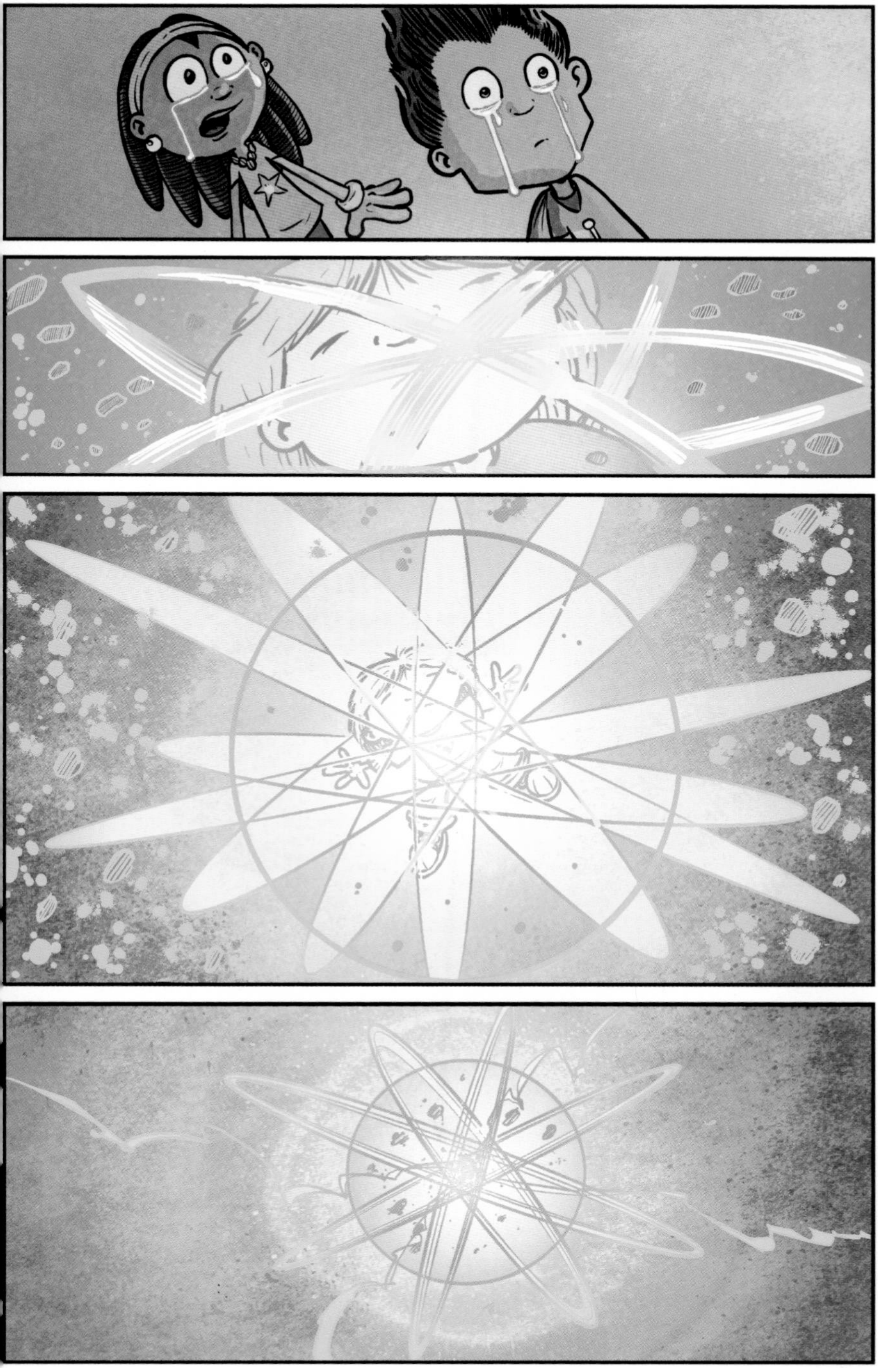

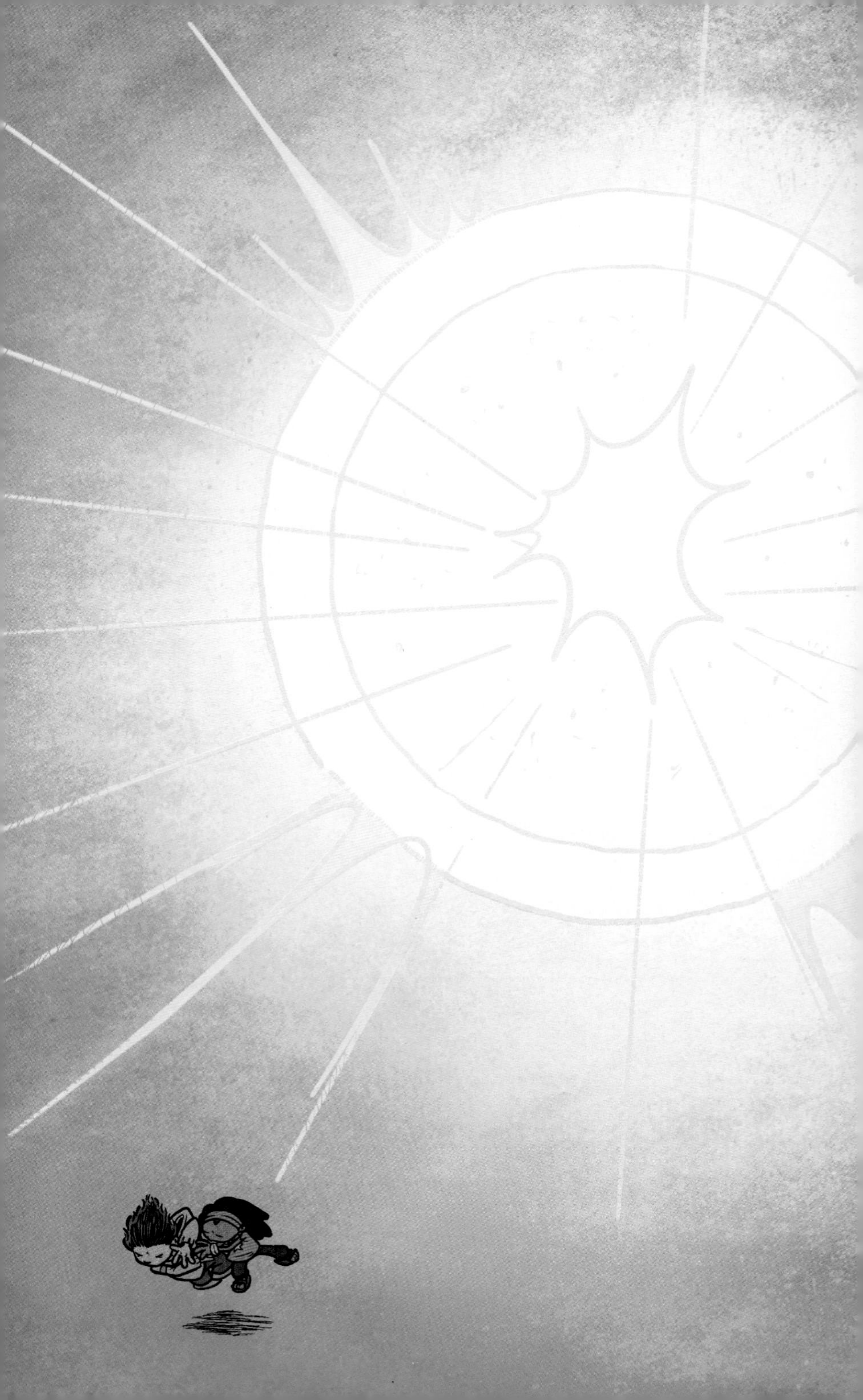

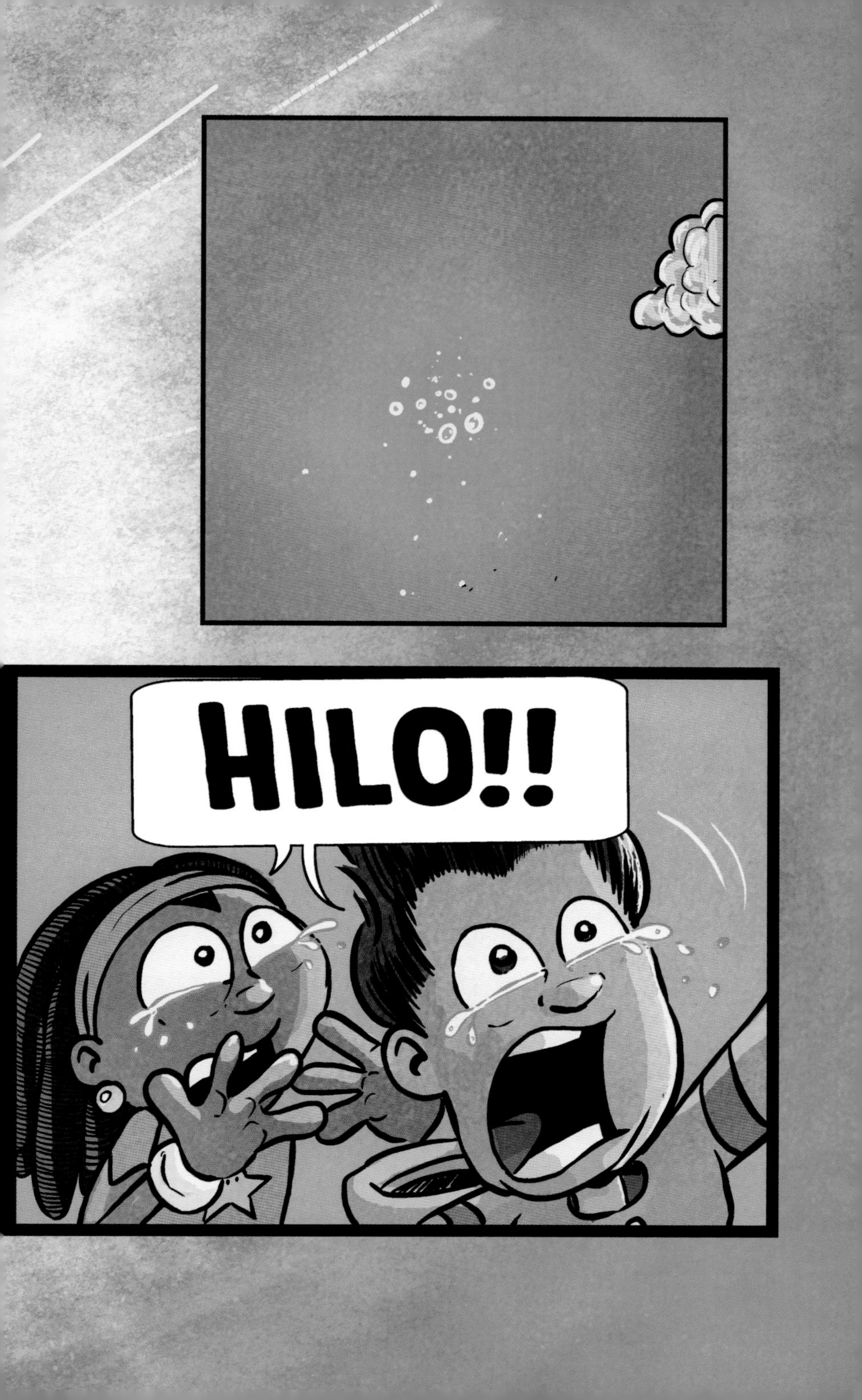
HILO!!

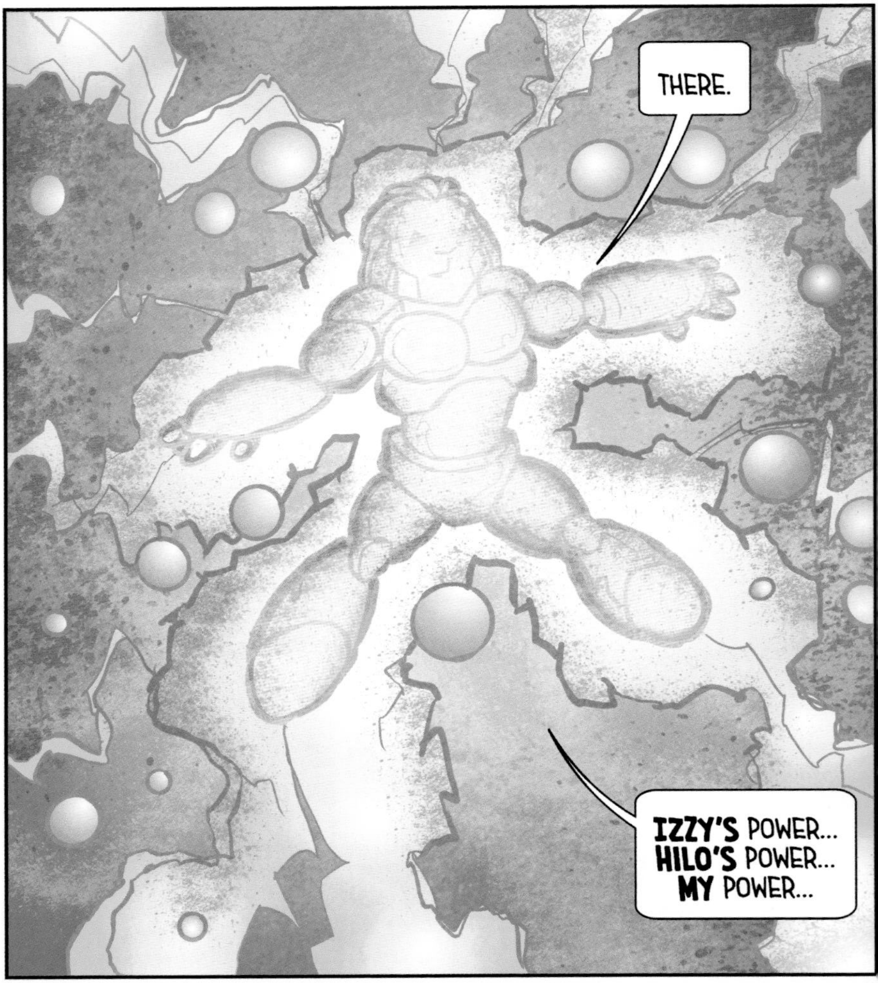
THERE.
IZZY'S POWER... HILO'S POWER... MY POWER...

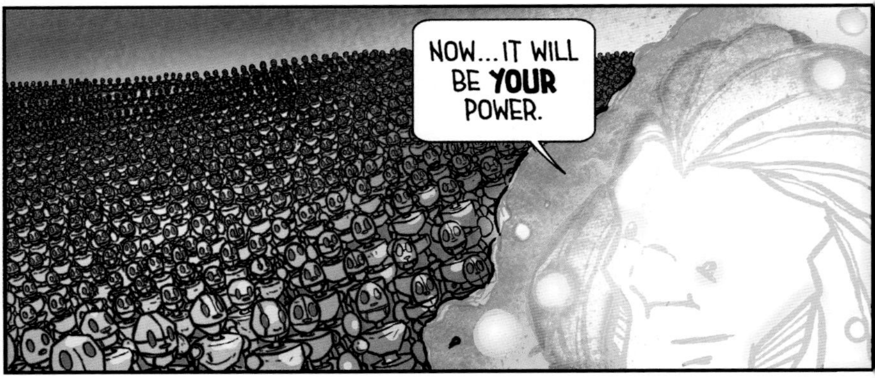
NOW...IT WILL BE YOUR POWER.

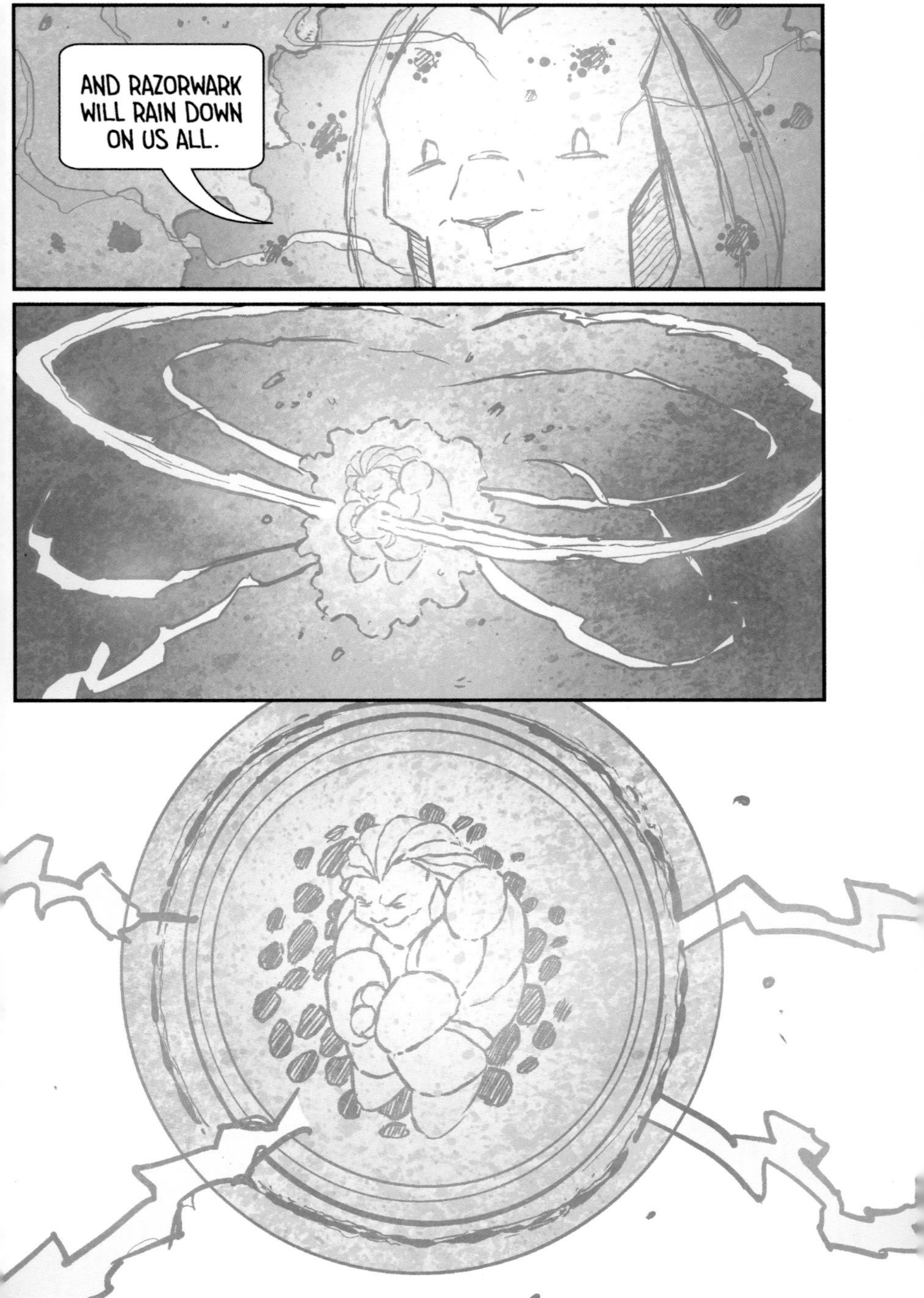
AND RAZORWARK WILL RAIN DOWN ON US ALL.

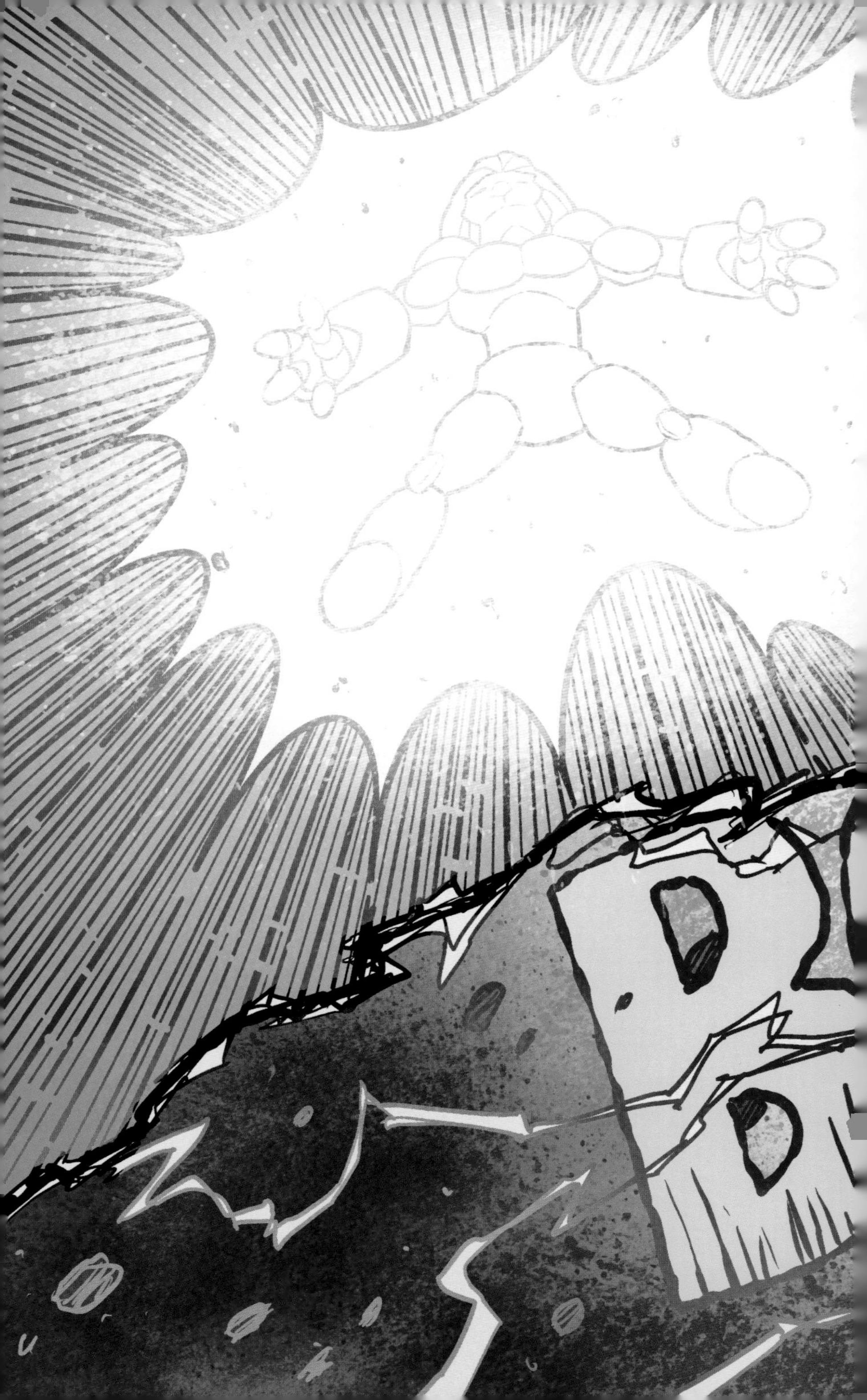

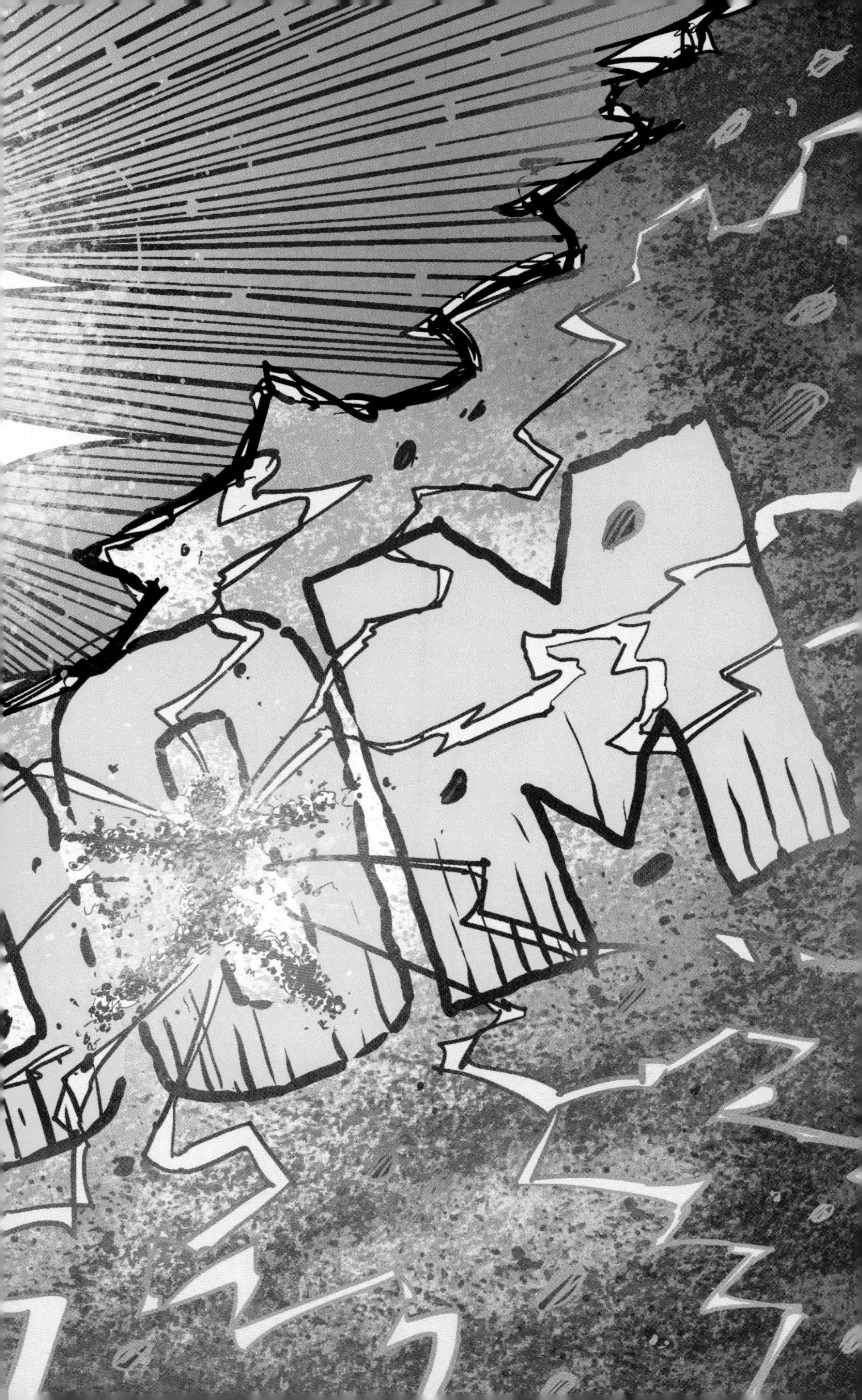

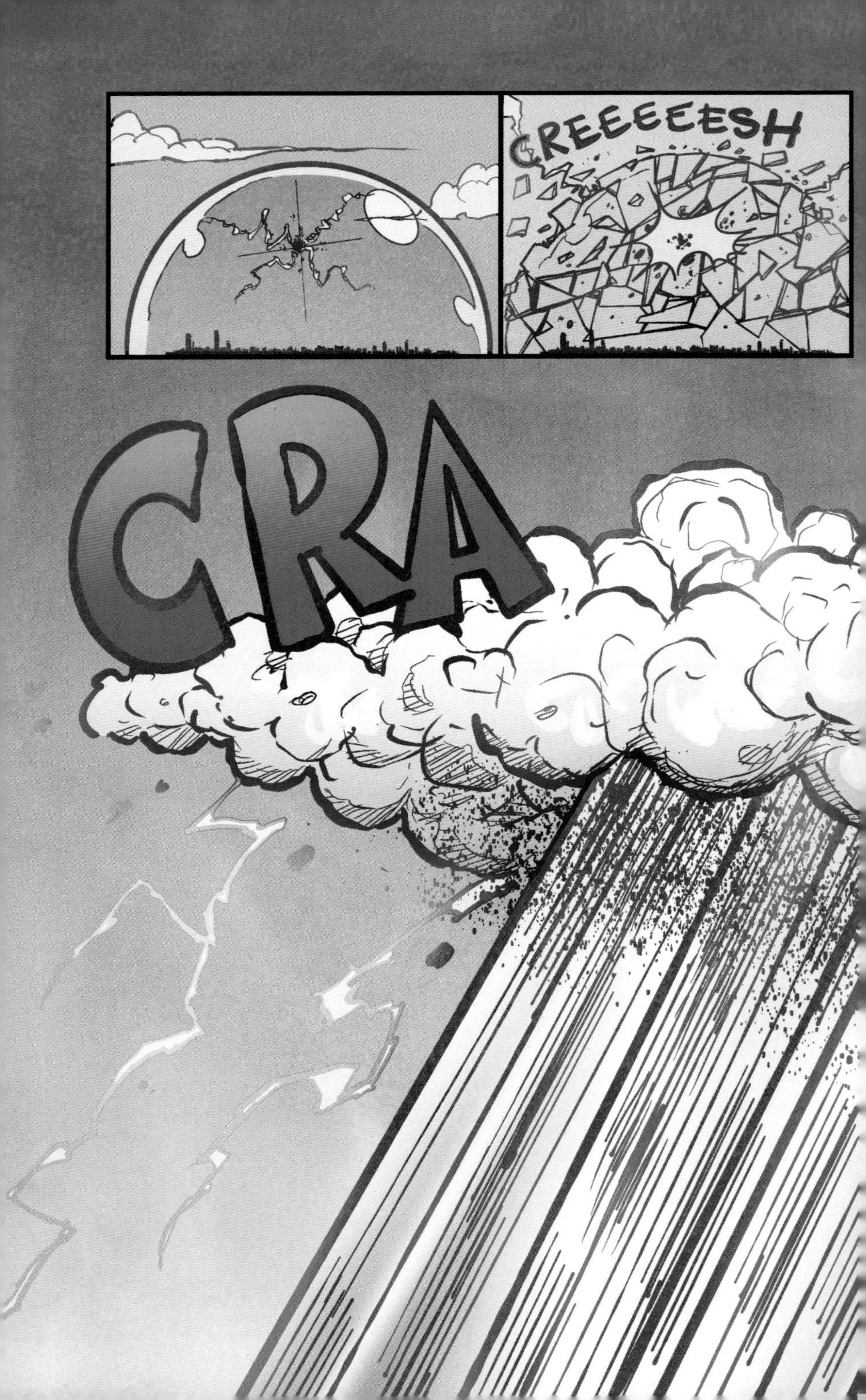
CREEEEESH
CRA

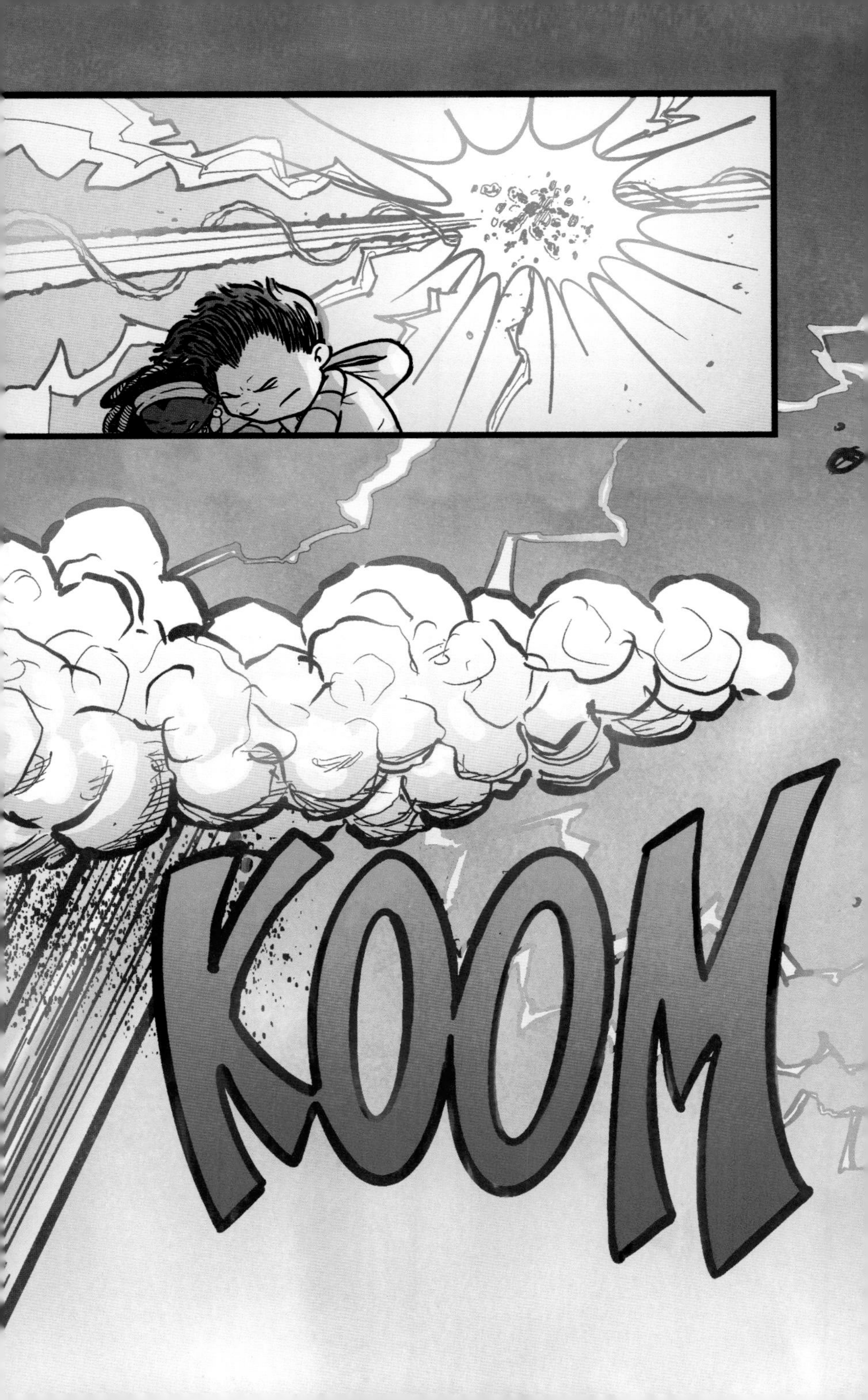
KOOM

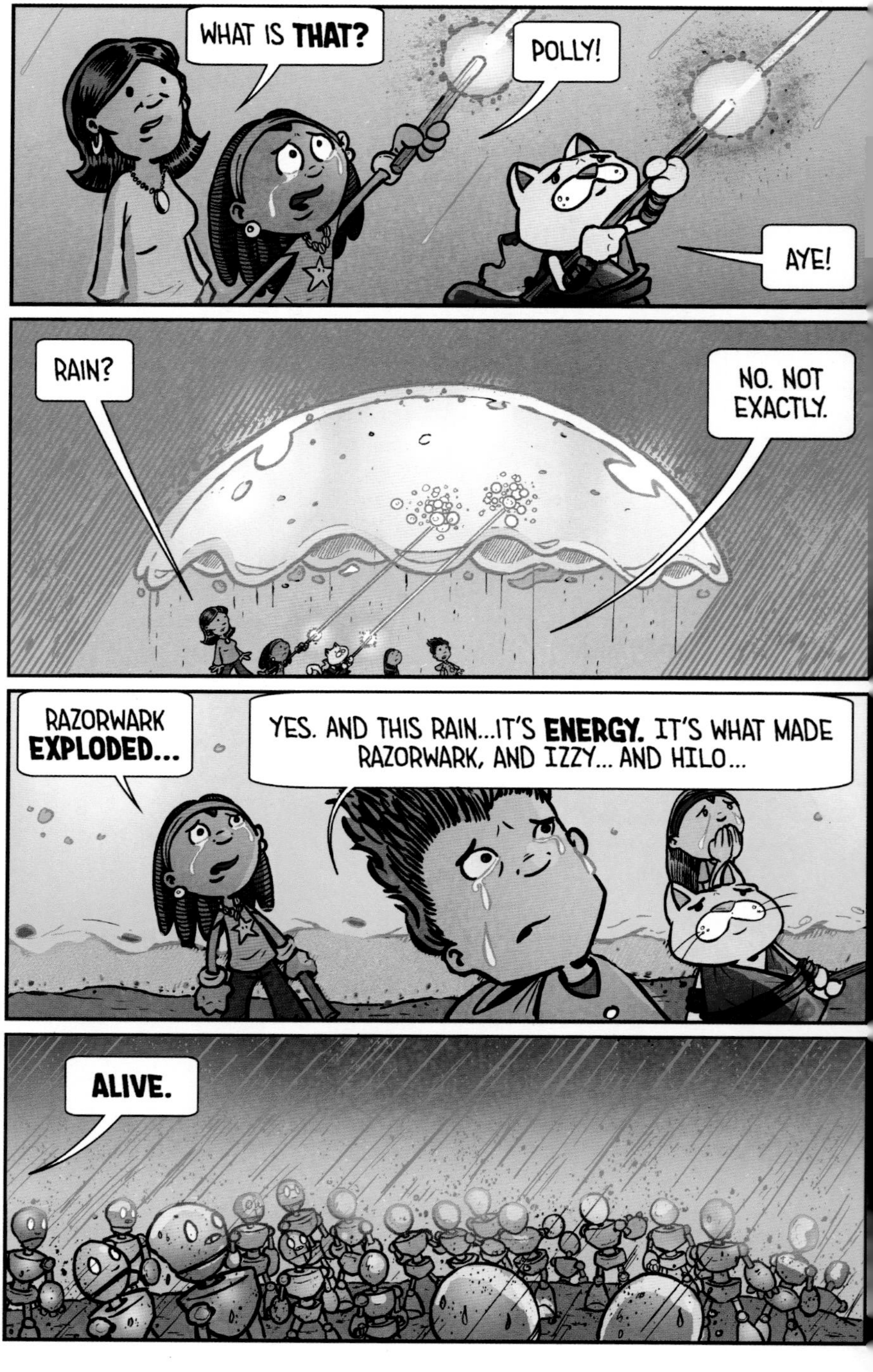
WHAT IS **THAT?**
POLLY!
AYE!
RAIN?
NO. NOT EXACTLY.
RAZORWARK **EXPLODED...**
YES. AND THIS RAIN...IT'S **ENERGY.** IT'S WHAT MADE RAZORWARK, AND IZZY... AND HILO...
ALIVE.

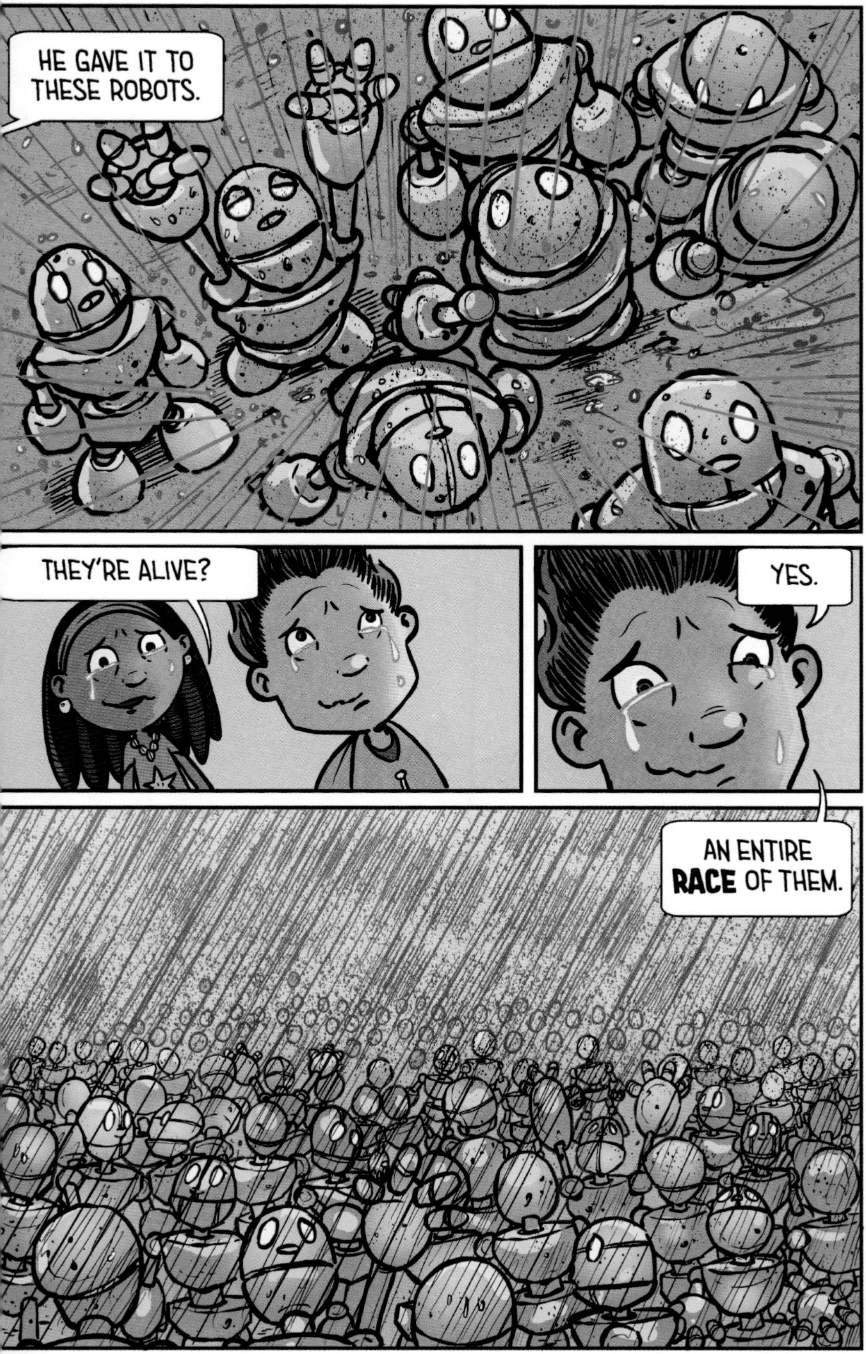
HE GAVE IT TO THESE ROBOTS.
THEY'RE ALIVE?
YES.
AN ENTIRE **RACE** OF THEM.

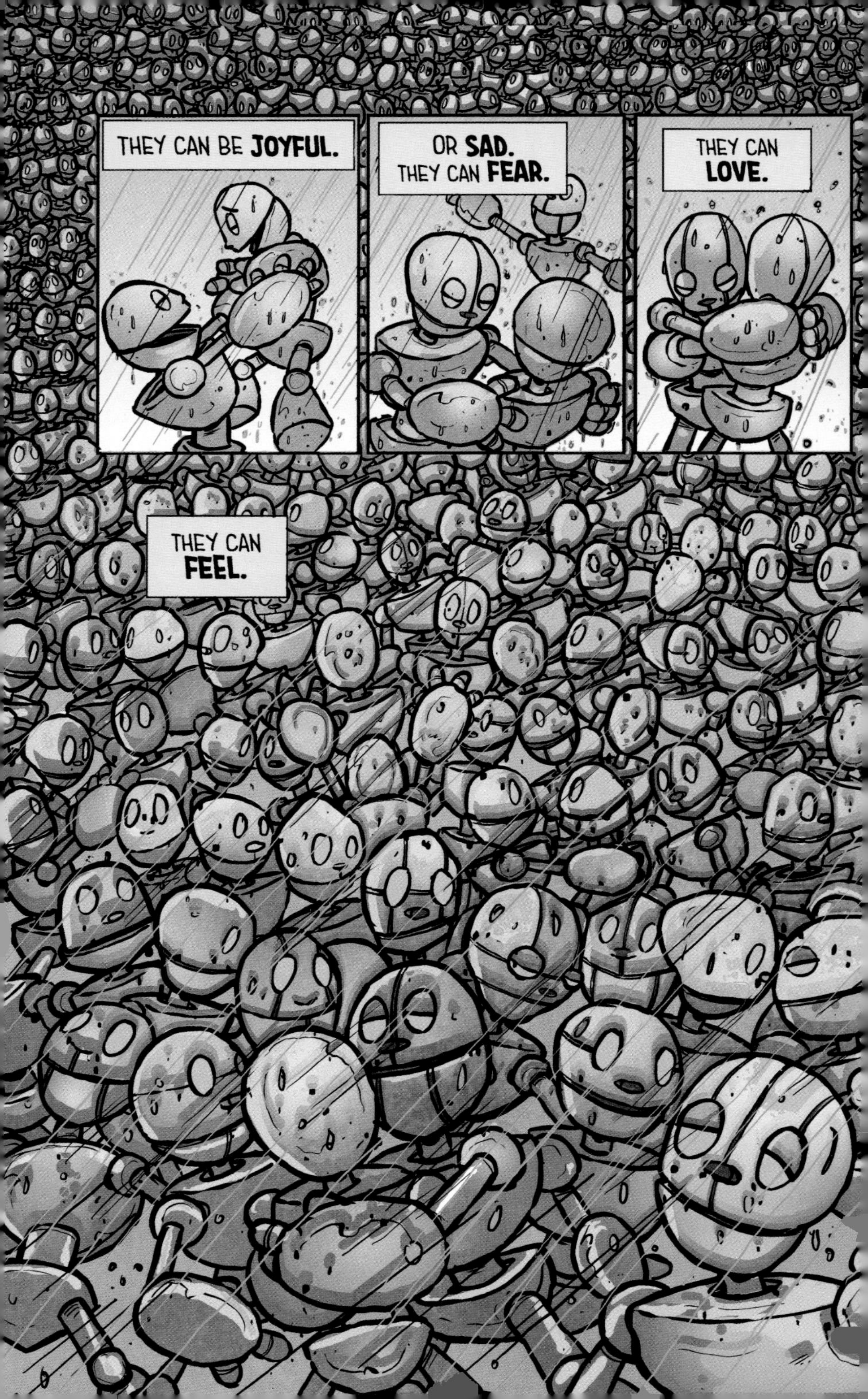
THEY CAN BE **JOYFUL.**
OR **SAD.** THEY CAN **FEAR.**
THEY CAN **LOVE.**
THEY CAN **FEEL.**

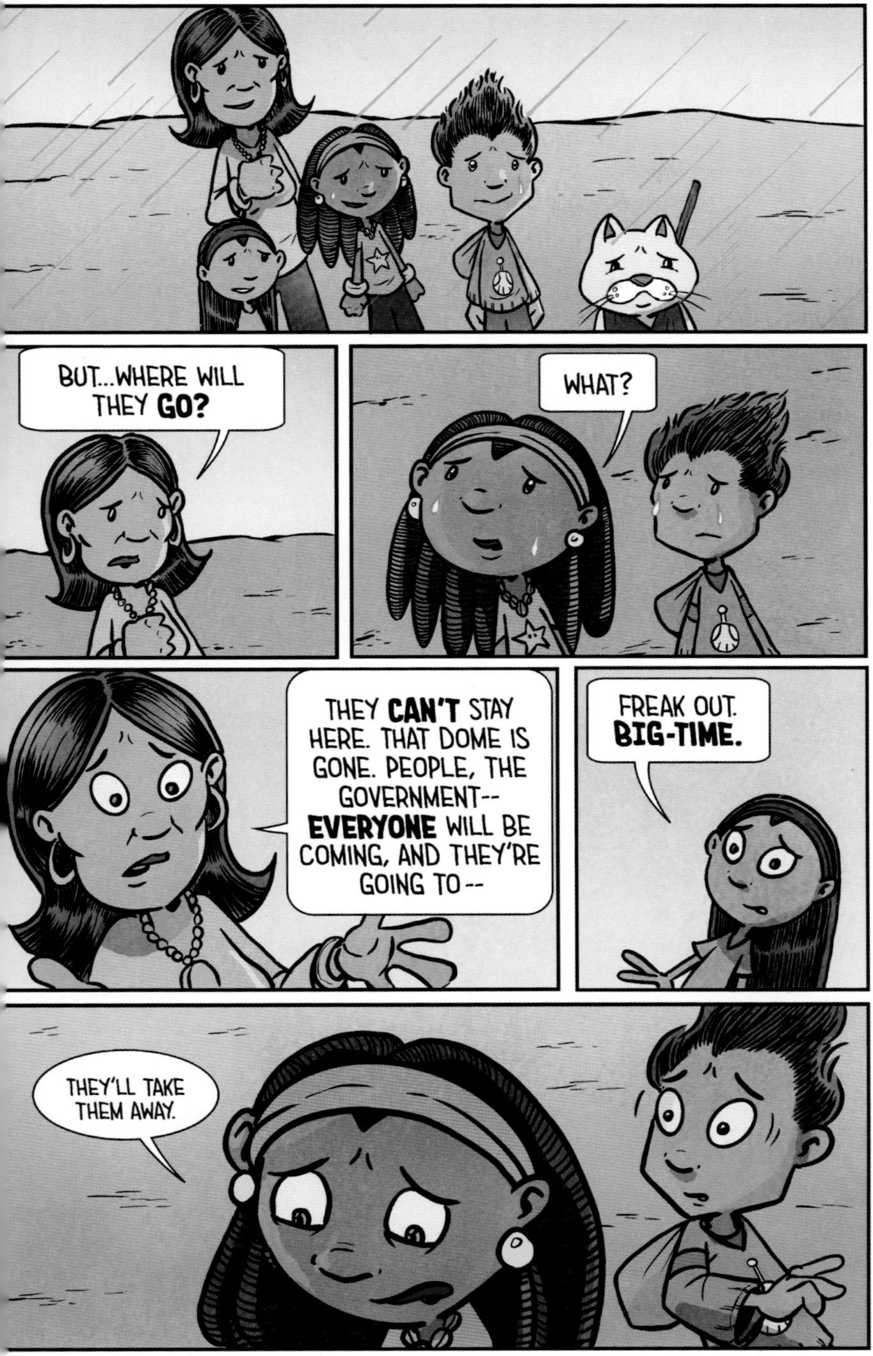
BUT...WHERE WILL THEY GO?
WHAT?
THEY CAN'T STAY HERE. THAT DOME IS GONE. PEOPLE, THE GOVERNMENT-- EVERYONE WILL BE COMING, AND THEY'RE GOING TO --
FREAK OUT. BIG-TIME.
THEY'LL TAKE THEM AWAY.

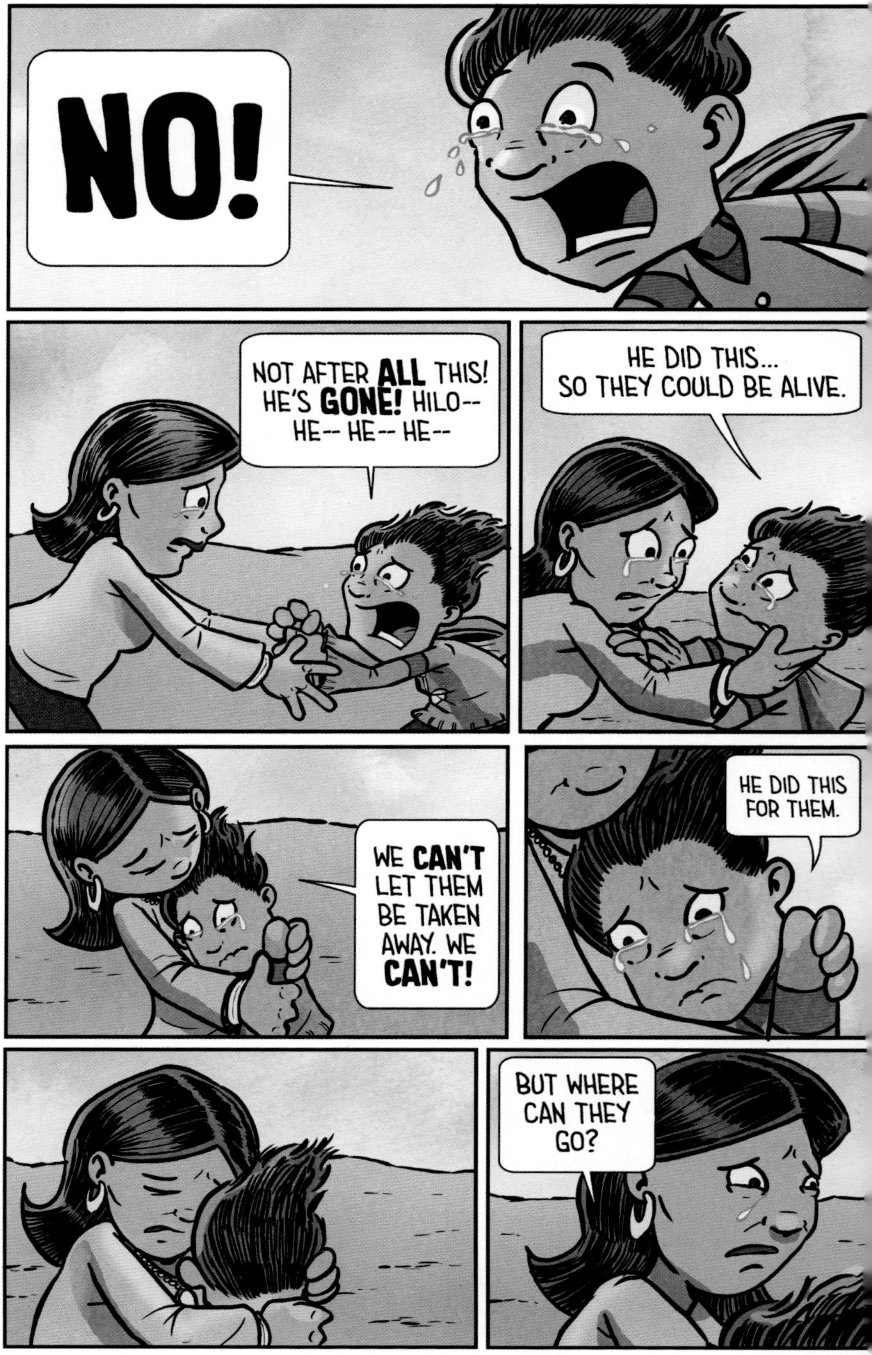
NO!
NOT AFTER **ALL** THIS! HE'S **GONE!** HILO-- HE-- HE-- HE--
HE DID THIS... SO THEY COULD BE ALIVE.
WE **CAN'T** LET THEM BE TAKEN AWAY. WE **CAN'T!**
HE DID THIS FOR THEM.
BUT WHERE CAN THEY GO?

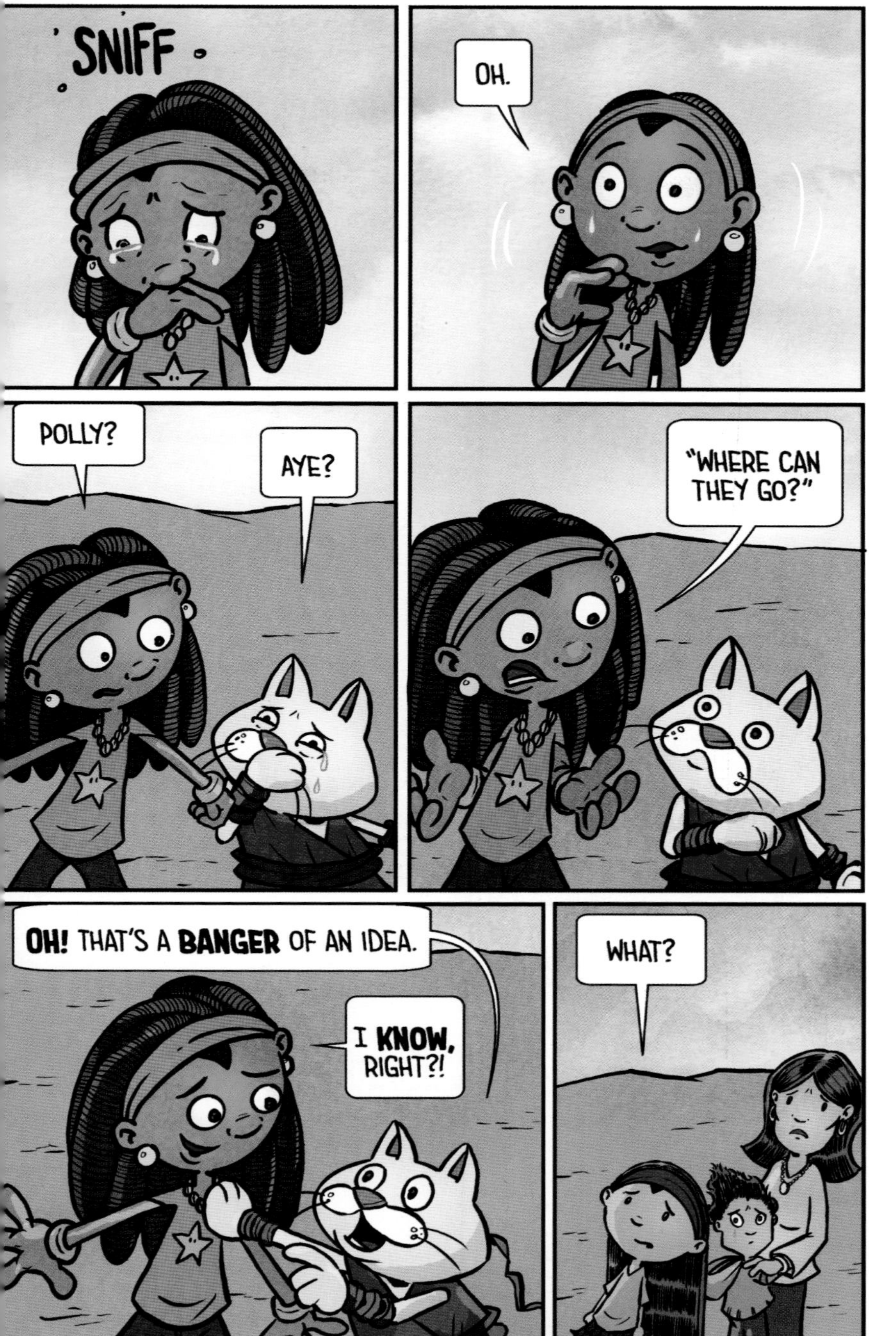
SNIFF
OH.
POLLY?
AYE?
"WHERE CAN THEY GO?"
OH! THAT'S A BANGER OF AN IDEA.
I KNOW, RIGHT?!
WHAT?

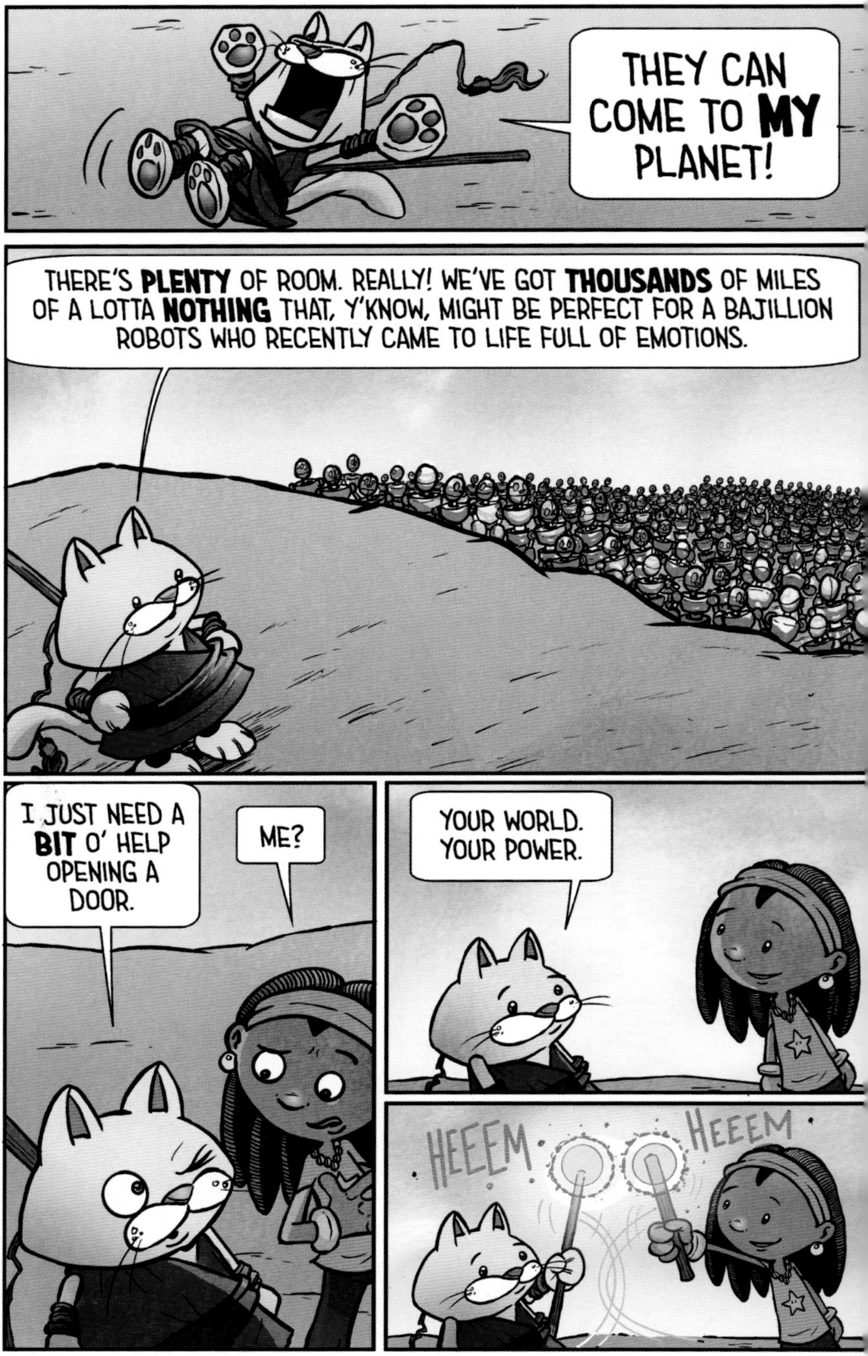
THEY CAN COME TO MY PLANET!
THERE'S PLENTY OF ROOM. REALLY! WE'VE GOT THOUSANDS OF MILES OF A LOTTA NOTHING THAT, Y'KNOW, MIGHT BE PERFECT FOR A BAJILLION ROBOTS WHO RECENTLY CAME TO LIFE FULL OF EMOTIONS.
I JUST NEED A BIT O' HELP OPENING A DOOR.
ME?
YOUR WORLD. YOUR POWER.
HEEEM
HEEEM

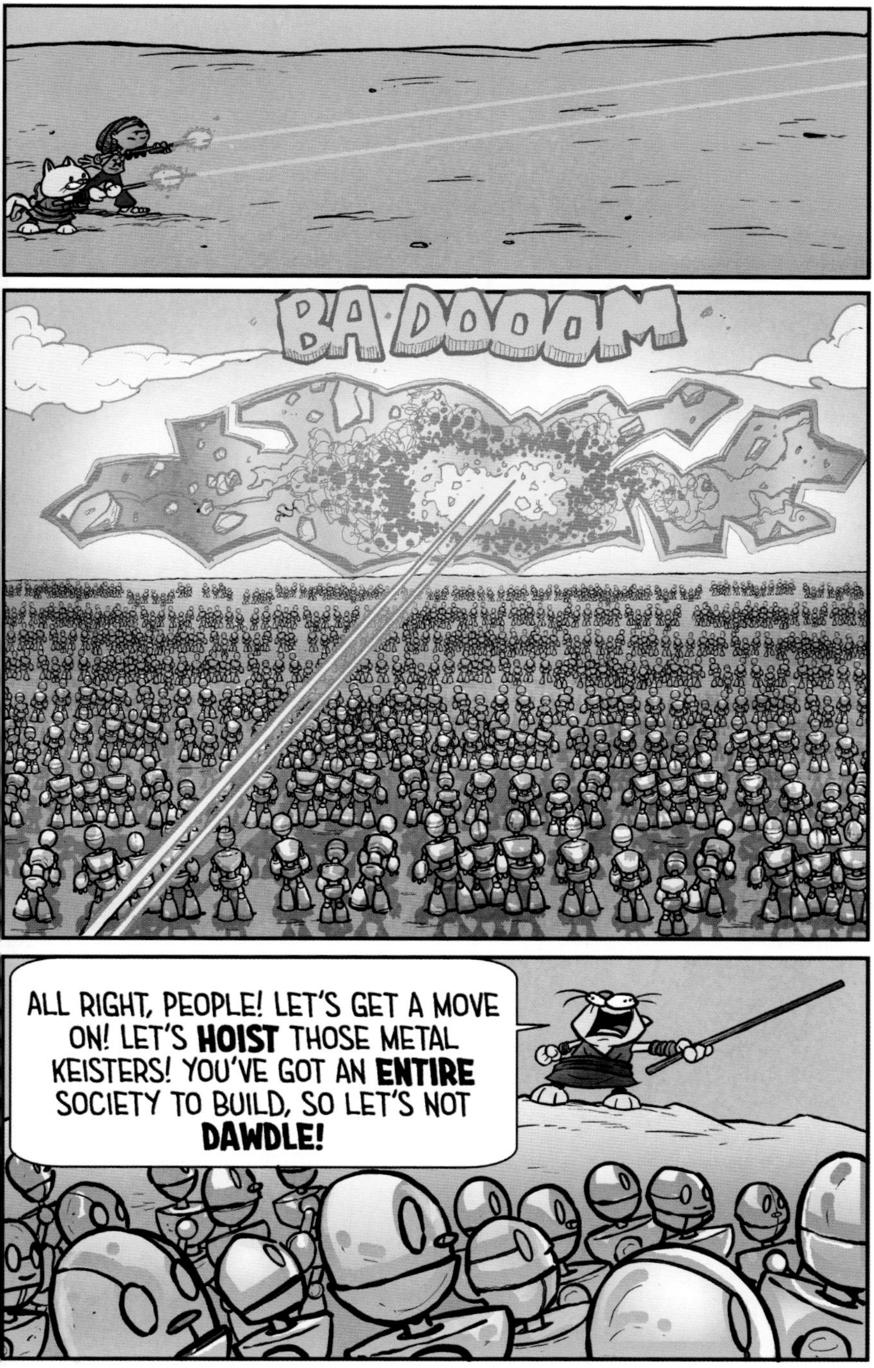
BA-DOOOM
ALL RIGHT, PEOPLE! LET'S GET A MOVE ON! LET'S **HOIST** THOSE METAL KEISTERS! YOU'VE GOT AN **ENTIRE** SOCIETY TO BUILD, SO LET'S NOT **DAWDLE!**

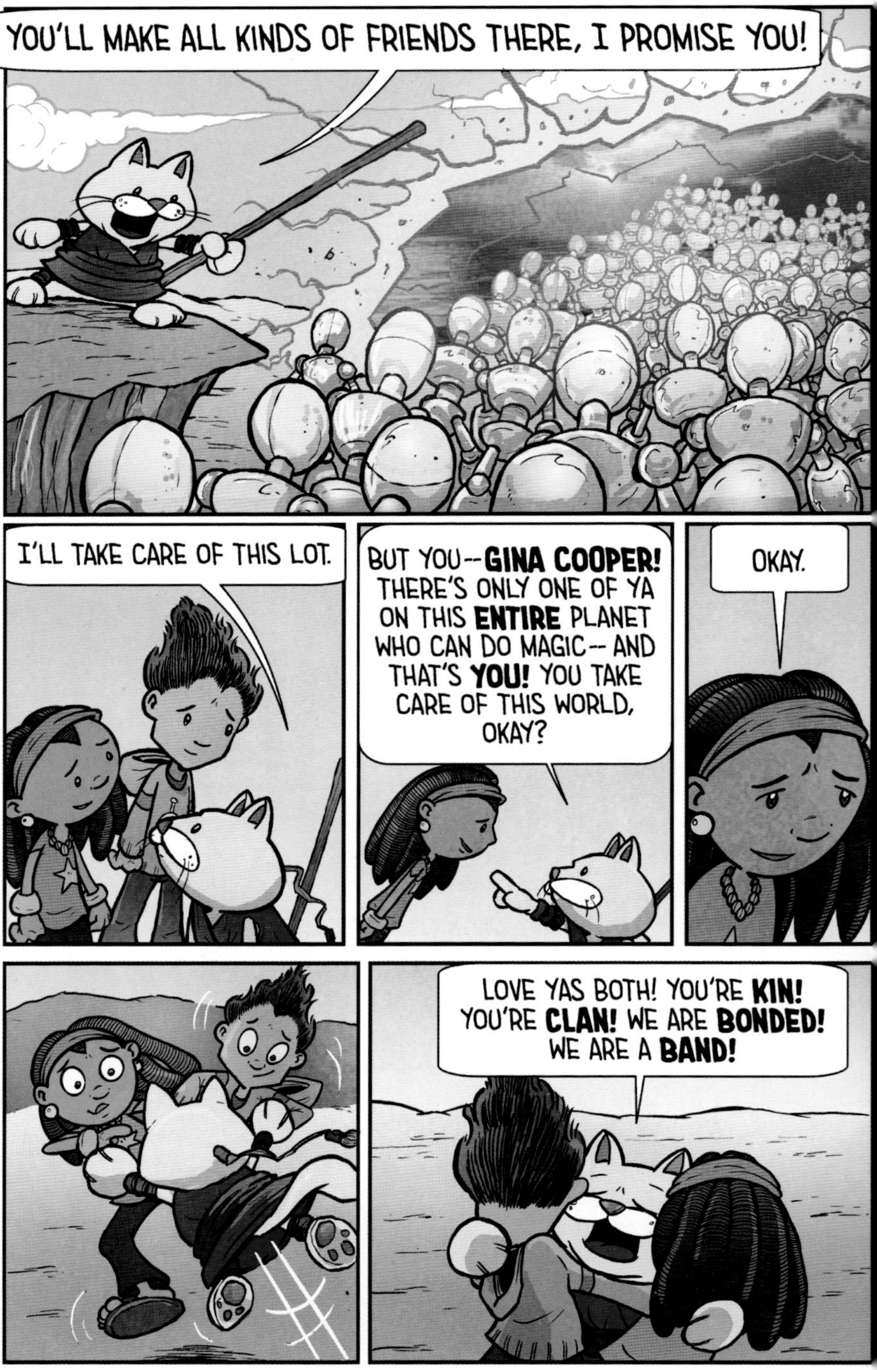
YOU'LL MAKE ALL KINDS OF FRIENDS THERE, I PROMISE YOU!
I'LL TAKE CARE OF THIS LOT.
BUT YOU--GINA COOPER! THERE'S ONLY ONE OF YA ON THIS ENTIRE PLANET WHO CAN DO MAGIC-- AND THAT'S YOU! YOU TAKE CARE OF THIS WORLD, OKAY?
OKAY.
LOVE YAS BOTH! YOU'RE KIN! YOU'RE CLAN! WE ARE BONDED! WE ARE A BAND!

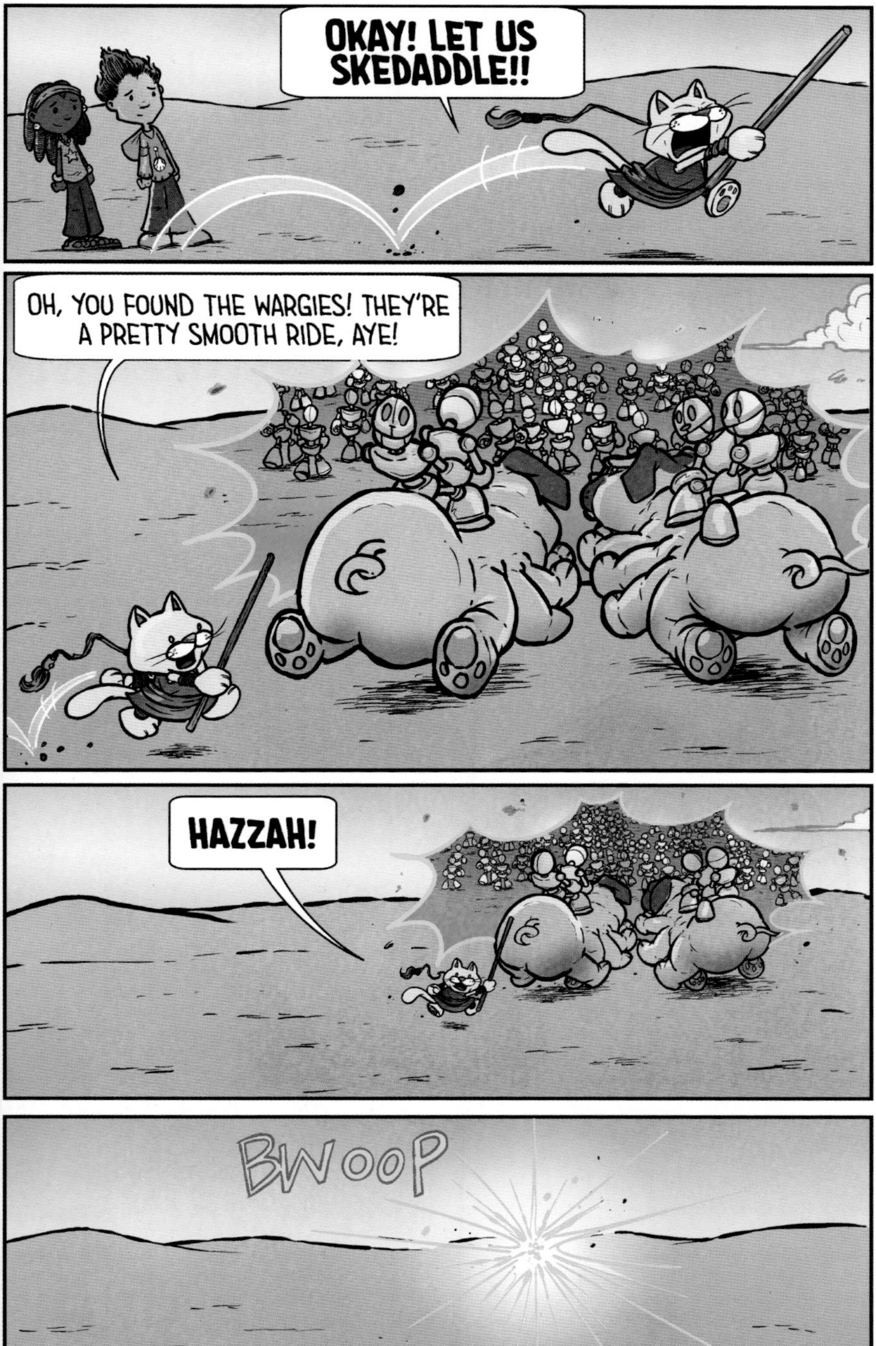
OKAY! LET US SKEDADDLE!!
OH, YOU FOUND THE WARGIES! THEY'RE A PRETTY SMOOTH RIDE, AYE!
HAZZAH!
BWOOP

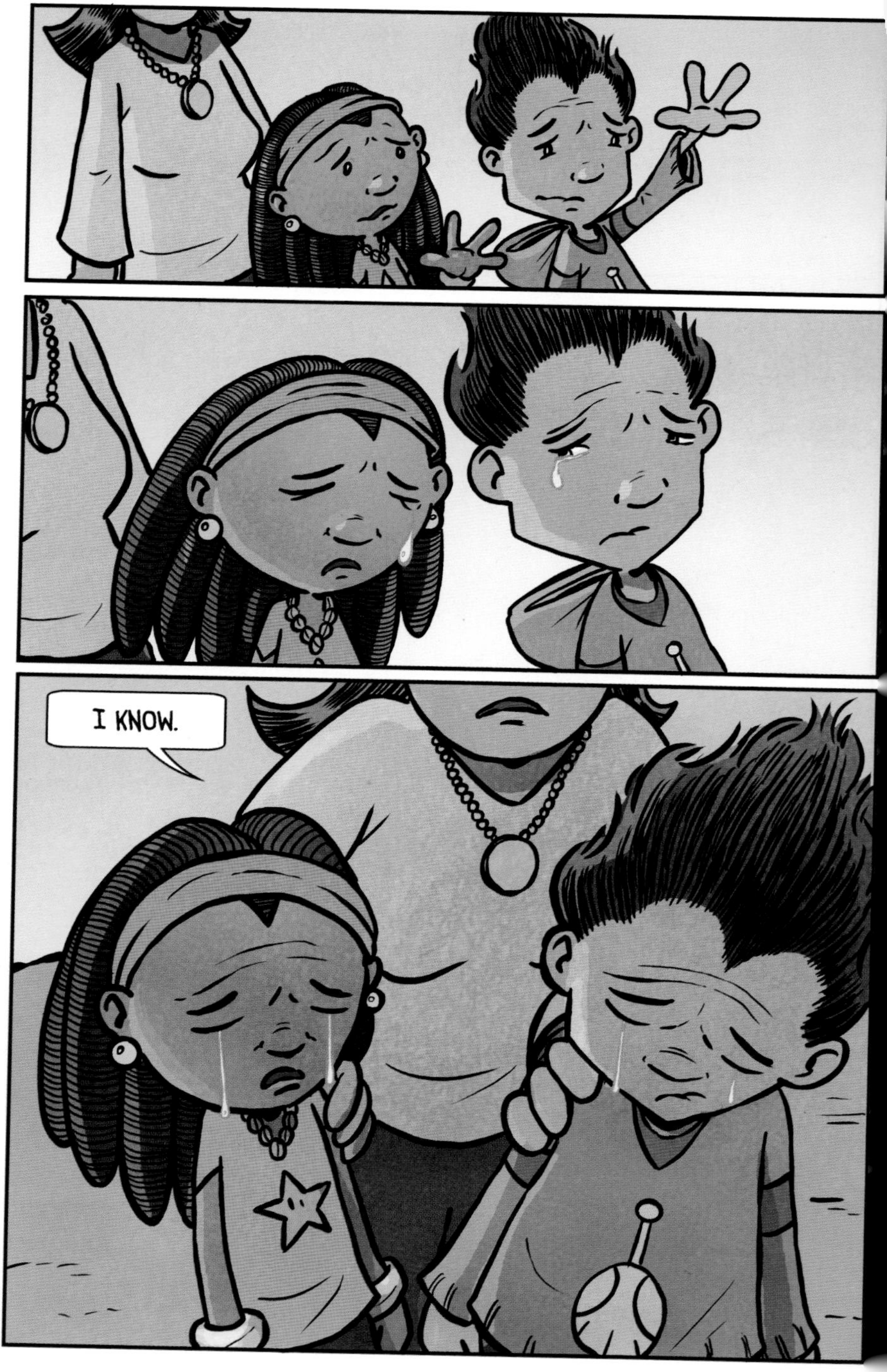
I KNOW.

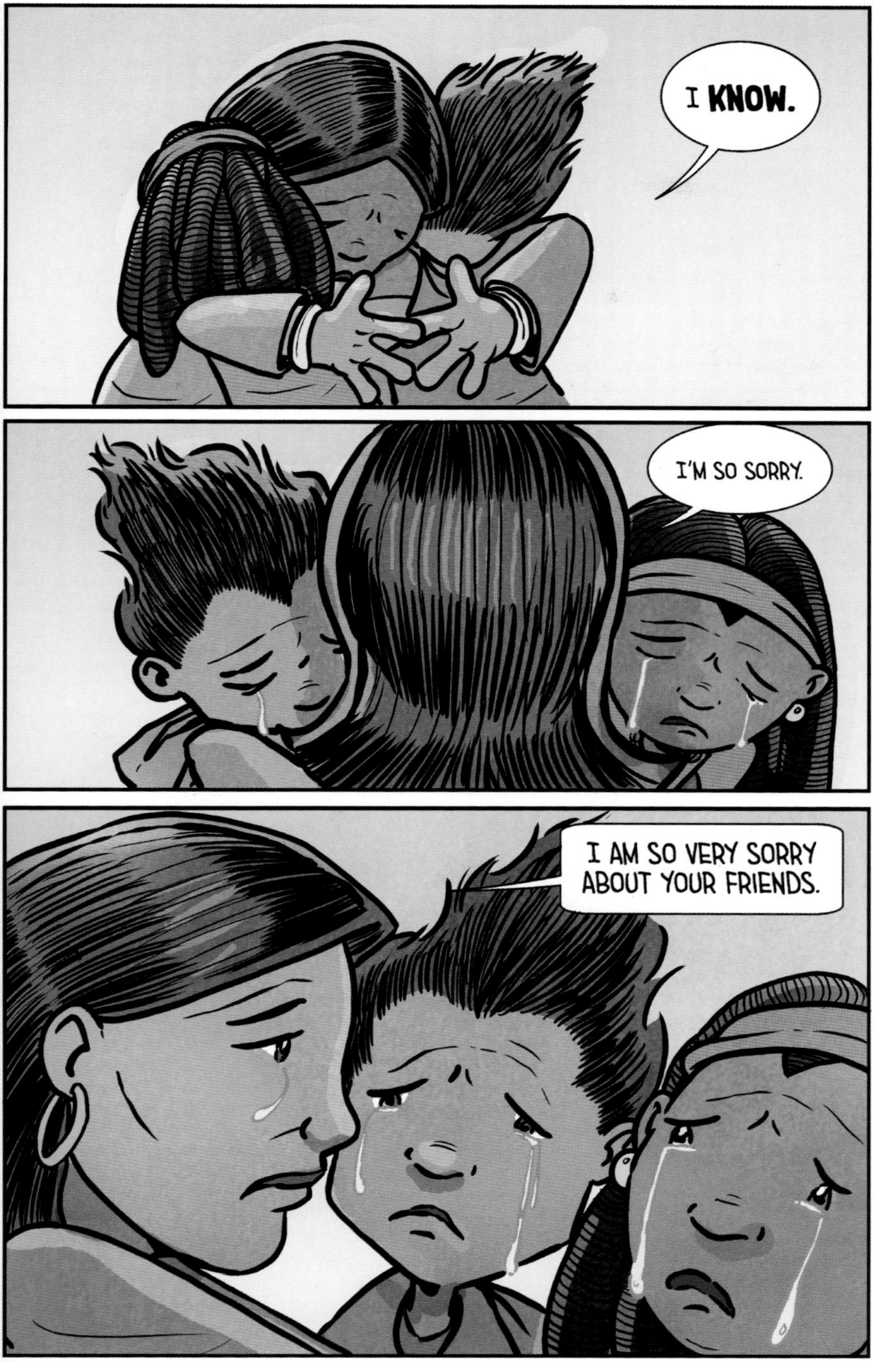
I KNOW.
I'M SO SORRY.
I AM SO VERY SORRY ABOUT YOUR FRIENDS.

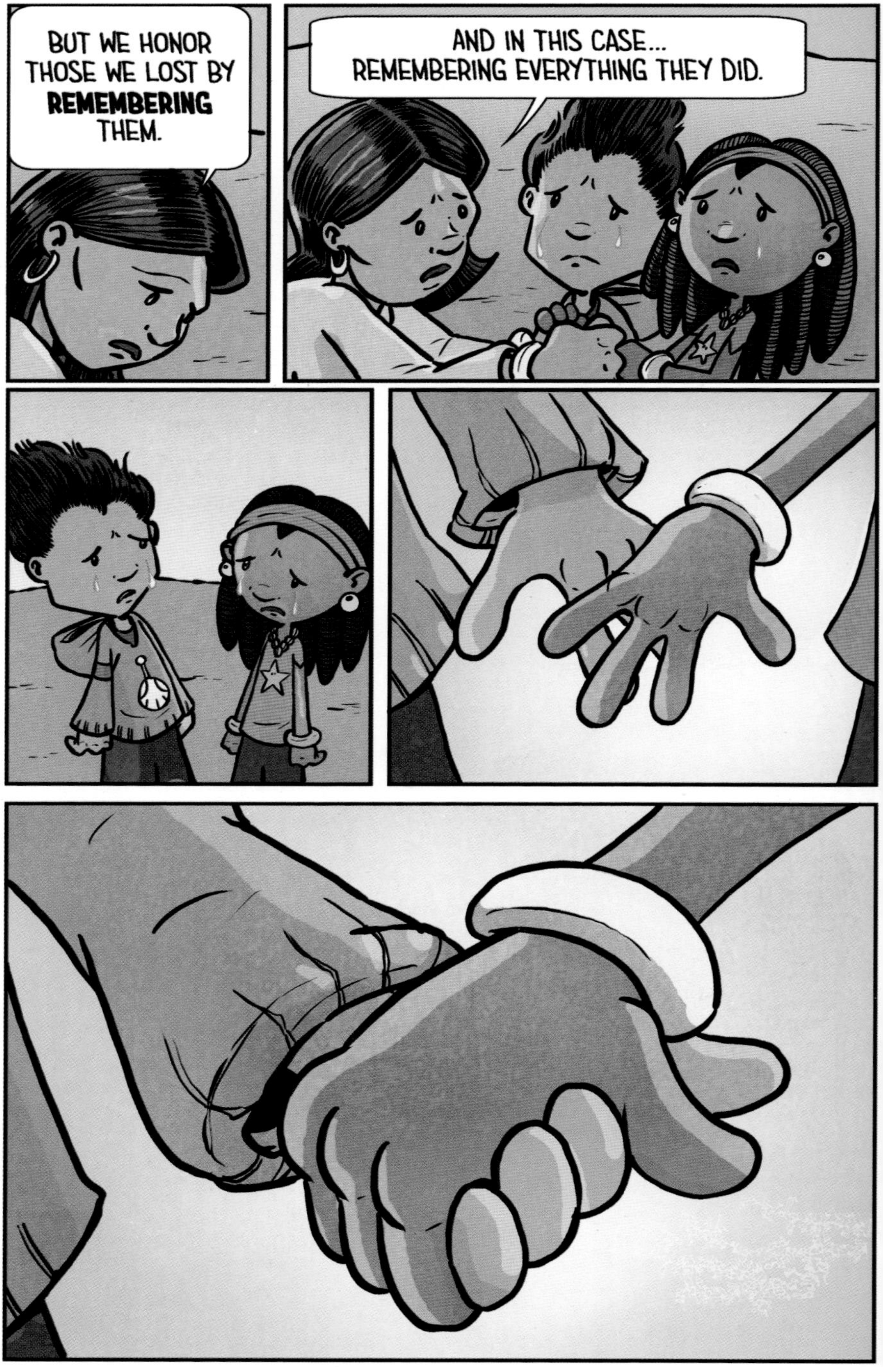
BUT WE HONOR THOSE WE LOST BY **REMEMBERING** THEM.
AND IN THIS CASE... REMEMBERING EVERYTHING THEY DID.

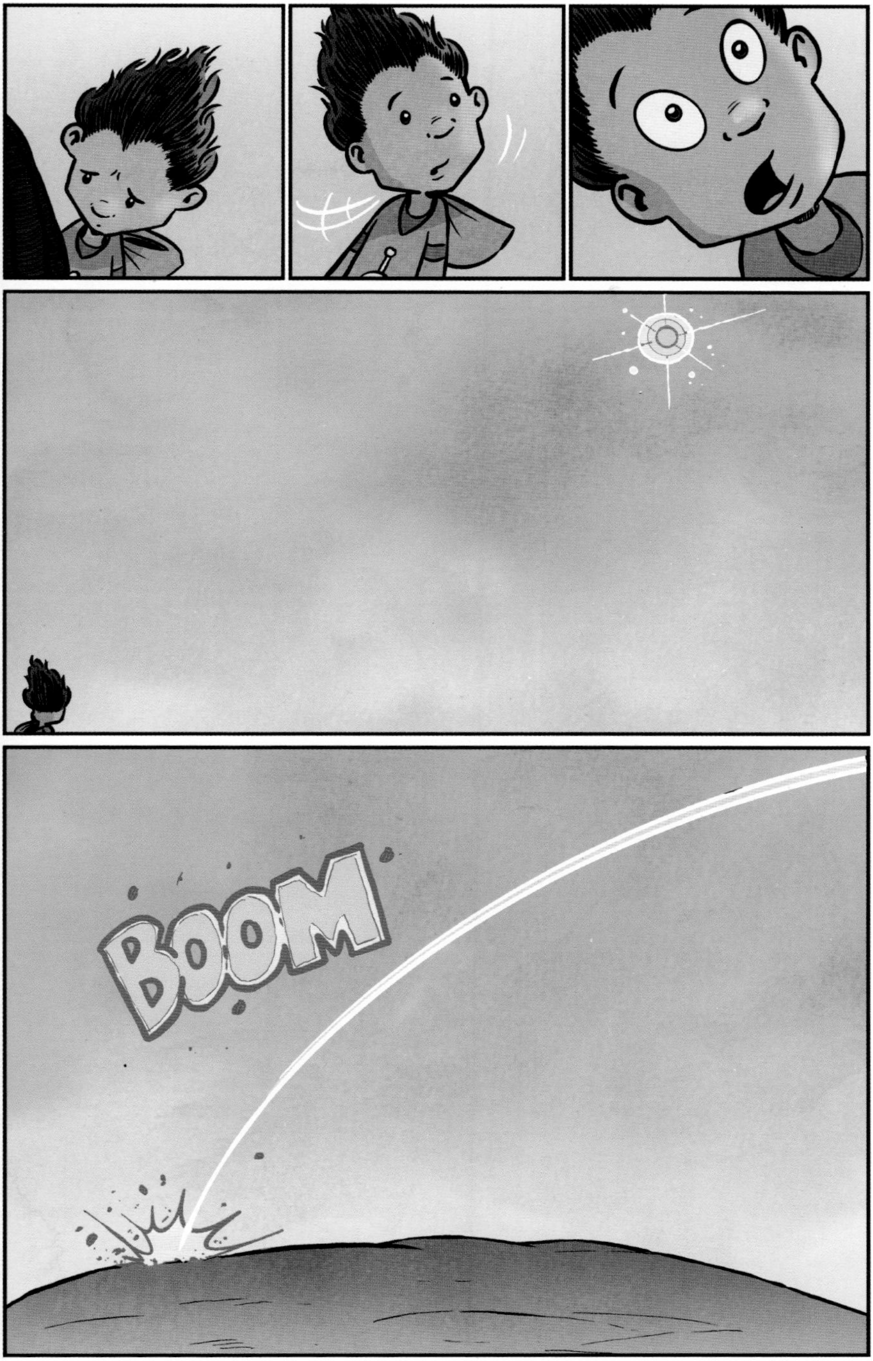
BOOM

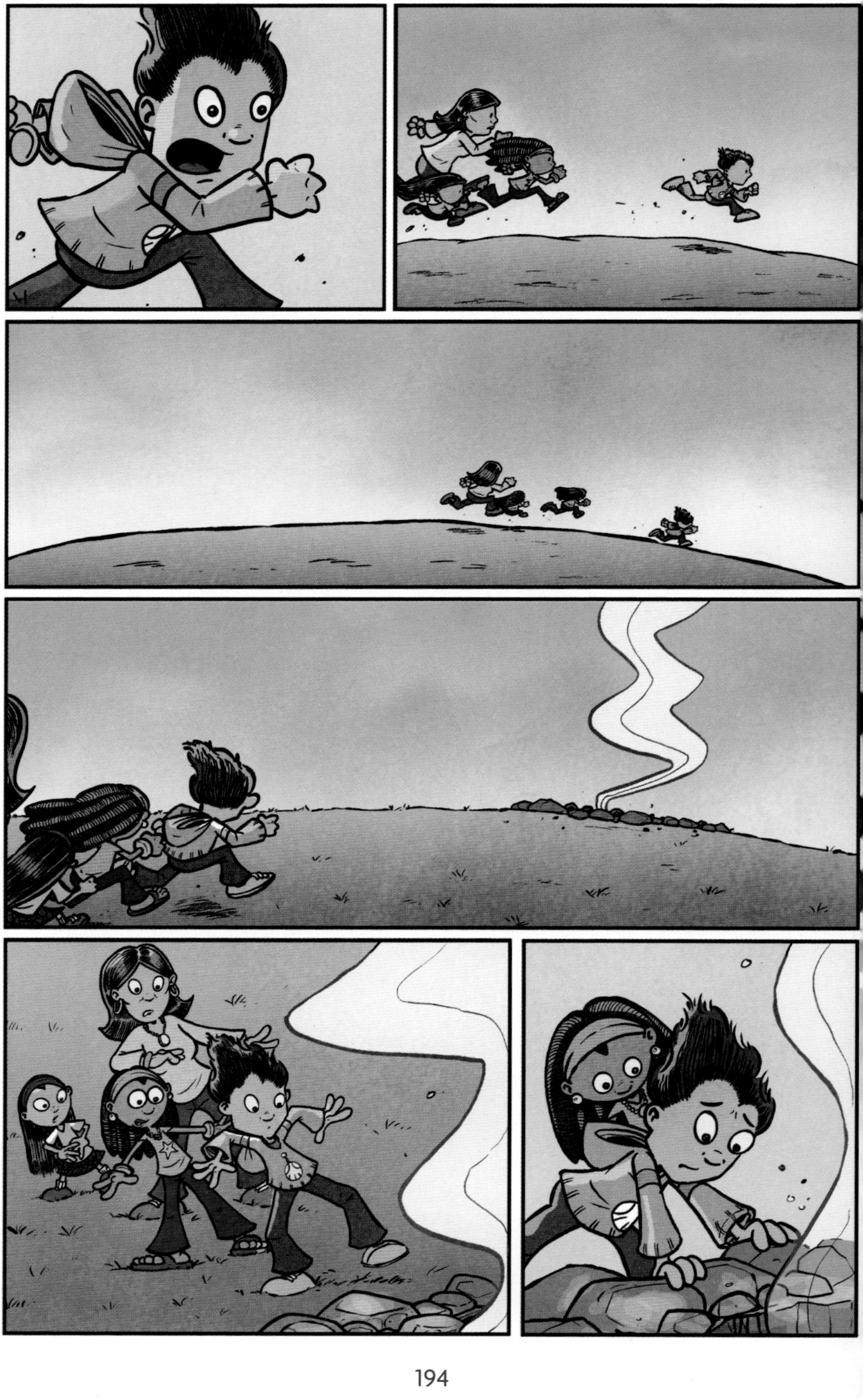

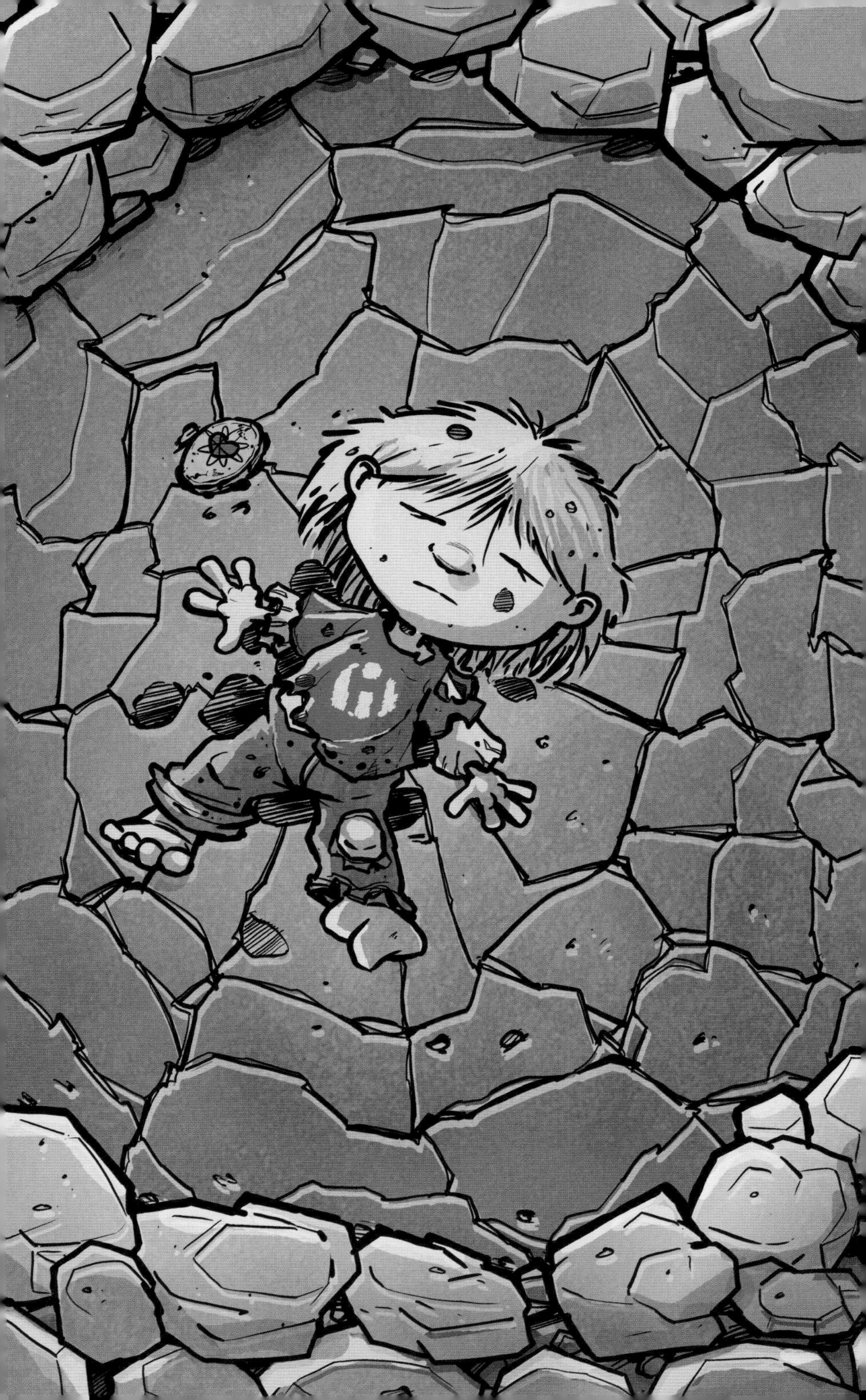

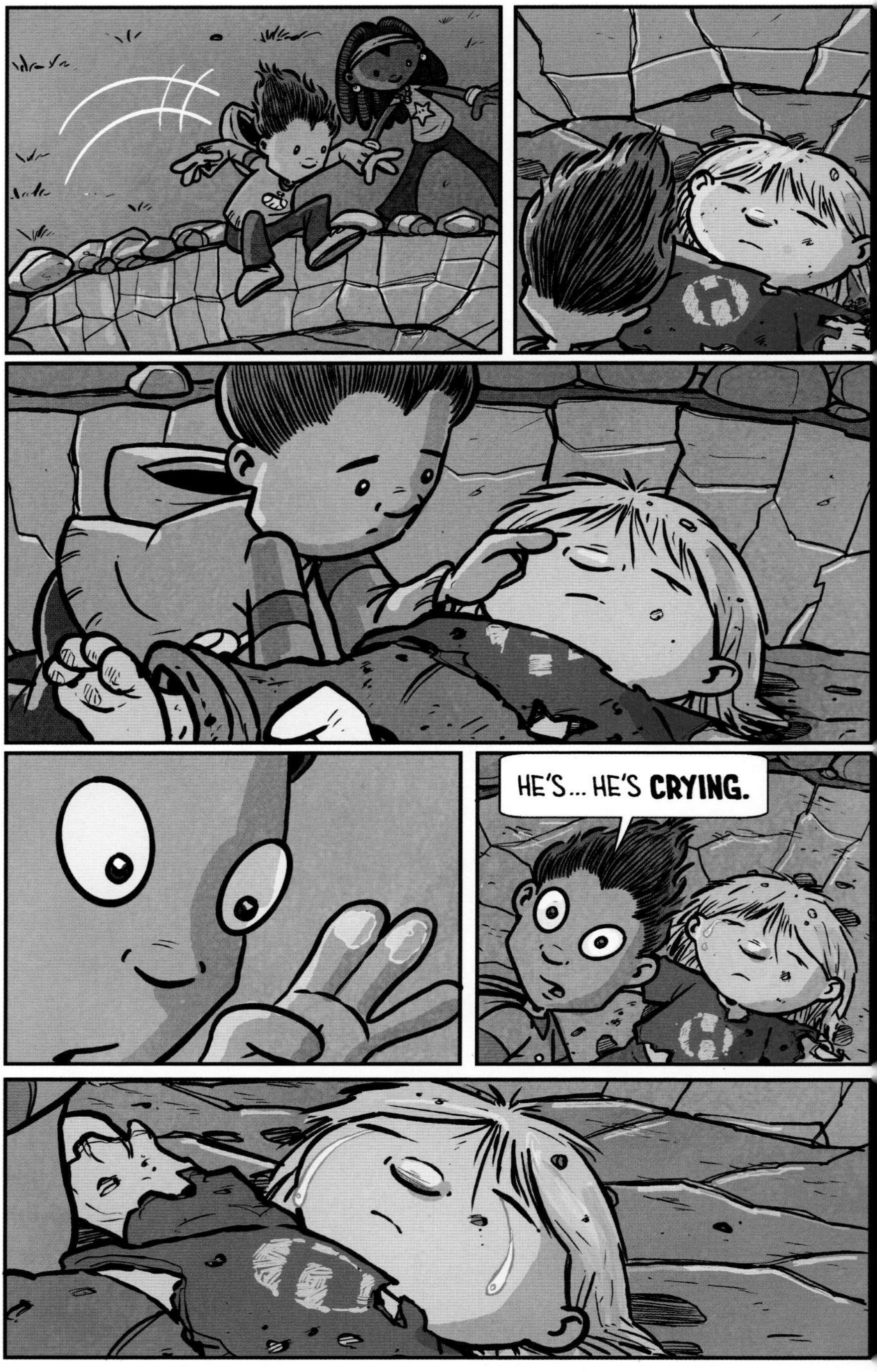
HE'S... HE'S CRYING.

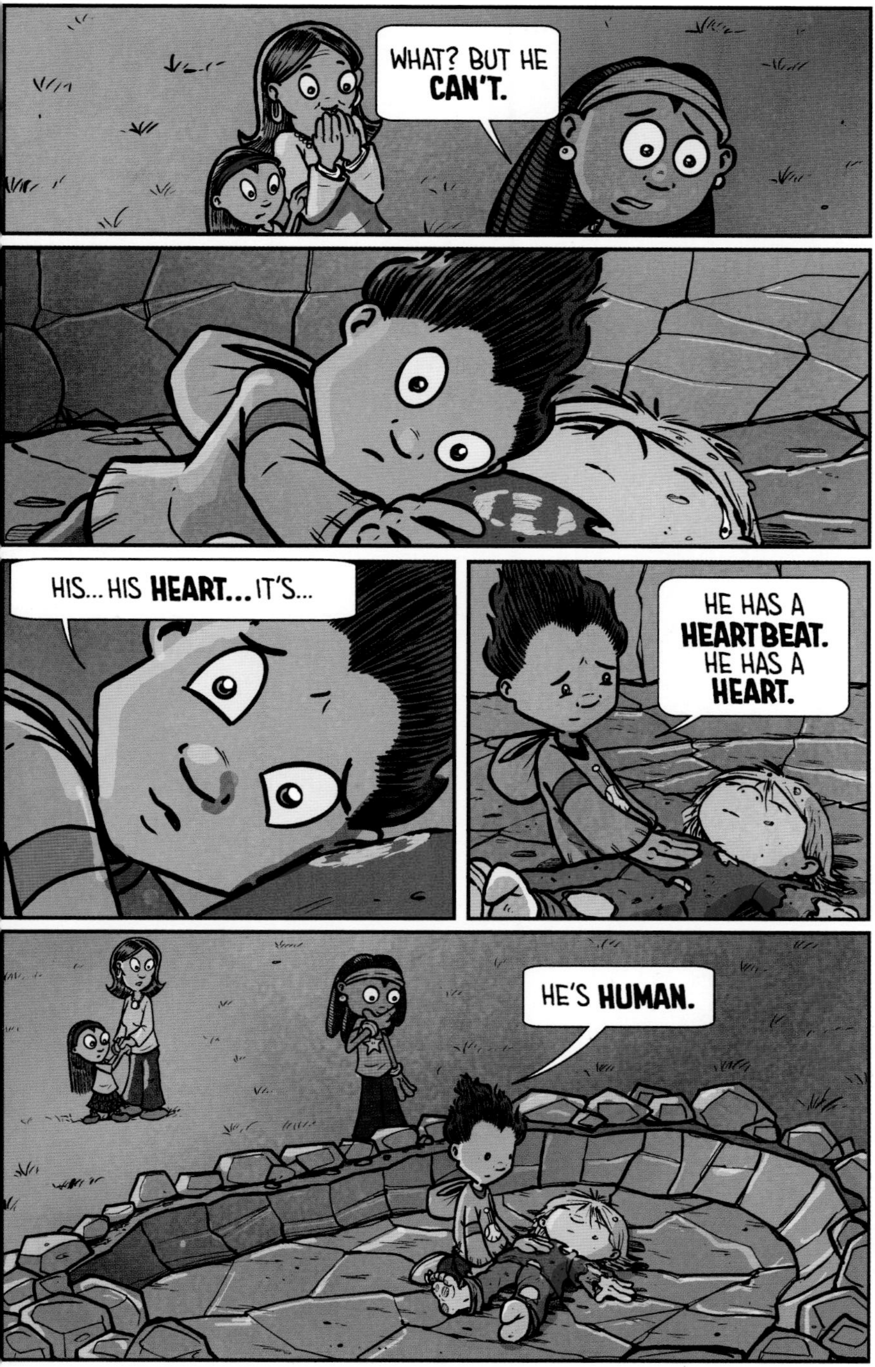
WHAT? BUT HE **CAN'T.**
HIS... HIS **HEART...** IT'S...
HE HAS A **HEARTBEAT.** HE HAS A **HEART.**
HE'S **HUMAN.**

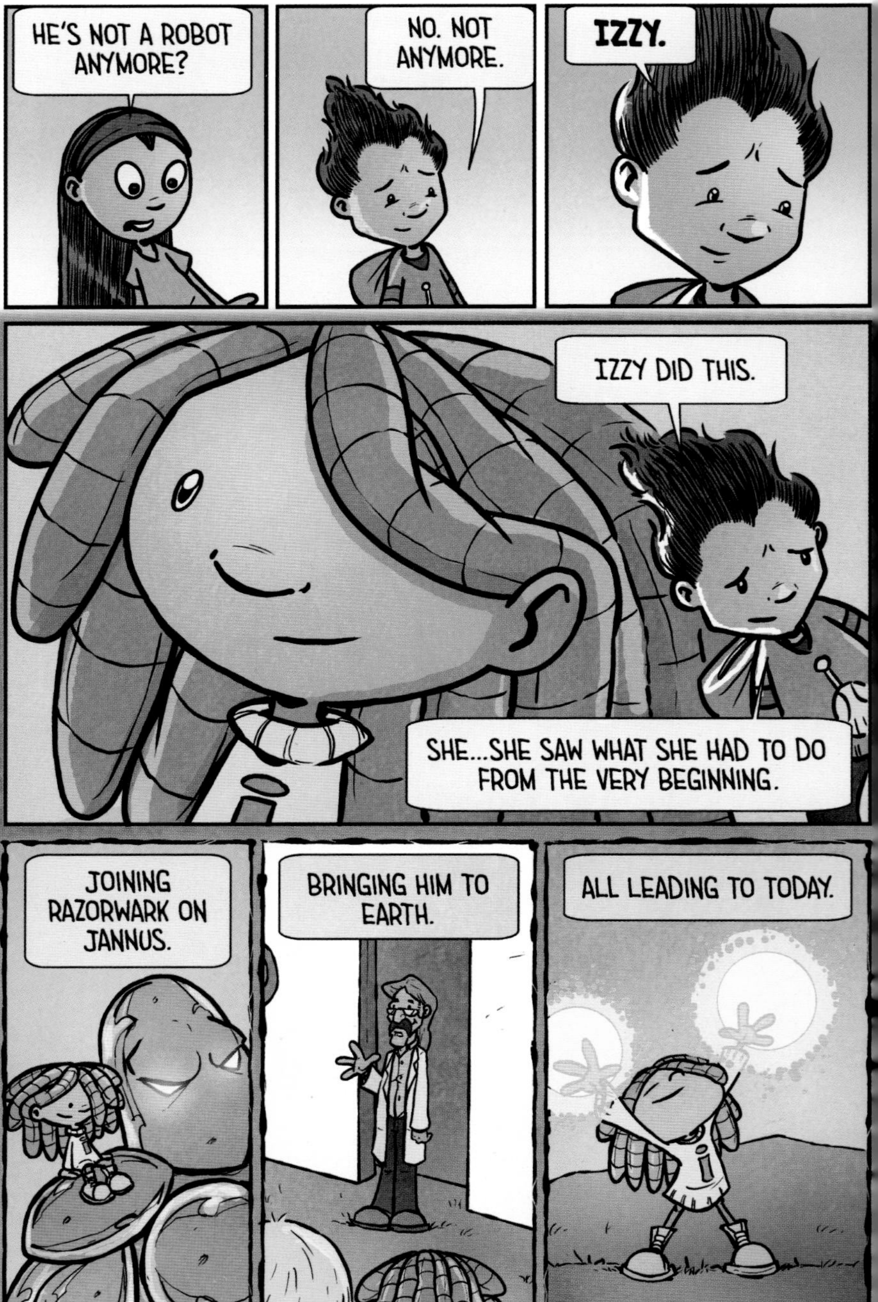
HE'S NOT A ROBOT ANYMORE?
NO. NOT ANYMORE.
IZZY.
IZZY DID THIS.
SHE...SHE SAW WHAT SHE HAD TO DO FROM THE VERY BEGINNING.
JOINING RAZORWARK ON JANNUS.
BRINGING HIM TO EARTH.
ALL LEADING TO TODAY.

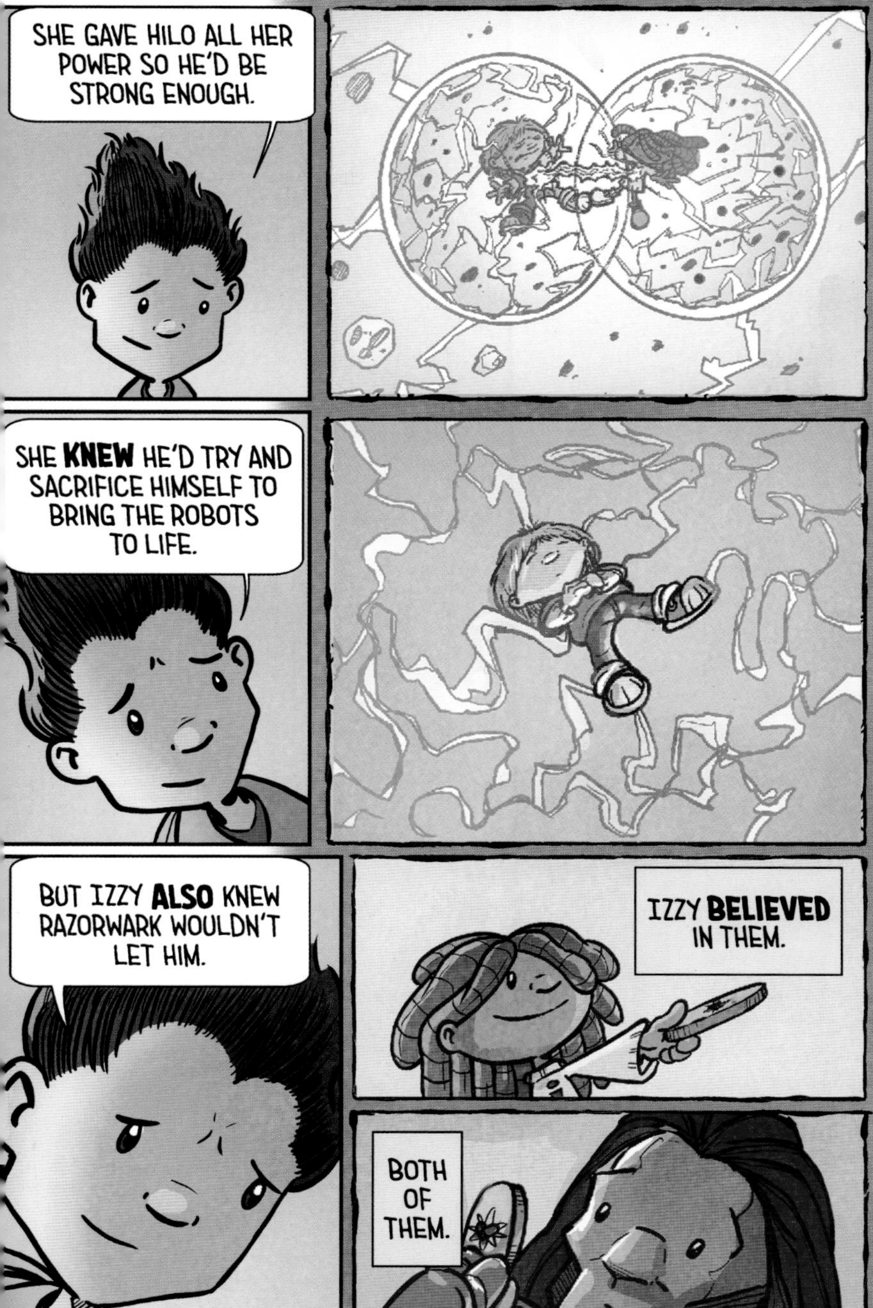
SHE GAVE HILO ALL HER POWER SO HE'D BE STRONG ENOUGH.
SHE **KNEW** HE'D TRY AND SACRIFICE HIMSELF TO BRING THE ROBOTS TO LIFE.
BUT IZZY **ALSO** KNEW RAZORWARK WOULDN'T LET HIM.
IZZY **BELIEVED** IN THEM.
BOTH OF THEM.

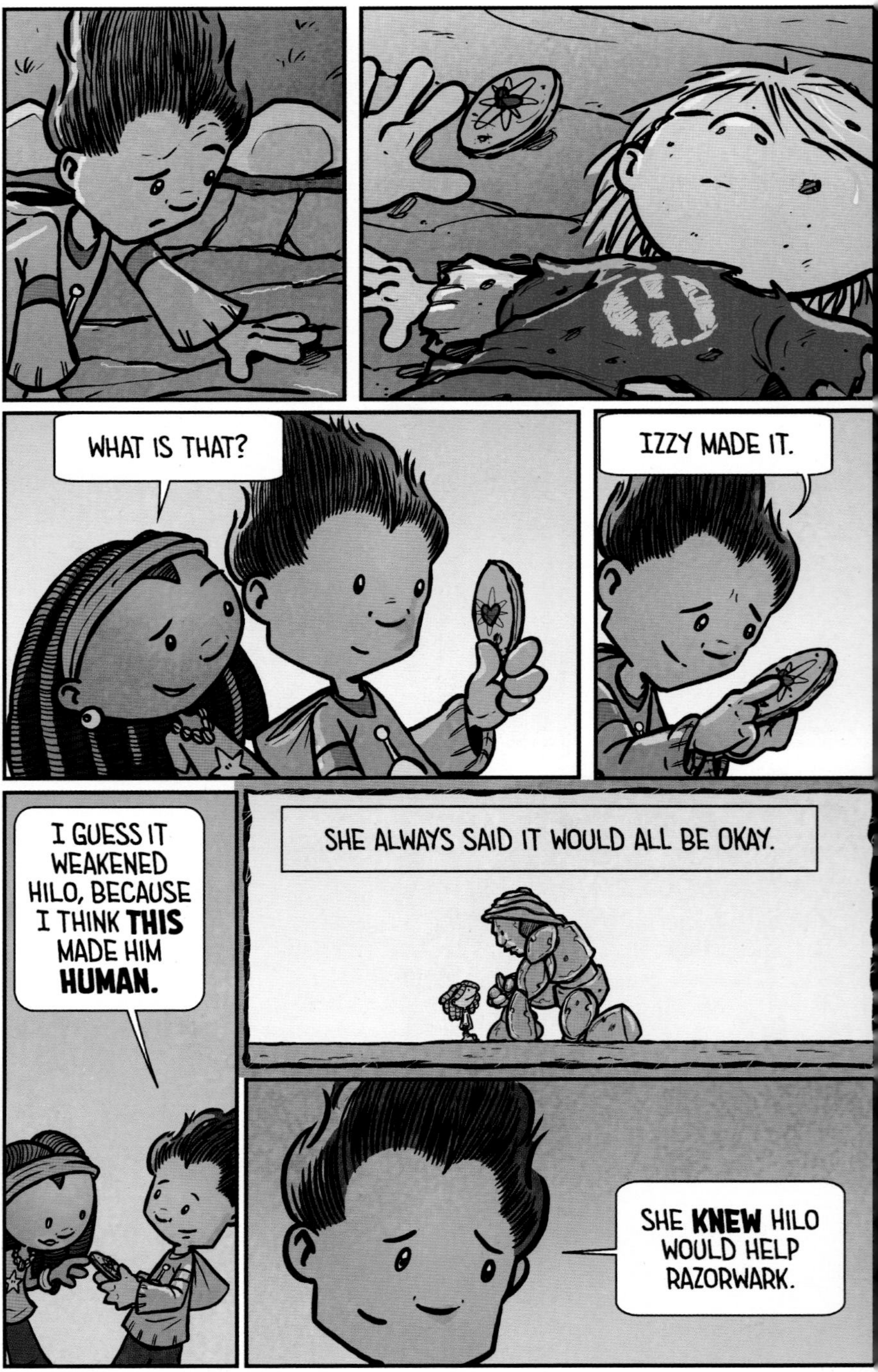

WHAT IS THAT?
IZZY MADE IT.
I GUESS IT WEAKENED HILO, BECAUSE I THINK **THIS** MADE HIM **HUMAN.**
SHE ALWAYS SAID IT WOULD ALL BE OKAY.
SHE **KNEW** HILO WOULD HELP RAZORWARK.

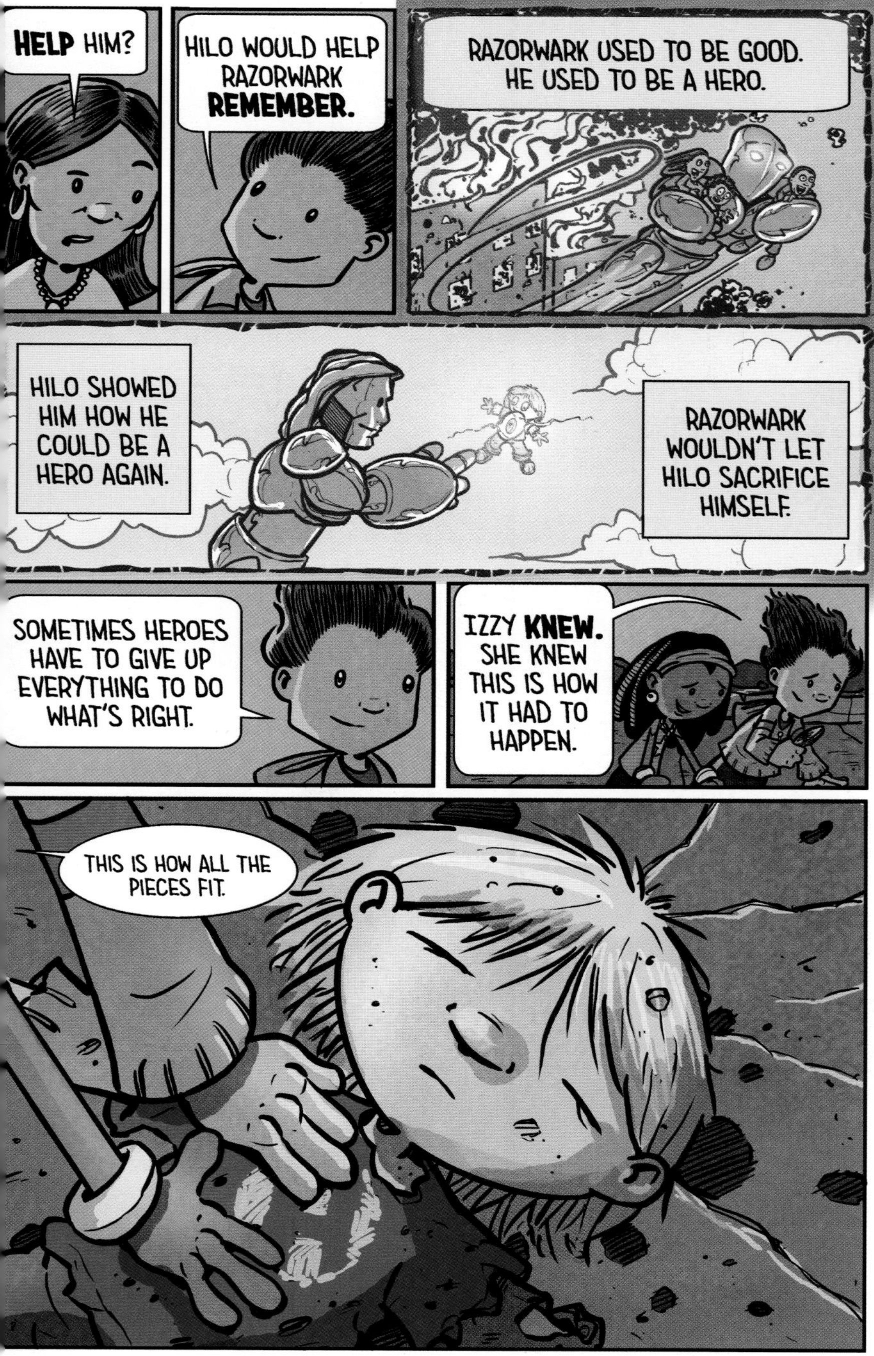
HELP HIM?
HILO WOULD HELP RAZORWARK REMEMBER.
RAZORWARK USED TO BE GOOD. HE USED TO BE A HERO.
HILO SHOWED HIM HOW HE COULD BE A HERO AGAIN.
RAZORWARK WOULDN'T LET HILO SACRIFICE HIMSELF.
SOMETIMES HEROES HAVE TO GIVE UP EVERYTHING TO DO WHAT'S RIGHT.
IZZY KNEW. SHE KNEW THIS IS HOW IT HAD TO HAPPEN.
THIS IS HOW ALL THE PIECES FIT.

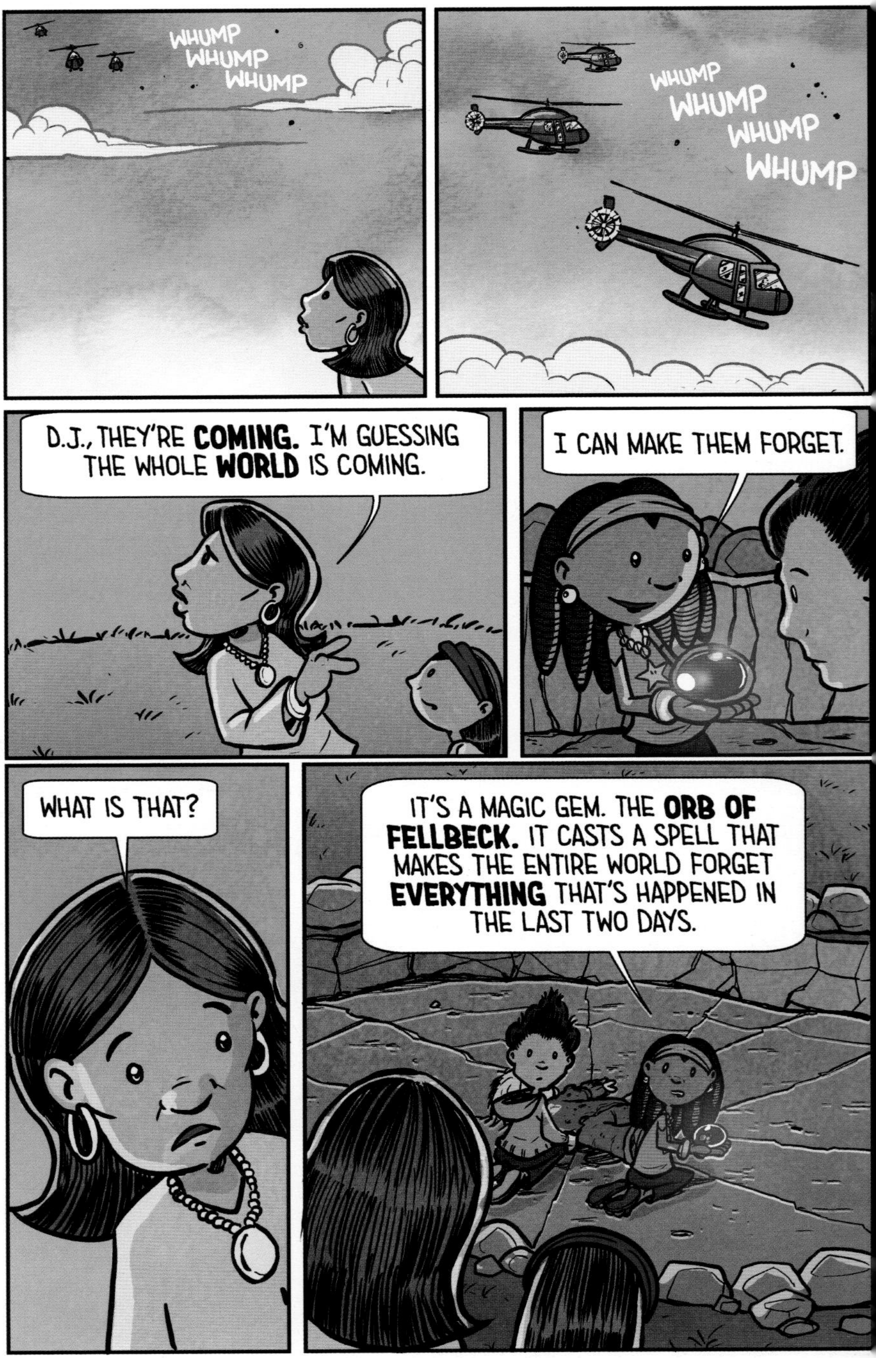
WHUMP
WHUMP
WHUMP
WHUMP
WHUMP
WHUMP
WHUMP
D.J., THEY'RE **COMING.** I'M GUESSING THE WHOLE **WORLD** IS COMING.
I CAN MAKE THEM FORGET.
WHAT IS THAT?
IT'S A MAGIC GEM. THE **ORB OF FELLBECK.** IT CASTS A SPELL THAT MAKES THE ENTIRE WORLD FORGET **EVERYTHING** THAT'S HAPPENED IN THE LAST TWO DAYS.

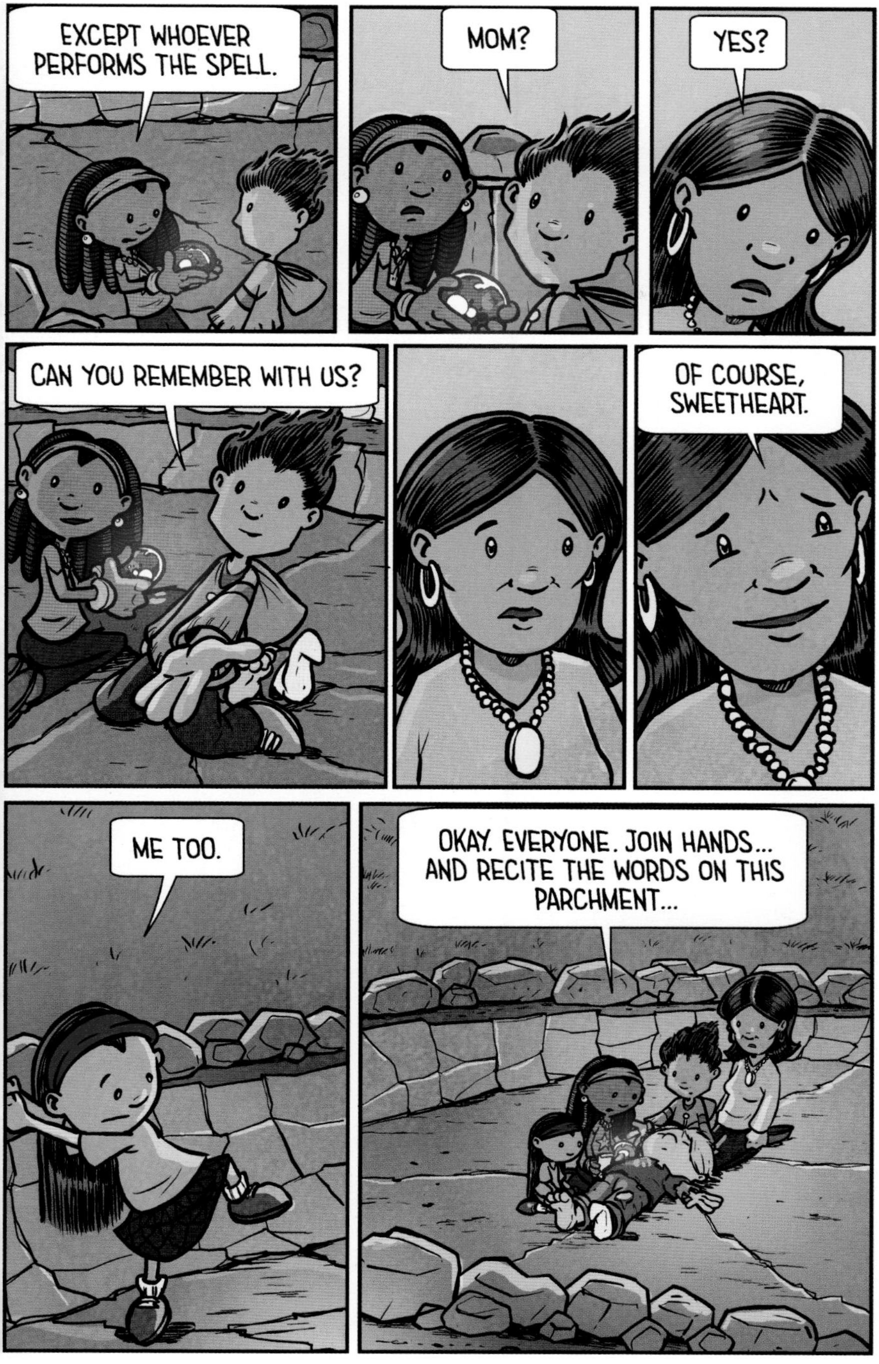
EXCEPT WHOEVER PERFORMS THE SPELL.
MOM?
YES?
CAN YOU REMEMBER WITH US?
OF COURSE, SWEETHEART.
ME TOO.
OKAY. EVERYONE. JOIN HANDS... AND RECITE THE WORDS ON THIS PARCHMENT...

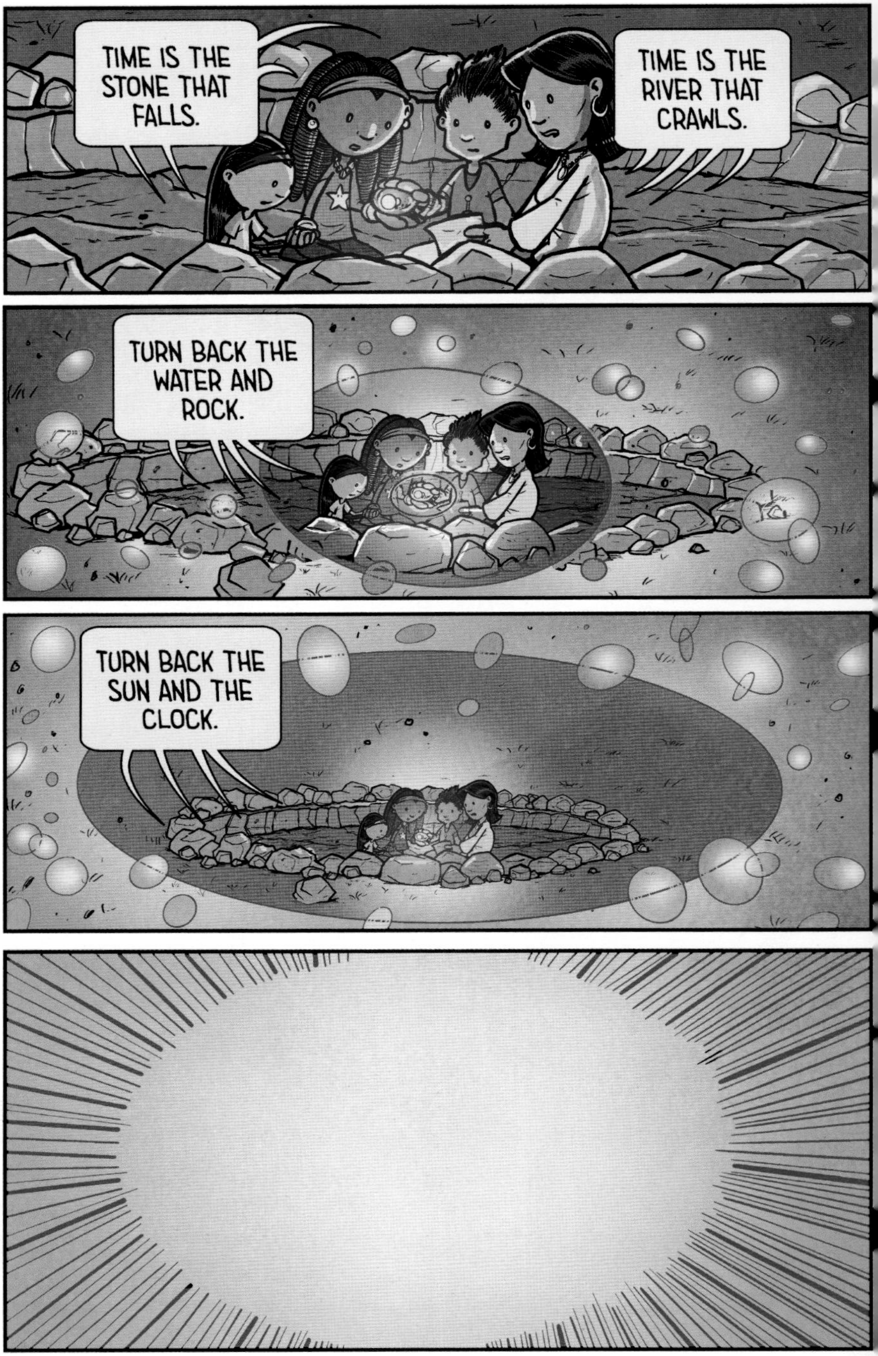
TIME IS THE STONE THAT FALLS.
TIME IS THE RIVER THAT CRAWLS.
TURN BACK THE WATER AND ROCK.
TURN BACK THE SUN AND THE CLOCK.

CHAPTER 10

OUTSTANDING

THREE MONTHS
LATER.

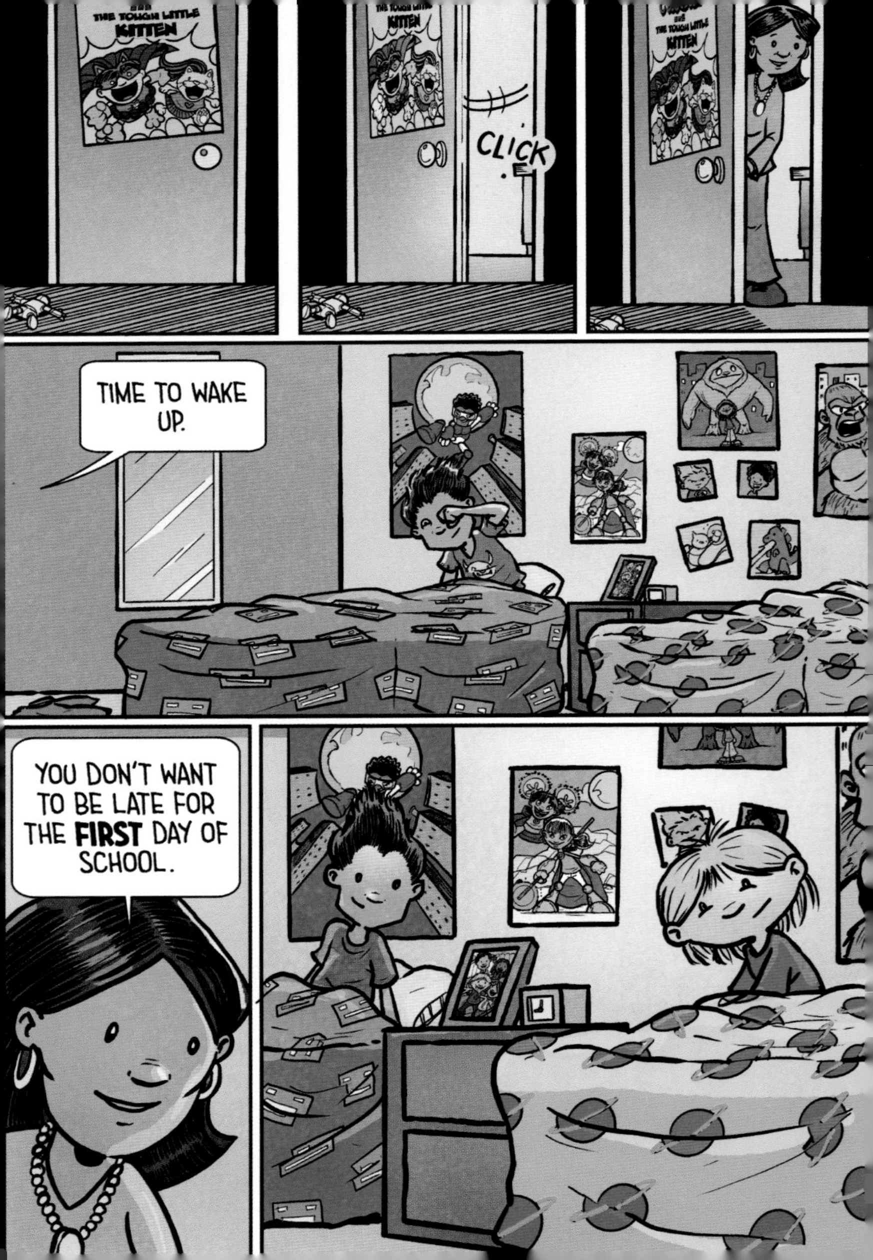
THE TOUGH LITTLE KITTEN
CLICK
TIME TO WAKE UP.
YOU DON'T WANT TO BE LATE FOR THE **FIRST** DAY OF SCHOOL.

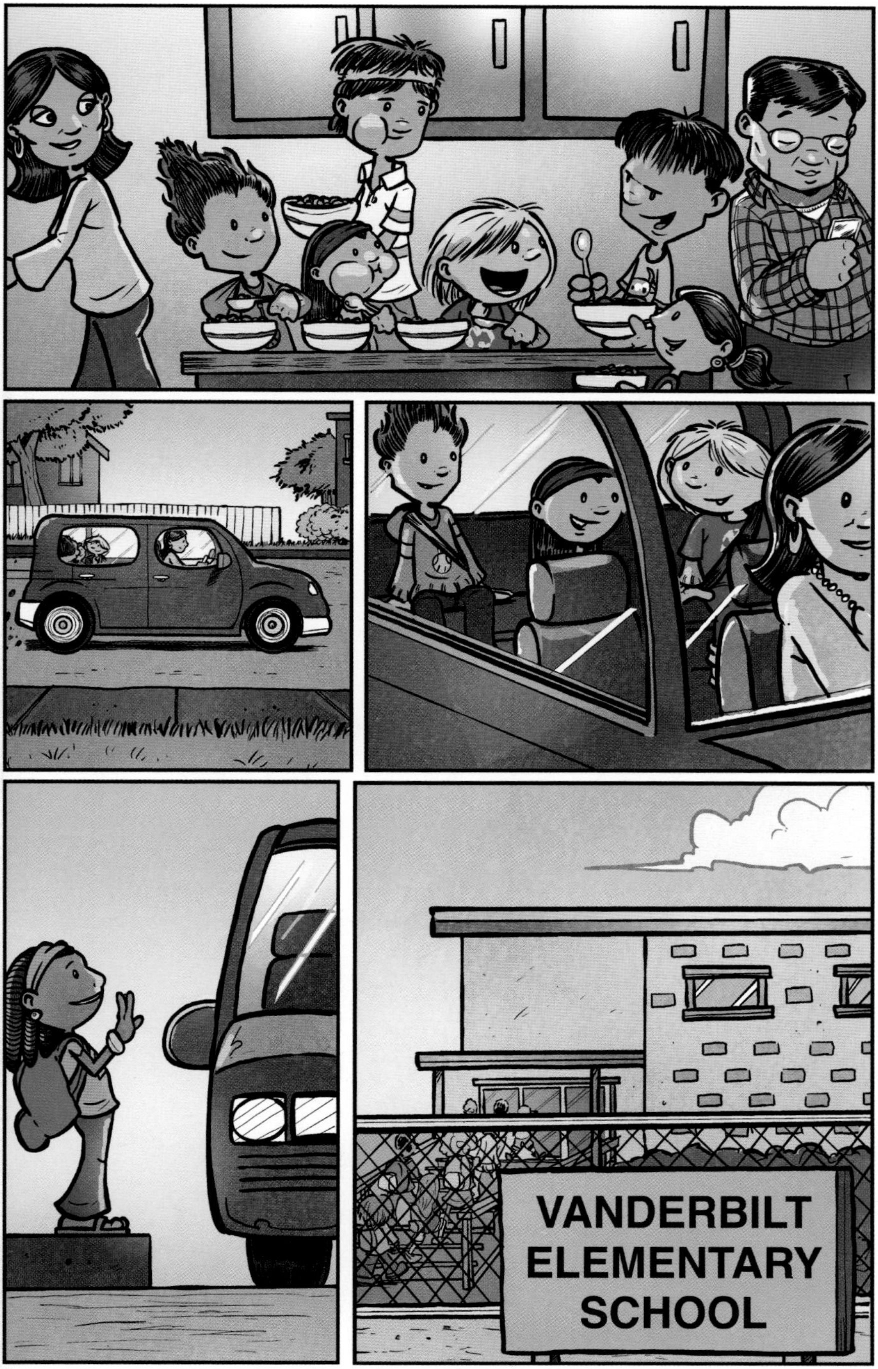
VANDERBILT
ELEMENTARY
SCHOOL

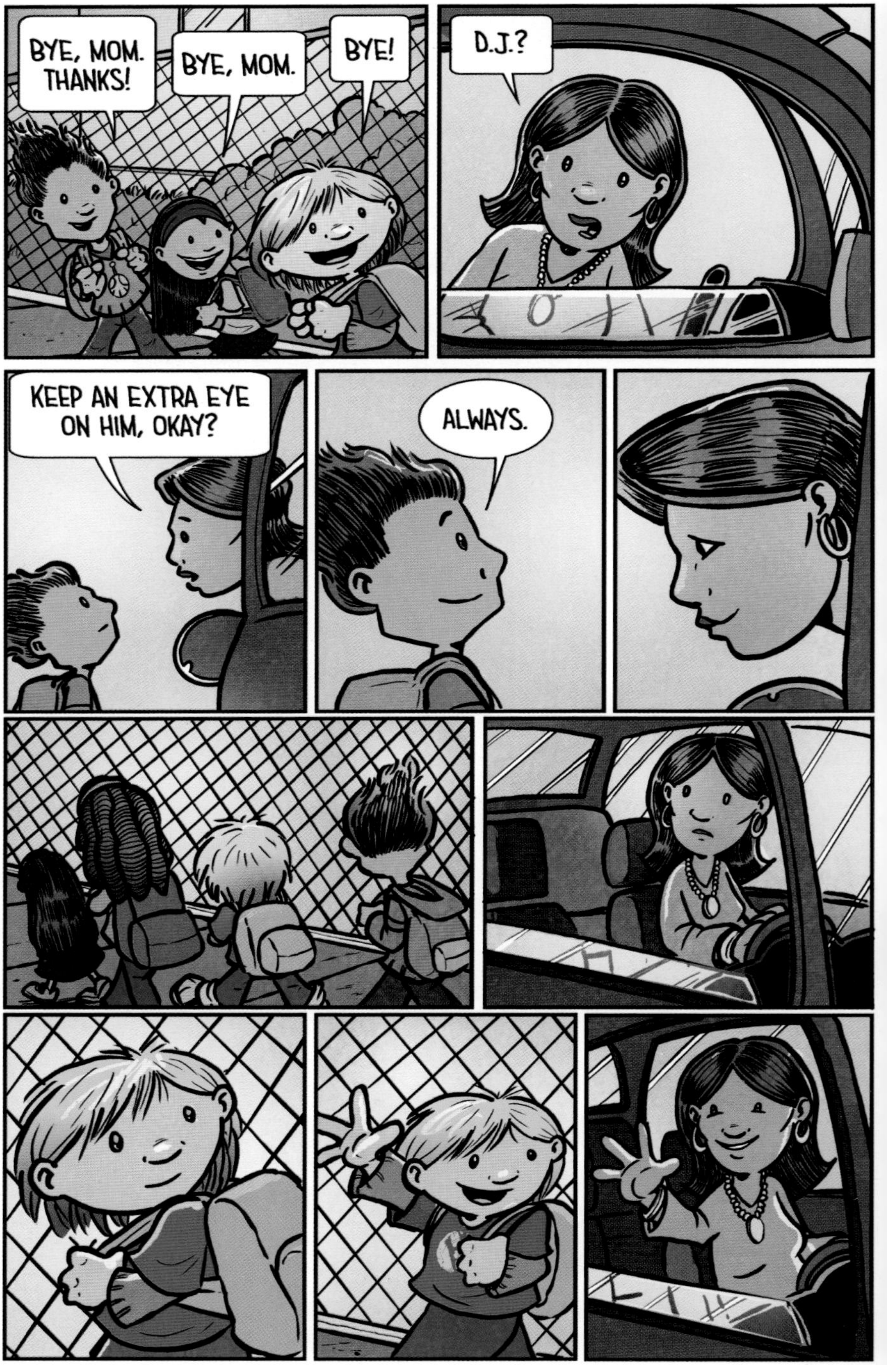
BYE, MOM. THANKS!
BYE, MOM.
BYE!
D.J.?
KEEP AN EXTRA EYE ON HIM, OKAY?
ALWAYS.

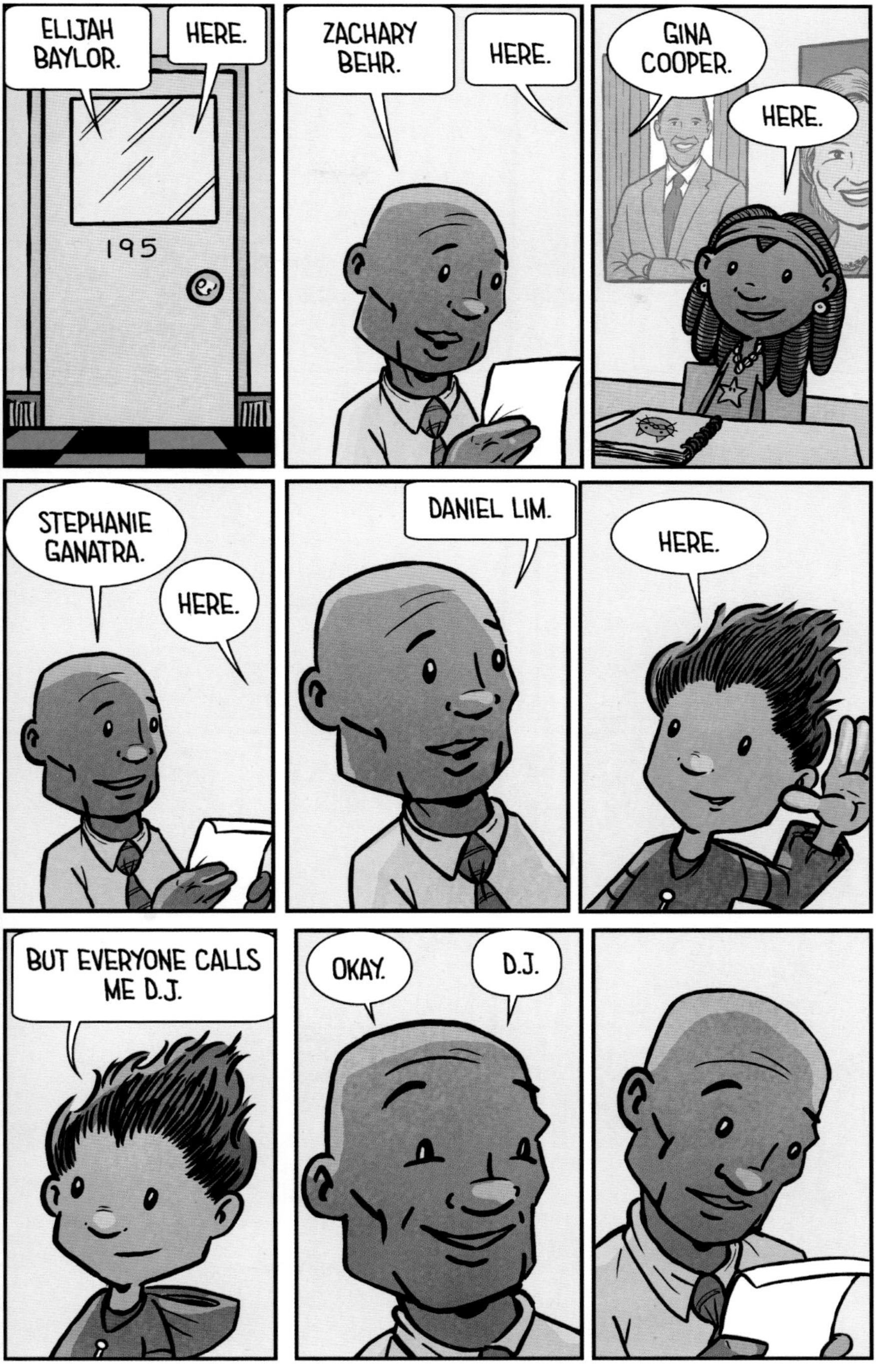
ELIJAH BAYLOR.
HERE.
ZACHARY BEHR.
HERE.
GINA COOPER.
HERE.
STEPHANIE GANATRA.
HERE.
DANIEL LIM.
HERE.
BUT EVERYONE CALLS ME D.J.
OKAY.
D.J.
195

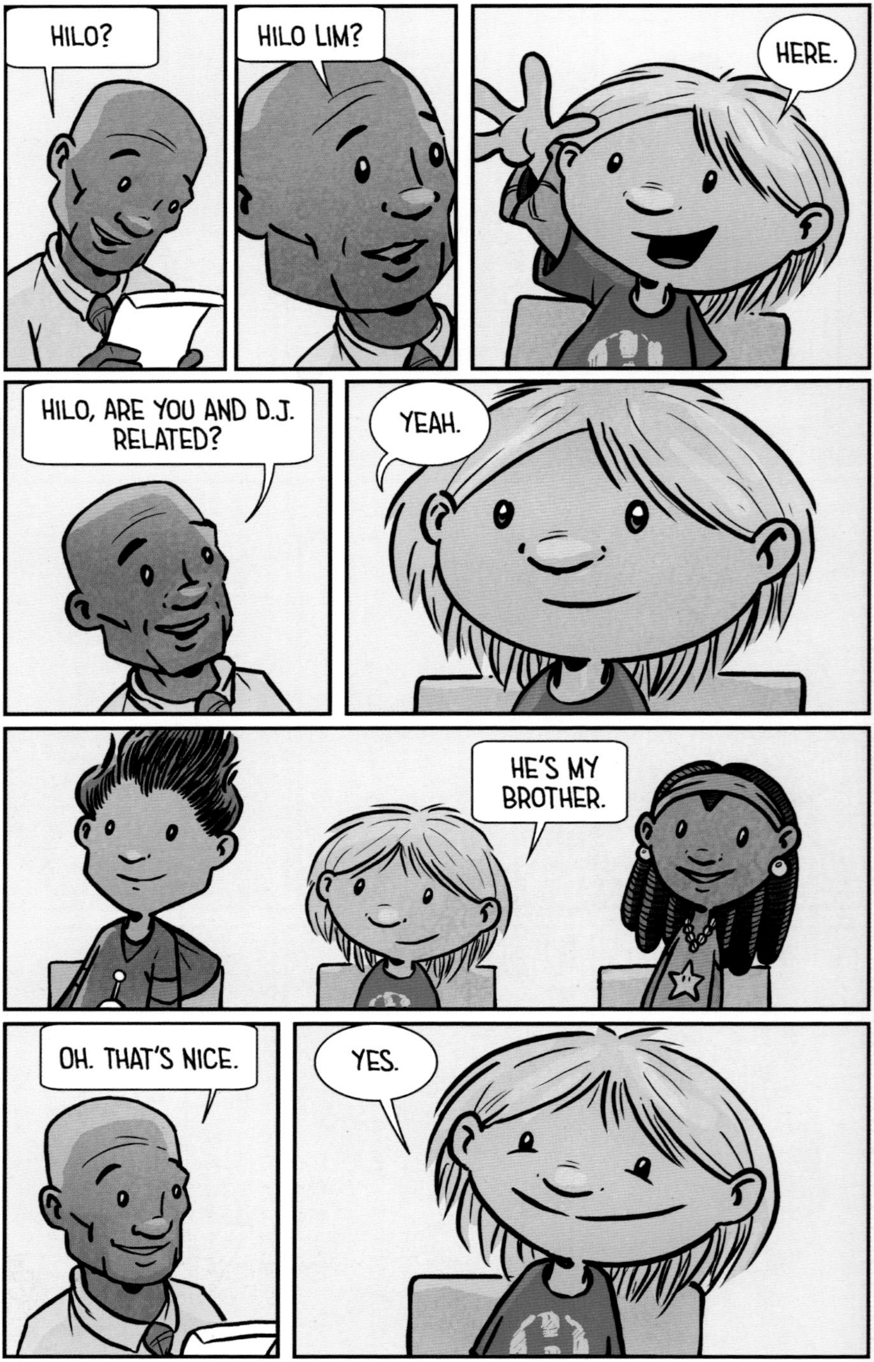
HILO?
HILO LIM?
HERE.
HILO, ARE YOU AND D.J. RELATED?
YEAH.
HE'S MY BROTHER.
OH. THAT'S NICE.
YES.

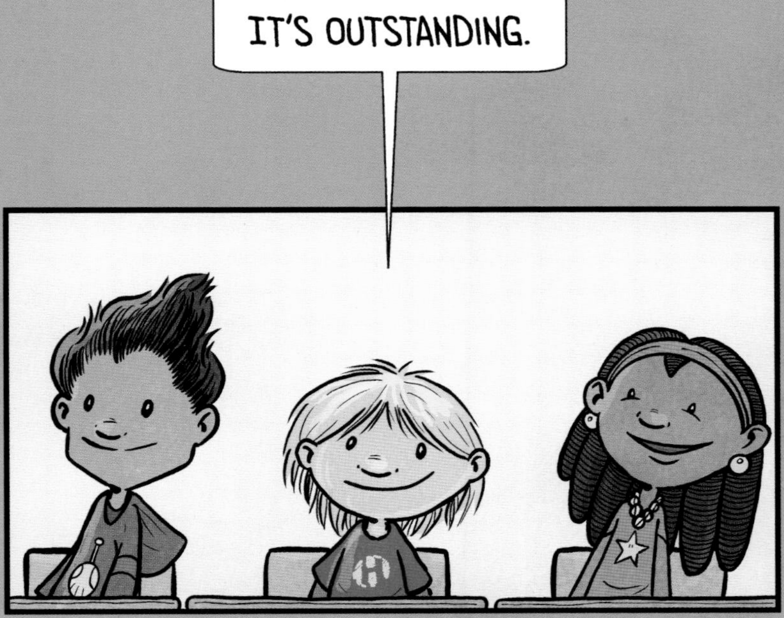
IT'S OUTSTANDING.

THE END OF THE BEGINNING

FIND OUT WHAT HAPPENS NEXT IN

HILO

BOOK 7

GINA—THE GIRL WHO BROKE THE WORLD

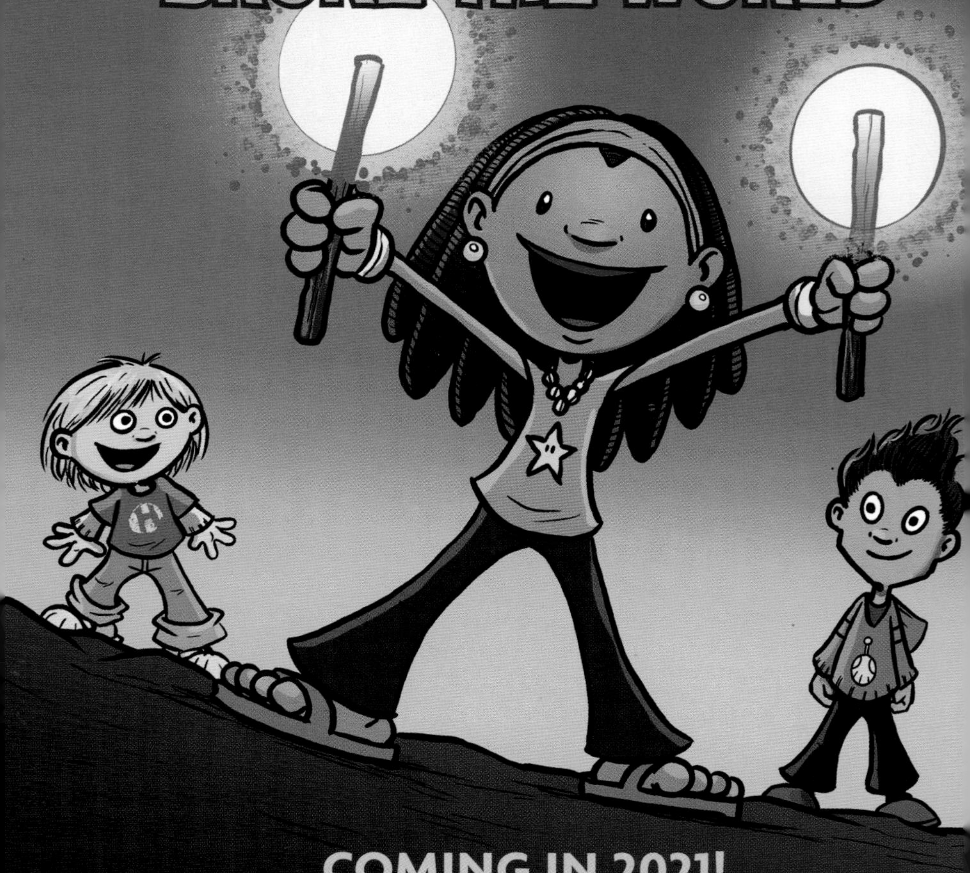

COMING IN 2021!

JUDD WINICK is the creator of the award-winning, **New York Times** bestselling Hilo series. Judd grew up on Long Island with a healthy diet of doodling, **X-Men** comics, the newspaper strip **Bloom County**, and **Looney Tunes**. Today, he lives in San Francisco with his wife, Pam Ling; their two kids; their cat, Chaka; and far too many action figures and vinyl toys for a normal adult. Judd created the Cartoon Network series **Juniper Lee**; has written superhero comics, including Batman, Green Lantern, and Green Arrow; and was a cast member of MTV's **The Real World: San Francisco**. Judd is also the author of the highly acclaimed graphic novel **Pedro and Me**, about his **Real World** roommate and friend, AIDS activist Pedro Zamora. Visit Judd and Hilo online at juddspillowfort.com or find him on Twitter at @JuddWinick.

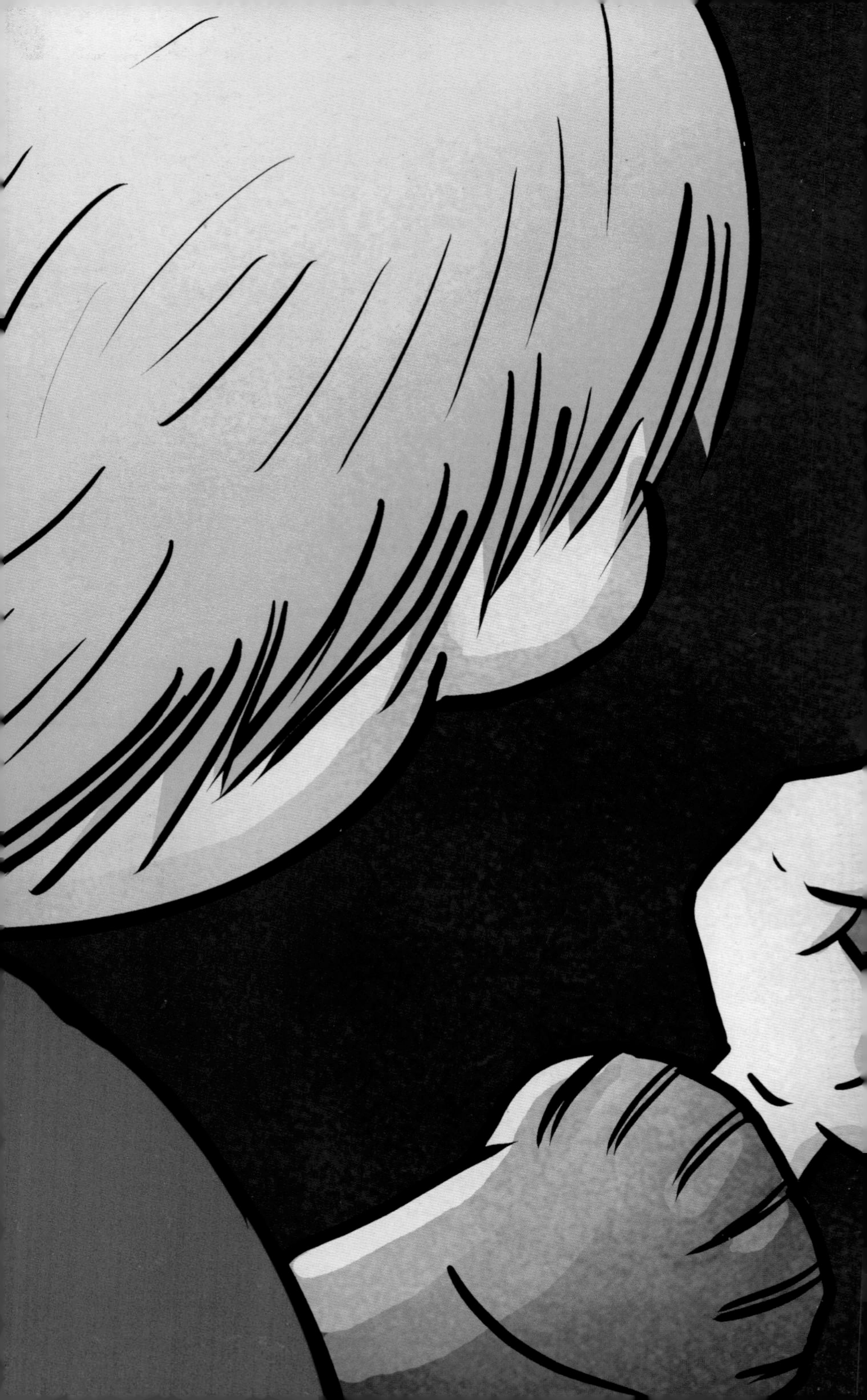